JANET HUMPHREY

Jed

a DUST prequel

First published by Ducklet Publishing 2023

First edition

ISBN: 978-1-73-927951-6

Cover art by Warren Wong

This book was professionally typeset on Reedsy.
Find out more at reedsy.com

Dedicated to the memory of our cat Robert
who supervised the writing of this book
Rest in peace 'our boy'
we will always love you

Her absence is like the sky, spread
over everything.

C S Lewis

Contents

Preface

JED became a side stop on the writing of the DUST series for me.

DUST Book One had been published in September 2019 to great sales and reviews but in the back of my mind I wanted to know why Jed has become the person he was at the time of infection by the DUST.

I also wanted to explore his early years and how he overcame the shadow of the Cetin brothers alongside Kitty to start a new life invigorated and refreshed.

He was a great character who deserved his own story to be told.

And here it is...hope you enjoy!

Acknowledgement

To my first readers, Val and Stan, Liz & Byron.

Thank you all for taking a chance on me and DUST

I hope you enjoy this prequel as much as I have enjoyed

bringing Jed's story to you.

1

Clare and Jed

Jed didn't know when he first realized his mum Clare was sad.

He knew the difference even from a young age between being sad because your chocolate bar was finished and how his mum was from time to time.

He knew she loved him, that was clear from the way she protected him from those around her but inside he also knew that she was sad more often than she was happy.

Sometimes he would catch her looking at him with a mixture of pride and something else. It took him a lot of years to realize what the other was.

It was fear. They had lived in squats for most of his young life, going from one derelict building to another, being pushed out time and time again by the same group of bailiffs.

He had started to like one of two of them, especially Mr James. Mr James was always nice to him and his mum.

One sunny spring day the bailiffs came again.

"Come on now Clare, you know the drill" Mr James would smile kindly at them and say as the bailiffs entered yet another cold and draughty squat. "Pack up your things, now, it's time to leave"

Jed's mum would smile wanly and start to shove clothes and food back into the carrier bags and make sure Jed had his coat on, and his belongings with him before being guided back out into the sunshine outside.

Once they were outside, Mr James always produced a lolly from his pocket and handed it to him after giving his mum a questioning look of approval.

She always nodded yes, and for the next few minutes Jed would watch more and more people exiting the same squat where they had come from.

It was magical almost. When he was old enough Jed would make a game of counting the people as they came out of each place they were evicted from. This morning he got to twenty eleven.

He didn't know his numbers after twenty so he started again. That was a big building, the twenty-eleven. A large and very dusty warehouse that had been sold for development which had never come. It had become a blot on the landscape in the city of Exeter and eventually, after being sold again, the new developers had engaged Mr James and his colleagues to move on the community of squatters who had made this building home.

This would be the last place Jed would live with his mum, but as he sat on the wall in the sunshine licking the lolly and watching his mum as she fumbled in her coat pocket for a piece of paper he had no idea how his life would change forever.

"Is that good Jed?" Clare said as she came back to sit on the wall with him. Jed nodded.

"Where are we going now, Mum?".

"Not sure love, just waiting for Big Mike to come back" she replied. "Some of the others mentioned a boarded-up shop down on the old parade but I think some of these know about that one too"

She nodded at a group who had set off purposely towards Cathedral Square. Big Mike was one of the nicer people in the squat. Jed had known him all his life. Big Mike was a very tall man with a bushy red beard. Jed had thought that Big Mike was a Viking, and this had made him laugh when Jed had asked him one evening in the squat. Big Mike had roared with laughter but said, no he actually came from Stoke on Trent.

"What about Mrs Hilston?" Jed asked as he looked around at the people walking by them.

Mrs Hilston was their social worker and although she was nice, the council didn't have enough accommodation for all the rough sleepers in Exeter. Mrs Hilston had been in their lives since Jed was four and a half. Mrs Hilston had tried to help Clare both in support and advice.

Most of the time Clare managed, but she was still using drugs and alcohol which banned them from most of the shelters, though the Salvation Army shelter would let her and Jed in as long as she promised not to kick off.

She had kept the promise for three nights the previous year until one of the other residents had stolen a £10 note she had stashed away in her bag. Jed had been asleep and hadn't seen who had taken it. Clare and Jed were escorted to an office upstairs where Jed was allowed to sleep on a dusty sofa until morning. Clare curled up in a chair beside him. They were not welcome there after that.

Jed and his mum picked up the carrier bags and put them into a nearby abandoned shopping trolley and started off toward the council offices. Clare knew that it was not likely that they would be given a permanent home, but she was hoping for at least a hotel room for a few nights. Jed desperately needed a bath, as did she, but in the squat, the best she was able to manage was a quick strip wash in a local pub's disabled loos once or twice a week.

As they walked along Jed noticed other people they passed gave them a quick look over and then glanced away. Jed was used to this staring and ignored it. . His mum pushed the supermarket trolley loaded with their possessions but Jed carried his school bag and a rucksack. He was strong and wiry for his age, and he was proud he could help his mum carry things now. When he was younger she would pop him into the child seat and push him along.

After a short walk, they arrived at the council offices. Clare parked the trolley at the foot of the stairs and patted Jed on the head.

"Right Jed, you are in charge of our stuff until I come back out. No talking to strangers OK?"

Jed nodded and sat down on the low brick wall next to the stairs. He wished he'd still had his lolly but the sun was warm on his face.

As he sat there more people came and went from the council offices. Several stared at him as he waited but no one commented or spoke to him. After a long wait eventually, his mum came back down the stairs. Jed looked at her, she'd been crying he realised. Behind her was Mrs Hilston the social worker who looked sad as well. Clare sat down beside her son and cuddled him fiercely.

"Jed, Mrs Hilston is going to look after you for a short while. I need to get some help, and she can look after you better than I can at the moment". Jed squirmed in her grasp

"No! NO!" his voice got louder which made more people stare at him. Clare took his face in her hands.

"Yes Jed, this is what is best. Once I am well again you and I can be together but she's right, you need more than I can give you at the moment."

Jed sobbed as she looked at him with such love that it broke his heart. Mrs Hilston came down the stairs and stood beside them quietly.

"We've got a lovely room all set up for you in a home just down the road."

Clare looked up at Mrs Hilston and nodded. Mrs Hilston then looked and Jed and said

"Come on Jed, bring your bags and we will go and get you set up"

"Mum? You are coming too?"

Clare shook her head sadly "No Jed, I'm going to the hospital now"

She nodded at a tall man who had come out of the offices. Mr Cooper here is going to take me to the hospital for a stay. Jed looked at their possessions in the shopping trolley

"Our stuff Mum, what happens to it?"

"Mrs Hilston is going to have it stored for us both until we can come together again. It will be safe, I promise."

Clare stood up and Jed hugged her again.

"Now be a brave boy and go with Mrs Hilston". She smiled at her son who was getting so tall for his age. She turned him around and Mrs Hilston then took his hand.

"Come on Jed, let's get you settled"

He turned back and waved at his mum, tears running down his dirty face making clean tracks as they fell. They went up the steps together and into the offices.

Mrs Hilston turned and smiled at Clare as the man came down to help her move the trolley to the back of the building.

Jed was staring up at the massive staircase in front of him. The building was one he had never been inside before and there were loads of people all moving around looking very busy and important. To one side was a reception desk and behind it was two ladies who were answering a bank of phones. The phones rang and each one was answered with

"Exeter Council how may I direct your call?"

They listened and then pressed a button before the next call came in. Mrs Hilston took his hand and directed him to the back of the room where a long corridor stretched out in front of them.

On each side, multiple doors lead to more offices and more noise. Jed didn't like this place, he didn't like the people but he couldn't go back now. He had to be brave for his mum, so he walked and looked and eventually Mrs Hilston stopped at a blue door with her name on a plaque and went inside, Jed followed her in.

"Sit down there Jed, I need to make a call before we go"

Jed did as he was told and sat down on the chair Mrs Hilston had indicated putting his rucksack and school bag down. Mrs Hilston sat down behind a small wooden desk. On each side of the desk and piled up around it were cardboard files.

Jed looked down at the pile beside him. The top file had the name "Sarah Foster" written on it in black pen. Jed wondered if all of the files had names on them, he also wondered if he had a file in this office, and if so what would it say?

Mrs Hilston picked up the phone and dialled a number. The person who answered the phone had a loud voice but he couldn't hear the words. As Mrs Hilston spoke into the phone Jed continued to look around at the office and the files. He wanted to get up and walk around but he had agreed to do what Mrs Hilston wanted. He was a good boy and he was brave for his mum.

After a short while, Mrs Hilston smiled at him and walked back around the desk to where he was still sitting.

"Right Jed, we need to get you settled in your new temporary home"

She held out her hand, "Come on, bring your bags"

Jed stood up and put his bags back on his shoulder and walked out with Mrs Hilston back into the corridor. They walked back to the reception area which was still busy and full of people moving around. Jed followed Mrs Hilston back outside and down a path to the side of the building into a car park.

She walked to a small car which Jed knew was a Ford Escort. It was black and quite dirty. Jed liked cars but he hadn't been in many as a passenger.

His mum didn't drive and they took buses or walked when they needed to get somewhere. Mrs Hilston opened the car and popped the passenger side lock for Jed to get in. Jed put his bags by his feet and watched as Mrs Hilston took off her nice shoes and popped on a pair of brown moccasin shoes. She smiled as she did so

"Don't like driving in my other shoes, they get scuffed " she said with no further explanation.

She put on her seatbelt and helped Jed on with his one, before starting the car and pulling out of the car park onto the road. As they drive along the streets Jed spotted some of the people he had watched come out of the squat earlier. They were sitting on a bench in the sunshine. They looked happy and contented. Jed wondered where his mum was now.

"Where's my mum going ?" Jed asked as Mrs Hilston went around the roundabout at the bottom of South Street. Mrs Hilston smiled and didn't reply immediately. When she was across the roundabout she said

"Your mum isn't well Jed, she had gone with my colleagues to a special hospital where she will get the help she needs" She added, "I'm sorry that this has happened Jed, we did hope that your Mum would be OK, but she needs help and you need more stability than she can give you now".

Jed didn't reply but watched the cars as they drove.

"What's sta-bility? Can I visit her?"

"Stability is where you have a safe and permanent place to live, and no you can't see her not until the doctors are finished making her better. Do you understand what withdrawal is Jed?"

Jed thought about the question. In all the years living with his mum, there was one guy called Kimmy. His mum had explained as several of the other squat residents helped Kimmy onto a bed, that he was sweating 'the bad stuff out'

Jed had been curious about the bad stuff. He couldn't see anything coming out of Kimmy lying on the mattress but sweat. He did smell bad though. Later on his mum had explained that Kimmy had taken too many drugs and his system was dependant on them. When Kimmy had tried to stop, the drugs had made his body crave them.

Jed nodded. He didn't think his mum was like Kimmy. "Is my mum like Kimmy?" He asked.

"Who's Kimmy?" Mrs Hilston replied puzzled. Jed explained as she drove.

"Yes and no. Your mum is addicted to alcohol more than drugs, although its mostly the same results. The doctors will try and help her to not need it any more, which should make her feel better. Does that make sense.?"

"Yes, sort of"

Mrs Hilston turned left and pulled up on the side of the road. Jed looked out at a large house behind gates which had a sign on the fence 'Methodist Children's Home, - saving souls since 1902' and underneath 'Manager Charlie Gibbons'

Mrs Hilston turned off the ignition and took off her seatbelt.

"Right Jed, this is where you will be staying for a while" She helped him off with his seatbelt and they got out of the car. Jed took his bags and put them back on his shoulder and followed Mrs Hilston to the gate. She pressed a button on a small panel near the gate and Jed could hear a buzz. After a short while, a voice came out of the speaker

"Hello?"

"Hello" replied Mrs Hilston "It's Jenny Hilston, I've brought Jed Long ".

The gate buzzed and Mrs Hilston pushed the gate open

"Come on Jed" she urged as he followed her inside.

As Jed walked through, Mrs Hilston closed the gate which shut with a bang. Jed jumped at the noise of the gate but Mrs Hilston ushered him onwards to a big blue door which was already open. Inside a man was stood waiting.

"Hello Jenny, hello Jed," said the man who was watching them as they came closer. Jed didn't like the man, he wasn't sure why perhaps it was the brown cardigan he wore with chunky shoes and grey trousers.

Mrs Hilston replied "Hello Charlie" as she passed the man and walked into the house.

Inside there was a staircase to one side of the hallway, Mrs Hilston seemed to know where she was going as she walked past the staircase and down a short dark corridor into a kitchen area. Sat around a large wooden table were three other children all eating sandwiches.

"Hello Katy, Hello Sam, Hello Ben," said Mrs Hilston as she went into the room.

All three children smiled and gave a cheerful thumbs-up as each of them had a mouthful of a sandwich.

"This is Jed, everyone, he's going to be staying here whilst his mum is in hospital".

Jed came in behind Mrs Hilston and smiled at the three children.

"Sit down Jed, sit down then, now would you like cheese or ham in your sandwich?"

"Cheese please Mrs Hilston"

Jed put down his two bags on the floor and pulled out a spare chair and sat down.

Jed realised he was very hungry indeed. Mrs Hilston took off her coat and started to make a sandwich for him, adding a small packet of crisps to the plate as well. She put it in front of him and Jed began to eat.

"OK Jed, I'm going now to see how your mum is doing so Charlie will show you where you will be staying once you have had your food OK?"

Jed nodded, he was trying to eat his sandwich politely but it was the best food he had eaten for days.

When Jed was with his mum, food was something that they didn't have access to often. Clare had developed a relationship with some of the local restaurants and takeaway places where she would clean and do food prep for a few hours in exchange for a hot meal for her and her son.

Jed tried to think back to when was the last time he and his mum had eaten and realised it was two days ago in the evening. No wonder he was hungry. Jed finished his sandwich and crisps as the other children left the room.

Once his meal was finished, Jed followed the lead of the other children who had put their dishes and cups on the side of the sink and sat back down. The man came back into the room and stood near the door looking at him.

"Right Jed, there are a few rules you need to follow, and if you do, we will get along just fine. " Jed stared up at the man who looked mean.

"Rule number one is no fighting with the other kids. I've got enough to do here without dealing with bickering kids"

Jed looked up at him without showing any emotion. Jed had learned on the streets that to look scared meant you would be picked on.

"Rule number two is you don't bunk off school. You'll be enrolled at the Methodist School down the road tomorrow and Mrs Cooper won't take any rubbish from any of her students either. She will make sure that you spend your time right and do your homework. Rule number three and this is the most important one - do not cross me, Jed. I can be an evil bastard if you do, and you will regret it."

Jed nodded as he realised this was expected of him he added

"Yes Sir" Charlie Gibbons smiled but Jed noticed it wasn't a nice smile like Mrs Hilston gave the children.

"Good, right bring your bags and I'll show you where you will be sleeping."

* * *

2

The Home

Jed got on the 'wrong side' of Charlie Gibbons within a day. The other children were very quiet sitting in a big lounge reading books as Jed and Charlie went upstairs to find his room.

The house was huge, spread over three floors, the downstairs was living space and study rooms, plus the kitchen and utility room. As they walked upstairs Charlie Gibbons waved his hands at some of the rooms they passed. On the second floor, Charlie walked down a dark green painted corridor and stopped at the last door on the right.

"This is your room Jed" as he opened the door. Inside was a small metal bed with a mattress, two small pillows and a pile of blankets and sheets. Alongside the far wall was a small chest of drawers and a hanging rail

"You'll be making your own bed every morning and I do regular inspections to make sure it's tidy. You will also keep your room clean and tidy, and no eating in your room."

Jed walked into the room and stared at the bed. He turned meekly and said,

"How do I make my bed sir. I've not made a bed before? My mum and I had sleeping bags"

Charlie huffed and said "Put down your bags then, you're be doing it"

Jed dropped his bags on the floor near the bottom of the bed. Charlie then instructed Jed to put the blankets, sheets and pillows on a nearby chair. Jed then took one of the sheets and laid it down on the bed.

"Tuck the corners in Jed, it keeps it neat"

Jed then added another sheet on top followed by the blankets and tucked those in too. The pillows had fresh covers on them, and they were added to the top of the bed. Jed had to admit this was a lovely bed, even if the room was gloomy and a bit cold.

"Right see that?" said Charlie. Jed nodded "That is how your bed needs to look EVERY morning before you come down for your breakfast. No exceptions, if you don't then you lose a blanket, so don't moan and say I never warned you about this!"

Jed nodded again. His neck was starting to get sore, but he knew that this man was someone you had to defer to.

"Right, put your stuff in there," said Charlie pointing at the chest of drawers and the rail. "How many clothes do you have?"

Jed picked up his bags and started to unpack them as Charlie stood over him. Jed pulled out two woollen jumpers which were darned but clean, five pairs of underpants and three tee shirts.

"No trousers?" said Charlie

"No sir, these are my only pair. Mum said I keep on growing like a weed" replied Jed

"OK well there are a pile of donated clothes, let's get you kitted out, and you'll need a school uniform and some books too. Follow me"

Jed followed Charlie down the corridor to another room which was lighter and brighter than his room. More hanging rails were set up around the room and piles of clothes were laid out on another bed. Charlie looked Jed up and down and went over to one pile picking up some more trousers and other items. He handed these to Jed

"Try those on, if they are too long then they can be taken up by Miss Goodwin - she's the cleaner and the cook here"

Jed slipped out of his trousers and tried on the pair handed to him. They were too long but fitted him well everywhere else.

"OK, that's good," said Charlie "Here's some more in the same size".

Jed held onto the trousers as Charlie rummaged around in some other piles. Jed was handed some white shirts which fitted well, more underpants though these looked a bit worn, plus a pack of socks and a pair of worn but clean shoes. His arms ached with the weight of the items but Charlie wasn't finished yet.

Charlie went over to another rail which held some bottle green jackets with 'Methodist Church School' embroidered in white thread on the breast pocket.

These also looked worn and Charlie noticed Jed looking at them.

"Donated by the families of other kids at the school once they leave" he commented. "Right put that lot down and try this one on"

Charlie said handing him one of the smaller jackets. Jed complied and tried on the jacket. It smelt a bit musty like something left in a charity shop but as he stood there Charlie cracked a rare smile.

"Fit's you well," he remarked. "That's handy as we don't have anything smaller than this size"

Jed picked up the rest of the clothes and followed Charlie back down to the room where he was going to be staying.

"Put all your clothes away and come downstairs, we've got to give you a haircut and get you some school books, you start tomorrow".

Jed gulped, he'd not been to school for a long time. It was difficult to attend when you didn't know where you would be living, and yet his mum had made sure he learned to read and write.

She had also been keen to expand his knowledge and they had spent many happy hours in the library learning about dinosaurs or space. These had been the happiest times with his mum, and he missed her dreadfully.

Jed wondered where she was and how long he would have to stay here. Mrs Hilston had said she was going to the hospital but she didn't look ill to him but then he remembered what Mrs Hilston had said about addiction. Jed wondered if his mum was going to be sweating and shivering on a mattress somewhere.

After putting away the clothes and his possessions in the room, Jed walked downstairs to where the other children were sitting reading in the living room. As he walked in, they all looked up at him, then back down at their books.

"Hello, I'm Jed"

The girl smiled at him then indicated herself "Katy", then pointed at a skinny boy "Sam" and then a small chubby boy "Ben,"

"Can I sit down?"

Katy pointed to a large bookcase in the corner of the room

"Better get yourself a book before Charlie comes back. He likes to see us all reading, it makes him believe we are behaving ourselves" she giggled as she pointed.

Jed went over to the bookcase and looked at the books there. Most of them were Bible Stories, he realised. No stories about space or dinosaurs. Jed picked up a book that had a bright cover picturing a bearded man sitting on a donkey. He walked over to the only spare chair and sat down.

"Oh that one is a doozy," said Katy as she saw the book Jed had picked up "Children's Bible in 365 stories. Charlie will be pleased" Jed was puzzled but before he could ask Katy what she meant, Charlie had come back into the room.

"Right Jed, you come with me, lets get your school books all sorted, then you will be ready for tomorrow" Jed put down the book on the chair and followed Charlie back outside and down the corridor to another room near the kitchen.

"This is my office Jed, do not enter here unless you are asked to, no poking around OK?"

Jed nodded again. His head was starting to spin with all these rules. Charlie plucked a key out of his trouser pocket and unlocked the door. Inside was a warm and cosy space, with a desk and chair, a table with a kettle and coffee mugs and a radiator near the window.

Charlie walked over to a cupboard and opened it with another key. Inside were piles of books. Charlie sorted through picked out several and put them down on the desk. He added a small pile of pens, pencils, an eraser, plus a small bag with a patch in the same logo as the jacket Jed had tried on earlier.

"These are your school supplies, do not lose them, we can't afford to keep replacing them" Jed put all the items into the bag.

"Dinner is in an hour, so you can go back and read until Miss Goodwin calls you for dinner, then after dinner, I will give you a hair cut"

Jed returned to the living room and put down the bag beside the chair. Katy looked up and smiled at him

"Been in the room of DOOOOOM have you?" Jed looked puzzled so she explained "The charity clothes and other stuff?"

"Oh yes, I've got some more trousers, a jacket and some school stuff. What's the school like?"

Sam sniggered but Katy shot him a fierce look.

"It's OK. The headmistress Mrs Cooper is a bit fierce but the French teacher Mr Wall is tough but fair. Don't get on the wrong side of the RE teacher though"

Ben added

"Religious Education. Miss Cartwright is a Methodist teacher from the 1930s. If it's fun, or something happy then it's forbidden. Sweets except on Sunday, playing hopscotch or even laughing. She'll be down on you before you can say Prayers for the wicked"

Ben finished his speech with a roar of laughter. "My aim in life is to send her packing. I'm doing a good job aren't I?"

Katy agreed then they all went back to their books.

* * *

Jed settled into the home quickly. His first experience of a group meal came a couple of hours later. Charlie came into the room, and Jed could tell he was pleased to see all the children with their noses deep in a book each.

"Grub's up. Wash your hands and come and eat".

Jed followed the others into a wash room off the ground floor with multiple sinks and washing machines. He followed Katy in scrubbing his hands clean then marched behind her to the kitchen where he had eaten his sandwich earlier. A tall blonde lady was putting dishes of food on the table and Ben was already helping himself.

As Charlie walked in, Ben paled then dropped the ladle he was holding.

"You know better" growled Charlie as he sat down at the head of the table.

"Grace first" Ben looked stricken but Jed couldn't understand why. He didn't know what Grace was. Perhaps she was another child? His confusion cleared as all the rest of the children sat down and grasped their hands together their eyes tightly shut. Charlie noticed Jed's confusion.

"We say Grace here in this house, before every meal Jed. Thanking the Lord for putting food on our table though we are all sinners."

Jed shut his eyes and mimicked what Katy had done.

"Elbows OFF!"

Jed opened his eyes in shock. Across from him Katy mimicked moving his elbows off the table. He moved them , clasped his hands together and shut his eyes again. Finally Charlie started to intone.

After a couple of minutes of him berating how unworthy they all were and thanking God for the food, he finally said

"Let's eat"

Jed opened one eye and saw Ben had picked up the ladle again. The food smelt good. Beef stew with mashed potato. Jed was handed the ladle by Ben and he helped himself, piling on stew and mashed potato. Jed looked over at Katy who smiled at him. As they ate, Charlie talked to the tall lady who Jed realised must have been Miss Goodwin.

"Got some trousers that need taking up Hilda. That one there" Charlie said pointing at Jed. The lady replied in a strong Devon accent

"No problem, I'll do that after dinner "

She turned to Jed and said

"Come and see me in the kitchen after your haircut Jed, and we can get these trousers sorted"

"Thank you".

"You're welcome my dear".

Once the meal was over, the children put their plates and cups on the counter top near the sink. Katy, Sam and Ben went back into the living room and sat down again with their books. Charlie followed with Jed behind. Charlie walked over to another cupboard and got out a large white sheet which he put down on the carpet.

"Grab that chair" indicated Charlie. Jed did so, and Charlie put the chair on top of the sheet.

"Sit down then" Jed did so and Charlie produced another sheet that he wrapped around him. Charlie then turned back to the cupboard and produced a set of clippers. "Number four I think"

Jed didn't know what he meant but after the shouting about his elbows he thought it best not to ask. As he sat there, showers of hair started to fall. Jed's hair wasn't long but there was lots of it. On the rare occasions, his mum had noticed, she had tried to cut his fringe but in the end, she had taken him to the barbers when funds allowed. Jed tried to think how long it was since his last haircut. He remembered it was February, and it was nearly summer now. After a few minutes, the shower of hair started to fade. Jed was sitting facing away from the rest of the children and yet he knew they were watching him.

"That's better," said Charlie as he turned off the clippers. "Neat and tidy. Right off you go and get your trousers fixed then it will be bedtime."

Jed went back out into the kitchen where Miss Goodwin was getting out an old fashioned sewing machine and setting it up on the table in front of her. Jed was fascinated as she deftly threaded the machine before turning to him holding out a pair of trousers. They were turned inside out.

"Try those on then pet, it's easier to turn them up inside out"

Jed did so and as he stood in the kitchen his thoughts turned again to where his mum was and whether she was OK. Miss Goodwin glanced over at him

"It will be OK Jed, your mum is where she needs to be"

Jed felt his eyes welling up with tears but he didn't say anything. His throat was tight and he concentrated on putting on the trousers. Miss Goodwin took him over to a chair near the table and said

"Get up onto the table, makes it much easier to pin these"

Jed complied and stood watching her as she picked up a box of pins and started to pin the trousers to fit.

"You'll be growing out of these soon enough, but for now let's get them looking right". After a couple of minutes, she asked him to get back down and out of the trousers onto the next pair. Four pairs of trousers pinned later Miss Goodwin said

"I'm making hot chocolate for the other children, would you like a cup too?"

Jed had never had hot chocolate before but he thought it sounded nice.

"Yes please Miss Goodwin".

"OK then, back into your other trousers and I'll bring you a cup through before you go to bed" Jed did as she asked and went back into the living room where the other children were again reading.

"Is there a TV?" Jed asked looking around the room

"Special occasions only" replied Sam looking up

"Oh and Songs of Praise on a Sunday" chipped in Ben.

"It's over there in that cabinet"

Katy said pointing at a large wooden cabinet by the window. Jed walked over to the cabinet which had two fancy doors on the front of it.

"It's locked," said Katy "Charlie has the only key".

Jed was disappointed. Some of the squats he and his mum had lived in, had been wired up for electricity, and one or two of them had portable TV's.

His mum hasn't minded him watching cartoons on a weekend, but only if he had done his homework she had set. Jed had not been to 'proper' school even though he was nearly nine years old.

His mum had said that she would enrol him when they arrived at the last squat but she came back from the school furious because they wouldn't accept her address as valid.

The social workers had been in their lives since he was nearly five years old but he knew that things had got worse for them to take him away. Mrs Hilston had spoken to the school at the time but they had been clear that without a fixed address they couldn't take Jed into their school.

So in the end Jed had always done his homework and school work with his mum and he preferred that. Miss Goodwin came into the room with a tray of steaming mugs. She put the tray down and passed the drinks around.

"Be careful it's hot" she said to each child as they accepted the mug. Jed accepted his mug and immediately loved the smell. He took a small sip, mindful of the warning and felt warm and toasty. It was delicious, like a liquid hug. He sipped his drink and watched the other children drinking theirs.

"Good eh?" said Sam "Miss Goodwin is the best at making the hot chocolate. Unlike Charlie she gives us each a good spoonful of cocoa rather than just waving it across the top of the cup before putting it back in the tin".

"Is she not here all the time?" asked Jed

"No only four days a week in the evening. Most of the time she is gone by dinner time, then we have to be very quiet for Charlie" said Katy looking worried.

She brightened as she carried on drinking "But he's OK as long as you don't annoy him. We'll look after you Jed, make sure you know stuff"

Jed finished his drink and put it back on the tray. The others were still drinking so he went back to the chair and took out the book again.

"Can you read?" asked Ben

"Course I can" replied Jed fiercely "Why wouldn't I?"

"Just you haven't turned a page of the one you are reading since you picked it up" replied Ben reasonably. "It's not a bad book once you get into it".

Jed said "I prefer space stories"

"We all prefer other stories, but Charlie and the home think we need to repent so they fill the bookcase here with all of this" replied Ben indicating the bookshelf next to them. "You'll get a chance to take out a book from the school library tomorrow".

Charlie came back into the room

"Bedtime kids, no chatting, brush your teeth and straight to sleep".

Jed followed the others upstairs and when he got inside his room, he found three pairs of altered trousers lying on the bed with a note in careful script

"Taken the final pair home to finish, I'll bring them back in the morning Miss Goodwin"

Miss Goodwin had been busy.

Jed thought as he got out of his clothes and into a brushed cotton pair of pyjamas that. were lying on his new pillow.

They smelt lovely and clean Jed's mum had never insisted on pyjamas for him. Jed had always worn a long tee shirt in his sleeping bag, and sometimes a jumper too depending on how cold the squat they were in was.

Jed took the toothbrush and paste Charlie had left for him and walked down to a large bathroom where Sam and Ben were already there brushing their teeth too. Jed was pleased when Sam moved over so he could start to brush his teeth.

Ben turned and his mouth was filled with foam, he made a "gaaaaaaaaaaa" sound which made the other boys giggle but mindful of Charlie's warning Jed got on with brushing his teeth before returning to his room.

He took some coat hangers and carefully put the three pairs of trousers on the rail next to the new blazer. Jed then got into bed and switched out the light. His last thoughts before drifting off were to say a 'goodnight' to his mum and he hoped he would see her very soon.

* * *

The next morning Jed was rudely awakened by Charlie walking down the corridor swinging a large loud bell whilst saying.

"Wake up kids" Jed wondered for a second or two where he was, then it all came back to him. He got out of bed and walked down to the bathroom again where Sam and Ben were standing washing their faces with flannels and soap.

Sam indicated a flannel beside him "Charlie left that for you".

The flannel was rough on his skin and the soap was medicinal in smell.

"Coal Tar," said Sam as he noticed Jed's reaction to the smell. "Charlie buys it because it's cheap. We get a bath three times a week at the moment, but Charlie expects us to wash daily."

Jed followed the other boys lead in stripping off and using the flannel to clean themselves.

"Katy gets her own bathroom at the moment, but expect there will be other girls coming soon".

Jed got dressed in the uniform he had been given and followed the other boys downstairs to the kitchen.

"Leave your blazer off, for meals," said Ben, "Don't want to start your first day with breakfast down it".

Jed returned back to his room and put his blazer on the bed before dashing down the stairs to the kitchen where Miss Goodwin was handing out plates of scrambled eggs and toast to the rest of the children.

"Eggs for you Jed,?" she said as she turned to him smiling.

"Yes please, Miss Goodwin," said Jed as he sat down next to Katy.

Charlie came into the room as Miss Goodwin was pouring juice for them all. He sat down and accepted a plate of the food before saying grace again. As he finished all the children started to eat. Jed was famished. He ate all of the eggs and three pieces of toast and would have had more but he saw Charlie watching him and decided not to.

"First day at school Jed," remarked Charlie as he drank his juice. "The others will show you the ropes but be aware Mrs Cooper sends me regular reports on all our wards and if any of you misbehave there will be hell to pay. Now back up to clean your teeth before school"

Jed followed the others back upstairs and brushed his teeth again. He'd never been forced to do this by his mum, but he had to admit he did like the clean teeth sensation. He went back to his room and gathered his blazer and the school bag Charlie had given him before going back downstairs to the living room where the others were standing waiting for him. Katy looked nice, her hair had two clips holding it back from her face. Jed refrained from remarking as he knew from previous experience girls didn't like to be called nice.

Charlie came into the room. "Right back home by 4.30 pm at the latest and do not dawdle!"

* * *

3

Exeter Methodist Church School

The children trooped out of the front door and walked down the road, joining other groups of children who were also walking towards a large red-bricked building at the end of the street. Ben turned to Jed and whispered.

"Watch out for Mrs Cooper. Sam reckons she is Charlie's sister" Jed sniggered at the thought of a female Charlie but as he was escorted into Mrs Cooper's office, he realised that Sam was probably right.

Mrs Cooper was even more stern looking than Charlie was. She was thin and waspish, with wispy grey hair arranged in a tight bun which made her face look even more pinched. She appraised Jed with a frown as he stood in front of her, his bag by his feet.

"Jed Long," she said looking at him. "No formal education and you are almost nine? date of birth is 22-10-1990 "

"Yes, Miss" replied Jed

"Why have you not been to school?" she asked

"My mum and I didn't have a home"

Mrs Cooper looked at him expecting more.

Jed added, "The local school wouldn't take me until my mum and I had a home, and we couldn't find one". Mrs Cooper looked a little less stern as she heard this.

"Well, our first job is to assess you to find out what you do know, follow me"

Mrs Cooper guided Jed into a classroom next to her office. Inside was a small elderly man sitting at a desk in front.

"This is Mr Wall, he teaches French but he has agreed to assess you for grading"

Mrs Cooper looked at the man who smiled at Jed

"Come in young man, sit there, what's your name?"

"Jed, Sir" replied Jed sitting down on the chair behind one of the desks. Mr Wall came over and placed a small pile of papers down on the desk in front of Jed.

"Maths, English, RE and this one is for your IQ -IQ, or intelligence quotient, is a measure of your ability to reason and solve problems. Do you have a pencil? Oh, good"

Jed took out the small case and produced a sharp pencil.

"First of all write your name at the top of each page of each paper Jed, then READ them all as you tackle each one. I say that because sometimes there are trick papers and you can end up wasting a good while only to find out you should have just ticked a single box and stopped."

Mr Wall went back to his desk and picked up a clock.

"One hour for each paper Jed, I will tell you when it is time to move on to the next one".

Jed looked pensive but he gripped his pencil hard and waited for the first signal

"And start!" said Mr Wall as he placed the clock facing Jed so he could see.

Jed picked up the first paper which was Maths. Jed liked maths, his mum had bought a book of puzzles every week and as he got older the puzzles got more complex. She had always given him the money to pay for goods and used that as a lesson asking if he knew how much change he should get back. Before Jed had finished the first paper Mr Wall said

"Onto the second one please Jed" as he came to collect the maths paper from him. Jed wrote his name on the second paper which was English, and then again he read the whole paper first. He couldn't see any trick questions and decided to complete the third essay about his favourite book.

The book was called Islands in the Sky by an author called Arthur C Clarke. He had taken the book out of the local library when he was seven years old. His mum had told him that the author had written a lot of books but this one was about a little boy who wins a TV contest to visit anywhere and decides to go to the moon.

The TV company say that the moon isn't anywhere on earth but Roy is a clever boy who points out that the rules don't specifically exclude the moon. Eventually, they agree and the boy is trained and goes to a moon base. Jed had loved the book and one day his mum brought home his very own copy from a charity shop. The book was dog-eared and well-thumbed but Jed had managed to put it into his rucksack before he and his mum were evicted. Jed started to write the essay and again before he knew how much time had passed, Mr Wall came over to collect his paper

"Onto the next one Jed please" Jed looked at the next paper which was RE Religious Education. He could answer some of the more basic questions but was confused about some of them, he did his best and eventually, the hour for that paper was over. As Mr Wall collected the RE paper he smiled

"Just one more to go Jed then you can go and join the others for lunch in the canteen"

Jed added his name to the final paper and then read through the questions. No trick ones here either so he started to answer the questions which he realised he enjoyed. Some were simple like what is the colour of blood? or what are clothes made of, but as he went through the questions they started to get harder. Jed did his best and finished the questions before the hour. He put down his pencil

"Finished already Jed, well done. Right now I will show you where the canteen is then I will get marking your papers."

Jed put his pencil back into his bag and followed Mr Wall down the corridor and across a walkway to another building. The smell of cooking chips filled the air and Jed was pleased when they arrived to see Katy, Ben and Sam waving at him from across the room.

"Off you go Jed, I will collect you later for your grading"

As Jed arrived at the table the others were sitting down at Ben and Sam was tucking into a plate of chips. Katy was eating lasagne and salad. She said

"Just go and help yourself, give them your name, they know you are at the home, Charlie gets billed every month, but they don't say what's been eaten which is why" nodding at Ben and Sam "THEY don't eat anything not deep fried".

Ben grinned whilst adding more chips to his fork. She then nodded towards a stout woman by the trays

"That's Miss Cartwright RE teacher, she's the one to look out for"

Jed glanced over at the woman. His mum would have said she looked like she was chewing on wasps. Jed walked over to the kitchen area and copied the children in front of him by taking a small wooden tray and putting it on the counter top.

Looking at the dishes on offer, Jed decided to compromise and have both lasagne and chips. He wasn't too keen on vegetables but he could see the lasagne looked like it had been stuffed with some grated veg anyway. After he had collected his plate he followed the other children down the line to the till. Most of them produced cash and were given change for their meals. When Jed arrived the young women looked at him.

"I'm Jed Long". The woman consulted a list and nodded, adding a tick by his name. As he walked away one of the other children that were in front of him said

"Another orphan" with a sneer, his friends standing around.

"I'm not an orphan!" said Jed fiercely. "My mum's in hospital"

"Yeah right" replied another one in the group "Orphan!".

Jed looked stricken as more and more of the group started to chant "Orphan, ORPHAN!".

Katy stood up and came over and planted herself behind them.

"Simon Thomas, your dad is a drug dealer and your mum steals from the local supermarket".

The first boy whirled around and faced her his face turning bright red.

"That's why you can supposedly afford school meals because your dad is peddling shit and your mum is mugging Tesco's! Come on Jed your food is getting cold"

She turned with a spin and Jed followed in her wake to the table.

"Well done," said Ben forking another mouthful of chips.

"Well, he deserved it!" Katy replied. "The other kids here all know we live at the home, but sometimes ones like them" she indicated the group who had slunk back to another table and were looking back over at them "need a little lesson in humility".

Jed took up his knife and fork and started to eat. When they had all finished and taken their trays over to the tall storage unit in the corner, Katy said

"Right Jed let's go and sit in the library and you can tell us all about your first morning".

The four of them went back out into the corridor and Jed followed them upstairs into a large room filled with books. He loved libraries, they were the warm safe happy places he'd spent many days with his mum when they had been evicted. His mum loved reading too and had passed on her love of books to him. Katy walked over to the large desk in the middle of the room and spoke to the man sitting down.

49

"Mr Matthews, this is Jed - can you please issue him a library card?".

Mr Matthews was a tall man with short grey hair. He looked ancient indeed but had a nice crinkly smile.

"Hello Jed, yes Mrs Cooper mentioned you are a new starter" He turned to a Rolodex and flicked through the files before plucking a small piece of card from one of them.

"Here you are," he said handing Jed the card. "Sign your name on the bottom there" Jed took the card and the pen Mr Matthews handed him and signed his name on the bottom. He handed the pen back.

"You can take out up to ten books at a time, any damages must be paid for, so please look after them". Jed turned to Katy, Ben and Sam with a huge grin on his face.

"Come on then, let's choose you some books so you don't have to face 365 Bibles stories again tonight," said Sam.

Jed followed them to the fiction books and looked carefully along each aisle until he came to the section for space. He took down a large book which was titled 'Space Wars Fact and Fiction' He tucked that one under his arm and continued his search. When he had collected five books he went back to the desk and carefully put them all on the top. Mr Matthews smiled as he checked all of the books out.

"You've got three weeks to read those, but I suspect you might be back sooner than that, just like young Katy here"

Katy blushed and didn't comment. Jed tucked the books into his bag and followed the others to a set of sofas in the corner where Ben and Sam then asked

"So how were the exams, Jed?"

"OK, I think" replied Jed." Didn't know much about the RE questions but I tried."

"Sam nearly gave Miss Cartwright a heart attack once," said Katy "He came into the class saying he had seen Jesus in the boy's toilet. You got a detention for that one didn't you?"

Sam smirked. "One of many, one of many".

"Well, the classes are streamed so you will be with different people for each subject". As Katy finished Mr Wall came into the library

"Ah there you all are," he said kindly. "Jed can you come with me please to Mrs Cooper's office. I have finished your grading. Off to class the rest of you, Jed will be joining you for French next lesson".

Katy, Sam and Ben trooped off to their next lessons and Jed followed Mr Wall back up to Mrs Cooper's office. As he entered he noticed she was smiling more than she had been earlier.

"Come in Jed," she said smiling. Jed was worried but he walked into the room and took the chair indicated. Mr Wall sat down next to him.

"We've compiled your exam tests and we are thrilled that you are with us"

Jed looked even more confused as she continued

"It seems that your IQ score is very high which is very good news for our funding - money we get for each pupil"

Mr Wall added, "Most of the children here are in the middle IQ range, but your score means that Exeter Methodist School will now receive extra funding and you will benefit from some of that money".

Mrs Cooper handed over a piece of paper to Jed

"This is your timetable for home, and here is one which has been laminated so you can carry this in your bag at school. On the back is a map of the classrooms and each lesson is marked here. Mr Wall is going to be your form teacher for this coming year"

Jed followed her directions across the laminated timetable she held and saw that as Mr Wall had mentioned he was to be in French class for the next period.

"Welcome again to Exeter Methodist School and we look forward to seeing your progress over the next few years. Mr Wall will take you to get settled in your form room"

Jed stood up and awkwardly shook Mrs Cooper's hand she held out, then followed Mr Wall out into the corridor. Jed turned to Mr Wall

"Was my IQ high then?"

He smiled and replied as they arrived outside a noisy classroom

"Yes Jed it was impressive, but IQ is only a small part of a person".

As they entered the room the noise level dropped dramatically. Inside were about thirty pupils, and Jed was heartened to see Katy, Sam and Ben all sitting at desks on the far side of the room.

"Good morning Form 4L," Mr Wall said as he ushered Jed to a desk adjacent to Katy. "This is the first day of a new term. Some of you may know me already as your French teacher from last year but this year I will be your form teacher in addition to that subject."

From the back of the room a small groan went up, Jed along with a few others looked back to see Simon Thomas the boy Katy had raged against back in the canteen. Simon winked at Jed and blew him a kiss.

"Simon peut-être que ton français s'est amélioré depuis l'année dernière - oui ?" said Mr Wall in a stern voice to the back of the room.

"Oui un peu peut-être monsieur" replied Simon in a sulky voice before sliding down in his chair.

"Bon bon, peut-être que nous pouvons maintenant nous mettre au travail. Right class books out, let's begin"

Jed's first experience with the French language didn't go well. He had come across other nationalities in the squats he and his mum had lived in but most of them spoke Polish or Romanian not French. He was asked to try some basic phases but he was distracted by the sniggers behind him. He screwed up his face and tried again. Mr Wall was kind and didn't focus too much on him for the rest of the lesson but Jed felt deflated.

As they were packing their bags up Ben nudged him and whispered

"Don't worry Jed" Jed smiled back at him and looked at his timetable for the next lesson.

"You're in RE with us," said Sam "Come on"

They walked down the staircase and into a long corridor

"This is the new block, built last year with funding from the church".

Jed followed them into a large spacious room with more desks than the French classroom had. Standing next to a table was Miss Cartwright who handed them each a bible as they entered.

Jed accepted his copy and followed the others this time sitting behind Sam. Ben and Katy were sitting two rows in front of them. Jed was fascinated to see what Ben meant back in the home about sending Miss Cartwright packing but he could see her looking across at Ben with an expression that suggested that he was not her favourite in the class.

Miss Cartwright focused on him he quickly turned it into a cough and looked down at his bible. At the front of the room, there was a very impressive-looking whiteboard that had a single word on it.

'God'

Miss Cartwright tapped her ruler on her desk which made a very loud noise. As she turned to the whiteboard to add more Jed noticed out of the corner of his eye Ben leaned over with a pair of scissors in his hand and appeared to cut something in the air. Jed couldn't see what it was at first until suddenly a small plastic toy swung within Miss Cartwright's view.

Jed realised it was an Action Man doll but instead of it being dressed in the latest commando outfit, it was dressed in a white robe and appeared to have long hair.

The classroom erupted into noisy appreciation. Jed realised this was possibly what Ben had been planning. He looked over at his friend and saw he was poker-faced, unlike all the other children who were whooping and laughing at the sight of the action man swinging just out of Miss Cartwright's grasp.

Jed smiled but just watched Miss Cartwright get more and more frustrated at both the toy which was swinging back and forth like some sort of holy symbol just out of reach and her class's loud cheering as she tried again and again and failed to wrench the toy down.

Eventually, she brought her chair underneath and managed to wrench the toy down. Her previous tidy appearance was now dishevelled hot and sweaty, and her grey bun released from its confines lay limply around her face.

"Who DID this!" she hissed turning to the class and brandishing the doll in her hand "this evil".

Ben raised his hand

"Miss, that's not evil - that's our Lord," he said in a sweet voice, Jed thought worthy of a choir boy. Jed like the others was trying not to laugh but it was increasingly difficult to keep a straight face.

Eventually, he dug his fingernails into his palm and the sharp pain made him calm down. The noise had attracted attention as the door opened and Mrs Cooper strode inside startled not to find a class in an uproar but her RE Teacher stood on her chair and waving a toy.

"June, what is going on?!" said Mrs Cooper sternly as Miss Cartwright staggered from the chair back down onto the ground and faced her supervisor.

"The, the children" replied Miss Cartwright "They set this THING up to humiliate me!"

Mrs Cooper took the doll from Miss Cartwright and examined it "It appears to be Jesus" said Mrs Cooper softly. She turned and focused on the class

"Does anyone know anything about this?" she looked directly at Ben as she spoke. To his credit and Jed's amazement, Ben looked calmly back at Mrs Cooper despite her laser focus without a reply. Jed would have shrivelled under her gaze he knew but Ben continued to just look ahead without any fear or embarrassment.

Mrs Cooper then turned back to Miss Cartwright. "Perhaps you should go and tidy yourself up June, I can take over for this lesson"

Miss Cartwright nodded and picked up her books and left. Mrs Cooper then turned back to the class.

"Let me make it very clear, if I find out who did this, you will be in detention with me for a month". She turned back to the whiteboard and said "The lesson today will be on the subject of God in your lives"

The class started to get out their notebooks and the lesson started. At the end of the lesson as all of the children were leaving Mrs Cooper said

"I want no more nonsense from any of you towards Miss Cartwright please". Outside in the corridor, a few of the pupils gave thumbs up towards Ben who accepted the accolades calmly. As they walked down to the canteen however Katy caught up with Ben and said

"That was really mean Ben. Ben turned back to her, "You said you were going to set it up so she could grab it"

Ben laughed back "But that was more fun wasn't it?" Katy shook her head

"No, it wasn't she was humiliated"

"Perhaps that will teach her to not give me detention for getting my classwork wrong by a point then"

Katy turned and caught up with Jed "You knew about that?"

"Sort of yes but it was mean not to let her catch it as it swung down. Ben knew how tall she was and it just made it horrible"

Jed didn't have an opinion but he could see Katy was upset about it. He could see that Katy was a fair person and he too thought towards the end of the incident that Miss Cartwright looked like she might cry.

Over lunch Ben had a few more of his fellow classmates give him the thumbs up. Jed could see he was enjoying his moment in the spotlight but he also saw that Simon Thomas and his friends were interested in all this and Jed suspected that Ben would be targeted by them all next. Nothing happened until the following day when during English class, Mrs Cooper came into the classroom and walked quietly over to the teacher Mr Hughes

"Ben Rogers, can you please go with Mrs Cooper please?". Ben gulped but tried not to look guilty and meekly followed Mrs Cooper outside into the corridor. She led him to a room at the end which was empty. Jed later found out that she had turned to Ben on shutting the door and asked in a quiet voice.

"Why did you do it, Ben?"

Ben was disarmed by her soft tone and didn't reply immediately.

"Did you know what Miss Cartwright did after your little stunt yesterday? She came to see me and gave in her notice Ben. She felt that she had lost the confidence of the school and wanted to leave. I, however, persuaded her to stay and I have been given information that suggested that you were behind this. Am I wrong?"

Ben looked at the floor and nodded.

"The information came to me anonymously which I particularly dislike, but it does appear to be true then. You will apologise to Miss Cartwright who is in her classroom marking papers immediately and you will be in detention with me for a month. Mr Gibbons will be informed of this as you will not be back to the children's home before his curfew and I expect you will also have consequences with him.".

Ben did as she asked of him, and realised when he saw Miss Cartwright again that she was indeed distraught about the situation. However, she accepted his apology with good grace and even wished him a good day as he made his way back to the English class who were awaiting his return. Later, Katy, Jed and Sam heard the full story and the consequences of his actions.

"Charlie is going to be mad at you Ben," said Sam "That's the third detention this year"

Ben slumped into a chair and groaned.

"I know!" he said "Last time I was given the job of clearing out that basement room, cobwebs everywhere, AND he knows I hate spiders!!"

Katy tried not to look satisfied but she was pleased that Ben had been caught.

"Who told her?" asked Jed

"My bet is on Simon Thomas," said Sam "He's never liked the fact that you are more popular than he is, even though he had that birthday party in the nightclub last month"

"Night club?!" asked Jed

"Yeah Simon's dad works for that drug dealer Mr C, the Turkish guy who owns that new development down by the Quay. Simon persuaded his Dad to allow him to have an 11th Birthday party with cocktails in the club for his birthday."

"Baby cocktails" laughed Katy" all sweet syrups and piles of fruit. His mates seemed to think they were getting alcopops"

"They drink?" said Jed puzzled. His mum and the other people in the squats he had lived in often were drinking but he'd never seen kids drinking.

"Well they all say they do, but I'd doubt it," said Sam. As they walked home Ben was lagging behind.

"Come on big man!" said Sam "Face the wrath of Charlie, and then it will be all over"

"No it won't, "said Ben miserably. As they all arrived back at the home Ben was further behind them.

The others waited for him and they walked inside the front door, taking off their shoes and coats. Charlie was waiting outside his office and gestured to Ben without a word. Ben walked down to meet him his demeanour that of someone walking the plank. Jed didn't realise at the time how close this was to the truth. Later in the year when he had started to catch the wrath of Charlie, he realised how much of a bully he was.

* * *

4

Grief

Life became routine for Jed in the home. He got used to the different rules that Charlie had set, and was enjoying the regular work at school. Each afternoon as they got back to the children's home, they would go into the living room and start their homework.

Jed began to thrive at the school despite his late start. He still didn't enjoy French but Katy would help him by teaching him the French words for objects such as pencils or sponges. Miss Goodwin always made sure to slip him an extra sausage or egg at breakfast when Charlie was in his office taking a call. Jed had asked Charlie about his mum a couple of times, but Charlie had told him there was no news of her.

The other kids in the home made a special effort the day Jed mentioned it was his birthday. Miss Goodwin passed him an extra sausage at breakfast and although it was a school day, the dinner that evening was extra tasty. Miss Goodwin had cooked a roast chicken. Charlie had commented

"Bit posh for a Friday isn't it Hilda?"

Miss Goodwin just shrugged and said

"Fishmonger was a bit short today and my parent's neighbour had a bunch of chickens just going to market. I got a bargain with this one"

One cold morning in mid November just as the children were finishing off their breakfast Mrs Hilston appeared at the kitchen door. Miss Goodwin looked up as she was pouring juice.

"Hello Jenny, what's up?"

"Is Charlie around Hilda?"

Miss Goodwin said "in his office"

Mrs Hilston walked down the corridor and knocked on the door.

"Finish up you lot," said Miss Goodwin, "No gawking now, you'll be late for school". A few minutes later Charlie came into the room

"Jed, can you come to my office please?"

Jed stood up "Leave your plate lad, I'll clear it," said Miss Goodwin. Jed followed Charlie into his office where Mrs Hilston was sitting. She looked very sad.

"Sit down Jed" he did so on the chair by the window. "Your mum has not been very well Jed, and the hospital have been treating her for a while now. She has been very sad, and..." Mrs Hilston stopped then gulped "They found her dead in her room this morning. I am so sorry Jed".

Jed stared at her in shock

"She's not dead she was ill".

Mrs Hilston replied,

"She was ill Jed, and it looks like she had a heart attack. Do you know what that is?"

Jed nodded "Your heart breaks, we learned it in class yesterday".

"Sort of yes".

"And she is never coming back to collect me?"

"No". On hearing this finality Jed's whole body was racked with sobs and Mrs Hilston took him into her arms and let him weep. She looked over at Charlie.

"He won't be at school today, can you let them know?" Charlie nodded and went out of the room.

Outside the other children were crowded around on the stairs trying to hear what was happening. Jed's sobs clearly echoed around the hallway.

"Come on now, get ready for school" Charlie gruffly said to them all "Jed's had some bad news so he won't be at school today".

The children were visibly upset, Jed was the only one of them still with a parent that might have one day collected him, which had given them all hope of adoption in the future.

Katy's parents had been killed in a crash when she was three, Ben's mum abandoned him at the church when he was a baby, and Sam's parents had adopted him from Russia but their lifestyle wasn't suited to children and they gave him up back to the authorities.

The last time Sam had seen his parents, they were telling him they would see him soon. Charlie had confirmed they weren't coming back for him during a blazing argument.

Over the years all of them had been living in the home, occasionally Mrs Hilston had visited with prospective parents, but most of these candidates wanted cute babies, not kids who in a few years would be teenagers. As they got ready for school Katy hissed to the others

"We are THERE for Jed, you hear? No one bullies him ever, especially that snake Simon". The boys nodded their heads in solemn agreement.

* * *

Jed spent the day in his room and refused to eat despite Miss Goodwin coming up with a sandwich which was one of his many favourites.

He felt hollow and empty and didn't think he would ever feel happy again. He knew his mum wasn't in the best of health but in his mind, he thought of her being in the hospital like a spa day or a holiday to get better so they could be together again.

He had not even managed to give her a proper hug goodbye. He had no one now to protect him. Mrs Hilston had told him that the doctors needed to examine his mum to make sure how she had died. She didn't expand on that information but Jed knew that doctors cut dead people up. He tried not to think about his mum lying cold and alone, but the thoughts kept on coming into his mind until in desperation he went downstairs to the kitchen where Miss Goodwin was making a pie. He startled her as he dashed into the kitchen and collapsed onto a chair.

"My head hurts" he complained.

"Not surprised Jed" she replied calmly.

"I think you need a nice mug of tea" He shook his head no.

"Well my pie is just about to go into the oven so I am having one, with biscuits!"

On hearing this word Jed looked up "Oh yes, we have a stash of lovely custard creams" she grinned. "And Charlie doesn't know where I keep them!".

She turned and got out two mugs and popped in a couple of tea bags, and a spoon of sugar. After brewing the tea in the mugs and fishing the bags out, adding milk and stirring she put one down in front of Jed.

"I'm sorry about your mum Jed. what was she like?"

Jed started to tell Miss Goodwin about his mum, all that he could remember. He finished with "I don't want to forget her, but I already am".

She looked at him calmly and said.

"Well in that case you need to write it all down, as much as you can remember. Things she told you, things she liked or hated. Her favourite songs, all of it. Then you can never forget because it's all written down. Then she will be with you forever".

Jed realised that this made a lot of sense. He took a custard cream biscuit and nibbed on the edge of it as he thought. He picked up the mug and dunked the biscuit into the hot tea. He ate the rest of the biscuit and took another one.

"Help yourself, Jed, these are for you today". They sat in comparative silence, the clock on the wall ticking away. After drinking his tea and eating another two biscuits, Jed stood up and said.

"Could I have an exercise book please?"

Miss Goodwin smiled "To write about your mum?"

"To remember, yes" agreed Jed. She walked into the office and after a few minutes came out with a ruled notebook. It was pink and had a metal spine.

"Charlie said you could have this one. It came as a free gift when the school sent a load of books over".

Jed took the notebook

"Thank you for the tea and biscuits, I'm going to write now". He headed up the stairs with the notebook in his hand.

Miss Goodwin sighed.

He was so young like all of them, all alone.

Jed spent the rest of that first day writing his memories of his mum down. He heard the other children come up the stairs after arriving home from school, and then a small knock on the door.

"Come in". Katy and Ben were standing at the doorway looking scared. Jed realised that Sam must have been in detention

"You've heard?". Katy nodded then came in and sat on the bed.

"WE," she said fiercely pointing to each of them in turn including Jed "are FAMILY! No matter what" Jed nodded.

"You're writing about her?"

"Yes, Miss Goodwin suggested it".

"We all did too, it helps when you can't remember. Mrs Cooper is coming a bit later Jed, she wants to check in on you. Dinner is in fifteen minutes, its chicken pie smells amazing"

"Yes I was with Miss Goodwin for a bit" replied Jed putting down his pen and shutting the book.

He followed the others to the bathroom to wash his hands and face, then went downstairs where Charlie and Miss Goodwin were talking quietly.

Jed could tell they were talking about him, but he didn't really care. He felt hollow and washed out. Miss Goodwin pulled the pie out of the oven, which Jed had to admit did smell great. She added large bowls of mashed potatoes and carrots to the table and then started to slice up the pie onto plates.

Jed took a small bite of his pie, but couldn't really taste much. He was glad that the others came and saw him, but he was content just to sit with them all and hear about their day at school. In the back of his mind, his thoughts churned over

Everything is the same for them, my life has stopped.

He put down his knife and fork and looked down at his feet. His eyes started to fill up again and he choked back sobs. Miss Goodwin noticed and nodded to Charlie.

"Come on Jed, I can put your dinner back in the oven again." Jed stood up and followed her out into the hallway. She ushered him into the living room where the voices of the others in the kitchen were a quiet murmur.

"Sit down," she said kindly. "Now my advice is to not try to be brave, this is a time for you to show how much your mum meant to you, and if that means crying, then so be it. My old mum calls it 'tears for the dead, tears for the left behind' and that's a very good way of looking at it. You're sad because she'd gone and you are sad because you are left behind."

At hearing this Jed stood back up and hugged Miss Goodwin hard. She returned the hug and let him weep until he was exhausted. Jed thought

She smells of pie and flowers

He was strangely comforted by the closeness. As they stood locked in an embrace the doorbell went. Charlie went to open it, noting that Miss Goodwin and Jed were in the living room. Jed heard Mrs Cooper's voice and turned to see her coming into the room.

"Jed, I wanted to come and tell you I am so sorry about your mum"

Jed felt like crying again, hearing people acknowledge the fact, whereas he was hoping it was all a giant mistake but instead he said in a low voice.

"Thank you, Miss".

"You will not be expected back to school for two weeks"

Jed looked startled at this

"It gives you time to grieve Jed and if you need more time, just let Charlie or Miss Goodwin know".

Charlie indicated to Mrs Cooper to follow him and Miss Goodwin ushered Jed back to the kitchen where the others had already finished and left their plates by the sink. She fished out his dinner and said "Could you manage a bit more dinner?"

Jed nodded and tried to eat. It didn't taste of anything but he felt sad that her lovely pie was going to waste. His mum was always keen to use up food, Jed knew as they didn't have a lot of money. He managed about half before putting down his knife and fork again.

"I'm sorry"

"Don't be Jed, it's not a problem." She swept up his food and popped the leftovers into a bin.

"It will go to the pigs"

Jed laughed "You have pigs?"

"Yes, my family own a small farm on the outskirts of the city. Maisie and Jasper, are fine pigs and had a litter just last week. I can speak to Charlie and see if you can come and see them if you would like to?"

Jed nodded. "Yes please".

"OK then, well as you are not at school for the next two weeks you are going to be my helper OK? You can start by scraping those other plates into the bin as well."

Jed followed her instructions and started to scrape the leftovers. He noted that most of the plates were cleaner than his plate was. He felt bad again, but then reasoned that the pigs would enjoy the chicken pie more than he had. He put all of the plates onto the counter top.

"Thank you, Jed, now go and read in the living room until I bring in your hot chocolate".

Jed went into the living room where the other children were already reading. Katy had the latest 'Famous Five' story. Jed had been told all about her obsession with Enid Blyton. Sam had confirmed that Katy had persuaded Mr Matthews to buy the whole collection and she was now engrossed in the story.

Jed picked up his book but couldn't concentrate on 'Space Wars Fact and Fiction' He stared at the pages but nothing was going in.

"When is your mum's funeral?" asked Katy.

"Don't know" replied Jed. "Mrs Hilston said something about finding out what went wrong with her"

Charlie came into the room with the hot chocolates, and it was clear he had heard the conversation.

"Jed, as soon as we know when the funeral is, we can make arrangements."

"What's the arrangement?" said Sam confused.

"The service" hissed back Katy.

"Yes, the service" agreed Charlie. "Mrs Hilston and the council are making the arrangements for your mum Jed, she will be along again tomorrow".

He put down the hot chocolates and patted Jed on the shoulder. Jed didn't feel comforted by Charlie as he did Miss Goodwin. He felt safe with her but he didn't think Charlie really cared. The children sat in companionable silence sipping their drinks.

"You are all orphans like me then?" asked Jed.

He'd never really thought about the subject before, the other kids had just been there. He had assumed that all of them too had family that would be along to collect them, as he had been. Not now. Katy nodded.

The others shared their stories, Sam was the most emotional of them all, despite Katy's fierce outburst earlier. All of them realised that Jed had experienced real and true love from his mother for longer than all of them.

Katy commented that she still sees flashes in her dreams of her mum and dad bent over her cot.

"I'm not sure it's even real, but it helps me".

Jed told the others about the memory book he was writing.

"That's a really nice idea, Jed," said Katy. I've said this to the others, and now to you "You are OUR family, no matter what OK?".

Jed felt tears well up. He'd always wanted brothers or sisters and now he had them. "OK," he said softly trying not to look at them.

* * *

5

Cherrywood Farm

The following day Jed woke up to find a baggy pair of dungarees, a sweatshirt and a pair of wellington boots by his bedside. Laid on top of them was a note

'These will keep you warm and dry today'

He recognised Miss Goodwin's script-like handwriting. He had seen her shopping lists which looked like gothic church manuscripts.

He quickly washed and dressed and joined the others downstairs in his socks, the wellington boots held in his hands.

He dropped them by the front door and went into breakfast. He realised he was really hungry and after grace, Jed accepted a large portion of scrambled eggs and toast.

Katy, Sam and Ben said goodbye as they dashed back upstairs to get ready for school. Jed sat in silence, enjoying the creamy eggs and buttered toast. Charlie was nowhere around, which was unusual in the mornings. Miss Goodwin noticed him looking at Charlie's empty chair.

"He's off to the Church meeting in Winchester this morning. Early start and won't be back until tomorrow Jed. Now do those wellies fit you?"

"I think so, but I don't have any thick socks - just these" Jed put up one foot encased in a thin cotton sock for Miss Goodwin to see.

"Well those are no good for anyone, you will get blisters." She turned to a drawer and pulled out a sock.

"Now these will keep you both warm and comfortable today. My mum knits socks for charity, family and friends, and I asked her to make you a pair".

Jed goggled at the blue and silver sock, Miss Goodwin held in her hand. It shimmered and sparkled and the silver thread looked like stars.

"Just one?"

"No, no" she laughed retrieving the other sock from the same drawer. "Two socks. They are made from wool and nylon so they will be strong, warm and breathable. A hug for your feet from us. Here, try them on, over your other ones. The best cure for blisters is two pairs of socks"

Jed put down his toast and went over to the sink to wash his hands, then sat back down and tried on the socks. They felt magical, soft to the touch and immediately his feet felt warmer.

"Thank you, and thank you to your mum," Jed said delightedly as he picked up his toast again and continued to chew. "Are we going to the farm today?"

"Yes once all the washing up is done. You can help me." Jed stood up after finishing his breakfast and brought his plate over to the sink. "Now, you stand on that stool there," Miss Goodwin said "and here is a tea towel. Now when I put something here in the draining rack, you wait a moment then pick it up and dry it off. OK?"

Jed nodded. Standing on the stool he could see Miss Goodwin move gracefully as she cleaned off scraps into the bin Jed thought

the piggies' bin

submerged the plate, or cup into the warm soapy water. Jed had never lived anywhere where washing up was done. His mum had lived off takeaways or meals in exchange for cleaning work, so this was a whole new world to him.

Miss Goodwin chatted as she washed, explaining that her family had lived on their farm for over one hundred years. Her great-grandparents had moved to Exeter from Ireland via London to start a new life.

"Did you like growing up on a farm? Isn't it smelly?"

"Oh my yes" she chuckled. "Sometimes the stink of the cows is a bit much, but it's my life and I still love it." Jed continued to concentrate on each plate, cup or cutlery as he carefully dried each piece.

"Do you have a boyfriend?" he asked, "a farmer?".

Miss Goodwin smiled gently. "It's hard to find a man who wants to be or is a farmer," she replied. "Most of the farmers in the area, are older than my dad, and these days women can make great farmers too. My mum does a lot of the work my dad does, they are a team".

Jed thought that sounded lovely. As they washed and dried the plates, and cups Jed started to feel at peace. His mum had always said that some boring things were good for you, and he supposed that maybe washing up dishes was one of these. After a short while, the job was done. Jed went back upstairs to collect his coat before joining Miss Goodwin in the hallway. She produced a fluffy cream wool hat and gloves from her bag.

"My mum went a bit mad with the wool from Dolly" she commented. Jed looked confused. "Dolly the sheep, she gave the wool you are wearing, the sock wool got dyed but she didn't have enough time to dye and then knit up the other stuff "

Jed laughed. "Your sheep have names?!"

"Of course, there aren't that many of them" she laughed, picking up the piggies bin they made their way outside into the car park behind the home. Miss Goodwin walked over to a small white car. It was tiny.

84

"This is Yogi" Miss Goodwin announced proudly. "Perfect for the traffic around this city." She unlocked the car and got in, putting the bin into the boot. Jed got into the passenger seat. There were only two seats and despite its size, it was roomy on the inside.

"This is a TARDIS" Jed laughed.

He loved Dr Who but hadn't watched TV for a long time, not since the last squat with his mum. She too had loved the show, especially the Daleks. One of Jed's favourite memories was watching with her, them both curled up under warm blankets on a sofa in the squat, as The Doctor tried to foil these enemies of the earth.

"Yes, it is a bit"

Miss Goodwin agreed as they buckled their seatbelts and she started the car. She drove out of the car park and into the city traffic. She drove carefully but expertly across the city. Jed loved watching people as they drove past them. He wondered how many people would be meeting pigs and sheep today. He realised not many in a city like Exeter.

After a few minutes, they got out of the city onto one of the country lanes that criss-crossed the county. The hedges were in full bloom, and the traffic started to ease in both directions.

Jed could see miles and miles of fields with sheep and pigs scattered across them. He also spotted horses standing on a hill and others running along a field at the top. After a short while, Miss Goodwin turned right into a long windy lane which led up to a farmhouse on another hill. The farmhouse looked very old. It was made of stone and wood. As they travelled carefully up the lane they passed a sign which stated 'Cherrywood Farm'.

"Your farm is called Cherrywood?" Jed asked.

"Yes Jed, there is a cherry orchard in the backfield too. We have to keep the animals out of there, otherwise, there is nothing left for us to make pies with. My dad likes making stuff out of wood as well. You'll see" she added laughing.

She pulled up in front of the house where a tractor was parked. Jed was amazed. He'd never been in the countryside, and although there was a scent in the air of

cow poo?

He liked the noises he could hear and the wind that blew across his face.

"Now get your coat, hat and gloves, and we'll go and see my mum first".

Jed got out of the car with his belongings and Miss Goodwin pulled out the piggies bin. She dropped it by the front door walked inside called

"Mum, I've brought Jed to see you". Jed followed her in shyly. He didn't really know how to meet people, and he stood behind Miss Goodwin. An older version of Miss Goodwin came into the hallway from a kitchen Jed could see behind her.

"Oh Hilda, it's lovely to see you again. Come here sweetie" Miss Goodwin's mum looked just as nice as she did, with an apron covered in flour and several spots in her curly hair. She had a warm smile and Jed immediately realised she was also a nice person. She turned to Jed and smiled warmly.

"Hello Jed, I'm sorry to hear about your mum, our Hilda said that you might like to spend some time with us. I've got a nice glass of warm milk for you to start with. Hilda, a cup of tea?"

All of this was said in a soft west country lilt which Jed realised made him feel safe. She wasn't expecting a reply but Jed nodded as did Miss Goodwin beside him.

They followed her out into a large kitchen which was filled with pots and pans and in the corner was an Aga. Jed knew all about Agas from John one of the other people in the squat who told him about them, and how he would have a house one day of his own with an Aga.

Jed's mum and the others in the squat just smiled at the tales John told. They knew that like them he was unlikely to ever have his own house and certainly not an aga. Jed sat down where he was told, at the massive wooden table in the centre of the room. The table looked old and worn, but also looked like it had been scrubbed very well. He was passed a glass brimming with milk, and as promised it was warm. This confused Jed until the others noticed

"It's straight from Daisy," said Mrs Goodwin, "She's just been milked this morning."

Jed took a small cautious sip. It was delicious. Not like the milk he normally drank at home, creamy and fresh.

"Bit different from what you get from the milkman eh?" added Mrs Goodwin.

"Yes Miss," said Jed taking another long sip. He finished the milk whilst Miss Goodwin and her mother sipped their tea and chatted. He liked being with them, it took his mind off his troubles and thinking about his mum.

He was also grateful he didn't have to go to school for a while and deal with all the stares and the comments behind his back. He was glad that when he did, his friends

family

in the home would be there to support and defend him. Jed soon polished off the milk and carefully put the glass back down on the table.

A few minutes later a tall stout man walked into the kitchen through another door. He was over six feet tall and wore a baggy woollen jumper and cord trousers tucked into warm-looking woollen socks. He didn't seem surprised that they had visitors and Jed supposed this was Miss Goodwin's dad.

"Hello," he said "You must be Jed. My name is Gary, and you have already met my gorgeous Millie here" indicating Miss Goodwin's mum. Miss Goodwin and her mum giggled. It seemed that this was a common phrase said here in this warm and cosy room. Jed liked them straight away.

"Hello," said Jed shyly. "Thank you for the milk".

"Our pleasure Jed, I'm just going to have a cuppa then we'll take you out and show you the farm". Mrs Goodwin

Millie

Jed thought, got up and poured a cup of tea for her husband. Their routines and habits were comforting to Jed, and he watched them fascinated.

He'd not been exposed to many people who liked each other during his time with his mum. Some of the other squat inhabitants were keen to be together but these relationships rarely lasted more than a few weeks before one or other of them would yell and scream and leave. He could see that both Millie and Gary and Hilda all liked and respected each other very much.

His mum had not had any partners for many years, and Jed knew that his dad had been another resident of a squat back in London.

He'd once asked his mum about his dad, but she had not given him any information and had been sad for the rest of that day. Jed learned not to ask awkward questions as he grew up, and his mum provided for him all he needed. Jed suddenly remembered his new socks, hat and mittens.

"Thank you for my socks, hat and gloves" Millie laughed

"My pleasure Jed, it's nice to have someone to knit for. Gary and Hilda can only wear so many things I make. They will keep you warm on the farm today."

* * *

Twenty minutes later Jed and Hilda pulled on their wellington boots, coats and gloves and followed Mr Goodwin out into the yard behind the house.

Miss Goodwin had the scraps bin from the home, which she carried out into the sunshine. On this side of the farm, the wind was stronger and Jed was glad of the warm clothing he was wearing.

At the top of the yard was a large tractor with a trailer behind it. Jed gawked at it. It was bright yellow and had huge wheels which were taller than any of them. Mr Goodwin however lifted his leg up and hauled himself expertly into the cab of the tractor, then looked down at Jed who felt very small indeed.

He held out a hand and Jed took it, feeling himself be pulled easily up into the cab beside Mr Goodwin and sat down on a small pull-out seat. Miss Goodwin, popped the scraps bin onto the trailer, then got in as well and wedged herself behind her dad

"Right off we go". said Mr Goodwin as he released the brake and started the engine. The tractor moved off out of the yard and onto a track across a field behind the farmyard. Jed had not been in the countryside at all before now, and the wide-open fields and space left him in awe.

Both Miss Goodwin and her father had grown up here, spending their days walking these fields. He felt completely calm as he sat beside Mr Goodwin as he expertly navigated the track down to a stream at the bottom of the fields.

There were a collection of cows in one field and sheep in the other one. The tractor stopped and Miss Goodwin got out from behind her father's seat. She walked around to the other side and opened the door, helping Jed out onto the grass. She walked back to the trailer and helped her dad pull off the feed for the cows.

Jed knew Miss Goodwin was strong, he had seen her put heavy loads of laundry down at the home, but she lifted each sack without any apparent effort. Mr Goodwin pulled out a penknife and slit the bag, picking it up as easily as his daughter did, and started to lay a trail out for the cows who had gathered around. These were small cows, brown in colour with white blotches. They had big wide eyes and lashes which made them look like Disney characters.

"They're Jersey cows," said Mr Goodwin. "Great milkers, and no problems".

"Have you always had these cows?" Jed asked as one of them came up and nuzzled his shoulder. He didn't feel scared or worried. He was nearly as tall as most of the cows, and apart from the one, the others were more interested in the trail of feed Miss Goodwin was laying down.

"Pretty much so, yes" replied Mr Goodwin. "My grandparents came here from Ireland back in the early 1900s, they had been farmers in Ireland but the owner of their land wanted more money which they couldn't afford. So they came to England seeking a new life, and this" Mr Goodwin lifted his hands indicating the fields and house "was the result after many years of hard work".

Miss Goodwin came back after emptying the sack and took down another one. "Enough chatter" she joked. "Jed want to help me get these out?"

Jed nodded and walked over to where she was cutting into the sack.

"I'll hold it until it's about half empty, then you can take it over OK?"

Jed did so, following her as she laid another trail of feed on the grass. She stopped then handed him the sack showing him how to dispense it evenly. Jed walked along with several cows walking behind him laying the trail as he'd been shown. When the bag was empty he grinned and turned. Cows were eating along the trail.

"Well done lad!" said Mr Goodwin "Fine work. Right onto the sheep next".

Both Mr Goodwin and his daughter picked up a different sack each and opened a gate to where the sheep were crowded around waiting for their turn. All of them had only a limited fleece coat, and Jed thought they looked a bit cold and strange. Miss Goodwin pointed out one of the sheep which had a blue mark on her flank near her leg.

"That's Dolly, who donated the wool Mum made your socks, hat and gloves from".

"Don't they need a lot of fleece to keep warm?" Jed said feeling a bit guilty in his warm woollen items but Miss Goodwin didn't laugh.

"No Jed, If one year's wool is not removed by shearing, the next year's growth just adds to it, resulting in sheep that overheat in summer. If they are not sheared, they have greatly decreased mobility and are in much greater danger from fly-strike, all of which causes suffering and possible death."

"What's fly strike?" asked Jed puzzled.

"Fly strike is a painful, sometimes fatal condition caused by flies laying eggs on another animal, which hatch into maggots and eat their 'hosts' flesh," said Mr Goodwin.

Jed was shocked. It sounded like something from a horror movie.

"We have to shear the sheep so that doesn't happen. Lots of what we do on the farm are to give our animals a better life whether that's getting the vet out for a lame animal to helping them when they are having little ones" Miss Goodwin came back for a second bag.

"Better give Hilda a hand " chuckled Mr Goodwin.

Jed helped Hilda with the rest of the feed for the sheep who like the cows were happily munching on the trail that had been left for them. When all the bags were emptied and were back on the trailer, Mr Goodwin indicated that they should get back onto the tractor.

Jed found it easier after watching Miss Goodwin easily climb back into the cab, and he followed her lead and was soon back in the seat. Mr Goodwin climbed back in and after starting the tractor again, they made their way along the trail, towards more fields in the far corner of the farm.

Jed could see trees in a high orchard ahead of them. As Miss Goodwin had already said, there was a strong fence all around the trees. The trees were in straight rows but they didn't have any blossom on them.

"Those are the reason our farm is called Cherrywood," Mr Goodwin said. "My grandparents planted these trees in their first years here and they have been fruiting ever since."

"Can you eat them?" Jed asked. He had only ever had a cherry on a cake, his mum had bought for him in a bakery near the squat.

"Yes these are sweet cherries, Jed" replied Miss Goodwin. "Mum makes amazing cherry pies with them".

Mr Goodwin looked out at the trees.

"A long time ago Jed, down the coast there was an area called the Tamar Valley which was so famous for its cherry blossoms, that Queen Victoria visited them."

"Has she visited your orchard?" Jed asked.

"Oh no" laughed Mr Goodwin, "She died in 1901, and my grandparents didn't make the trip over until 1903".

Mr Goodwin started up the tractor again and moved off down the trail back to the house. Jed could see on the other side of the farmhouse a large field with a barn in the middle of it. The barn was mostly just a roof over the area. As they approached Jed could see pigs in pens underneath. He could also hear them, rapid squealing as the tractor approached.

Mr Goodwin pulled up to the gate and got out to open it. Jed was surprised when Miss Goodwin hopped into the driving seat and started to move the tractor expertly through the gate. Jed's mouth was agape and Miss Goodwin looked over with a chuckle.

"Been driving these things since I was younger than you Jed" she chuckled. She drove carefully over to the barn, Mr Goodwin closing the gate and following on foot. She parked up.

"Come on then Jed, let's give these piggies their treats". They both got out and picked up the scraps bin from the trailer then followed Mr Goodwin into the barn where the pig's noise got much louder. Inside were five pigs and the noise was tremendous.

"They know they are in for a treat" yelled Mr Goodwin. Miss Goodwin opened the bin, which was very smelly and tipped it up into a trough on the other side of the pen. The pigs immediately gathered and shuffled for a spot and started to eat.

The noise levels went back down to snuffling which made it easier for Jed to hear what Mr Goodwin was saying.

"These are British Landrace pigs, Jed. They are the best pigs for our needs. That's Lucy" he said pointing out one with a grey spot on her back "Samuel is the one with the yellow and blue mark, Kenny is the biggest one at the trough, and Harriet is the smallest one there - she's got a bit out of her ear. And finally, Hilda's favourite Maggie is the one snuffling around for the leftovers there on the ground"

"I bottle-fed Maggie," said Miss Goodwin as she came back over from the trough. "Her mother rejected her as she was a runt".

"Doesn't look much like a runt now does she Jed?" said Mr Goodwin laughing.

"Do they get eaten?" asked Jed sadly. He knew from some of the people who were in the squat about vegetarians and how they hated to see animals being killed for food. A couple of the people in the last squat were very vocal in their beliefs and had been arrested a few times protesting outside the local burger shop.

"No they don't Jed, but we do have some pigs that are reared for meat" replied Mr Goodwin. "That's the life of a farmer, unfortunately. We grow stuff and some of those things are animals. When these pigs have babies, we do move those pigs to a rearing shed for slaughter when they are six months old".

Jed looked at the pigs in the pen and suddenly burst into tears.

"Oh Jed, what's wrong?" Miss Goodwin put down the bin and came over, bending down. Jed was mortified. He'd not cried since his mum died, but watching the pigs and knowing that their babies were dead had just overwhelmed him. She hugged him softly until he was able to talk.

"Their babies" he sobbed.

"Yes Jed it's a hard lesson, I'm sorry, maybe this wasn't such a good idea". Jed pulled away and gulped.

"No," he said. "I'm sorry Miss"

"Don't be Jed, you are in shock with all that's happened. The pigs are not awake when they are killed, Jed. They don't know anything. We don't send them to just any abattoir, we have one who we know will look after them as carefully as we do, because we do care about them. All farmers care Jed, but at the end of the day, we raise them to make us money, and unlike the sheep and cows, pigs aren't useful for anything other than meat and eating the scraps"

Mr Goodwin looked kindly at Jed. Jed nodded and wiped his face with his sleeve. He knew that this was right and that the pigs that the Goodwin's looked after would have a good life. Mr Goodwin passed over a hanky so Jed could wipe his face and blow his nose.

"It's clean, Millie gives me a fresh one every morning, and I haven't used it yet" he chuckles as Jed tried to give it back.

"No that's OK, we have loads, you keep it". Jed tucked the hanky carefully into his coat pocket, as Miss Goodwin closed the gate to the pig pens.

"I think we need to get back to the house for lunch," said Miss Goodwin "Mum's been baking this morning". Jed followed Miss Goodwin back to the house, whilst Mr Goodwin parked the tractor behind the house again.

"Boot's off" called Mrs Goodwin "Lunch is nearly ready, get your hands washed please". Jed followed Miss Goodwin's lead in getting her boots off and trotting into the kitchen before heading for the scullery where there was a large stone sink. They washed their hands before joining Mr & Mrs Goodwin back at the kitchen table.

"Pie is steak and kidney, there is mash potato and greens," said Mrs Goodwin as she cut into the pie. Steam billowed out and the smell was amazing. Jed hadn't realised how hungry he was but accepted a huge slice of steaming pie. Jed was used to waiting for Charlie to say grace and he was surprised that didn't happen here.

"Go on Jed, tuck in," said Mrs Goodwin.

"You don't say grace?" said Jed a little surprised.

"We worship God by looking after his animals and his land, and each other" replied Mr Goodwin gently.

He smiled at his wife and daughter. Jed picked up his knife and fork and nearly moaned out loud. The pie was amazing. The others also started to eat and the room was filled with silence until Miss Goodwin said.

"Dad, I was going to bring Jed here for a couple of weeks, is that OK? You could do with an extra pair of hands."

Mr Goodwin nodded.

"If that's OK with you Jed? Hilda's right, we are coming into a busy time here on the farm. There will be plenty for you to do." Jed was delighted but remembered to finish his mouthful before nodding.

"Yes sir, please"

"OK then, that's settled then. Jed realised he was truly content. Although the pain of his mum, and the earlier crying had made him feel drained, the warm and comforting food and these people had calmed his fears about being alone. He knew he was safe her with them.

* * *

And so for the next two weeks, Jed's routine became much different to his friends in the children's home. He had breakfast with Katy, Sam and Ben, but as they left for school Jed got into the overalls that Miss Goodwin had adjusted for him. She had brought them back with her on the first day, and after measuring Jed up she had taken them in and adjusted the length so they fitted.

"These were a pair of Dad's old ones so they will be fine," she said as Jed once again stood on the chair, whilst she pinned and clipped the overalls.

Each morning after breakfast Jed accompanied Miss Goodwin back to the farm, to be treated to another glass of warm milk and a hug from Mrs Goodwin, as she started her morning bakes. One day near the end of the two weeks Mrs Goodwin stopped her baking and turned to him.

"Your mum's in heaven with the Lord".

"How do you know?" asked Jed. His mum had never been religious but being at the school, he had learned that sinners went to hell.

"Because she loved you, Jed, she brought you up to be a fine young man, and that means that in the eyes of God she is sin free."

Jed thought about this over the next few days and realised that in his heart he believed her. Better that than the furious God that the Church School suggested.

Each day Jed was led by Mr Goodwin to a different part of the farm and did his best to help. After a few days, Jed was strong enough to manage the feed bags almost by himself.

He enjoyed the process and being out in the fresh air brought colour to his skin. He also enjoyed visiting the pigs in the barn and was quickly able to distinguish them from each other. Their noises of contentment when the piggie bin appeared made him laugh. As the final day approached Jed was sitting on a bale of hay watching Lucy snuffle in the trough for treats she had missed. He was going to miss this place. Miss Goodwin came and sat down beside him.

"What were your mum's favourite flowers, Jed? Mrs Hilston needs to know as the council wants to put some flowers on her coffin?" Jed knew the answer immediately

"Freesia's," he said confidently. "Mum loved the displays of them in Cathedral Square by the church".

"OK, then freesias it is" she replied "I'll let Jenny know".

"You can come back at weekends if you would like. But you also need to get back to school as well Jed. I'm sorry because I know Dad would have loved to get you working here, but you are too young at the moment".

Jed knew she was right, but he wasn't looking forward to going back at all.

* * *

6

Simon Thomas

Simon Thomas was waiting for Jed on his first day back at school just before the Christmas holidays. The class had been told he was returning and Simon nodded at his gang. They all knew what this meant. Simon had primed them during the time Jed was not at school.

"We're going to give him a good welcome back lads," said Simon one break time. He and his fellow bullies had taken over the bench at the back of the playground. "Thinks he's something special" he added with a grunt as he scuffed his shoes on the tarmac." Well let's welcome the little orphan boy back!" he finished as the bell for the next class went off.

Jed had truly dreaded his first day back, but Katy, Sam and Ben had walked with him and Ben had tried to fly down the road to make him laugh. The sight of his friend frantically flapping his arms as he careered down the road did make Jed smile a bit.

Jed went to Mrs Cooper's office as he arrived. She was kind and asked him how he was feeling. Jed couldn't really answer her. His last two weeks were sad but also the best he had since before his mum died. She had been kind to him but explained that apart from the day for his mum's funeral which had finally been arranged, he was to be at school full-time for now.

She knew that his mum's funeral was on Thursday and said he would not be expected back until the following Monday. After leaving Mrs Cooper's office he walked down when the rest of the class was waiting outside Mr Wall's room.

Katy made room for him in the queue despite mutterings coming from Simon Thomas and his friends about 'jumping in'. Things only got worse from there on in.

As they made their way into the room, Jed heard Simon hiss 'Orphan' behind him. Jed didn't turn around but Katy glared at Simon as they walked to their desks. During Mr Wall's French lesson, Simon and his friends continued to hiss at Jed but made sure that Mr Wall's back was turned at the time. The noise levels in the class disguised their bullying until at one point the teacher happened to turn around just as Simon was mimicking crying into his hands.

Mr Wall swiftly walked up between the desks, Simon being the only one who was not paying attention despite the gasps coming from those around him who could see what was coming. Suddenly his arm was wrenched upwards. Simon was startled to find himself looking into the furious face of his French teacher.

"Simon Thomas, you are a pathetic bully who is going to spend the next month with me after school!" said Mr Wall with barely concealed rage. "Mrs Cooper will be writing to your parents, and if this continues you WILL be expelled!".

Jed and the rest of the class looked at Simon who was trying not to cry but had an expression of fury on his pinched face.

"Now go and see Mrs Cooper and tell her what you have done. I will be checking on you later". Simon gathered his books and bag and stomped out of the room.

"Now class, onto the next chapter" Mr Wall said as he walked back to the front of the class. The room settled down, but Jed knew that this was going to make Simon and his friends more frantic about getting their revenge. He started to wish he was back at Cherrywood Farm. He daydreamed through the rest of the lesson, imagining he was back scratching Daisy behind the ears again, listening to the others grunting as they hunted for more scraps in their pens. During break time, Katy dragged Jed, Sam and Ben into the library.

"He is pathetic" she announced "but he is going to be even more furious now" Jed looked confused until she added. "Sara Roberts who lives down the road from Simon told me that the police were called last time Simon got detention. His dad beat him and his mum up, and was arrested. If that happens again I think he will try and take it out on you".

Jed groaned. "Why me?" he asked. "What have I done to him?"

"Nothing!" Ben replied "He picked on me last year just because he saw me wearing something he said was from a charity shop. When I told him I didn't care, he started on me, calling me 'charity boy' every time he could. Nightmare".

"So, we have to make sure that Jed isn't alone" Katy mused. "We are fine for the walk to and from school, but we aren't in your English or Maths lessons with you. Leave it with me, Jed we will make sure that Simon decides to pick on someone else".

They walked to the next lesson which was RE. Miss Cartwright was on extended leave due to the incident with the Action Man/Jesus incident. She had not returned to the school the following day and Mrs Cooper had been forced to call the Church Board for a substitute. Mr King was an experienced Religious education tutor and the class had quietened down when he first arrived.

"I will be looking after your class until the end of term" he announced, looking directly at Ben who blushed "and as I am much taller, please note that any tricks will have to be higher than the last attempt". Ben looked sheepish and got out his books.

The rest of the day passed without incident. Simon and his friends were sat at the other end of the canteen during lunchtime, and Katy did as she had promised. Jed was not alone in any of the classes or the times moving between them. She had asked one of his classmates in English and Maths, a ginger-haired boy called John to 'look after Jed'. John had a crush on Katy and readily agreed.

John was one of the taller boys in their year and was currently the hero of the under 11's rugby team. Jed felt a bit embarrassed at first but walking with John to and from the classes his other friends couldn't protect him in, was comforting as well.

Jed also found that he liked John as well. They had a love of space and science in common. John told Jed as they walked to their maths class, that he had done an experiment in his mum's kitchen with a magnifying glass and her favourite lipstick, which rapidly melted all over her kitchen table.

"I was grounded for a week," he said with a chuckle "and no pocket money for two months until she was able to buy another lipstick in the same shade. It was worth it though. I'm sorry about your mum" Jed looked at John who blushed "Katy told me hope that's OK?" Jed nodded. He couldn't really speak when people were kind to him at the moment.

* * *

7

Twenty Eleven

The day Jed said a final goodbye to his mum was a bright and frosty one in early December. . Jed had received a visit from Mrs Hilston the night before, explaining that the council had made all the arrangements for his mum, and what would be happening. They sat at the kitchen table with a cup of hot chocolate each.

"I will be picking you up Jed at 9.30 am tomorrow. Miss Goodwin and Charlie will also be there, along with some of your mum's friends"

Jed looked surprised at this.

"Who's Mum's friends?" he asked.

"Someone called Big Mike" she replied "Came into the council offices the day after your mum died and asked the receptionist for the person looking after you. He's definitely a big chap, isn't he?" Jed nodded. "Anyway I came out into the reception and he explained that he and some of your mum's other friends from the squat would like to be at her funeral. He came back yesterday and was told where and when so you can expect some more people than just us there".

Jed knew that the people in the squat were kind, but hearing that they would be coming made him feel warm and a bit teary. Mrs Hilston noticed but didn't comment. "Anyway" she turned to see Miss Goodwin coming into the room. "Hilda found a suit which she has cut down so you could look your smartest". Jed turned to see Miss Goodwin holding up a black jacket and trousers. In her other hand was a clean white shirt with a black tie.

"Can you try this on Jed, if it needs taking in any more I can do that before tomorrow?"

Jed nodded and quickly tried on the suit. It fitted him perfectly. Both women looked like they might cry but Mrs Hilston just gulped loudly and said softly

"It looks perfect Hilda, well done"

Miss Goodwin nodded. "Your school shoes will have a good clean and polish too".

Jed hugged Miss Goodwin tightly. "Thank you," he said, trying not to cry down his new suit.

Miss Goodwin hugged him back without a word. He quickly got back out of the clothes which Miss Goodwin then hung back up. She went out of the room "These will be on your hanger in your room" she said as Jed sat back down with Mrs Hilston.

"The council is also arranging flowers, I understand from Miss Goodwin that your mum loved freesias?"

"Yes, she did" Jed replied looking into his hot chocolate.

"Well, that's what will be on her coffin.

After finishing their hot chocolate Mrs Hilston said. "I will see you tomorrow Jed." she hugged him around his shoulders and then left. Jed went into the lounge where Katy, Sam and Ben were trying to pretend they hadn't been listening to the conversation.

"We wanted to come tomorrow," Ben said, "but Charlie said we had to go to school." Sam added, "but we are going to be thinking of you".

Jed sat down and took out his book, but he couldn't concentrate. His tummy felt like he had drunk snakes, not hot chocolate.

* * *

Jed was unable to eat anything for breakfast the next day, but Miss Goodwin just nodded and passed him a cup of tea. He tried not to look at the other children who were quieter than normal. Even Ben just ate his eggs and bacon without a constant commentary about them, life, and the birds who had laid the eggs.

Before they left Sam, Katy and Ben just placed their hand on Jed's shoulder without a word and left. He was glad they hadn't tried to do more to comfort him, but he knew that they would be there for him tonight and forever.

Miss Goodwin started to clear the plates from the table and Jed helped. Keeping busy was good and he concentrated on making sure each of the plates was scraped clean into the piggie bin, and then placed on the counter ready for washing.

Eventually, that job was done, and Jed realised that he could delay no longer. He went up into his bedroom where the suit was hanging up on the rail. His school shoes lay clean and polished beneath the suit. He looked at his suit and then sat down on the bed heavily.

He picked up the notebook he had been writing all his memories of his mum and started to read it. His eyes started to fill up and tears dropped onto the pages, but he didn't stop reading. Miss Goodwin knocked on the door and entered.

"Your mum would be so proud of how brave you are being, but you know that being brave is not the bravest thing you can do for her?" Jed looked up, his eyes still full of unshed tears.

"Your mum would be even more proud of you for showing how much you care about her, how much you miss her, and how each and every one of these tears will keep her close to you forever. So don't think you cant weep for your mum, she knows how much these emotions will help you in the future"

Jed looked at Miss Goodwin though he still didn't really understand what she meant, he did know that by crying he did feel a little bit better, and the weight in his tummy was a little less hard.

"So now, go wash your face and clean those teeth of yours. I'll help you into your suit"

Jed did as he was asked and came back into the room where Miss Goodwin had laid out his suit. He quickly changed out of his tee shirt and trousers into the clothes.

"OK, Mrs Hilston will be here in a few minutes, go and sit in the lounge to wait for her." Miss Goodwin said. "I need to get changed too."

Jed sat in his chair and waited. Miss Goodwin appeared a few minutes later. She had changed out of her apron and dress into a black dress that flowed around her like silk with a matching black jacket with silver buttons. She looked beautiful Jed realised. She had tied back her blonde hair with a black clip and she had a small arrangement of freesias in her right lapel tied with a black ribbon. In her hand was another arrangement.

"This is for you Jed," She said holding out the buttonhole. Jed stood still whilst she deftly placed the flowers on his lapel in the same place hers was. "Over your heart so you never forget her" she added.

The doorbell rang and Charlie went to answer it. He was also wearing a suit, but unlike Jed's one, it was a dark grey and it didn't really fit him well. Charlie almost never wore a suit at the home. The only time Jed had seen him in one was when the Circuit Superintendent Ministers had come to the home for an inspection and a meeting.

Charlie looked uncomfortable being in the room. He was never a source of comfort for Jed or the other children and he didn't look like he wanted to start now either. Mrs Hilston came into the room. She too was wearing a black dress but her one was longer than Miss Goodwin's. Miss Goodwin passed her a buttonhole too.

"Thank you, Hilda," she said softly as she put her buttonhole on her dress. "OK Jed, are you ready?"

Jed nodded though he really wanted to go back up to his room and never come out again. They all walked out into the car park. Miss Goodwin got in Mrs Hilston's car with Jed in the back. Charlie walked over to his car. Mrs Hilston set off towards the east of the city.

The city was busy with cars and buses and pedestrians but a short time later the cars pulled up outside the Crematorium on Topsham Road.

Mrs Hilston parked in a space near the front door where there were a few people standing around and talking. Jed looked over at the group of people. He recognised Big Mike immediately though he wasn't wearing his favourite denim jacket and jeans. Big Mike was wearing proper trousers which looked a bit tight and a nearly white shirt with a grey tie. He looked nearly as uncomfortable as Charlie was.

Some of the other people Jed also recognised but he didn't know their names. All of them were also wearing clothes he had not seen before. People in the squat rarely wore good clothes. The conditions they lived in meant that clothes didn't last very long either from the dampness or being nibbled by the rodents that also made their home there.

Jed got out of the car followed by Miss Goodwin and Mrs Hilston. Charlie pulled up his car next to them and got out. He glared at the group by the door but didn't say anything. He shuffled behind the group and followed them all in. Mrs Hilston nodded at Big Mike and the others before leading Jed into the chapel.

* * *

Jed had never been in a chapel before but this one was beautiful. The entranceway lead into a large room with wood panels on the floor, the walls and the ceiling which rose upwards into the roof. It was light and airy and didn't look like a church. Jed followed Mrs Hilston down the aisle to where a young woman dressed in a dark blue suit was waiting for them.

She smiled at Jed and said, "My name is Jane, and I will be conducting the service for your mum today".

"Are you a vicar?" asked Jed confused. She didn't appear to be wearing a dog collar. She laughed politely and shook her head.

"No, I am a celebrant . That means that because your mum wasn't religious, we can talk in the service about her without religion, or we can include hymns if you would like".

"She liked Morning is broken" replied Jed firmly.

"The hymn or the pop song?" asked Jane.

"I don't know" replied Jed confused. Mrs Hilston nodded to the celebrant.

"It doesn't matter but as long as we can have it?" Jane nodded.

Jed's head was hurting. He didn't want to make a decision and he was glad that both Mrs Hilston and Miss Goodwin were there for him. Mrs Hilston looked over at Charlie who was by the front door and said

"Jed, your mum's casket is coming, we need to go outside to meet it".

Jed followed Mrs Hilston outside with Miss Goodwin and Jane behind.

In the distance coming down the same driveway was a sleek black funeral car. In front of it were two men in suits and top hats walking slowly in time with each other. They matched their steps to each other and the car behind them crawled along.

After a few minutes, the men and the car arrived at the entrance to the chapel. Big Mike and the other people from the squat bent their heads. Jed carried on looking at the car. His mum was inside that box in the back. He could see flowers on top of the box. The men walked to the back of the car, and the driver and a passenger got out too. Together the four of them, all dressed in dark grey suits opened the back of the car, and

Mum

in her box was lifted onto the shoulders of the four men. In unison they turned and walked into the chapel with the box on their shoulders, moving slowly. Jed wondered if the box was heavy. His mum had been a small woman, barely taller than he was, and wiry thin.

Mrs Hilston ushered him beside her and they followed them into the chapel again. Jed looked back to see Miss Goodwin and Charlie behind and Big Mike and the others bringing up the rear. Jed had never seen Big Mike upset before, even when his dog had to be put down at the PDSA. Yet now Mike was walking behind the coffin trying not to look at anyone, tears running freely down his face.

The men arrived at the end of the aisle and put the box down on a tall stand behind an arrangement of flowers. Jed was pleased to see the flowers on the coffin and in the tall vase were freesias. His mum called them 'bunches of sunshine' whenever she saw them in the florist's window displays. There were blue, white, yellow and even pink ones.

Jed followed Mrs Hilston to a bench at the front of the aisle and Miss Goodwin and Charlie sat down beside them. Jed looked around again and saw Big Mike being passed a large handkerchief from one of the other people there whom he thought was called Sid. All of the people Jed had seen in the last squat were there. He thought.

Twenty Eleven, there are more than Twenty Eleven people here for Mum.

Jed looked back at the front of the chapel. The box his mum was in was a dark brown colour and had handles on the side. The celebrant Jane cleared her throat and announced.

"We are here to celebrate the life of Clare Long. Her family and friends are here to say goodbye".

Jed looked down at his shoes as she continued to talk. Miss Goodwin slipped her hand into his and squeezed. Jed didn't look at her but felt better for her doing that. He could hear Big Mike behind him, sniffing. Jed turned his attention back to Jane who was still talking about his mum.

She had talked to people who had known her, Jed thought as she commented on his mum's love of family and friends and her joy in being a mother. Jed listened more carefully to what the woman was saying now. He liked to hear that his mum loved him. He knew that she did, but sometimes when he was not being good, she would get annoyed with him. Yet when she had calmed down, she had hugged him and kissed his forehead. He missed her dreadfully and despite trying not to, he followed Big Mike with tears running down his face. Miss Goodwin fished a handkerchief out of her bag which wasn't as big as the one Big Mike had received and passed it to him. Jed held it in his hand but didn't wipe his face. He remembered what Miss Goodwin had said and let his tears show how much he missed and loved her.

* * *

After the service was finished, the people attending started to drift up to the coffin and many placed flowers on top of it. Most were freesias but Jed saw Big Mike place a single red rose onto the top of the pile.

Jed realised that Big Mike loved his mum, and that made his throat tighten again. Miss Goodwin, Mrs Hilston and Charlie were the last to go up, and Miss Goodwin lightly touched the top of the coffin and silently mouthed something. Jed could not make out the words but when she turned and saw Jed, he noticed that her eyes were full of tears again. Jed was the last to go up and he placed his hand on the coffin. Was his mum still in there, or was she in heaven as Mrs Goodwin had said? He still thought Mrs Goodwin was right. He turned and joined the others outside. Big Mike came over to him and bent down.

"I'm so sorry about your mum Jed. She was a lovely person". Jed looked up at the big man and said

"Thanks. Have you found another home?"

Big Mike nodded and put his finger to his nose, in a gesture of confidentiality. He whispered back. "Nice place just down from the local Church. been empty since the owner died. Doesn't look like it will be sold anytime soon." Miss Goodwin came over to Jed and said.

"We need to go now, Jed". Jed turned and followed her back to the car where Mrs Hilston and Charlie were waiting. Charlie looked like he didn't want to be there, but Mrs Hilston was smiling at him. Next to her was the celebrant Jane. She held out her hand and shook Jed's small hand, then turned and went back inside.

* * *

Back at the home, Jed went back upstairs and changed out of the suit, carefully hanging it back up again. He put on his sweatshirt and trousers plus the socks Mrs Goodwin had made for him then went downstairs where Mrs Hilston and Miss Goodwin were chatting in the kitchen.

"Sit down Jed," said Mrs Hilston. Jed did so. "When your mum's ashes are ready, you have a choice on where you would like them to be scattered or buried". Jed knew all about cremations. His mum was going to be or had been burned.

He knew she didn't want to be buried. They had talked about things like that when he had been with her. Not often, just when a movie came on the portable TV where people were dead and coming out of their graves. Jed realised he probably shouldn't have seen these sorts of films but he always felt safe with his mum, and he knew from her that this was make-believe. Jed thought on the matter for a few minutes, he needed to make sure she was in a pretty place.

"scattered, in the Cherry Orchard" he finally announced, adding "Please?" looking at Miss Goodwin.

She took a deep breath, Jed knew she was trying not to cry again. She nodded.

"It would be our pleasure" she finally said.

Jed was pleased. He knew his mum would have loved the view out over the hills with the pink blossoms falling on the ground. Mrs Hilston passed Jed a cup of hot chocolate.

"Tell us about your Mum Jed?". Jed did, he spent an hour talking about her until he thought he had said everything he could remember. He was glad Charlie wasn't there. He didn't understand.

* * *

8

Laid to rest

A week after the funeral Jed was collected by Mrs Hilston and Miss Goodwin and driven back to Cherrywood Farm. There was snow on the hills, but they made good time on the roads.

On Jed's lap was a grey plastic container that contained the ashes of his mum. Jed was wearing his funeral suit again, and in the jacket pocket, he had got his mum's memory book. Miss Goodwin had asked him to bring it with him, but he was confused as to why. She just smiled and said

"You'll see soon enough"

Jed cradled the container on his lap as the city streets gave way to the glorious countryside. As they drove up the lane to the farm, Jed could see the cherry trees on the hill but they were bare of blossom still, their branches twisted. Jed hoped that there would be blossom in the spring.

As the car pulled up outside the farmhouse Jed could see Mr & Mrs Goodwin come out to greet them all. Mr Goodwin had a clean pair of overalls on, and Mrs Goodwin had a pretty dress on, though she was wearing a practical pair of shoes with them.

"Hello," said Mrs Goodwin, as they all got out of the car. "We've done some tea for you all for afterwards"

Jed was confused but Mrs Goodwin added

"We're going to have a wake for your mum Jed, just us all. Is that OK?"

"What is a Wake?" asked Jed.

Miss Goodwin turned to him and said.

"A Wake is for you Jed, for the living. It's a chance for you to share your memories of your mum with us all so we can remember her with you".

Jed remembered the memory book and realised why Miss Goodwin had asked him to bring it. Mr Goodwin smiled at Jed

"We've got a lovely day for it".

After a few minutes of chat in the yard, the group walked up the hill to the cherry orchard. Jed could hear the pigs grunting in their pens as they walked by. The container felt cool in his arms as he walked. Around him were people who understood and didn't try and make him do anything. They just were.

As they got to the orchard, Mr Goodwin went ahead and opened the gate. Inside the trees were bare. Mr Goodwin walked to the last row of trees which looked out over the countryside and the farm down below.

"Is this a good spot Jed?" Jed nodded. The sunshine on his face felt comforting. He knew his mum wasn't in this container, but he also wanted the place her ashes would lie, to be perfect. This spot was. Miss Goodwin helped Jed to take the lid off the container and then turned him around slightly so the light breeze was behind him facing down the rows of trees.

"What do I do?" he asked suddenly frightened he was going to make a mistake.

"Shall I show you?" she asked gently.

Jed nodded. She took the container and turned it slightly downwards. Grey-white ash started to fall out of the container and was immediately taken by the breeze down the row of trees. She tilted the container back up.

"Like that," she said. Watched by the Goodwin's and Mrs Hilston Jed mimicked her actions and watched as his mum's ashes fell down and were picked by the breeze moving like wisps of smoke onto the ground. He turned the container back upright again, then repeated the move again.

This time the breeze took the dust and Jed could see it dancing in the wind as it swirled and then landed on one of the smaller trees. Jed turned to Mrs Hilston offering her the container. She stepped up and took it from Jed.

"Goodbye Claire, we'll take care of Jed" she whispered as she turned it downwards. Miss Goodwin was next. Jed could see that she was trying not to cry. Jed turned to the Goodwin's.

"You both?"

Mr Goodwin accepted the container from his daughter and flicked it so the dust coming out went high into the trees. Mrs Goodwin like her daughter was visibly upset but also accepted the honour.

Before Jed was aware, the container was passed back to him for him to finish scattering his mum in the beautiful orchard. He lifted the container and tipped out the remaining ashes which lifted up higher than any had done before. He watched as they sparkled and shone and moved off in the breeze down onto the trees. They stood for a short while watching the trees move in the wind, their branches creaking and groaning.

Jed was calm and felt the warm sun on his face. He believed this was his mum bringing light to him. She was finally at peace in this beautiful place.

"Thank you," Jed said.

"For what?" asked Miss Goodwin

"For letting my mum be here" he replied. "She would have loved this place".

Miss Goodwin was unable to speak, her throat had constricted but nodded. Mr Goodwin indicated the furthest tree in the row.

"We thought that your mum's container could go there".

Jed could see a spade leaning up against the tree which was the nearest one to the view. He could also see that a patch of earth was piled up next to the spade.

"If that's OK with you Jed?"

Jed walked over to the tree and touched the bark which was gnarly and old.

"Yes„ this is perfect" he agreed turning around to face them all.

He carefully placed the container, now empty into the hole with the lid back on again. Beside him Miss Goodwin stood, followed by Mr and Mrs Goodwin with Mrs Hilston standing slightly further back.

"It's traditional, for family members to scatter soil," Miss Goodwin said.

Jed picked up a handful of the soil and dropped it into the hole, where it landed on the container.

"Goodbye Mum"

The others followed each putting a handful on top of the container. Finally, Mr Goodwin started to carefully put the soil back into the hole. Jed could see a patch of grass turf next to the hole.

"There are wildflower seeds in that patch Jed, so each and every year, wildflowers will grow here".

Jed liked that idea. Once the hole was filled again, Mr Goodwin carefully placed the grass turf onto the hole and pressed it down with his foot. He looked over at Jed for approval and was relieved to see he was smiling. They made their way back down to the farmhouse, and after washing their hands Mrs Goodwin brought out a feast of sandwiches, pies, cakes and cups of tea for everyone. Jed was famished. He accepted sandwich after sandwich until he felt he looked like one.

After the meal was over, Mr Goodwin lead them all into the warm cosy living room. In the hearth, a fire was burning which warmed the chilly room.

"Jed, why don't you bring out your memory book for us to see, if you are happy with that?" asked Mrs Hilston who had been told about the book by Miss Goodwin a few days earlier.

Jed took out the book from his pocket and opened it up. He started to read.

"My mum was my best friend. She was sometimes sad but made me feel safe" Jed looked at the people in front of him. All were enraptured by his words and even Mr Goodwin appeared to be struggling with tears. He read in a clear voice, his memories of his mum, her friends, and funny things she had done or said and finished with

"and she wanted me to be a scientist, so that's what I will be". Jed looked up from the book.

"I believe you will be a great scientist Jed," said Mrs Hilston.

The others nodded in agreement. The rest of the afternoon was spent talking about Clare. Mrs Hilston had known Clare the longest of all of them, even before Jed was born, and she shared memories of Clare which Jed thought he would also write down in his book later that evening.

As the sky darkened Mrs Goodwin brought more cups of tea into the living room, and they talked about the orchard and Jed's mum. Jed thought it had been a really lovely day. Eventually, Mrs Hilston looked at her watch and announced.

"I must get Jed back to the home otherwise Charlie will send out a search party".

Jed wasn't convinced that was true. Charlie didn't like the children in the home, he had realised. Charlie liked his job because most of the time there wasn't much for him to do, other than arrange the supplies of food and other items a busy home needed.

Miss Goodwin did all the work, the cooking and often the cleaning too. Jed stood up to say goodbye and Mrs Goodwin held out her hand. Jed ignored this and hugged her which made her gasp in surprise. Looking up at her he said

"Thank you for the wake" Mrs Goodwin looked down and said sincerely

"Our pleasure Jed, everyone should have a wake". Mr Goodwin also held out his hand but Jed thought better of hugging him and accepted the handshake solemnly.

"Come back in the spring and see the flowers Jed"

Jed then turned to Miss Goodwin who was not coming back to the home that night.

"Goodbye Miss, see you tomorrow".

"You will indeed" she replied accepting a hug like her mum. Jed then collected his memory book and followed Mrs Hilston out to her car, where Mrs Goodwin was passing her a large box of food.

"For your office Jenny, all those council workers need a good feed up".

Mrs Hilston accepted the box with a laugh and put it into the boot of her car. Jed got in and buckled his seatbelt. Mrs Hilston waved at the Goodwin's and started the car, carefully manoeuvring it down the lane and back onto the main road.

After about twenty minutes Mrs Hilston pulled up outside the children's home. Jed could see lights on in the living room and knew Katy, Sam and Ben would be waiting for him. As he came into the hallway and carefully took off his coat, the door to Charlie's office opened and Charlie came back out.

"Hello Jed, Hello Jenny". Charlie looked awkward. "Jenny, can I speak to you please?".

Mrs Hilston looked surprised but followed Charlie into his office where the door was shut. Jed went into the living room where he wasn't surprised to see Katy, Sam and Ben reading. Jed did spot that Ben's book on dinosaurs was upside down. Katy smiled as he entered and walked over to his chair before sitting down heavily.

"How did it go?" she asked.

Jed paused before speaking. He was exhausted but he knew that the others wanted to make sure he was OK.

"The Goodwin's arranged a wake," he said.

"What's a wake?" asked Ben.

"It's a sort of party to celebrate the dead" replied Sam who knew all sorts of things.

"Sort of yes, we talked about my mum, I told stories I remembered and" pulled out his memory book "I read from this"

.Jed was about to add something else but the noise coming from the hallway startled them all. It was the sound of the front door slamming. They waited to see if anything else would happen. Nothing else did until Charlie came back into the room. His ears were bright red but he didn't comment further, just placed their hot chocolate on the table and then left.

* * *

9

Changes

It wasn't until the following day that the children came down for their breakfast, they learned what had happened. Instead of a cheerful Miss Goodwin passing them a plate of bacon and eggs, instead, they found Charlie standing at the stove cursing as he attempted to fish four boiled eggs out of the pan of hot water.

"Where's Miss Goodwin?" asked Katy "Is she sick?".

"She's not coming back" replied Charlie gruffly "Now eat your egg quickly" Charlie replied curtly.

The children looked at their plates which held a boiled egg. They were not used to this for their first meal of the day but Ben gamely cut open the top of his egg and was dismayed to find it was practically raw inside.

Charlie looked over and didn't comment further. None of the children could eat their breakfast and Jed, in particular, wondered whether this is what Charlie and Mrs Hilston had been arguing about the previous night.

They drank their juice and went back upstairs to get ready for school. Ben beckoned the others into his room and fished out a tin behind his bed.

"Miss Goodwin gave me these a few days ago - want one?"

Katy, Jed and Sam looked longingly at the scones which lay in the bottom of the tin. Each grabbed one and sat on Ben's bed trying not to get crumbs on the floor or on them.

"Man that is good," said Sam with a sigh as he finished his scone first.

"Let's hope whatever happened Miss Goodwin comes back soon" added Katy who looked worried. "Charlie doesn't like working for a living and we'll starve to death if he is in charge of breakfast every day".

During the school day, Jed wondered more about the row that they had witnessed. He knew that Mrs Hilston would have normally been polite enough to say goodbye to him, especially after the day they had spent together.

* * *

When the children arrived home after school, they were greeted with the smell of boiled cabbage. The smell arrived in their noses as they walked into the hallway and rose around them as they walked into the kitchen. Charlie was standing at the stovetop again, stirring a large pot.

"Hello Charlie," said Katy. "What are you making?"

"Cabbage soup" he replied gruffly. "The market was selling them off cheaply" He turned to the children and said. "Sit down".

They all complied though the smell of the cabbage was starting to make them feel very sick.

"The Church Committee has instructed me to save money in the coming year. We are running over budget in every area." The children looked bemused but realised that this was not good news for them.

"And as such Miss Goodwin has been let go, the food budget has been slashed and you will all have to wear your clothes for longer in future. You will also have to help clean this place, starting with your rooms, but there will be a rota up in the kitchen from tomorrow".

Katy looked particularly distressed to hear Miss Goodwin would not be back.

"What about our homework?" asked Sam

"You can do both" replied Charlie gruffly. "An hour a day, each and you will still be able to do any homework that's been set. Now eat your dinner"

Charlie scooped out the soup from the large pot and placed a bowl in front of each of them. Jed noticed that several pieces of the cabbage in his bowl looked burnt as if the pot hadn't been stirred. Despite feeling hungry on getting home, none of them ate more than a few mouthfuls before asking to be excused. Back in the living room they huddled together and whispered so Charlie couldn't hear them. They needn't have worried as they heard Charlie swear loudly as a metal pot landed on the kitchen floor with a loud clunk and spatter.

"Hope that's the cabbage soup," said Ben fervently.

"What IS going on?" asked Sam.

"No idea, but we'd better step up and try and find out" replied Ben.

* * *

The next morning the children walked into the kitchen which still smelt of cabbage. Stood at the stove was a stern grey-haired woman.

"I'm Mrs Foster" she announced not looking around at them. "Mr Gibbons has asked the ladies of the church flower committee to help out to feed you. Miss Taylor and I have taken on this thankless task so sit down."

The children sat down not sure whether this was a good development or not. She turned and placed the pot she had been stirring onto the table. Inside was a grey watery mush that still seemed to smell of cabbage.

"Good and hearty porridge" she announced. "Cheap and filling".

She took a bowl and ladled some of the stuff into it, placing it before Katy. The porridge looked nothing like the stuff that Miss Goodwin had made for them in the past. Hers was rich and creamy and she had added a spoon of honey to each bowl. This was lumpy and yet also watery at the same time and also somehow tasteless. Despite the appearance, each of them tucked into their portion as all were ravenous from the night before. Ben had shared out the remaining scones before bedtime but there was less than one each.

As they were eating Charlie came into the room. He looked happier than the previous night.

"Ah I see you have met Mrs Foster!" he announced with a smile. "Miss Taylor and Mrs Foster here have very generously agreed to add to their pastoral duties and help out the home through its financial crisis".

Jed thought that Mrs Foster had the same expression on her face that Miss Cartwright had his mum would have said 'like she was chewing on wasps'.

The thought made him smile but he quickly looked back down at his bowl so Charlie wouldn't notice. They continued to eat in silence. Ben noticed that Charlie had not joined them for the meal.

"Are you not eating?" he asked.

"No, no" Charlie replied with a smile that none of them liked the look of "I've been asked to attend a progress meeting at the Church committee today". He held a piece of paper in his hand which he placed on the table.

"These are going to be your duties each week. Ben, you are Green, Sam, Blue, Katy pink and Jed is Orange"

They looked at the sheet of paper. It was filled with tasks ranging from 'washing dishes(Green) to 'laundry (Pink), with plenty of blue and orange as well. Tasks had been listed by day and time of day. Jed could already work out that most of their spare time not taken up by school, homework or sleep would be used in these tasks.

"Any questions? No? right off to get ready for school" Charlie announced "We'll begin tonight with dinner prep. That's you, Jed"

Charlie said with a smile. The children trooped back upstairs to clean their teeth and get ready.

"That was horrible" Sam announced shuddering dramatically as he cleaned his teeth more thoroughly than normal "The toothpaste takes the taste away but what about that gritty texture?"

Jed's first session for dinner prep, that evening didn't go well at all. Mrs Foster had been replaced by Miss Taylor, a small woman who didn't appear to like children very much either.

She spoke only to criticise Jed for cutting the potatoes into bigger pieces than she liked, but when he made them smaller, that too was wrong.

Eventually, with a sigh she took over the task, directing Jed to peel carrots instead. That evening the children were presented with stew. Jed had not seen what meat the stew had been made from but when it had been cooked it went very grey and stringy.

Katy, Ben and Sam had been on a variety of cleaning duties before their dinner, and Katy, in particular, looked distressed at the meal in front of her. As before Charlie didn't join them for the meal. This was becoming a pattern that all of the children had noticed. Miss Taylor also didn't join them for the meal, citing a need to

"feed my cat and attend evening prayers"

The children all sat gloomily looking at the food in the bowls in front of them.

"We need a plan," said Ben stirring his bowl with a spoon

All of the children made sure that their lunchtime meals were hearty as they had begun to realise that relying on the meals provided at the home was not going to be enough.

Katy in particular became very good at asking for extra portions of portable goodies such as fruit cake and by the end of the week, they were used to eating more in the canteen at school, plus whatever they could sneak into the home for sustenance until the following morning.

They had found a cupboard in the attic which had not been cleaned out for many years. Behind the old textbooks and piles of clothes that had been forgotten, was a small box that became their salvation.

Over the course of a few weeks, each of them added more items to the box, and when Charlie had gone to his room for the evening, they sneaked upstairs and had a feast before bedtime. They were careful not to leave any traces of their food, and now they were responsible for cleaning of the rooms, this became easier.

* * *

10

Revenge

With the changes at the home, Jed had nearly forgotten about Simon Thomas and his vows of revenge.

Distracted by the busy days both at school and at the home, Jed knew that Simon was just biding his time, but with everything else going on, it wasn't until several days into the new term, Jed had been asked by the teacher to take a book back to the library for him.

Jed had agreed as he also wanted to get more books out. As he walked along the corridor back from the library, his new borrowed books in his bag, he wasn't paying attention to the corridor ahead. As he turned he spotted Simon Thomas and his gang standing at the entranceway back to the science block. Unfortunately, Jed's next lesson was chemistry. He stopped and looked at the boys ahead of him.

"Ah look who we have here lads it's the orphan boy himself. My dad beat me when he heard about my detention, so it's only right that we pay it forward, eh lads?".

Jed was terrified but tried not to show it. He knew that classes were about to finish, but he wasn't sure whether to just push past them or wait. He decided not to move forward. Simon turned to one of his buddies, a spotty lad called Neil.

"You wanted first dibs Neil" pushed him forward. Neil looked petrified but moved forward towards Jed with a menacing air. He cracked his knuckles and growled.

"Orphan Boy, you are getting it". Jed stood still. He had no idea what to do, but as Neil's fist came towards him, he instinctively moved away, which unbalanced Neil to the point he then stumbled forwards before landing in a heap on the floor. Jed laughed but he knew this was not going to help. Simon looked furious that his friend was scrambling to get back up on his feet.

"Get him!"

Jed turned and ran back to the library block, arriving just as the lesson bell sounded. Behind him in the corridor, classes excited in a chatter of noise. The corridor filled with the sound of children moving to their next classes.

Jed turned and saw that Simon, Neil and the others were on the far side of the crowd. Simon looked furious and Neil looked sheepish. Jed followed some of the other kids out into the playground, then dashed around the building until he could enter the science block through another door. He knew that Simon and the others wouldn't be in any more of his classes today, but he also knew that this wasn't finished yet.

* * *

When Jed arrived out of breath into his chemistry class he saw Katy look worried. "Simon?" she asked. Jed nodded. He was still out of breath but finally added

"Yes, caught me in the corridor from the library"

"I TOLD, you to be careful Jed," she said fiercely but quietly as the teacher was about to start the class. "Simon's dad beat on him for getting a months detention and he wants to pay you back for that".

Jed didn't know what to say. It was Simon's fault for being a bully but Katy seemed to be blaming him. He took out his class books and tried not to think about it anymore. Later during a recess, Jed attempted to explain to Katy but she brushed him off with

"I tried to help you but you"...she trailed off looking exasperated.

"Look I'm sorry but it's not my fault," said Jed. "He's the bully, why should I hide from him?".

"Because he's dangerous Jed" she replied frustrated. "He will beat on you until there is nothing left".

"Well perhaps I should let him" retorted Jed "Once I'm dead I can be with my mum!". Katy looked distraught at this but didn't comment further.

* * *

Jed spent the next few weeks avoiding the protection of John and trying not to engage Katy. The latter proved more difficult because she would try to bring up the subject both in the children's home, on the way to and from school, and also in the classes they shared.

Ben and Sam tried not to get involved but they found it as tricky as Jed did. Eventually Jed, frustrated and angry turned on Katy one evening

"Look, I know you are trying to protect me, but I don't need you to baby me. If Simon is coming for me I don't care. I want to be with my mum".

Sam and Ben hadn't heard this from Jed and they both put down their books in shock.

"You don't mean that do you Jed?" said Ben looking pale.

"Why not?" retorted Jed, "My life is pants, If Simon isn't trying to wail on me, I'm getting earache with her trying to be my mother, and the life here is crap!".

Katy sobbed and dropped her book running out into the corridor just as Charlie came in with their evening hot chocolate.

"What's going on here?" he asked looking back as Katy ran up the stairs.

"Nothing" muttered Jed turning back to his book. His head was swimming and he knew he had upset Katy who was only trying to help. His tummy was tight and he felt bad but he knew if he went after Katy now she would just say more stuff. He couldn't cope with her.

* * *

During the next few weeks, Jed spent a bit of time with John, not for protection but to get some tips on how to fight. Jed knew that as well as being a rugby player John also knew how to fight and had done martial arts.

Jed had not apologised to Katy after his outburst and he was still trying to avoid her whenever he could. Jed knew that once he had taken Simon down, the bully would move on to someone else instead.

John showed Jed some basic moves to unbalance an opponent and some others to prevent them from hitting. He refused to show Jed the proper moves but explained some basic defensive tactics which he could use. Jed practised on his own as much as he could and eventually one lunchtime John declared him ready.

"Not much else I can teach you," said John after the fifth time Jed had laid him out on the gym mat they had borrowed during recess.

"You're pretty good Jed, wiry and fast. Just floor him and make sure he doesn't get back up". Jed felt more tuned into what he could do, and he realised that knowing this stuff made him feel better.

* * *

11

Showdown

The big fight or "humiliation of Simon" as Ben later kept referring to it later started at the end of the following day. Katy and Sam were staying behind in class to help the science teacher clear up, so Ben and Jed walked out of the school gates turning into the road with the home at the top of it. As they walked Ben mused on the coming meal

"Can you not burn the fish tonight Jed?"

They knew that Mrs Foster was keen to observe the 'fish on Friday' rule and for the last three weeks, a selection of strange fish had become their Friday meal.

None of the children had minded the fish, but the bones left in had become a talking point, especially when Sam had nearly choked on one. Only the prompt bash on his back by Ben had prevented a major catastrophe.

Sam had retched for most of the remaining mealtime and was first up to the secret stash once Charlie had retired for the night.

"Chip's would be ace too" he added. Jed knew that Mrs Taylor didn't approve of 'junk food' as she referred to it.

"No chance" replied Jed, "Boiled potatoes, she's already told me I am peeling a bundle when I get home. My fingers will be wrinkly for ages"

Jed waved his hands in front of Ben's face to emphasize before mimicking Mrs Taylor's voice

"Oh, and you children are SO ungrateful for the home the church has provided for you, the food that you eat..blah blah".

He finished with a flourish before looking ahead to where a group of children was standing. This was unusual but Jed had seen groups of his peers gathered to trade game cards or marbles or other stuff.

As they approached Jed's thoughts were still on the pile of potatoes awaiting him at the home. Suddenly a voice called out from behind him

"Orphan Boy, you are going to get beat!".

Jed inwardly groaned, turning to find Simon Thomas and his gang. The children ahead of them must have been told there was going to be a fight, which is why so many of them were standing around near the tree which was halfway back to the home.

Simon had been clever in making sure this fight happened off school grounds as he was aware that Mrs Cooper was often on-site until late. The children standing behind Ben and Jed were starting to jeer but Jed wasn't sure whether this was for him or whether the lack of blood and gore was directed at Simon. The noise motivated Simon to come closer and add

"I'll take on both of you - Orphan Boy and Child of a Whore" Simon indicated to Ben whose face went a strange shade of red.

"My mother was not a whore" said Ben with gritted teeth, his fists clenched by his side.

"Was according to my dad" jeered Simon. "he called her two for a £1 back in the"

Simon's words suddenly stopped replaced by a whoo as Jed launched himself into the boy toppling them both onto the ground. Jed was on top of Simon and started to pummel him in the chest. Neil and the other members of Simon's gang could only stare as the smaller boy gave their leader a thrashing. The crowd of children gathered closer so they could see the fight. Simon appeared dazed as he gave little resistance to Jed who was muttering under his breath.

"What IS going on!" said a voice behind Jed.

Jed looked behind him still sitting across Simon's chest to see Mrs Taylor standing with her hands on her hips. The crowd of children has parted and was starting to disperse.

"GET OFF" she yelled.

Jed complied whilst Simon was helped to his feet by Neil who looked sheepishly at the ground. Jed could tell Simon was hurt but he didn't care at that point. Jed's arm was wrenched back making him yell out loud.

"And you lot can get off home before I call the school on you" Mrs Taylor held Jed's arm tightly.

"Get off me!" Jed yelled as he twisted out of her grasp.

"Fighting! Wait till Mr Gibbons hears about this!" Mrs Taylor stalked off back to the home.

"Who does she think she is?" asked Ben as he came over to where Jed was standing.

"Thanks for that Jed". Ben said

"Shame she came along, I was going to start pounding on his head next," said Jed ruefully.

* * *

Jed was sent to his room on arrival back at the children's home.

"To reflect on what you have done" added Mrs Taylor.

Jed was glad that Charlie wasn't there but he was sure that Mrs Taylor would give him the incident from her perspective. The bonus was that Mrs Taylor had to deal with the potatoes herself which made Jed smile. He saw as he took off his school uniform that the trousers had a large rip near the knee. He wished Miss Goodwin was still there. She would have taken the trousers and repaired them, brought him a hot chocolate, and listened to his side before hugging him. He missed her.

Two hours later Charlie arrived back from his latest trip. The children were eating their boiled fish and potatoes with little enthusiasm.

Katy had been shocked to learn of the fight when she got back from after-school sewing club. Initially, she had been angry with Jed until she learned why he had attacked Simon.

"That boy is evil," she concluded "Are you OK Jed?"

"I'm fine but my trousers are ripped".

"Give them to me" Katy sighed. "Miss Goodwin was teaching me invisible repairs and left me her sewing kit"

Jed was relieved but just nodded. The children had heard Mrs Taylor and Charlie talking for several minutes.

"Couldn't wait to put the boot in?" said Sam softly

Charlie came into the kitchen "Jed, come with me".

Jed stood up and followed Charlie into his office. "Mrs Taylor informs me you were brawling in the street earlier?"

"The school bully was" Jed started but Charlie held up his hand.

"I'm not interested in why I'm punishing you for fighting in the street. The Church has a lot of opposition to this home being sited here, we have had complaints from the neighbours. You will be helping out at the church after school Mrs Taylor had a list of jobs including clearing out one of the basement rooms. That should stop you from getting into mischief. Now go and finish your dinner".

Jed trailed back to the kitchen where the others were waiting.

"Got to go and clear out some stinky basement room at the church," Jed said as he sat back down. He trailed his fork through the remaining cold fish and potatoes.

"I'll tell Charlie it was my fault," said Ben.

"No, thanks, appreciate the offer but he's not interested" replied Jed.

* * *

165

The following day Jed was surprised that many more children nodded and acknowledged him. He was used to being invisible but even some of the more popular and older children nodded and gave him the thumbs up. This didn't last. In the form room, Simon was absent which Jed was relieved about it. This lasted until Mr Wall was taking the register Mrs Cooper came into the classroom and murmured softly to Mr Wall.

"Jed Long, can you please go with Mrs Cooper?". Jed stood and followed her out into the corridor. She walked without comment until they arrived at her office. Jed followed her in.

"I've had a phone call from Simon Thomas's father this morning that he won't be in school as he was beaten during an after-school fight last night".

"But Miss" started Jed.

Mrs Cooper held up her hand but she didn't look angry "However Jed, I am well aware that Simon Thomas and his little band of thugs have been targetting you and the other children in the children's home for some time. I understand you were defending your friend from some rather nasty slurs about his mother?".

Jed gulped and replied, "Yes, Miss".

"I thought so" she added, "I made it clear that defending your friends from such horrible slurs was a noble thing to do, and that I would not be inflicting any further punishment on you, as I understand you are going to be helping at the church for the next month?" Jed nodded again.

"Mr Thomas had been misled by his son, which alas means that Simon will find further penalties coming from his father." Mrs Cooper continued "I am telling you this, so you understand that a bully is often a victim of a bigger bully. Mr Thomas Senior is not a nice person, and his wife and son have often been victims of his. Simon Thomas is a bully, but with the guidance of the school, and the occasional shock, like yesterday, he might be saved from himself."

Jed didn't really understand most of what she was saying, but he did understand that Mrs Cooper knew what the real reason for the fight was. He also realised she didn't blame him for defending Ben.

* * *

Later in the library, the children gathered to hear what Mrs Cooper said.

"She is firm but fair" declared Katy.

"What did she mean about Simon's dad?" asked Sam

"He's a brute" replied Katy, "He's been arrested for beating his wife up" added Ben.

"How do you know this stuff?" asked Jed.

"Simon was out of school for a month, he and his mum went to a shelter in Plymouth last year," said Ben. "When he came back he was worse. More beatings of the first years, taking his anger out on everyone else".

Jed felt sad about Simon but he didn't regret standing up to him either. During the rest of the day, Jed wondered where Simon was. He found out the following day when Simon arrived at school with a plaster cast on his right arm, and a sling covering the shiny white plaster. His mother was with him, and she sported dark glasses and a soft brown fur coat. Simon shuffled into the school building with his mum.

Twenty minutes later she came back out on her own. She avoided looking at anyone and walked swiftly out of the school grounds to the car which was waiting for her. It was a dark blue sleek Mercedes that looked brand new. Jed could see the driver, who was clearly Simon's father. He had the same slicked-back hair but also an air of menace that Simon had yet to master.

* * *

Simon Foster appeared that morning in their form room, but he was a shadow of himself. He was clearly in pain from his broken arm but didn't comment on the reason for the cast. He also avoided looking at Jed or the others from the home, preferring to huddle with his gang and whisper menacingly over at them.

For the next month, Jed's life became boringly routine. With the threat of Simon Foster dissipated, after a full day of school, Jed would change into some old clothes Charlie had found for him, then walk across the estate to the church, where Mrs Foster was waiting for him.

Each afternoon for two hours, Jed would open boxes, and on Mrs Foster's instructions move them to one of three piles.

"Keep, dispose and sell".

The disposal area to the far end of the room was much bigger than the keep or sell ones. This was because most of the boxes contained old books which Jed realised were probably full of mould. The basement was cold and damp, and Jed was convinced also contained massive quantities of spiders who didn't want their boxes moved. However, he carried on with the task of daydreaming when he got a chance about his latest space book.

Each evening once the two hours were up, Jed was released from his penance and walked back to the home where Charlie instructed him to go and wash. He then joined Sam, Ben and Katy for his dinner which had not improved in quality or taste over the last few weeks. A succession of watery stews, fish pie (bones left in), and cheap fatty chicken. Rarely did any of the children enjoy their meals but eventually they realised that they could not carry on eating smaller portions or Charlie would start to suspect them of hoarding food.

* * *

12

New arrival

Three months later the children were in the sitting room finishing off their homework when they heard the bell go on the front door. Charlie came out of his office and answered the door. The children recognised the voice of Mrs Hilston but the door to the hall was closed so they didn't hear what she was saying.

Twenty minutes later she came into the sitting room with Charlie behind her and behind him was Simon Thomas.

"Hello Katy, Sam, Ben. I think you know Simon?" Jed nodded but didn't say anything. "Simon is going to be staying here for a while".

Jed finally exploded "He's a bully!" he said furiously "He tried to beat me up from day one of school".

Charlie replied "Quieten down Jed"

"I will not" Jed replied.

All the anger and frustration of dealing with Simon at school boiled over. "It's his fault I had to clear out that stinking basement in the church for the last month, and now he's living here too?"

Mrs Hilston looked shocked "You have Jed clearing out a basement?" she turned to Charlie questioningly

"He was fighting in the street" replied Charlie sulkily.

"I was defending my friend from his slurs about his mum from HIM!" shouted Jed pointing at Simon who was smirking behind Charlie. The white-hot rage he felt boiled over.

"If he stays here, I'm leaving". Mrs Hilston turned back to Jed.

"You can't leave Jed, you are a child in the care of the council". Jed turned to her.

"Since Miss Goodwin left, this is a hell hole. Bad food, horrible punishments.". Mrs Hilston looked aghast but let Jed continue. "I hate it here".

She looked at the other children who were looking down at the floor.

"Is this true?"

"Foods pretty cruddy" added Ben not looking up.

"The church budget got slashed, you know that Jenny. We've had to make some cutbacks" Charlie said defensively. "Back to basics, and the two ladies from the church, well they do their best, but neither is a gourmet cook".

Mrs Hilston looked at the children.

"He's right I'm afraid. The budgets have been slashed, and the council have had to withdraw some funding that paid for Miss Goodwin to come and cook. However" she drew out a card "This is my personal office number, if ANY bullying goes on I want you to call me immediately".

She turned to Simon who was also looking at the floor, his cast now grubby and covered in graffiti "Any bullying will result in removal".

Simon carried on looking at the floor and nodded. She then turned and followed Charlie back out into the hallway. Simon stood not looking at any of the others who went back to their homework.

After a few minutes the front door opened and closed and Charlie came back into the room. "Right Simon follow me, we need to get you sorted for the night." Simon followed Charlie out but gave Jed and the others the finger before he left.

"How is he here?" asked Sam. "Where's his mum and dad?". "Don't know don't care" replied Jed sulkily dropping back down into his chair.

* * *

The following day at school the full story became clear. Mr Wall called the form to attention before the beginning of school. Simon was nowhere to be seen. He had been called in to see Mrs Cooper before the class had fully assembled.

"Right quieten down you lot" called Mr Wall tapping his pen on his desk, which made a surprisingly loud noise. The class settled down and looked ahead.

"Some of you might be aware that there had been an incident in the town last night." Mr Wall looked kindly but stern and was looking directly at Ben, Sam Katy and Jed who was looking down at his desk.

"Simon's father has been taken into custody last night and we understand he had been charged with the attempted murder of his wife". Jed looked up startled. "Mrs Thomas is currently in the local hospital under police guard and is in critical condition. Simon has been taken into the care of the local council. I tell you this not so you can all gossip about it, but so you are aware of the facts. The school is supporting Simon, as is the Methodist Children's Home which for the time being will be Simon's home until a relative can be contacted to take him in. I ask you all to allow Simon the time to grieve for his change in circumstances. That is all".

Jed looked over at Katy who was mouthing behind her hand "He tried to KILL her?".

Jed thought about what Mrs Cooper had said to him about Simon's father. He realised that she was very close to the truth of it. He still hated Simon but he could also have some sympathy for him.

* * *

On the walk home that evening Katy caught up with Jed who was walking ahead of them all.

"Don't you feel sorry for him?" she asked.

"No!" replied Jed fiercely turning to face her, Sam and Ben who had stopped. "He's a bully, it's sad his mum nearly died but that doesn't stop me from hating him".

"Oh Jed," said Katy with a sigh. As they arrived back at the home, Sam was pushed aside by Simon who had come up the path behind them.

"Make way squirt," said Simon shoving Sam almost into the rose bush by the front door. Simon turned the handle to see Charlie coming to greet them.

"Hello, Mr Gibbons," Simon said with a broad smile. The others followed in behind him trying not to laugh as Charlie beamed at Simon.

"Can I help you at all?" added Simon with a beatific smile.

"No thank you, Simon, go and do your homework". Simon grinned at the other children and walked into the sitting room, bagging Jed's chair.

"That's my chair!" said Jed

"Mine now orphan boy" hissed back Simon before he added in a loud voice, hearing Charlie coming in

"Can't I borrow this one please Jed?" in a polite voice.

Jed was shaking with rage but turned and walked away. Charlie looked in on the group not seeing or understanding the dynamics. Simon got out his homework and started but as soon as Charlie left he started to hiss at Jed again. Jed who was sitting on a spare chair next to Katy started to rise before she grabbed his arm.

"He's not worth it," she said softly "He wants you to get into trouble and you are letting him bait you" Simon smiled and gave Jed the finger again. Katy's hand on his arm tightened further. She pulled him back down and said "Now explain this science fact to me again".

Jed knew she was trying to distract him but he also knew her understanding of science was not good.

* * *

13

Runaway

It took Jed only three weeks to decide to run away. Simon had ingrained himself with Charlie to such a degree, Charlie cited Simon as an example when chastising the other children for some issue. Katy, Sam and Ben didn't see what Jed did. Katy had tried to make friends with Simon and Jed knew that turning his friends

his family

against him was part of Simon's plan.

Katy continued to try and pacify Jed but his rage grew as they started to include Simon in their activities in the home. He started to hate them as well.

Simon's relatives had been contacted in the weeks following his father's assault on his mum. Katy mentioned to Jed one evening when they were alone that one distant uncle who lived in Scotland had been contacted but he wasn't interested in taking on his sister's child.

Simon's dad had been remanded in custody awaiting trial and Simon's mum was still on a life support machine in the hospital. Simon had been taken regularly to see her by Mrs Hilston and on his return, Jed thought his behaviour became viler than before. Jed realised that Simon blamed him for the situation, for making his dad so angry that he attacked his mum. Jed couldn't understand this and didn't care much either.

Jed started to plan his escape. He knew where Charlie kept the petty cash box in his office, and over the next few days when he got the chance, he sneaked in and pocketed a small amount from the tin. Jed knew that Charlie rarely tallied up the box, and seemed to add more cash to it each week.

In the fourth week, he checked to see how much he had got. £16 and some small change. Jed knew that a ticket to London from Exeter for a child was about £2 so he would have money for food for a while. He tucked the money back into the socks Miss Goodwin had given him. He knew stealing was wrong but he also knew he would end up fighting Simon again if he stayed.

The following week Jed became aware that Mrs Foster would be sleeping at the home over the coming weekend. Charlie has persuaded her to stay as he would be attending a church conference in Manchester.

Jed had overheard her telling Charlie that she wouldn't be late for bed. This gave him an idea. As none of the other children would be awake after 9 pm, Jed knew he could sneak out and make his way to the train station to catch one of the last trains to London before anyone missed him.

During the week Jed took some of the tuck box supplies into his room. These weren't missed either. Jed was appalled to see that Simon was brought into the tuck club after he commented to Sam about the awful meal they had just had. He was bragging about his dad allowing him to have spicy curries when Jed interrupted him with a curt

180

"Well that's not happening ever again is it?" Katy looked shocked as Simon turned to face Jed.

"Did you say something Orphan boy?"

Katy said, "Simon, that's not nice!"

Simon looked back at her.

"Sorry," he said before turning back to Jed and saying in a false contrite voice

"I'm sorry Jed" whilst maintaining a smirk Jed knew the others couldn't see.

Later Katy and Ben took Simon up to Sam's room to show him where the tuck box was. Jed didn't go with them but resolved to make sure that suitable supplies were in his bag before the weekend. Jed didn't speak to the others during the rest of the week. Sam tried to engage him but Jed just shrugged him off with a curt

"I'm busy"

Jed was ready to leave this all behind, despite knowing that leaving would break his friend's hearts. On Friday night Jed ate his final meal of boiled fish and potatoes without comment. Katy was concerned about him, he knew but hopefully, she wouldn't realise what was coming.

Jed took himself off to bed at the normal hour, brushed his teeth, said goodnight to Sam who was in the bathroom too, and then got dressed for bed. He turned out his light and waited. The small alarm clock on the table read 20.15. He had about an hour to wait. The other children filed off to their rooms. Jed heard Simon wish the others a good night. He had never hated someone so much as this boy, but soon his life would improve.

* * *

Jed heard Mrs Foster come up the stairs panting slightly as she paused on the landing just before 9 pm. He carefully got out of bed and started to dress as he heard her move up to the top floor where the spare bedrooms were located. He left his shoes off but sat on the bed, his bag filled with his possessions including the copy of Islands in the Sky and his memory book of his mum. He had also packed the socks, hat and gloves given to him by Miss Goodwin whom he missed terribly. The gloves still smelt a little of the feed Jed had spread out on the field for the cows. He sat breathing in the smell which calmed him.

As the clock ticked towards 9,15 pm Jed put on his coat and carefully opened the door to his room. He listened but couldn't hear any noises coming from the other rooms. He heard Sam snoring and carefully stepped out into the hallway with his bag in one hand and his shoes in the other. He made his way carefully down to the ground floor.

He knew the front door was double-locked, but he had observed that the back door next to the kitchen only had a single lock, and the key was kept on a hook beside the door. Jed crept towards the back door, trying not to make a sound. He arrived at the back door and took down the key, putting it into the lock. He knew the door creaked slightly so he carefully opened it without making too much noise. Jed walked out of the door, turning to carefully close it. Someone would notice the key in the door, probably in the morning, but by then he would be out of Exeter and in London. He put on his shoes and started to walk.

Jed had been brought up by his mum Clare to be street smart. She had told him many times to be aware of people, and what they wanted. Jed knew if he looked busy no one would bother him. Jed knew the trains to London went on the hour, so he walked down the path to the street and turned to head into the centre of town. He walked along Topsham Road purposefully ignoring the other people who passed him walking or in cars.

He arrived at the train station just as the clock across the square ticked to 8.45 pm. Jed walked into the train station and looked for the ticket office. It was at the far end of the room. He walked to the counter and looked at the man behind the glass who was reading his paper.

"Hello," Jed said.

"Hello, young man," said the ticket seller. "Where are your parents? Isn't it a bit late to be out?"

"Oh mum is paying the taxi man outside," Jed said quickly. "She asked me to get the tickets to save time. One adult and one child please to London Paddington". Jed knew that if he didn't buy two tickets the seller would be even more suspicious.

The ticket seller who had a badge on his shirt saying 'Keith' looked at the front door, then put down his paper and started to produce the tickets.

"She'd better be quick" he commented as Jed handed over the money, and got back change. "The London train leaves at the hour, and the doors shut two minutes before."

"Yes, we know" replied Jed putting the change back into his bag and holding the tickets before walking back to the other end of the station. Keith watched him for a couple of seconds before turning back to his paper. Jed took the opportunity to walk quietly down to the gate where the display showed the London train was on time. He showed his ticket to the gate attendant who didn't comment on the lack of adults with him before going onto the platform to wait for the train.

Right on time, the train pulled into the station. Jed had walked quickly to the far end of the platform so no one would see him from the station concourse. The doors unlocked and passengers got out. Jed waited then got onto the train finding a seat in one of the carriages. Not many people were on the train so Jed made himself comfortable across two seats. He got out his book Islands in the Sky and started to read. He also got out some of the shortbread he had taken from the tuck box in the home and nibbled on a piece as he read. The train left Exeter St David's station on time as the ticket man had said. Jed continued to read and eat his shortbread until he spotted the ticket inspector who had entered the carriage at the far end. Jed continued to read and eat until the inspector said as he drew level with Jed

"You're not travelling alone are you son?"

Jed replied with a winning smile "Oh no sir, my mum is in the loo, here are our tickets". Jed handed over both tickets which disarmed the inspector "Tummy trouble" added Jed with a wince.

The inspector clipped both tickets and moved on. Jed returned to his book and took another piece of shortbread. He didn't think about the home or Simon. The train stopped at many places during the journey but Jed didn't notice these until at last Paddington Station came into view.

The station was busy despite it being after midnight. Jed knew that he had to find somewhere to stay and he realised he knew exactly where that was. Jed's mum had occasionally told him about a squat she had stayed at in London close to Paddington. It used to be a commercial office, but when the landlord increased the rent it became unoccupied and then derelict. The owners had never developed it, so the homeless in West London had taken it over and used it for their purposes. Jed thought he remembered where it had been, so as he left the train, he set off towards Edgeware Road.

After about ten minutes of walking, he arrived at the building he had been told about. There was fencing around the edge closest to the road, but Jed noticed that a hole had been carefully cut into the edges of the fence, so it was accessible despite looking like it was fixed in place. Jed lifted the edge of the wire and scrambled through.

Beyond the fence was a large building with fixed grates over the windows on the ground floor. Jed walked around to the back where there was a young man sitting smoking a pipe. He looked young, probably only a few years older than Jed was. He wore a grey baggy shirt over jeans and work boots.

"Who are you? what are you doing here, are you lost? " he asked in a strong Scottish accent. He looked surprised to see a young boy coming into the squat.

"I'm Jed"

"Hello Jed, are you lost, mate?"

"No, I've run away" replied Jed deciding that telling the truth was the best thing to do "I lived in a children's home but it was awful there, so I have run away to London. My mum died a few weeks ago, and she told me about this place"

"Oh right," said the lad taking the pipe back out of his mouth. "What was her name?"

"Clare Long" replied Jed.

"Don't know her" he said, "but Billy might. Come with me".

Jed followed the man, back into the building through a fire exit that had been propped open with a concrete slab. Inside the rooms were lit with paraffin lamps. They gave off an eerie glow that flickered as they walked past. Jed could see people huddled down in rooms as they passed, most were asleep but some were awake and talking or eating from tins. No one paid any attention to him. He was comfortable in places like this. Jed followed the man through to the other end of the building into a small kitchen. Sat at a table was a tall black man with dreadlocks who was sipping from a mug.

"Billy, found this one outside, says his mum knew this place?" Billy turned to look at Jed.

"Hello," he said. "Who are you?"

"I'm Jed".

"Bit young to be walking the streets aren't you Jed?"

"I'm nearly eleven," said Jed defiantly. "Really,?" said Billy with a grin. "I would say nearer nine". Jed didn't reply. "And who is your mum who knows this place?"

"Clare Long" replied Jed.

Billy smiled. "Clare Long, now that is a name I haven't heard for a while"

"You knew mum?" asked Jed.

"Oh yes, quite a fierce lady" Billy replied. "You can go now Matt" he added to the man still standing in the doorway. "Now sit you down there," said Billy" and tell me why you are here".

Jed sat down and realised he was feeling very weary. He told the story of his mum, growing up in squats, and eventually being parted from her whilst she went into the hospital. When he got to the part of hearing she had died, tears fell from his eyes, but he continued to talk until eventually he ran out of effort and stopped. He looked back up at Billy.

"A fine fierce woman your mum was Jed, and I am truly sorry for you, but you won't be able to stay here."

"Why not?" he said

"Because we are about to be evicted too" Billy replied. "You can stay until then, but the police and social will be around, and having a small child here, will attract too much attention. Have you eaten?" he added

"Shortbread" replied Jed.

"Well I think we can do better than that" replied Billy. "There is some Chinese in that fridge, cold but still edible" Jed walked over to the fridge where indeed there was a cardboard container with some Chinese veg in sauce inside. "Fork is over there in the drawer," said Billy. "I'll find you a sleeping bag"

Jed sat back down at the table and ate the veg with relish. Despite being cold he was ravenous and ate every scrap. After a couple of minutes, Billy returned with a sleeping bag and a pillow.

"You can bunk down in here," he said. I'll have a think about where you can go when the bailiffs arrive"

Jed finished the food and put the container in the dustbin in the corner, washed the fork in the sink, and placed it back in the drawer. He then took off his coat and shoes before putting the sleeping bag on the floor. He got into the sleeping bag and put his head on the pillow. He fell asleep in moments

* * *

Jed woke to the noise of people moving around the next morning. He was up and out of the sleeping bag, folding it neatly over a chair. Gradually people came into the kitchen though none seemed surprised to see a young boy standing there. Billy came into the room yawning and announced

"This is Jed, his mum was one of us, he's one of us, and no one messes with him - understood?".

Those that were there nodded.

"Pass it on" added Billy before he walked over to Jed. "Did you sleep well?"

"Yes sir" replied Jed, which caused a ripple of laughter from one of the men standing in the kitchen.

"Sir"

"Yes Leon?" replied Billy looking sternly at the man known as Leon. Leon looked down at his tatty trainers and didn't reply.

"Right you lot, we're expecting the bailiffs either today or tomorrow. Duke has a contact on the inside of the council who has passed on these dates, so we need to make sure the building is secure"

Billy asked puzzled "How did you get in Jed?"

"The fence was cut, I could see it" replied Jed.

Billy slapped his leg which generated a loud noise.

"Come on people, get some cable ties and get that closed up"

Leon and one of the other men dashed out of the room, presumably to secure the entrance Jed had used the previous night. Billy turned to Jed

"Not scared of bailiffs are you?"

Jed shook his head. He knew most of the bailiffs who had dealt with evictions in Exeter.

"Right, well we have stockpiles of food and plenty of water so they won't starve us out."

Jed's stomach rumbled at the mention of food. He was very hungry indeed.

* * *

Ten minutes later a small blonde girl came into the kitchen yawning. She was dressed in a tunic smock and loose cotton trousers.

"This is Amy" announced Billy "She's my lady"

"Huh, you wish" Amy replied with a grin, but it wasn't a mean smile. Jed liked her immediately. She reminded him of Miss Goodwin, only smaller.

"And who is this Billy?" Amy asked as she came towards them.

"This is Jed, he's run away from a home in Devon"

"Hello Jed," said Amy holding out her hand. Jed shook it blushing. "I ran away from a home too" she added. "Fifteen I was and found this place. What's your story?"

Jed told her, as she started to prep for a meal.

"Can I help?" Jed asked.

"Can you?" she smiled. Jed took up a potato peeler and said

"I can peel potatoes"

"Okay then" Amy laughed. "Good job we had a huge bag from the market last week". Amy showed Jed where the potatoes were stored and gave him a large washing-up bowl to put them in.

Jed carefully peeled the potatoes and chatted to Amy who was cutting up a small pile of onions, before adding them to a large frying pan.

"We're making corned beef hash" she announced.

Jed had never heard of it, but the smell of the cooking onions was making his mouth water. Amy showed Jed how to open three tins of corned beef using the key that was part of the tin. Jed didn't like the smell of the corned beef. He thought it smelt more like dog food, but he didn't comment.

Amy took the peeled potatoes out of the bowl and cut those up as well, adding them to the pan. She took a jug of water and added that before putting on a lid to cover the pan. The room started to smell amazing.

"Twenty minutes and the food will be done," Amy said as she took out a large sliced white loaf from a box on the table.

"Butters in the container over there, get all of those buttered then put them on this." Amy handed Jed a large plate. Jed stood at the table carefully buttering the bread, cutting each slice into two then placing them on the plate. Amy took off the lid, adding the corned beef before stirring it again and putting the lid back on.

She walked to the doorway where a large bell was strung from the ceiling. It reminded Jed of the school bell. Amy rang the bell, and suddenly people started to come into the kitchen from all directions. The room was filled with people and noise. Jed stood and watched them. It reminded him of the twenty-eleven back at the final squat in Exeter. He missed his mum, but he could see that this squat like his one, was a community. He wondered what Charlie and the others were doing now.

* * *

14

Alarm

Jed was missed at breakfast. Sam had knocked on his door which was shut but didn't go inside. He went down to breakfast where Katy, Simon and Ben were eating their boiled eggs. Mrs Foster had been persuaded to take on the breakfast duties by Charlie. She was better at boiling eggs, so the children accepted her for this. Her attitude hadn't changed, if anything it was worse. She obviously despised the children but hid it behind a veil of sarcasm. As Sam came into the room, Katy looked at him

"Where's Jed? Did he sleep in?"

Sam shook his head "Don't think so".

Charlie came into the kitchen and hearing Sam's reply asked "What's wrong?"

Katy said "Jed's not come down to breakfast"

"Well he knows when it is, he can just go hungry then" replied Charlie, sitting down at the table.

Ben glanced at the others. Simon was the only one who didn't appear worried. Even with the bad meals, the others knew Jed would not miss his meals. After they had finished, leaving Simon down in the kitchen dashed back upstairs and knocked on Jed's door. When there was no reply Sam opened the door.

"He's not slept in his bed."

Katy groaned. "Oh no, where is he? Charlie's gonna be mad".

Ben opened the drawer. "His stuff is gone, his memory book".

"He's run away" concluded Sam. The children went back downstairs where Mrs Foster and Charlie were clearing up, helped by a smiling Simon.

"Jed's gone," said Sam

"Gone where?" asked Charlie distractingly

"He's run away" added Katy. Charlie looked around at them.

"He's done WHAT?!". Charlie went upstairs and walked into Jed's bedroom. The children followed him.

"He's gone," said Katy.

"Bloody boy!" announced Charlie as he stomped back downstairs to his office. He slammed the door, just as Simon came into the hallway. Simon decided wisely not to comment but he was thrilled. He liked the other kids, but Jed had made life difficult for him. He was happy that the orphan boy was gone, and he sincerely hoped it would be for good. However, he decided to fake mild concern, which started Katy crying. He patted her back, before Sam took over, handing her a tissue. After a short while, Charlie came back out

"You lot, off to school, I've called the council and the police and I'll be ringing the school in a bit".

The children trooped upstairs to their rooms to collect their bags and coats before going outside to join the other children making their way to the school. Word spread quickly that Jed had run away, mostly fuelled by Simon who was trying not to look too pleased about it. His gang knew he hated Jed and having him leave home was a bonus. In public, however, Simon managed to look as worried as the other children as to where Jed had gone.

* * *

Back at the home, Charlie was fielding calls from the council, Mrs Hilston was on holiday but her colleague Mr Cooper had already called twice.

Charlie was fed up with his job. First the budget cuts, and the moaning kids, then this. The phone rang again. It was the leader of the Church Council who had been informed of the issue. Charlie sank back into his chair as the voice on the other end of the phone made it clear that this needed to be sorted.

Twenty minutes earlier a WPC Turner had arrived at the home to make a report on the missing child. Charlie was not impressed as she asked lots of awkward questions that Charlie didn't know the answers to. She was interested in hearing about Jed's mum's death.

"Do you think he is trying to find relatives?" she asked

"None around" replied Charlie curtly. "Council looked into it, but the boy's mum was the only relative".

"Does he know anyone outside of Exeter?" she asked making notes in her book with a pen

"Don't think so, they lived in that big office block squat for years. Now, are we done?" Charlie was frustrated. He had plenty of work to do without this.

"For now," WPC Turner said with a frown "We'll be back if there is any news"

"Right O," said Charlie escorting her out of the office and into the hallway. "Goodbye".

He turned on his heel and back into his office. WPC Turner frowned.

Nasty man to be in charge of a home for kids

* * *

WPC Kim Turner had been a policewoman for three years. She had joined straight out of college after deciding that being a secretary wasn't for her. Unlike some of her colleagues, she still retained the ability to care about the people she was there to protect, and this case was worrying her. She decided to keep looking for Jed, even if the case was shelved. She had one more stop to make.

Mrs Cooper had been expecting a visit from the police ever since Charlie's call that morning. Her secretary announced the arrival of WPC Turner just as she was thinking of calling Charlie back to see if there had been any news.

"Hello," said WPC Turner. "You know why I am here?"

"Yes, yes come in, we're all worried sick about Jed" replied Mrs Cooper ushering the policewoman to a chair.

"Tell me about Jed" WPC Turner started with. She left her notebook in her pocket. She was aware that letting people talk unimpeded was the best way to get to the truth. Mrs Cooper clarified the situation with Jed's mum and her early unexpected death. She also touched on the bullying started by Simon Thomas and his gang.

"And he's now living at that home" Mrs Cooper finished. "Simon Thomas is living at the Exeter Methodist Church Home?" asked WPC Turner astonished.

Yes, his dad is on remand for attempted murder, and his mum is not expected to live"

"And this is the boy who had bullied Jed?"

"Yes," Mrs Cooper looked forlorn. "I did plead with the council not to place him there, but they have no other places available. Budget cuts".

"Is Simon Thomas here in school today?" asked WPC Turner, realising she might have found the reasons for Jed deciding to run away

"Yes," said Mrs Cooper.

"I need to speak to him, please. Could you be the appropriate adult as he had no one else?"

"Of course" replied Mrs Cooper who pressed a button near her phone

"Laura, can you please arrange for Simon Thomas to come to my office". A few minutes later Simon arrived at the door to Mrs Cooper's office and knocked.

"Come in," said Mrs Cooper. Simon walked in, then stopped when he saw the policewoman sitting down on the other side of the desk.

"Come in Simon, sit down. WPC Turner wants to ask you some questions about Jed" Simon shuffled to one of the other chairs and sat down not looking at either of them.

"Don't know nuffing" he said.

"Look at me!" said WPC Turner. Simon glanced at her.

"Can't talk to the fuzz without my parents" he added

"That's your right Simon, but Mrs Cooper has kindly agreed to act as in loco parentis, which means that in the absence of your parents she is looking after your rights."

"You had been living in the home for about a month?" Simon nodded. "Had you had much contact with Jed?"

"Not much no" replied Simon still not looking at her.

"And before that, you had been bullying him?"

"I have not!" Simon stood up "That's a lie"

"Sit DOWN!" Mrs Cooper's voice was unexpectedly loud, startling even WPC Turner who tried not to show it. "You are lying Simon Thomas, you have been in detention multiple times for bullying and the last time was when you tried to beat Jed in the street near to the home." Simon sat but he was looking mute now.

"Do you know why Jed ran away?" asked WPC Turner kindly. Simon shook his head.

"OK, thank you, Simon, you can go now," said Mrs Cooper. Simon got up and walked out. "That is one troubled boy," said Mrs Cooper." You know of his father?"

WPC Turner nodded. "Everyone knows Mr C's team".

* * *

WPC Turner decided to check with some of the public transport routes out of Exeter. She felt that Jed wasn't going to be found in the city. Working on nothing but instinct she called the Central Bus depot and spoke to the manager who agreed to put out a call to the drivers asking if a small child with a rucksack had travelled on the buses the previous night.

"Probably after 9 pm" WPC Turner added, "So hopefully strange enough to be noticed".

As she left the bus depot office, she glanced at her watch. Her shift was ending in an hour, but she just had time to check with the train station's office as well. On arrival, she noticed the clerk behind the glass was reading the local newspaper. He didn't pay any attention to her until she rapped on the glass.

"Hello, is the manager here?" she asked politely.

"Blue door at the end there, just knock and they'll answer," the clerk said turning back to his paper. His badge said 'Keith'. WPC Turner walked to the blue door which had a peephole and knocked sharply standing back so they could see her uniform. After a few seconds, the door opened

"Yes?" The woman standing in the doorway held a pile of papers.

"Hello, my name is WPC Turner. Can I speak to you about a missing child please?".

"Come in dear, it's a bit cramped in here though," said the woman. "I'm Maggie the station manager, pleased to meet you".

She put down the papers on a side table and ushered WPC Turner to a chair next to a desk which she then sat at. "Trying to organise the rotas. Nightmare at the best of times."

"We have a missing boy, his name is Jed. He went missing sometime between 8 pm last night and 8 am this morning from the church home"

"Do you have a photo?" asked Maggie

"No sorry, but I have a description. Hopefully, if he got on a train, someone would have noticed?"

"Not sure" replied Maggie. "Keith was on last night and if he took his nose out of the paper more than twice I would be surprised. Still it's worth a try, follow me".

They made their way back out into the concourse area, and Maggie took out a bunch of keys, opened the green door next to the ticket window and ushered WPC Turner inside. The door led to a corridor and the left-hand door lead to the ticket office. Keith had put down his paper as he heard them coming in, pretending to study a pamphlet on the desk in front of him.

"Keith, did you see a boy getting on a train last night after 8 pm on his own?" Maggie turned to WPC Turner "description?"

"Four foot two inches, dark curly hair, small build, probably had a rucksack with him" replied WPC Turner. Keith blushed

"Well there was a lad who bought two tickets last night to London - the 9 pm train " he stated, "Said his mum was paying for the taxi and she'd sent him on to get the tickets so they wouldn't miss the train. Sounds like that boy" WPC Turner turned to Maggie

"Any close circuit footage?"

"System's down, been like that for a week or more, sorry" replied Maggie.

"Clever boy," said WPC Turner. "Buy one ticket, it makes you stand out. "Two tickets, my mum's paying for the taxi, no one notices. Thank you" she added turning back to Maggie. "London Paddington is the final stop, yes?" "

Maggie replied " Yes would have got in around 12.15 am. I'll send an alert to Paddington to see if they have seen him."

"Thanks" replied WPC Turner, "I'll pass this on to the Met, though I can't imagine that they would be pulling out all the stops to find him".

* * *

15

The Squat

Jed settled into life at the squat. He made himself useful around the building, cleaning and clearing rubbish with some of the others.

Billy found Jed to be a great little helper and made sure that the other residents treated him well. Jed rarely left the building. He knew that the alarm would have gone up once Charlie and the others discovered he was missing. Billy had told Jed that occasionally the local council would try and gain access, and there was an eviction notice in place. Billy was expecting the bailiffs within the month.

Jed spent his days being useful and was becoming a good sous chef to the resident cook Martin. Martin had confessed one day whilst Jed was peeling potatoes for the evening meal, that he used to work in a posh kitchen.

"Only lasted three weeks," Martin said "Head chef was a brute, used to be on that cooking programme. He comes across as all nice but he once threw an iron griddle at one of the workers in his kitchen for not making the green beans exactly 2 inches long".

"Did it hit him?" asked Jed

"No made a large hole in one of the workbenches, which set him off further" replied Martin. "He ended up being held back by two more of his minions, and the guy who had failed to measure the beans" Martin laughed at Jed's expression "Yeah really, he expected each bean to be measured before being cut precisely. Here if the food is edible its a triumph. Much more my thing".

Jed carried on peeling potatoes but he had already decided he didn't want to work in a posh kitchen.

Each night Billy spent some time with Jed playing snap and other card games. Jed liked Billy a lot. Nearly all of the people in the squat reminded him of the twenty-eleven from Exeter. He saw a lot of the same type of people here in the London squat. Billy had told Jed that most of the residents worked outside the squat in the "black economy".

Jed didn't know what that was, but Billy had explained that because none of the residents had a permanent address or tax details, they worked for cash in hand cleaning the local offices, working in the takeaway restaurants further down the road, or some of them also worked in a nearby factory packaging up fragrances.

* * *

Things stayed the same until the following week. Jed was cleaning one of the rooms on the first floor with Derri, an Irish girl with bright ginger hair. Derri was another of Jed's favourites. She brought him back a bag of pick and mix from the corner shop where she worked every week. He especially liked the boiled sweets as they lasted the longest. Jed was sweeping up some rubbish for Derri to bag when a whistle sounded outside.

"That's the alarm," said Derri throwing down her bag, "Come on Jed, the bailiffs are here" Jed followed Derri at a trot to the landing where some of the others were gathered.

"To your station's people," Derri yelled as she ran down the stairs.

Jed struggled to keep up with her but managed to arrive at the back door just as she was locking it up. She pulled chains across locking them with padlocks sitting on a shelf nearby, and bolts which looked new. Derri commented as she finished

"Billy went down the hardware shop last week, these should keep them out for the time being".

Jed had never experienced a siege, in all of the squats he had ever lived in, the residents' co operated with the bailiffs, and left when asked. This was exciting but also scary. He saw Billy pulling large pieces of plywood across one of the windows and nailing it to the window frame. The light faded as others started to do the same. From the outside, Jed could hear a megaphone. The sound was muted. He walked back upstairs where Martin was nailing shut another window in one of the rooms. Martin noticed Jed

"Not to worry little buddy, they aren't coming in here".

Jed said "I'm not worried", and it was true. He wasn't worried, just wondered what would happen next. Suddenly a large bang sounded downstairs which did startle him. "They've got a rammer," said Martin. "Two of the bailiffs and a steel pole".

The sounds continued until Jed heard a creak and then more sounds coming from downstairs. Yelling and the sound of heavy boots on the stairs. Jed watched as two men came up the stairs and stopped when they saw him.

"Hello," said one of them. "Where're your parents, little man?"

"Defending the house," Jed said without thinking. He knew he had to pretend he had a parent, so he stood his ground.

"Well sadly, we are taking back this building now, so you and your family, and all of these others" the bailiff looked at Martin who was standing holding a hammer. "Put that down mate" Martin complied but stood his ground. "Get your stuff, you're evicted".

More scuffles came from downstairs, Jed looked over the bannister to see Derri being lifted and moved out of the room she had been in, she was struggling and cursing the two female bailiffs, twisting and turning trying to get out of their grasp. Both women calmly moved onwards through the front door which was now completely smashed.

Behind them, Billy was collecting his bags and moving out. Jed realised that this was it for this place. Martin moved down the stairs closely followed by the two bailiffs. Jed went into the kitchen where another resident Lee was being cut free from the chains they had tied themselves to. One bailiff handled the steel cutters whilst the other lifted the chain away from Lee's hands before the chain was cut.

"Oww," said Lee

"Didn't touch you" said the bailiff with the cutters grimly "Now clear your stuff and go". Lee stood rubbing his wrists before giving Jed a wink and picking up his rucksack. Jed collected his coat, and bags before following the others outside. Billy, Martin, Lee and Derri were all standing on the pavement, their bags stashed on the ground. Jed went over to them

"You OK?" asked Derri

"Yeah" Jed nodded.

"Nothing we could do against their rammer," said Billy with a frown looking over to where a long steel pole with a metal block on the end was lying near the front door. "This lot has managed to access a few places with that".

"Where are you going to go?" asked Jed "Can I come with you?" Just as Billy was about to answer a voice behind him said

"And who are you, young man?" Jed turned to see a woman standing looking at him. She didn't look kind. Pulling out a wallet she said

"Irene Judge, Paddington Borough Council Social Services". Jed looked at her badge which had a photo of the woman on it. He didn't answer her.

"Who are his parents?" Irene said addressing the adults.

"We ALL are," said Derri.

"His legal parents" replied Irene dryly. No one replied.

"OK, a runaway," said Irene with a satisfied grin. She took hold of Jed's arm

"Let me GO!" yelled Jed, turning to the others who were as shocked as he was. She didn't let go.

"Officer!" she said trying to hold onto a squirming Jed. A police officer came over. "This boy is a runaway," she said as Jed managed to squirm out of her grasp, but before he could sprint away, the policeman took his arm, less forcefully and said

"Come on lad" turning and walking Jed away followed by Irene Judge who looked back only once at the residents. Jed heard Billy yell

"Good luck Jed" as he was led away.

Jed realised his time was up, so he didn't protest anymore. The officer took him to a patrol car and placed him in the back

"Can you bring him to the council offices please?" Irene said as she went back to her car, parked down the street. Jed watched as the bailiffs continued to evict the others from the building as the patrol car sped by. He thought.

More than Twenty Eleven

Jed arrived at the council offices to be greeted by Irene Judge. She dismissed the officer with a nod who got back in the patrol car without another word. Placing a hand on his shoulder which Jed shook off, Irene ushered him into the building which was much bigger than the one in Exeter. She escorted him to a lift and pressed the button for floor five, then tapped some digits into the keypad next to the lift buttons. The doors closed and the lift went up.

Stepping out into a corridor, Jed saw that the building had a great view of the city. He'd never been up so high, and he walked over to the window in the hallway. Irene followed him and said

"That's the Houses of Parliament, and Big Ben is the clock on the end" Jed knew all about them from his lessons at school. Irene opened a door next to the window and Jed walked in. There was a big sofa and a table.

"Would you like a drink? Sorry I don't know your name?"

Jed didn't reply. He shook his head. He was thirsty but didn't want to show this. Irene sat down on the sofa.

"Now it's obvious to me you have run away. Do you want to tell me your name?" Jed didn't reply. "OK, well I can't help you if you don't tell me who you are".

Irene stood up "Well I am hungry so I will bring you some food and drink and if you want it, great, if not I'm sure my secretary will have it".

She walked out and Jed heard a click. He went over to the door. The handle was locked. She had locked him in. He rattled the door angrily, then sat on the sofa. After a few minutes, the door clicked again and Irene returned.

"You locked me in!" said Jed angrily.

"You aren't cooperating" replied Irene. She held up two packets "Ham and cheese or egg?" she asked.

Jed looked mutinous but he was starving.

"Ham and cheese," he said. She looked at him quizzically

"Please" he added. She handed over one of the greaseproof paper packets.

"From the deli down the road", she said as she unwrapped the other one.

She also placed two cans of fizzy pop on the table. Jed started on one of the sandwiches which was delicious. The ham and cheese were plentiful and Jed almost moaned with relief. He realised his last meal must have been the previous afternoon. He wondered where the others were now and if Billy had managed to find another home for them all.

After a few minutes of eating Irene said.

"Now I know you have run away, what is your name?"

"Don't want to go back" Jed eyed Irene. "They were horrible to me".

"Who were?" she asked kindly "Your parents?"

Jed didn't reply immediately but he realised that he wasn't going to get away from this woman. "The home, my mum died".

"I'm sorry" Irene replied as she screwed up the packet and put it on the table. "My job is to look after children," she said looking directly at him. "But I can't help you if you don't tell me what has happened".

Jed sighed deeply. "OK," he said. For the next forty minutes, Jed told Irene the story of the last nine months. She listened without interruption. Eventually, Jed stopped talking and looked down at his feet.

"Well, there is a lot I can do" she offered. "For a start, I need to get in contact with your social worker in Exeter - Mrs Hilston?" Jed nodded. "OK then, leave it with me. Did you want another sandwich?"

Jed shook his head. Irene got up

"I won't lock the door Jed, but the lift is key coded so you can't leave. I want to help you, so please stay here."

Jed slumped back into the sofa. He was exhausted. When Irene returned to the room twenty minutes later she found Jed curled up under his coat fast asleep. She carefully closed the door again. She went back an hour later to find Jed awake and sitting up again.

"Looks like you needed that sleep" she commented. She held out another greaseproof packet to him. Jed realised he was hungry again.

"Thanks," he said as he opened it up and started on his sandwich.

"I've spoken to Mrs Hilston," Irene said. "They were very worried about you Jed". Jed was embarrassed but he tried not to show it.

"She was nice," he said between mouthfuls of ham and cheese "But the home was horrible".

"She told me it didn't used to be for you?" Jed nodded. "Miss Goodwin was lovely, but the bully from my school ended up there, Miss Goodwin was sacked, and it just got horrible" Jed looked at Irene "I don't want to go back there, I'll run away again".

Irene looked pensive. "I don't know what's going to happen Jed, but Mrs Hilston is on her way here now". Jed was surprised. "She's coming to London?"

"She's getting the next train up Jed." Irene looked at her watch "She'll be here in about two hours".

* * *

Mrs Hilston wasn't sure what would greet her when she arrived at the council offices in London. She knew from speaking to Irene Judge that Jed had been found in a condemned squat that had been reclaimed that morning. It was now nearly 4 pm, and Mrs Hilston was concerned about getting back to Exeter before nightfall.

She signed in at the front desk and was directed to the fifth floor. Waiting for her was a woman who introduced herself as Irene Judge. She was ushered into a room, but Jed was not there.

"I think it's best to have a chat before we go to see Jed," Irene said sitting down at a table "Have a seat, would you like a coffee or tea?".

"No thanks" replied Mrs Hilston.

"I'm concerned about Jed's circumstances. He's said that the home mistreated him, a school bully was placed there?"

"That is true about the bully" admitted Mrs Hilston "against my advice" she added.

"Well Jed is adamant that he will run away again which is a major concern for us"

"Budget cuts mean we cannot place either child away in a different location. The bully was placed in the same home after his father brutally attacked the mother and she is not expected to live for very much longer. The father is on remand, expected to be charged with her murder sooner than later, and there are no other relatives willing or able to take him. What do you suggest?"

Irene looked at Mrs Hilston calmly. "We cannot offer either child a place in London, we have the same issues you do in Devon. All I can suggest is regular monitoring of Jed to try and defuse any tensions between him and this other boy".

Mrs Hilston sighed. "I hope that is enough" They stood up.

"OK let's go and see Jed," said Irene.

Mrs Hilston steadied herself for this. She was fond of Jed, and it broke her heart to know that he preferred to be in a squat rather than in a home. They walked down the corridor, towards another set of rooms on the other side of the building. Irene stopped at the first door and opened it

"Jed, Mrs Hilston is here"

* * *

16

Fury

Jenny Hilston had never been faced with utter fury before but she knew it now. As she entered the room, Jed stood up shaking with rage and fury.

"I TOLD you!" he said fiercely, "I TOLD you I would run, and I will again. I hate you, I hate Charlie, and most of all I hate Simon." he sat down again the energy had run out of him.

He started to sob. Jenny Hilston walked over and sat down beside him.

"I know you are angry with me Jed, and I am truly sorry. This cannot happen again though. You've had the police, the council and everyone else looking for you. "

"I DON'T care" yelled Jed again "I won't go back, and if you make me I will run again and this time you won't find me". Jenny looked imploringly at Irene who shook her head. There were no answers either woman could give the boy.

Jenny stood up decisively. "I can only promise that I will call in on you every week Jed."

Jed looked up at her. "How is that going to help?"

"If we don't try how can you be sure it won't?" Jenny replied reasonably. Jed thought about this. Maybe with more oversight from Mrs Hilston, Simon might show his true colours and get moved.

He stood up resolutely. "OK then,"

Jenny breathed out. She hadn't realised she had been holding her breath and mentally crossing her fingers for luck. She also wasn't sure how she was going to manage this, her casebook was expanding every week. Irene smiled at Jed and held out her hand.

Jed shook it "Thank you for the food"

"You are very welcome Jed" she replied "Goodbye".

Jed picked up his bags and followed Mrs Hilston back to the elevator. They both got in and stood awkwardly not looking at each other. Finally, as the lift moved downwards Jed said simply

"I'm sorry"

Jenny Hilston looked at the young boy standing in front of her. His courage and tenacity were something she very much admired but she understood that if she didn't help him, he could be lost in the system again. As the lift descended Jenny Hilston mentally vowed that this would not happen.

* * *

17

More of the same

Jenny Hilston and Jed arrived back in Exeter just before 11 pm. They had missed the train Jenny had been hoping to get onto, and the final train for the night stopped at every station on the way back to Devon. Jenny sat looking out of the window as Jed slept on the seat beside her. He had fallen asleep straight after eating another sandwich she had purchased at the station. His face looked angelic as he slept, without any of the fury he had directed at her that afternoon. She knew she had let him down, but the options were very limited. She hoped she could keep her word to him but she was afraid that was going to be difficult.

* * *

Jenny and Jed caught a taxi from the station on arrival which wound its way through the packed crowds in the centre of the city. Jed had woken up just before the train arrived at Exeter, and he looked out of the cab window at the people milling about. He realised it was Saturday evening, the city came alive at the weekends with the students and other people packing out the bars and clubs. The cab finally stopped outside the Home. Jed was dreading Charlie's reaction but he resolved to try. As they were gathering Jed's bags and Jenny was paying the driver, the front door opened and Charlie was waiting there. Jenny took one of Jed's bags and walked up to where Charlie stood.

"Sorry we are late, the train was delayed," she said. "Can I come in?" Charlie stood to one side and didn't comment as they entered. The house was dark. Jed supposed that the other children might be asleep, but he thought it more likely they were hiding at the top of the stairs listening to what was going on.

"Drop your bags there Jed," said Charlie indicating the hallway, "Go on up and off to bed, we'll talk tomorrow". Jed was surprised Charlie was pleasant to him but did as he was asked.

"Good night Mrs Hilston, goodnight Charlie," he said as he went up the stairs to his room. He didn't brush his teeth, just undressed and got into his bed. Mrs Hilston followed Charlie into his office and sat down on the visitor's chair.

"You looked bushed Jenny" Charlie commented. "Would you like a coffee or tea?"

"No thanks," she replied. "We need to come up with a plan for Jed, we can't have him go missing again".

Charlie nodded his agreement. "What do you suggest?"

Jenny outlined her plan to visit Jed more frequently, causing Charlie to frown

"How is that going to help" he commented once she had outlined what was possible.

"I'm not sure it will" she agreed, "but without something in place, we are going to be having this conversation, or worse again".

Once the strategy had been confirmed, Jenny stood and said

"I am back on call tomorrow but I will call in after school to see Jed" then she walked out of the office into the hallway.

Charlie followed and let her out before closing and locking the doors. He had not mentioned that whilst Jed had been away, he had arranged for new locks to be fitted to the external doors. Jed was not going anywhere again, he vowed.

* * *

Jed woke to the noise of the other children getting ready for school. He yawned and walked to the door. As he opened it, he heard a squeak as Katy tore down the corridor and almost toppled them both over as she hugged Jed tightly.

"You're back You're back!" she giggled. Sam and Ben followed, slapping Jed on his back and joining in the group hug. Only Simon stood glaring at him, not speaking, not commenting. Jed knew he was not happy, he was back again, but he resolved not to care about Simon. He could deal with him later. Jed joined the others downstairs as Charlie was dishing up their breakfasts.

"Jed, you and I are seeing Mrs Cooper before school today," Charlie said as yet another boiled egg was placed in front of him. Katy looked worried but Jed knew that he would have to account both here and at school for his actions. Simon was looking triumphant, but Jed ignored him. The strategy worked, as finally Simon picked up his spoon and loped the top off his egg. Jed ate contentedly enjoying the bustle of the busy kitchen. Katy kept glancing at him as if to confirm he was really back. There would be time, later on, to catch up he knew.

* * *

Charlie and Jed walked to the school behind the other children. Jed attracted the attention of the other groups walking in the same direction. Out of the corner of his eye, he saw people nudge each other and one group pointed at him whispering softly. He took no notice of them, just stood taller and pretended it was a normal day. He was scared though. He liked Mrs Cooper and didn't want to upset her. They waited in the secretary's office for a few minutes before the phone rang, she answered and said

"You can go through now Mr Gibbons". Jed stood up and followed Charlie into the Headmistresses Room. Mrs Cooper smiled broadly and said.

" I need to speak to Charlie alone for a moment Jed, could you wait outside with my secretary?"

Jed nodded and went back outside and sat back down again. The secretary who had a nameplate on her desk was called Mary Whitaker. She smiled at Jed but then carried on opening letters from a pile on her desk. Jed watched as she slit open each letter, unfolded it and placed it on a smaller pile to one side of her.

Eventually, the phone rang again and Jed was sent back into the room. Jed glanced at Charlie whose ears looked pinker than before. He also had the same expression on his face as Mrs Foster had, the 'wasp sucking face' as Ben had put it. Jed sat down and waited.

"I am very glad to see you back safe and sound Jed. I have spoken to Mrs Hilston who has given me the background to your..." Mrs Cooper paused briefly "journey and I have instructed Mr Gibbons that as your Headmistress it is my duty to you, to make sure you are not bullied at home, just as it is my duty to you and all the other children in my care, to ensure you are safe at school".

She looked at Jed who was surprised that she wasn't giving him a hard time for running away. That explained Charlie's expression and his ears. She had given him a roasting for not looking after him. Jed looked down trying not to smile.

"I would like to see you at the end of each school day please Jed for a brief chat. Mr Gibbons has agreed to this. I will see you at the end of each day starting tonight. You may go to your form room now"

Jed stood up and left. Charlie was still in the room. He suspected that this might cause issues later, but for now, he felt better than he had in a long time.

* * *

Jed slipped into the form room and took a seat at the back of the class. Mr Wall smiled as he entered but made no reference to him other than acknowledging his name when it was called on the form register a few minutes later. Some of his classmates turned when he confirmed he was there, but Mr Wall sharply snapped

235

"Eyes front please!" which made all of them turn back to him at the front of the classroom. The lessons began. Jed knew Simon was sitting in the same back row of the class, but he didn't look at him or acknowledge him at all.

* * *

During the first break time, Katy grabbed Jed and pulled him to one side of the playground. Ben and Sam were also there.

"Tell ALL!" Katy said.

"From the beginning" Sam added.

Jed sat down on one of the wooden seats and began. As he talked he felt a weight lifted off him. None of the others interrupted him to ask questions.

Jed finished with "I'm sorry I left you all".

Katy grabbed his arm and said "Now listen to what happened when they knew you had gone"

Katy confirmed that Charlie eventually had called the police to report Jed as missing. He had also been called up to the Church Council who were very worried about the publicity if Jed had been found injured or dead. Ben had heard Charlie on the phone to the council

"He was bricking it" he said with great satisfaction "The council had told him that he could be removed from his role as the Home Manager if he didn't make sure that you were back in a week. As it went from a week into nearly a month, Charlie was getting more and more calls from the Church Council asking what he was doing to find you"

"A WPC came around the first day to speak to all of us" added Sam. "She was nice and told Charlie that you had likely caught a train to London".

"Charlie put a call out to some of the other Church homes near Paddington but they hadn't seen you," said Katy. "What were the other people like in the squat?"

Jed told them all about Billy and the others.

"They aren't scary really, just looking for a home" he finished.

The bell went and they walked back into the main building for their next lessons. During the day, Jed was settling back down into the routine of schoolwork and the homework that came with it. Simon stayed away from him, but Jed spotted him whispering to Neil and his other cronies across the room. Jed knew this wasn't done yet.

* * *

At the end of the day, Jed made his way back to Mrs Cooper's office again. Mary Whitaker indicated he could go in. Jed knocked and when he heard a

"Come in" he entered the room. Mrs Cooper was writing on a pad of paper

"Sit down Jed, I just need to finish off these notes". Jed took the seat that he had been sitting on, a few hours earlier. Mrs Cooper put down her fountain pen and smiled at him.

"How was your first day back?"

"It was OK, thank you"

"I understand that you are being given extra homework to catch up again?"

"Yes Miss"

"OK, then. Now I want you to be honest with me Jed, do you understand?" Jed nodded. "If anything happens to you at school or at the home, if Simon or anyone else bullies you, or you feel like you did before, I want you to come to me" Jed nodded again. "OK well, off you go". Mrs Cooper took up her pen again as Jed picked up his bag and left the office.

* * *

Jed walked down the main corridor and out into the playground. Sitting on the wall just out of sight by the gate were Simon Thomas and his fellow bullies. They watched Jed as he walked to the gate but didn't make any comments. They knew they were not visible from Mrs Cooper's office.

239

Jed walked swiftly back to the home. Waiting for him were Katy, Ben and Sam who had been pretending to read in the sitting room. As Jed opened the front door, he heard hissing. Turning to the sitting room door Katy was beckoning him forward. However just as he was about to go in, Charlie's office door opened.

"Need to speak to you Jed" Jed put down his bag and took off his coat before following Charlie into his office.

"Sit down," said Charlie who still had the expression from earlier on his face.

"Now, I have been told I need to make sure you are happy here. I haven't got time for this nonsense, so here is what will happen. You will man up Jed, nothing wrong with a bit of banter, you will not go crying to Mrs Cooper, and you will not cause me more bother, am I clear!"

The last sentence was accompanied by Charlie's hand slapping the desk in front of him. Jed was shocked. He had never seen Charlie so angry before. but he realised that despite the words of Mrs Hilston and Mrs Cooper nothing was going to change.

"If you do not knuckle down, I will have to make other arrangements for you" Charlie continued. "We have foster homes available which might become our only option, it's your choice. Now go and start your homework, Mrs Cooper said you had a lot of it".

Jed stood up, shaking with anger

"SO nothing changes then?" Charlie looked at him in surprise. He had expected Jed to comply but this boy standing in front of him looked much older than his age.

"You allow a bully in here, who makes my life hell? What sort of a manager are you?"

"Don't you give me that lip Jed, otherwise you will have hell raining down on you. Now get OUT!"

Jed left the room still shaking. Katy, Sam and Ben were peering around the door frame of the sitting room. Jed could see all three of them were shocked by the raised voices coming out of Charlie's room. Just as Jed was about to go to them, the front door opened and Simon Thomas came in. He saw the look on Jed's face and smirked broadly.

"Oh you are still here then?" he said with a nasty grin on his face.

241

"Leave him alone Simon," Katy said.

Simon smiled more kindly "I was glad to see him, that's all".

Charlie came out and saw them all standing there.

"Homework - now!". Jed picked up his school bag and followed the others in. Just as he came level with Simon the other boy hissed "I give you a week orphan sneak boy". Jed knew that Charlie was not going to help him. He started to plot his next escape in his mind, as he sat down with his school books to study.

* * *

During the next week, things went back to how they were before. Mrs Hilston managed one visit to Jed but he could see she was distracted. She kept looking at her watch, even as she was talking. In the end, he gave up on her too.

Charlie true to his word made no attempt to stop Simon from bullying Jed, even with the trips and pushes he witnessed. Katy, Sam and Ben did their best, but Simon was careful to give the impression, all was well. Only when he and Jed were alone, did Simon whisper threats and promises of harm.

Jed had noticed quickly that the security at the home had been upgraded, especially the back door from the kitchen. There was also an alarm fitted which was new. Charlie made much of this every evening, setting it with a beep before retiring to his bedroom at the back of the house. Jed started to plan again, it was the only thing that kept him from going mad, the chance to escape all of this. Jed realised he needed to plan more carefully.

One of the suggestions from the church committee, which Charlie had reluctantly implemented was to allow the children to visit the city centre in groups during the weekend. An allowance was also given to them for sweets and pocket money toys. Each Saturday morning, Charlie handed over £2 to each of them. They then walked down to the city to spend it. Jed was happy to go along, but he had another plan. As they walked around, eating ice cream or looking in the toy shop, Jed was looking out for some of the twenty eleven, especially Big Mike. On the fifth weekend, Jed suddenly spotted him walking down Cathedral Square.

243

"Sorry, I just need to speak to him," said Jed indicating Big Mike "He was a friend of my mum". Katy, Sam and Ben looked on, as Jed rushed over to him

"Big Mike!"

"Jed! how are you?"

"I need to get away," said Jed quietly so the others wouldn't hear him

"Oh, Jed, you can't," Mike said bending down. "It's not good for a young lad to be out on the streets, you've got a warm bed, food, and I hear school as well? Your social worker was out looking for you. She said you ran away?"

"And I will again, it's rubbish, nothing has changed, they said it would but it hasn't"

Big Mike noticed the mutinous expression on Jed's face.

So much like his mum, fierce

"I'm sorry Jed," Big Mike said gently. I can't help you". Jed stalked away back to the others

"What's wrong?" asked Katy who saw how upset Jed was.

"Nothing, let's go," said Jed who was reeling from the rejection by one of the people he believed would save him. Jed didn't see that Big Mike was watching him as he walked away. Jed refused to comment on what had happened despite Katy and the others trying to get him to talk.

* * *

Jed continued to plan as the weeks went by. He realised he would have no exit once he was back at the home every evening, due to Charlie locking down the home so he changed his focus to the time during the weekends when the children were given more freedom.

In the back garden of the home, Jed spotted a hiding place behind an abandoned shed. He had explored this one afternoon whilst Charlie was out collecting paperwork from the church committee.

None of the other children was outside, they were all playing a game of snap in the living room. Jed opened the creaky door and saw that the shed had been used to store old books and other junk from the house. There was a folding bed, mouldy and wet, and behind that was a chest of drawers. Jed creped over to the unit and attempted to open one of the drawers. It was stuck fast but Jed spotted a large screwdriver which he used to prise open the top drawer. Inside it was a little damp but clean. Jed had found his hiding place.

* * *

Over the next few weeks, Jed squirrelled away supplies and cash for his next attempt. The thought of an escape lightened his mood. The secret of it warmed his soul, and he managed to give an impression to all including the other children that he was done with running. He avoided Simon whenever he could, he knew that getting into trouble with Charlie could scupper his plans. On the Friday afternoon of the sixth week, Jed crept out to the shed and surveyed his stash. It was enough. His plans were ready. He was ready. He was going.

* * *

18

Escape

The following morning, after breakfast Jed lined up with the others to be given their pocket money. Jed has been careful to stash only a small amount of his every week, using the remainder to buy sweets, but not to eat, but to take with him. As Charlie handed over the money he commented

"Don't spend it all, haha" in a jovial voice that wasn't like him.

Jed wondered why he was so upbeat, but realised it didn't matter. Jed got his coat and followed the others outside. Simon had already left, walking down the road with his friends. He never joined them on their visits to the city centre, preferring to spend his time smoking outside the local burger restaurant on the main road out of Exeter. As they approached the main shopping area, Jed stopped and said

"I've left my hat behind, you go ahead, I'll catch you up".

Katy stopped "We'll wait"

"No, it's OK you go ahead, meet at Cathedral Square in twenty mins?".

Sam nodded. Jed knew he was keen to get to the toy shop and browse the collections of stickers. All of the other boys had developed obsessions with the packs of cards and books to stick them in. Jed wasn't interested in any of that. He'd never been a collector.

Living in the squat had made him careful of any possessions as they needed to be carried on once eviction happened. Jed walked off quickly not looking at them. If he had looked back he would have seen Katy standing with a quizzed expression on her face. He walked back home but stopped just before reaching it.

As he watched he saw Charlie walking off in the other direction with a shopping bag. Perfect. Charlie would be at the local shops for a while. Jed waited until he was out of sight, then walked swiftly back to the home. He walked down the side path to the back garden and down to the shed. Nothing had been disturbed. He opened the shed door and levered off the front of the drawer where his belongings had been safely stashed. He grabbed his rucksack and added the cash he had just received to the bottom of it. He walked back out again, leaving the drawer as it was. No one would notice the damage he was sure.

Jed walked back up to the road and turned away from the city centre. He didn't want to be spotted by the others making their way back home, especially after they realised he wasn't coming back.

Jed walked down the main road away from the city centre until he got to a bus stop just outside the golf course. Cars turned into the golf course from both directions, mostly expensive-looking ones, with men at the wheel. Some of them had golf clubs sitting in the back of the car. Jed saw there was a path adjacent to the entrance, so he walked up to it. Further down the path, he could see a man with a dog.

Jed adjusted his backpack and started up the path. Just ahead of him, the man carried on walking ahead of him but the dog, a dachshund was very interested in Jed. As the dog came closer Jed lent down to stroke the dog. At this point, the man turned around as he reached the point where the path diverged into two.

"Winston - COME!" the dog ignored its owner. Jed stood expecting the dog to trot off but it didn't. Exasperated the owner walked back "I'm sorry, he's not as obedient as he needs to be".

Jed smiled. "That's OK, he's lovely," said Jed as he bent to scratch the dog's ears. The man looked around. "Who you here with?"

Jed replied, "Oh my mum's just chatting to the neighbour on the road" he indicated the road he had just walked up. "We're on our way up there". Jed indicated the other path

The man nodded and said "Well go careful", then walked back up the path in the direction he was going, "Winston!" the dog trotted off up the path.

Jed waited a while but the man didn't turn around again. The sun was warm on his back so he put down his rucksack and took off his coat, putting it into the bag before putting it on again. Once he saw the man had taken the other path, Jed made his way to the right-hand one. The path he had chosen ran alongside the golf course. He could hear the sounds of clubs hitting balls and the general chatter of people out enjoying the sunshine and fresh air.

As he walked along, Jed vowed to himself he wouldn't get caught this time. Simon had whispered to him one morning at breakfast that he would be in 'borstal ' by the evening. Jed did know what a borstal was. One of the other people in the squat had been kept in one during his own childhood.

Yorkie was made an orphan when his parents died in a horrible fire in a pub when he was only twelve. Yorkie had ended up in trouble with the police after trying to steal some cash from a local shop. He had been placed in homes, but eventually ended up in a particular place on the south coast that was run by a sadist called Mr Folke. Yorkie had been one of Mr Folke's main targets and had suffered during his early teens. Once released Yorkie had found comfort and friendship with the communities of squatters and had eventually made his way over to Devon working on the farms in the area.

Jed knew that he had to keep out of people's way and he had to find shelter. As he walked, the sounds of the golf course started to fade. He was getting tired now, and his legs needed a rest. Up ahead was a line of trees, Jed climbed the low ridge to one side of the path, and walked up into the shade of the trees.

He stopped under a large tree and sat down heavily. The sun was still bright in the sky but the dappled shade around him cooled him down. He reached into his bag and pulled out a can of fizzy drink, popped the tab and started to drink. Jed leaned back against the tree and looked around him. The tree line was just above the golf course. He could see people milling about purposefully below him, but he was partly hidden by the bushes that lined the ridge. No one looked his way, they were all too busy moving their golf balls around the course.

Jed sat for a while watching the people and trying to formulate a plan of where he could go. Big Mike wouldn't help him, and if he tried to get to London again, it was likely that the train station would be on alert for him. He needed to get out of Exeter. Jed suddenly realised he had a plan after all.

He stood up and put on his rucksack. He walked back
to the path and carefully climbed back down the ridge
onto the path. No one was around. He walked back
the way he had come to the main road, and then made
his way to the bus stop. There were three people
waiting there. A woman, a man and a young girl. As he
approached he heard the woman say to the girl

"Bus will be here in five minutes".

Jed smiled. He had enough cash to catch a bus, and
the stop indicated that this bus might go all the way to
Tiverton. Jed knew there was a train station at
Tiverton which wouldn't be monitored like Exeter
probably was now. He wondered if the ticket seller had
been told off for selling tickets to a child.

He stopped and waited behind the other people. The girl who was probably aged about six turned and smiled at him. Jed smiled back but didn't say anything. As he watched a bus approach from the main roundabout before the indicator came on, the driver pulled smoothly into the space adjacent to the road and stopped. The air brakes hissed and the door opened. The man got on first followed by the woman and the girl. Jed waited and then got on.

"Where to?" said the driver

"Tiverton please, child ticket," said Jed.

The driver frowned and said,

"Where's your parents?"

"Mum's in the hospital," Jed said looking down "I'm allowed to visit her today"

Jed looked up making sure he looked sad.

The driver frowned again before clicking the machine which produced a ticket. Jed handed over the money and took his ticket. He picked up a timetable from the display to one side of the ticket machine.

He took a seat near the back of the bus. He glanced around. No one was interested. The bus was nearly full, people off to their jobs, other children with their parents and the three other people who were waiting at the stop. The girl was sitting three rows ahead of him and kept looking back at him.

Jed ignored her and turned to look out of the window as the bus started up again and moved off. The scenery changed as Jed watched, from the outskirts of the city, into the countryside before meandering through villages, picking up more passengers until eventually arriving in the town of Tiverton. Jed opened the timetable. His mum had taught him how to read them from an early age. Buses had been their way of travelling around Exeter during his younger years, as Clare had never believed in prams or pushchairs.

He followed the diagram line for this bus and realised he could get to the bus station before catching another two buses to the train station. He put the timetable back into his pocket and watched the rest of the passengers get off the bus. As the bus pulled up on the road outside the hospital, Jed was careful to make sure that the driver saw him get off and walk towards the hospital, turning and waving as he did so.

The bus pulled away but Jed waited for a short while before walking back to the road again. On the back of the map, Jed had spotted a road map of the town. He traced the route from the hospital to the bus station. The next bus he needed to catch was just around the corner. Jed hutched his bag more comfortably on his back and started walking. As he turned the corner he could see the next bus approaching. There were a lot of passengers waiting for this bus including some family groups. He knew that the more people there were, the fewer people would notice him on his own. The driver this time was a woman, but as Jed had boarded the bus after a big family group she just sold him a ticket and started the bus up. Jed couldn't find a seat but he wasn't worried about standing. He made sure he was near the family group ahead of him, who were talking about going to London for the day.

Perfect

Jed knew that all he had to do was to follow this family all the way to the city. He smiled as he listened in on the chatter from the family. The parents were taking their two children, a boy and a girl, twins to the London Zoo for a birthday treat. The children were telling their parents about which animals they wanted to see. Predictably the boy wanted to see the fierce lions and tigers but the girl wanted to see the 'fluffy polar bears' Jed smiled as the mum explained that the polar bears were also pretty fierce and wouldn't want to be stroked.

The bus meandered around the town picking up and dropping off more passengers before arriving at the bus station. Jed followed the family off the bus and to the final bus before arriving at the train station. He tried not to attract attention but he could see that the family were completely absorbed in their own conversation. This bus was also quite full but Jed managed to get a seat two rows behind the family group. More passengers got on and off at the many stops before finally pulling into the train station.

As Jed got off behind the family, he could hear the sounds of cars but he couldn't see a road. The puzzle was answered as the boy child also commented on the noise of cars.

"That's the motorway over there Harry," said the father pointing into the distance where a line of trees was. "Goes all the way to London, but we will get there quicker".

They walked into the railway station and Jed was close behind them. This was the difficult part. Jed waited patiently as the father bought and paid for the family's tickets. As they moved off Jed walked to the counter and smiled broadly at the ticket seller who was a young woman who was chewing gum. She started at Jed

"I'm allowed to buy my own ticket," he said cheerfully indicating to the family group "Dad said it's good for me to be able to do maths". She looked at Jed but he realised that she really didn't care. "One child ticket to London please?".

He handed over the money and took his ticket before heading to the group who were standing near the kiosk in the entranceway. Jed walked over and asked the dad

"Excuse me, do you know when the train is coming? My mum is just paying for the taxi" The dad smiled kindly and said "It's going to be here in five minutes., Your mum better hurry"

Jed smiled his thanks and turned, The ticket seller had been watching him but talking to the dad had helped, he waved at her, going towards the toilets.

Jed quickly went to the loo before going back outside again. He glanced over at the ticket seller who was dealing with another group of people. He walked swiftly to the gate and showed his ticket to the guard

"Mum and Dad are already on the platform but I needed the loo" Jed said noticing the guard's frown. He saw the dad look back and waved, which reduced the guard's suspicion. He was allowed through but made sure not to go near the family group. He went to the kiosk and bought a bottle of fizzy pop.

The train was in view at the end of the line and as Jed sipped his drink standing out of the way, it pulled up next to the platform. Jed waited until most of the other people had boarded before selecting a middle-aged woman. He quickly walked to stand behind her, and then boarded the train. No one looked at him, he was invisible. Just another child going to London for the day with his parent. Jed had chosen well, the woman looked like a mum, dressed in a pretty dress with matching shoes. She walked down the carriage and sat down at a window seat. Jed decided to sit close to her but not next to her, so he wouldn't attract attention.

As the train pulled out of the station Jed sat back relieved. He knew the train would not go to Exeter, instead would cross to Taunton then onto Reading and London Paddington. Jed wasn't sure what he would do then, but the first thing was to disappear and he was now on his way. As the train trundled along, Jed took out his favourite book 'Islands in the Sky' and started reading again. He was so absorbed he didn't see the ticket inspector come into the carriage.

"Tickets please!" said the tall man wearing the GWR uniform. His waistcoat had very shiny buttons on it. Jed took out his ticket and handed it over as the inspector came down the aisle.

"Travelling alone?" said the man giving Jed a puzzled look "Mum's meeting me at Paddington" replied Jed quickly with a smile "Dad put me on the train,...he's living in sin"

The man smiled "Aren't we all"

Jed was confused but didn't ask what he meant. The story held so he was OK still. Jed turned back to his book. The train carried on through the countryside but Jed was absorbed in the story until eventually the train slowed down for the final time and arrived at Paddington Station. Jed picked up his rucksack and followed the rest of the passengers out onto the platform. He smiled relieved to be back where he could disappear again. He started down to the exit but before he could reach it a hand grasped his shoulder and a deep voice said

"And where are you going, young man?" Jed struggled but the hand clasped his shoulder firmly. He was roughly turned around to see Billy standing in front of him.

"Billy!" Jed wrapped his arms around him.

Billy pulled him away and said sternly again "Jed, you can't be here lad"

"I can't stand it there Billy, nothing changed, Charlie is worse, and Simon bullies me at home now as well as at school" Jed crossed his fingers behind his back. It wasn't strictly true but he needed to get Billy on his side. Billy sighed deeply.

"Oh man, you are a one, aren't you?" Jed wasn't sure what a 'one' was but Billy was now smiling a bit. "Come on then lad, can't leave you here like Paddington Bear".

Jed knew this related to the books which Jed's mum had read to him when he was younger. Jed picked up his rucksack and walked with Billy to the exit. "Did you find another squat?" Jed asked as they walked along the busy London street

"Found another office building back on Bayswater Road," Billy said as they stopped to cross the road. "Sited for development but the company went bust last year. We've already made it home"

Jed was thrilled. Finding Billy and the others was a stroke of luck and hopefully, this squat wouldn't get reclaimed for ages. Eventually, they arrived at a tall building set back slightly from the road. Like the last squat, there had been an attempt to prevent access but Billy took Jed down the alleyway beside the building to an emergency door. At first glance it didn't look like it could open, Billy pressed a switch near the top of the door and the lock clicked and the door opened. Turning to Jed he said

"New lad is a sparky, an electrician managed to fit an override switch to the door alarm" Billy opened the door and announced,

"Look what I found at the rail station!".

As Jed followed Billy inside he saw Martin standing in the doorway wiping his hands on a tea towel. The room was light and airy and it looked like the electricity was still connected.

"Ah, my sous chef's arrived just in time. Got a pile of spuds for you to scrub Jed me lad" Martin smiled kindly "But how did you get away this time?" he added.

Jed placed his rucksack on the floor and began his story after he had been taken by Irene Judge right up to when Billy had spotted him at Paddington.

"I was sure it was the rail police" he finished with a sigh. "Thought I was caught right and proper. Big relief when I realised it was Billy".

Martin chuckled. "Expect you are famished? Fry up before we start the evening prep then?... follow me!"

Jed willingly followed Martin back out into the room he had come from. The kitchen in this office was smaller than the last squat, more of a tea room than a proper kitchen, but they had set up several cooking and prep areas including what looked like a BBQ outside the kitchen fire escape. Jed sat down gratefully on a bench next to one of the prep areas.

Martin fired up one of the propane camping gas cookers and put a large frying pan on top of the flames. From a fridge next to the door Martin pulled out a pack of bacon and three eggs. He quickly fried the bacon before putting it on a plate next to the pan, then using the grease from the bacon he scrambled the eggs and placed them on top. He turned and put the plate down in front of Jed who was trying not to dribble. The smell was amazing. Martin added a slice of thickly buttered bread and a knife and fork to the table and Jed took them up and started on his first proper meal since leaving the home many hours earlier.

Between mouthfuls, he asked Martin what had happened to them all since he had been taken away. Martin confirmed that for a few days the group had been forced to split up, mainly to find a suitable place for them all again.

"Derri found this place in the end," Martin said "She'd been dating an estate agent over in Mayfair since last summer and they had been the agents for the landlord of this place. She had pumped him for information on his 'exciting' job and he had confessed that it was unlikely this place would get new tenants until next year at the earliest. She also got out of him details of the security company which we know are not the best at preventing access for people like us. They take the landlord's money, come and rattle a few doors and then collect their wages. Most of the guards are on minimum wage anyway and as long as we don't trash the place, they don't really care. They are predictable in their visits and we are all mostly out when they come around, so it looks secure and untouched".

Jed signed gratefully as he finished his meal.

"That meal was amazing, thanks Martin".

Martin smiled. "Well we can't put you to work on an empty tum can we?"

* * *

That evening Jed joined the others for a meal he had helped prepare. Billy had told Jed that the group decided things over their evening meals, such as chores, things to be done, and now what would happen to him. Jed had busied himself during the late afternoon with the potatoes Martin had given him. Jed scrubbed clean the potatoes and then under supervision was shown how to slice them for the meal which was layered potato pie. Jed had also prepared onions and sweet peppers and then had watched Martin turn these ingredients into another delicious dish.

Before the meal started as everyone had arrived Billy had called for a vote on whether Jed could stay. None of them had been pursued by the authorities for allowing him to stay in the last squat, but Billy pointed out that Jed was under thirteen and all it would take would be some nosy neighbour.

"I'll say he's mine" interrupted Derri with a grin. Jed realised up to that point, that he had been holding his breath and internally praying for a positive result.

"You'll need to get your story straight Derri" warned Billy "We can't have any um ms and ahas if the old Bill comes around. You need to both have a good strong story. and one that you both can tell outsiders if they ask" Derri winked at Jed

"We will eh Jed?" Jed grinned back at her.

* * *

19

Eleven to Fifteen

Jed's life for the next four years followed the same pattern as his early years.

Derri kept her word and between them, they came up with a simple storyline that each of them could recite should it be needed. Derri and Jed spent time asking and answering questions that Billy thought might come up should they be questioned in the future. By the time Billy was happy, Derri knew all about Jed's habits, interests and likes and dislikes, and Jed learned that Derri had grown up in Manchester. Billy explained that lies should be loosely based on the truth, and so their new life began.

The first occasion happened a few weeks later when Jed, his hair newly coloured went with Derri and Martin to the local shops for provisions. The shopkeepers in the local area were used to seeing the residents of the squat but when Jed stopped at a display of mangos outside an Indian food shop, the owner peered at Jed over his glasses and looked at Derri asking

"He's yours?" Derri smiled warmly and tugged Jed closer "My boy Jed - Jed meet Mr Singh, he sells great things". "Pleased to meet you, Jed," said the man.

Jed stuck out his hand and said "Hello".

Mr Singh chuckled and asked, "He's not been here long?"

Derri signed dramatically and confirmed "No, his dad had been looking after him for me, in Manchester but he found himself a girlfriend"

"Millie" added Jed

"Yes Millie" confirmed Derri ruffling his hair kindly " and she didn't like Jed being around, so now he's home with me instead". Jed looked up at Mr Singh who smiled.

"Well, welcome Jed. I hope you like living in London"

"Thank you sir" replied Jed then turned to Derri. "Can we have a mango?"

Derri laughed. "Yes, I think we can afford it."

* * *

Jed grew close to all of the residents of the squat. His favourite person was always going to be Billy who sometimes told Jed stories about his mum, which made him feel closer to her. Billy also took charge of Jed's schooling, explaining that it was important for him to be able to count, and also to have a wide range of knowledge for his adult years.

Derri would spend time with Jed each evening supervising his homework, making sure he washed and cleaned his teeth, and putting him to bed with his favourite books. Derri had found a big pile of space books in a local charity shop a few weeks later, and Jed loved to read each evening.

Another development happened a few weeks later. Derri had finished her relationship with the estate agent shortly after the squat was established and had started to grow closer to Martin. Jed loved to see them giggle and josh each other over the mounting piles of vegetables in the kitchen.

"Martin is nice isn't he?" Jed asked one evening as Derri was clearing up the table after dinner. She blushed fiercely as Jed started to clear some glasses. "He likes you" he added.

"Does he?" she asked

"Oh yes" confirmed Jed "It's obvious". Derri didn't reply but carried on moving more dishes to the sink area. He looked back. She was smiling.

* * *

The romance between Martin and Derri blossomed over the following months much to Jed's delight. They spent their spare time together and Jed was happy to see that happen.

Eventually, Martin confined to Jed that he planned to ask Derri to marry him the following evening, which was the longest day. Billy had arranged for a party to happen in the yard behind the building to celebrate the occasion. Jed helped Martin to cook a special feast including a pot roast and salads. Jed could see that Martin was nervous during the day but didn't comment knowing that to do so would make it worse.

The evening was a great success. Some of the other female residents had persuaded Derri to come with them for a drink, and when they all came back, the yard had been bedecked with handmade bunting and balloons. Jed loved these occasions.

This reminded him of another gathering, for Big Mike's birthday party just before the squat had been cleared. Big Mike had laughed and joked with everyone and had even asked Clare for a dance, which had made her blush fiercely. Jed's heart ached for his mum, but he also knew that she was always with him. He sat on the wall watching the others eat, and dance before Billy called out

"Quieten down you rowdy lot" which caused some at the back to jeer jokingly but they all complied. "Now Martin has an announcement to make" Billy nodded at Martin who looked to Jed like he might vomit at any moment. Martin gulped audibly then walked forward to the front of the crowd.

"Derri, you too," said Billy with a smile. Derri looked around puzzled to see a crowd of smiling faces. She joined Martin at the front of the crowd. Jed had pushed to the front, he knew what was coming. Martin turned to Derri and took both her hands. The people around them smiled but were silent.

"My darling Derri, I have loved you forever. Will you do the honour" Martin knelt before her "of taking my hand in marriage?"

The crowd waited for Derri's reply and as she nodded yes, her eyes stinging with happy tears, Martin lifted her up high in his arms turned and said

"My wife-to-be"

Derri was crying freely now, and Martin too had tears running down his face. They kissed to a roar from the crowd and then were enveloped by people wanting to congratulate them.

Billy stood to one side and yelled: "Hip hip hooray" to which the rest of the crowd joined in.

Jed stood next to Billy and asked "Did he get a ring?"

Billy shook his head. "He's taking her to Camden Market tomorrow to choose one. Best idea really, she's going to be wearing it for the rest of her life, so it needs to be one she loves". Jed thought about this, he loved the idea that someone would wear a ring forever.

* * *

The party went on till the early hours of the next morning, but by 10 am Martin was back in the kitchen with Jed making breakfast for the group. Jed realised that Martin was genuinely happy and when Derri popped her head around the corner, her ginger hair tangled, Jed realised that these two were probably also going to have children. He wondered what the children would look like. He realised he wanted to be around to see them. Later in the day Martin and Derri went off to Camden, and on their return, Derri had a beautiful ring to show them. It was a silver clasped pair of hands with a bright blue stone in the middle of it.

Over the next few weeks, Martin and Derri planned their wedding. Both of them were not religious, so they booked a slot at the local register office for the end of the following month. Mr Singh had agreed to allow them to use his upstairs flat address for the official records and Billy had offered Martin and Derri the use of a friend's flat in Richmond for a mini honeymoon.

"My mate Johnny owns the place" Billy had said to the happy couple. "I met him a few years ago when he was finding himself, and he's just about to go travelling in Spain with his girlfriend, so the place will be empty for a while.".

They both nodded happily "Right that's sorted then" Billy said with a wink to Jed.

* * *

Jed was peeling spuds when Martin came out into the yard and sat down beside him. "Do you know what a pageboy is Jed?"

Jed shook his head.

"It's a special job that a groom needs someone to do for him. I would, ...we would like you to be our pageboy, Jed. You would show people to their seats in the registry office, and also help out during the wedding. Would you do that for us?"

Jed dropped his potato and peeler and hugged Martin fiercely

"Yes," he said his voice muffled.

The rest of the wedding party consisted of Billy who had also been asked by Martin to be the best man, which had been happily accepted. Derri had asked two of the other residents Mandy and Laura to be her brideswomen and had spent many a happy afternoon browsing the local charity and thrift shops for outfits to suit.

Jed had accompanied Martin and Billy to another thrift shop that sold second-hand suits. Browsing the racks of men's suits, the group had arrived at the back of the shop where a collection of brightly coloured jackets were nearly hidden. Martin pulled out a red velvet jacket and tried it on. It fitted him perfectly. Billy browsed the rest of the rail and found a similar green jacket, which was a little bit too big.

"Judith can take this in for you Billy," said Martin admiring the jacket on his friend. Jed knew Judith to be a matronly-looking lady from Jamaica who was always crafting in the squat. She made socks and scarves for the group from wool she had found in the charity shops and had a hand-cranked sewing machine that fascinated Jed. He loved to watch her turning the handle whilst deftly moving the material from the front stitching precise lines, and making clothing for the group. Jed eventually found a stylish blazer near the back of the shop. It was tucked in a box of donations. Jed slipped on the jacket and turned to Billy and Martin.

"OK?".

Billy whistled "More than OK, Jed!"

* * *

On the appointed day Jed, Martin, Billy plus Derri and her two brideswomen Laura and Mandy arrived at the town hall. The sunlight dappled as it broke through the trees lining the road.

Martin looked slightly nauseous but Billy kept talking to him so it distracted him from what was coming. Jed knew Martin loved Derri and wanted to marry her. He couldn't understand why he was nervous. Billy had explained it to him the night before.

"He doesn't want to mess up Jed, he wants this day to be perfect for Derri. He wants to look back on this day as the best ever, but he told me he doesn't like being the centre of attention, never did, even from school days".

Jed looked over at Derri who was having her dress adjusted at the back. Judith had taken in the dress for Derri but had laughed at the last fitting.

"You gonna have to get some meat on your bones girl! I can't take this dress in no more."

Derri looked spectacular, the glittering pearls on the cream dress back enhancing her figure, the net underskirts flashing pink and white. Her brideswomen both wore similar dresses also found in the local charity shops Laura in pale blue and Mandy in pale pink. Each of them also wore similar net underskirts. Judith had been careful to make sure none of the men was around during the fittings, and the dresses had been tucked away in Judith's room after each fitting. Billy came down the steps and beckoned the group towards him.

"They're ready for us. Come on lads" Billy beckoned Jed and Martin to follow him up.

"You ladies wait here until Jed comes and gets you. You all look gorgeous by the way" Jed saw the ladies blush. He must remember that - compliment the girls. Jed followed Billy and Martin into the building.

"This way," said Billy ushering them both up the main staircase and into a long hallway. They followed him to the end of the corridor where a sign was marked

'King Wedding this way' with an arrow pointing to the corridor they were walking into. Jed realised this was Martin's last name.

"Why the sign?" Jed asked puzzled "Are there more guests coming?"

Billy smiled "Nah mate, but the wedding must be signposted. It's the law, just in case, someone wants to object to the marriage. Anyone who does has to be able to find the ceremony"

"Why would anyone object to a wedding?"

"Legal reasons," Billy said "If one of the two is already married, if one of them is being forced into the marriage, that sort of thing"

Jed was certain that neither of those reasons applied in this case, but he was also hoping that Martin hadn't heard what Billy had said. He could see Martin was looking even paler than he did outside. At the main door next to the sign was a woman in a pale grey suit holding a clipboard.

"Hello I am Mrs Helen Knox, I am the registrar for the local council, and I will be marrying you "she looked at her clipboard "and Derri today. Are you ready?"

Martin nodded.

Billy whispered to Jed

"Go get the ladies"

Jed turned and walked quickly back down the stairs and out to the steps where Derri, Mandy and Laura were waiting patiently

"It's time," Jed said.

"Take my arm," Derri said holding her elbow out. Jed complied happily and walked up the stairs to where the woman was standing.

Billy and Martin must have gone inside, thought Jed.

"Hello Derri," said Mrs Knox "Your bridegroom is inside waiting for you". Mrs Knox walked back into the room and closed the door.

Derri released Jed's arm "Better go inside then" she smiled.

Jed opened the heavy door and walked toward Billy and Martin. Behind him Derri, Mandy and Laura waited. From the back of the room, a tune began to play. Jed recognised it. He had heard Laura, Derri and Mandy playing this tune a few days earlier on a portable tape player. When he had asked Derri what the tune was called she had replied

"Arrival of the Queen of Sheba, Martin and I have decided on this for the wedding when I come into the room".

Jed listened to the tune and declared "I like it, you are a queen" This made Derri and her brideswomen giggle.

"Got you right on," said Mandy with a snort. And so the tune was confirmed.

As the room filled with the sounds of the classical tune, Derri and her brideswomen walked in unison into the room and saw that Martin, Billy and Jed were all looking at them at the top of the room where a large table was placed. Behind it, to one side another woman was sitting in front of a large leather-bound book and standing behind the table was Mrs Knox.

"Welcome to you all to this the wedding ceremony of Martin and Derri. My name is Mrs Knox and this" she indicated to the other woman who looked up and smiled at them "Is Mrs Kingston. She will be making sure that this ceremony complies with the law of this country."

Jed looked at the book in front of Mrs Kingston. It looked very old and very heavy. The book had been screened with only the top right-hand page visible. Jed turned back to listen to Mrs Knox explain how the ceremony would go. In less than twenty minutes Mrs Knox declared

"I now declare you husband and wife, you may now kiss your bride".

Martin smiled with relief and gathered Derri into his arms for a dramatic kiss. She giggled and returned the kiss. The music changed to a quiet classical piece of music which Jed also liked. The bride and groom were ushered to sign the register alongside Billy and Laura as official witnesses. Jed had been disappointed to learn that he was not allowed to be a witness but he waited patiently with Mandy whilst the register was done. Mandy pulled out a disposable camera from her handbag and took pictures as they waited including one of Jed who tried not to grin maniacally. She then passed Jed a small box.

"What's this?" he asked

"Confetti" Mandy whispered. "Don't open it yet, the council don't like to clear it up, wait till we are outside on the steps then scatter it over the couple. It is an old symbolic act to shower the couple with good luck, well wishes and love."

Jed peeled open the corner of the box to find small pieces of tissue paper in decorative shapes - bells, hearts, a flower. He liked the idea of this and tucked the box into his blazer pocket. As they all left, the bride and groom ahead of the others, Mandy slipped Billy and Laura similar boxes of confetti.

As they exited the offices and went down the stairs Billy, Laura, Mandy and Jed dashed ahead to the pavement where they turned in unison, opened their boxes and threw the contents over Martin and Derri who giggled in delight. Billy also managed to get a handful down the back of Martin's jacket and Jed managed to get some in Derri's hair.

Billy hailed a black cab that was passing them directing them to the local pub closest to the squat. Billy had planned a surprise for the couple and as they arrived a few minutes later, he directed them upstairs to the function room. As Martin and Derri walked in, they found the remaining residents of the squat plus their friends all waiting for them.

Judith and her friends had prepared a feast of Caribbean cooking. The food smelt amazing, Jed realised he was starving but he restrained himself until the others had collected their food. The party went on into the early hours with speeches and dancing. At the end of the night, Martin and Derri were directed to a cab alongside their suitcases to be taken to the Richmond flat. Jed helped Billy, Judith and the others clear up the party before they went to bed.

* * *

20

Kitty

Jed knew he loved Kitty from the first time he saw her.
She was busking in the square close to the office
blocks and coffee shops near the squat in his fourth
year of living in London.

Her dreadlocks swayed as she moved gently to the
beat of her guitar and she wore a complicated cotton
dress that had tassels around the hem. She played a
range of songs, mostly all ballads, which earned her a
regular tinkle as coins landed in her battered guitar
case from the passing pedestrians.

Jed sat on a bench watching her dance and sway. When the trickle of coins stopped she finished her song, bowed to the remaining couple of pigeons scratching around for a sandwich crust and then scooped out the coins putting them in her jacket pocket. She placed her guitar back into the case and locked it. As she stood Jed was standing in front of her, moving nervously from one foot to the other.

"You need the bog?" she asked with a grin "Nearest ones down there", she pointed back to the road. Jed shook his head "Cat got your tongue?" she added. She had noticed Jed watching her for most of her set, but she was a fierce woman who didn't fall easily for charming boys like this one.

"Can...Can I buy you a coffee?" Jed finally stammered. She appraised him sternly

"A coffee?" she quizzed. Jed nodded. He was going bright red and could see she had noticed. However, she smiled again, this time more warmly.

"OK" She looked at him "Nice one down this way," she said. "Come on mystery man...?"

"Jed"

"Mystery man Jed. that's a nice name" Kitty mused, as she led Jed away from the square and back onto the busy street. They walked to the coffee shop and Jed true to his word bought Kitty a coffee. He liked this coffee shop, it was warm and cosy with red leatherette booths where you could talk and not be overheard.

Kitty sat opposite Jed.

"Come on then, what's your story?" she asked

"What do you mean?" he replied

"Well you are definitely not from around here, your accent is cute though" she stirred her coffee "and you are not old enough to be out of school"

"Neither are you" Jed replied. He was starting to wonder about this girl, and she was a girl too. She was fierce but he also liked her vulnerability especially when she sang songs of love and loss.

Jed looked at his coffee "My mum and I lived in squats in Exeter until I was nine, then she went into hospital and I was taken to a home. She died" Jed paused and looked up at Kitty.

He wasn't sure what to expect but she looked at him with such a fierce love he nearly cried himself. He looked back at his coffee. "I ran away, lots of times, but kept getting caught and brought back to the home. I hated it there. Finally, they stopped chasing me, but I want to go back to Exeter" Jed looked up again.

"What's your name? How old are you?" he asked wonderingly

" Kitty and I am seventeen" she replied

"Yeah right," Jed said "and I am a famous film star"

She giggled and sipped her coffee "nice to meet you, Mr Film Star, gonna take me to the Oscars?"

"Come on" Jed urged "how old?"

"Fourteen" she admitted. "Foster care since I was six, the last one was the worst, I just upped and left,"

Jed said, "I'm nearly fifteen now, but sometimes I feel much older." Kitty nodded.

"Where do you live?" he asked

"I sleep on the floor of a flat above a chip shop, with friends who live in Acton. It's OK but the two oldest Simon and Matthew want to go travelling so they are giving up the rent, Lisa, the other is a children's nurse, and she is moving into the hospital nurse's home. I can't afford a place so not sure.."

"Why don't you come and live in our squat,?" asked Jed impulsively

"Moving in together, that's a bit random for a first date?" Kitty giggled.

"Date?" asked Jed blushing again

"Well, I think this is a date isn't it?" Kitty replied as she hugged his arm. They sat making their coffee last as long as possible before they reluctantly got up to leave.

Jed had never felt like this about a girl. The closest he had got to any female company before Kitty was being taught how to be kind to girls by Derri.

None of the other residents in the squat was Jed's age, the next oldest to Jed was a tall Scottish guy called Thomas who regaled Jed about his 'conquests' on a regular basis until Billy cut him off with a curt

"Don't be giving it all that man" Billy didn't like how Jed was starting to mimic Thomas in some ways, being less polite than before.

Billy had frowned at Thomas coming into the squat. He had suspected that Thomas was running drugs for a gang operating near the tube station but he hadn't managed to persuade the others of his suspicions. Billy had a few rules for residents and drugs was a big no. Billy had seen communities fall apart over them, and didn't want this one to go the same way. Billy also knew that Jed was finding his own way, but later spoke to Derri about Jed. This then led to Derri having "the Talk"

She had explained to him when he was twelve that girls were different from boys. Jed had blushed and wriggled when she started 'that talk' one evening after dinner. However, despite his blushes, between talks with Derri and Martin he had learned a lot of useful information about girls and also that the way Thomas was with them, and bad-mouthing them behind their backs wasn't a kind way to be.

Meet the (local) author

Janet Humphrey is the author of the bestselling DUST Book Series.

She's the wife of a laboratory scientist and cat mum to Bruce and Harry adopted from Four Paws in Oxford.

She's also been a casual worker, a part time student at the Open University gaining a BSc in psychology, a scooter rider and currently works a full-time job as an accounts assistant for JISC. She and her husband have spent a lot of time travelling the world in their spare time exploring places that could one day end up in her books like the original premise for DUST Book One.

She does her best writing in her sunny home office in Didcot. Janet loves to play with strong characters including her prequel character Jed, transporting readers to a place where the endearing flaws of the people are readily identifiable, but they are stronger than they look.

In her DUST Book One the tagline "The story humanity hopes never actually happens" Janet takes the prequel character Jed onwards from his downfall at the hands of the brutal Centin brothers Emil and Sly and gives him and seven other people a unique event which changes theirs and everyone else's perspective on how alien life might contact us.

For updates:
Facebook: DustBooksAuthor
Twitter: dustbooksauthor
Tiktok: dustbooksauthor
Instagram: dustbookauthor
Threads: dustbookauthor

Jed had learned a lot from Derri and Martin, both how they treated each other, and also supported each other. He wanted badly to see Kitty again, but when they had left the cafe, she had merely kissed his cheek and dashed off down the road before he could ask her out again.

Jed retraced his steps to the same square over the next few days but didn't see Kitty with her guitar. He was devastated and eventually confessed to Derri that he had met someone. Derri was a kind soul who could see Jed was heartbroken, so she took out a pad of paper and a pen, and handed them to him.

"Be a detective Jed, you have knowledge she shared, that will help you find her again". Jed was confused but took the items and sat down at the table in the kitchen. "Write all you know about her, what she told you, everything!" she emphasised. Jed started to write, the pen flowing with impressions of her, what she told him about her friends until eventually he stopped exhausted. The page was full of his neat script. He turned the pad around so Derri could read it. She didn't comment until she had finished.

"OK then, we start in Acton. Simon and Matthew and a nurse called Lisa, who is moving into nursing accommodation near a hospital. The flat is above a chip shop, there can't be too many like that in the high street. We start tomorrow". She smiled at Jed. "Now off to bed with you, and clean those fangs!"

Jed stood up and nodded. "Thanks, Derri" He hugged her as he walked by. She hugged him back. He was the closest thing she had to a son.

* * *

The following day Jed and Derri caught two buses from the squat arriving in Acton an hour later. Jed had remembered a couple of other things during the night, and he had added these to the page. One was an off-hand remark about one of the two flatmates who were going travelling.

Kitty had mentioned Matthew wore teeth braces and would leave these "to soak" in a cup in the kitchen overnight. Kitty had shuddered as she recalled going to the kitchen in the night, and nearly drinking from this mug.

"Horrible" she had commented.

The other was that Lisa had long ginger hair worn in a bun. Derri and Jed started at one end of the High Street, looking for chip shops which might have rental accommodation above them. They found three at one end of the street, but two were in single-storey blocks with no accommodation, and the third was in a block clearly marked as being offices of solicitors on the top floor.

"Ugh, can you imagine talking important business as the smell of chips and fish come wafting up the stairs into your offices,"

They carried on up the road, looking for more likely targets until eventually at the top of the road, Jed spotted the place. It was a chip shop, had what looked like flats above and more importantly, a sign was hanging off the building offering 'Rooms to let'. They walked across the road and stood outside the chip shop. The smell wafted under their noses, and Jed realised he was starving.

"Let's get a bag of chips then keep an eye on the place," said Derri who like Jed found the smell of the fried potatoes irresistible. She walked in and bought a large portion of chips, adding salt and vinegar to the order. They walked out of the shop and crossed the road to a low wall. As they sat down Derri sighed happily.

"I need some rest for my feet" as she opened the packet.

Steam billowed out as they each selected a chip. Derri clunked her chip with Jed's one in mimicry of toasting his health which made Jed giggle. They happily chomped the chips, as they watched the building. About half an hour later from the side gate next to the chippy a girl came out, wearing a short blue coat and with her ginger hair in a bun. Jed could see her dress under her coat looked like a nurse's uniform and she wore black clumpy shoes.

"That must be Lisa?" said Jed excitedly. "Should I go and speak to her?"

"Hold your horse young man" replied Derri handing him the packet, "I'll go and speak to her, wait here"

Derri got up from the low wall and hurried over to where the woman was standing next to the bus stop on the other side of the road. Derri tapped her on the shoulder and she turned around. Jed couldn't hear what Derri was saying but she gestured to Jed who tried not to look like he had eaten nearly his body weight in chips.

Eventually, she beckoned to Jed, who walked over to where the two women were chatting.

"So this is him?" said the woman who Jed knew now must be Lisa to Derri who nodded.

"Jed, this is Lisa, Kitty's friend. She told Lisa all about you, and is willing to pass on a time and date to Kitty for you to meet up with her again." Jed blushed bright pink but nodded.

"Where?" he asked simply.

"Well Kitty does art evening classes at the local polytechnic on Tuesday evenings, How about I say to her you will meet her and take her for coffee after that? 9.30 pm?"

Jed nodded again. Then it occurred to him "Where is the polytechnic?"

"Gunnersbury Lane" replied Lisa with a smile. "So I can tell her she has a date then?" Jed nodded blushing hard again. "Right, I need to be off now, my shift starts in an hour," said Lisa, "Nice to meet you, Jed" she walked off turning to wave at them both. Derri passed the chips back to Jed

"They're still hot, you can have the rest"

Jed was on tenterhooks until the following week. Derri has mentioned to Martin that their detective work had paid off, but Martin didn't comment to Jed about it, just passed him a crisp £10 note on the Tuesday morning after breakfast commenting with a sly wink

"Coffee's expensive in Acton"

Jed spent the day helping out in the squat fixing some broken floor planks in one of the main corridors with Billy. He was glad of the distraction and as they worked fixing and repairing, Jed was able to concentrate on the job. By lunchtime, they were done, with three new and two repaired floor planks now fixed. Jed spent the afternoon reading his memory book. He thought his mum would approve of Kitty, she had the same vulnerable air about her that his mum had but like Clare Kitty was a fierce person when provoked.

Jed was waiting outside the polytechnic by 9 pm. He was terrified of being late so had made his way to the location early. He watched as groups of adults walked out of a side gate on Gunnersbury Lane, some with books, some with large flat cases which he assumed were art supplies. Some were chatting outside the gate for a while but Jed watched and waited. Just as he was about to give up as the groups started to fade to a single person coming out, there she was. She had tied her dreadlocks up with a big piece of blue ribbon on top of her head, her dress this time was a shocking pink with blue flowers on it. On her feet were black Dr Marten lace-up boots.

They looked cute but he knew they were hard-wearing and protective shoes, not to be messed with. The effect was charming. He stood watching her put her case down and look around. He walked across the road and smiled as she realised he was there. She took off at a trot and ran into his arms. Her case was still on the pavement. He kissed her.

"Thought you weren't coming," she said burying her face now muffled by his clean white shirt." I was looking out of the classroom for you until the caretaker told me I had to go"

"I will always be here" he replied feeling that he meant every word. "You'd better get your case and we can go and get coffee, and you can show me what you do" Kitty walked back and collected her case then turned and grabbed Jed's hand.

"Best coffee is this way" she indicated a row of shops further up the road "Turkish coffee is the best".

They made their way along the street Kitty doing most of the talking. Jed was content to listen and hold her hand. They walked into the cafe, which was steamy and warm inside. They sat at a table and ordered coffee. Kitty took out her case and unzipped it taking out some paper. She turned one piece around at a time. Her art was breathtaking, with soft watercolours which swirled on the page as if alive. Jed wasn't sure it was of something in particular but the colours went together as if they were meant to be.

"I love it," Jed said simply which made Kitty blush. She showed him all eight pieces and each one made him happy to see it. Finally, as the coffee arrived she zipped the pages back into her case and placed it carefully propped up against the wall. She sipped her coffee and then said

"Lisa was impressed with you"

"Really?" said Jed "why?"

"She thought it was romantic, you and your mum coming to find me"

"Derri's not my mum," Jed said, "But she has looked after me for years".

"Well she was impressed"

"And you?" Jed queried "Were you impressed?"

"Well I'm here," she said simply "So yes Jed I am".

For the following month, Jed would wait outside the college for Kitty each week and take her for coffee, letting her chat about her art, and just watching how her face lit up as she described the joy of putting paint to paper. It was on their fifth official date that Jed saw the other side of Kitty. They were walking down the road to their favourite spot when on the other side of the road, a group of skinheads were standing on the corner.

"Come here darling," said one of the bigger lads to Kitty

"Leave him and come and see me," said another one.

"Fuck off" muttered Kitty holding Jed's hand even tighter. They continued to catcall until one said

"If we beat the little fucker up will you come and play?" Kitty turned and regarded them then loudly said

"I said FUCK OFF" she gave the group the finger which seemed to antagonise the biggest one who lifted himself off the wall he was leaning against and walked over to Kitty and Jed who had stopped.

Behind him, the other skinheads moved in a smooth formation. Kitty gripped Jed's hand tighter but kept the expression of contempt on her face. Jed tried to stand taller, but the skinhead didn't even glance at him.

"Come on now love, we can give you a REALLY good...."

Kitty balled her fist and whacked the skinhead in his jawline before he had a chance to finish his declaration. She turned, grabbed Jed's hand and set off in a run. Jed gripped Kitty's folder in his other hand determined not to let go of either one. As they ran they heard the skinhead holler to his mates to

"Get the little fuckers"

Kitty ran like the wind, and Jed kept up with her. They turned the corner arriving into a parade of shops, Kitty quickly ran down an alleyway which was half-hidden by some scaffolding. She came to a halt near a blue emergency exit door which was propped open by a chair.

"Come on" she hissed.

Jed followed her into the building which he realised was the back of the Turkish cafe. She weaved her way through the back room which appeared to be some sort of storage area, before finding themselves in the corridor where the toilet was. Kitty walked confidently through the corridor arriving at the counter. The owner Magnus was turned away from them so didn't realise they had arrived from the back of his cafe.

"Two coffees please," said Kitty with a smile as Magnus turned around.

"Sit down my dears" he replied.

They sat down at the table nearest to the counter. The windows of the cafe were steamed over so it would be difficult for their pursuers to spot them. The other customers were drinking and chatting and as they waited Jed looked at Kitty who was slightly flushed from the running.

"Impressive punch," remarked Jed who was beginning to realise that Kitty had done some boxing training in her past.

"Dirty fuckers" she replied "Lisa showed me some self-defence moves a while ago. She got mugged once and said it would never happen again, the first time I tried that one" she ended with a chuckle, just as Magnus brought their coffees. They sipped their coffees but Kitty was quieter than normal.

"Have you found somewhere to live yet?" asked Jed.

"No, and Simon and Matthew have now given notice on the flat" Kitty stirred her coffee, the swirling liquid mimicking her distracted thoughts. "Were you serious about coming to live with you?"

Jed looked at Kitty and realised how vulnerable she was. "I don't offer unless it's serious" he replied with a smile. "Did you want to ?"

She looked across the table at him and said simply "Yes".

* * *

And so their new life started. Jed spoke to Billy who was happy to have another resident to help run the squat, and the following day Billy and Jed borrowed Martin's van to collect Kitty and her belongings.

As they loaded her stuff, Kitty was saying goodbye to Lisa and Simon who were the only flatmates around. She had already said goodbye to Matthew who had already left for his final day of working in a local council office. Jed could see Lisa and Kitty were trying not to cry but failing with a lot of hugging. Billy watched as Kitty finally turned and came over to the van which had been packed with her stuff.

"Come on then," said Billy climbing into the driver's side of the van. Jed and Kitty squashed themselves onto the passenger side, trying and failing to get the seatbelt around them both. In the end, Jed pulled it across Kitty and held it down with his hand near his bottom. Kitty leaned out of the window to wave goodbye to her friends who were standing on the pavement still. As they moved off Kitty grinned at Jed and said happily

"New life" before she sat back watching the buses and other traffic as they drove back to the squat.

* * *

Martin and Derri were the only residents waiting for them when they arrived back. Jed and Kitty got out, and Jed took Kitty's hand and walked her over to introduce her to his family. Martin held out his hand in greeting but before Kitty could take it, Derri swept her up in a warm embrace.

"Lovely to meet you at last Kitty" "Jed saw that Kitty was a little overwhelmed but she was smiling as Derri finally let her go. Martin took her small hand in both of his, adding his welcome. Jed stood to one side watching as Martin and Derri both made Kitty feel welcome. Derri took Kitty's hand and led her back into the squat. Martin looked at Jed and Billy with a grin

"Looks like unloading is our job then?

* * *

Kitty set up her art stuff in a corner office of the building on the top floor. Jed helped her to clear the jumble of desks and other office equipment into one far corner. The room was perfect, the sunlight shimmering off the walls and giving the whole room a warm glow. Jed knew that she would make amazing pictures in this place.

The other residents met Kitty that evening over dinner. Kitty had offered to help Martin in the kitchen, which had been happily accepted. Between them, they had prepared a vegetable curry with crusty garlic bread. Even Thomas a hardened meat-eater had requested a second portion. Jed sat back his appetite now sated and realised for the first time, that he was happy again. He watched Kitty smile and chat with the others and knew that she was also content.

After the meal, Jed persuaded Kitty to get her guitar and play some songs for them. As the light faded in the room Derri lit some candles. Jed watched Kitty sing her songs and saw how the others were impressed. Billy was tapping his foot in time to the beat of each song. After a while, she stopped and received an enthusiastic round of applause which made her blush even more.

Billy had offered Kitty a room for herself, which was next door to the room where Martin and Derri slept. He didn't want to sleep with Kitty but knowing she was in the same building was enough for now. His room was further down the same corridor.

* * *

Over the next few months, Jed and Kitty fell into a routine which suited them both. Kitty was not an early riser so Martin had agreed she could deal with the evening meals, whilst he did the breakfasts. Most of the residents worked outside the squat, this being the only way they could afford to live in London.

Kitty would awake just after ten am each morning, coming into the kitchen where Jed was usually washing up the breakfast dishes under Martin's supervision. She didn't like to eat until later in the day but Jed would tempt her with a slice of granary bread and butter. She would sit and chew sitting on the back step near the kitchen and listen to the sounds of the crows in the trees surrounding the squat. She would then pack up her guitar and head for her spot to busk for the rest of the morning. She would return invigorated and happy after entertaining the commuters heading off to collect their lunches.

Most afternoons she would spend her time in her new studio creating colour and atmosphere on the paper. Jed had insisted on putting up her finished pieces in the room, which had attracted a few of the other residents to ask her to show them how to paint.

Eventually, she had a small class each day, Billy being one of the most enthusiastic to have a go. Kitty was a good teacher and the classes became one of the most popular in the squat.

* * *

21

Going Home

Although Jed had never been happier than he was during the first summer with Kitty he was also missing Katy, Sam and Ben. Jed wondered how they all were and how he could contact them. Kitty came up with the answer one evening whilst Jed was musing over the fate of his friends.

"Write to them," she said "Send them a letter".

"OK, but how do I make sure that Charlie doesn't intercept it?".

Kitty thought for a while then clicked her fingers.

"Use Mr Singh's address! He'd keep it a secret and pass on any reply".

Mr Singh had met Kitty the first week she had moved into the squat and always had a smile for her as she made her way to her busking spot. Jed realised that this was a good idea.

Over the next few days, Jed wrote a letter to Katy. He knew that if she got it, she would show Sam and Ben too. He'd already checked with Mr Singh to confirm that he was happy to pass on any reply and also field any checks should Charlie spot the letter. Jed had been deliberately vague about the location of the squat but had described the events of the last four years, including meeting Kitty.

Jed hoped that the letter would arrive and that he would get a reply back soon. Jed posted the letter on the last day of August, at a post box near the squat. Kitty insisted that they both kiss the letter "for luck".

Jed loved her quirky beliefs, crossing her fingers, never moving a spider and best of all wishing magpies a good day. Jed had initially laughed the first time she had docked an invisible hat to a noisy magpie on a branch overhead chanting

"Good morning, Mr Magpie, how are Mrs Magpie and all the other little magpies?."

Jed stopped laughing when Kitty turned on him with a fierce frown.

"Laughing at me?"

Jed gulped. "No, but why do you do that?".

Kitty turned back to the tree but the magpie had gone. "Think my dad used to do it," she said quietly. "It's an old superstition my mum told me. Something to do with that the magpie was the only bird not to sing to Jesus as he died"

Jed tried to keep a straight face and failed but he could see Kitty wasn't really offended.

"What do you remember about your parents?" he asked

"Loads" she replied simply. "We lived near the sea in Cornwall, Dad was a mechanic for a garage and mum stayed at home with me. Dad worked hard and always smelled of oil, but his hands were rough as well from the work he did. Mum liked to sing as well. She taught me the guitar when I was five, a proper one not a toy." she trailed off before taking a deep breath.

"Mum had issues. She was depressed after I was born, and it never really went away. Dad came home from work one day to find her still in her dressing gown staring at the wall. She hadn't moved since he'd left for work that morning. I was howling as I was starving and couldn't get any food myself. Social services came and assessed her and sectioned her that night. Dad couldn't cope as a single parent so I was fostered for a year before eventually ending up in permanent foster care. Five different homes in four years. Most around where I used to live but the last one was in Devon."

"Whereabouts," said Jed, "That's where I lived"

"Ilfracombe" Kitty replied. "There were fifteen of us in the foster home, but it wasn't a good place. I didn't have issues with the foster mum but I tried not to be alone with the foster dad. He was mean and nasty to all the fostered girls and spent all his time coaching the boys in a local football league. He laughed in my face when I said I could play. Got a beating for that. Eventually, I managed to work out how to get away and came to London last year. Met Lisa on a tube train. She noticed I hadn't got a ticket and was trying to avoid the inspector at the other end of the train. She bought me a ticket when he caught up to me, and bought me a coffee before her shift at the hospital. She was kind. She gave me a home"

Jed stayed silent as Kitty continued to look at the floor. He knew she was finding it hard to talk about her family. Suddenly she looked up at him, her eyes shining.

"Why don't we go back to Devon?"

"Why? Don't you like it here in London?"

"I do.." she stopped "But it's dirty and a bit tough here. I want to see trees and beauty, and there isn't much around here" Kitty scuffed her boot against the dirt in the courtyard.

* * *

The idea grew for Jed from that initial conversation. He wanted to go back to Cherrywood Farm and show Kitty where his mum's ashes lay. She would appreciate the beauty of the farm, and the Goodwin's would love Kitty in return.

Over the next few weeks, Jed and Kitty pooled their earnings. Kitty spent more time busking in the business district near the squat than painting. She also managed to find a local craft shop that was willing to display her art in exchange for a small commission on sales. Jed spoke to Mr Singh and was able to help around the store for a cash wage. Mr Singh hadn't received a reply back from Katy or the others and Jed knew that it was possible that the letter had been intercepted.

* * *

On the final weekend of August Jed was stocking up one of the storeroom shelves when he heard a very familiar voice. It was Charlie and he didn't sound happy.

"Where is this boy!" Jed moved carefully to the back of the store and opened the emergency exit door which he knew didn't have the alarm set. He then crept back to the door adjacent to the main store and listened to the conversation.

Mr Singh was talking quite softly at first in reply to Charlie's increasing frustration. From his vantage point Jed could see Mr Singh but only the back of Charlie who was much taller than Mr Singh. Jed spotted Mr Singh had seen him and quickly dropped down out of sight as Charlie spun around to see what Mr Singh was looking at.

"Is he here? Are you hiding this boy?" Charlie had been waving a piece of paper around, Jed realised that this was the letter he had tried to send to Katy, Sam and Ben.

"No Sir I do not know this person. Now if you do not want to buy anything I ask you to leave my shop before I am forced to call the police."

Charlie was a bully but Jed was aware that Mr Singh's family had come from India. One evening after work Mr Singh had explained the split between India and Pakistan and how his family home ended up on the wrong side of the line.

"It was called the partition of India and it happened a very long time ago, in 1947 my parents decided they had to leave. We came to England in 1950 and I was born in London the following year. I am 71 years old Jed and I have never seen my family's home, but we have lived a good life in England.

Jed continued to listen to Charlie's bluster and eventually the voice faded. However, Jed was very much aware that Charlie might still be lurking outside the shop waiting to see if he appeared. Jed crept back to the other end of the storeroom where he knew there was a door leading upstairs to Mr Singh's flat. Jed had often been in this flat at the end of the working day recently. Mr Singh was a kind man who often gave Jed slightly out of date food for the squat. He also was a generous employer.

"You work hard Jed, so you deserve a good wage" Mr Singh had said "None of my previous helpers had been so diligent."

Jed didn't know what diligence meant, but he knew it was a good thing. Jed waited until 8 pm when he knew Mr Singh would be closing up the shop. He heard him on the stairs coming up, slightly breathless. Jed put on the kettle for a cup of tea.

"He came," Mr Singh said simply

"Yes, I'm sorry" replied Jed getting out two cups, and teabags.

"This is not your fault Jed. He is a horrible man". Mr Singh came over to Jed who was trying not to cry. "I'm sorry you didn't manage to contact your friends but it changes nothing. You are welcome to work here, and if this man comes back I will send him away again."

Jed nodded and poured the hot water onto the teabags sitting in the cups. They sat and drank their tea and when it was time for Jed to leave, Mr Singh ushered him out down an alleyway at the back of the shop. "This leads back to the side road, you'll be able to get back home from there," he said handing Jed a carrier bag. "More things out of date" he added with a smile. "See you on Saturday".

Jed took the alleyway with the carrier bag in his hand. As expected the road was clear. If Charlie had waited, he was gone now. Jed walked quickly back to the squat. As he arrived Billy was making himself a coffee.

"Want one?" Billy said with a smile

"No thanks" replied Jed setting down the carrier bag he had been given. "But I need to tell you something". Billy sat down on the sofa at the back of the squat and listened as Jed told him about Charlie.

"And he found you today?"

"Well no, but I think he might come back and possibly come here".

"Well he won't learn about you from any of us" replied Billy with a fierce expression. "We don't grass up our people. What does this idiot look like?"

Jed gave Billy a full description and added "Oh and he speaks with a Bristol accent"

"Stand's out around here then" replied Billy with a chuckle.

* * *

Kitty was upset when Jed told her about Charlie the next day. They sat on the wall outside the squat with cups of strong coffee. Kitty yawned. She had been up late in her studio and Jed had decided not to disturb her.

"I'm sorry Jed it was a crap idea of mine". Kitty kicked her foot on the wall.

"No" replied Jed simply. "No it was a good idea, but it helps me now"

"How," asked Kitty

"Because I now know that Charlie is still at the home, and likely the others are too. He's checking their mail so all I have to do is watch the home to see when I can speak to them. How are the savings looking?"

Kitty smiled. "With your wages and my busking, plus I am expecting money from the art the shop has sold, we should have about £300 by the end of next week".

Jed grinned. "Right, so end of September then?" Kitty smiled back.

* * *

Derri and Martin were finishing washing the dishes when Jed and Kitty came into the kitchen.

"Derri, Martin, can we talk to you?" Jed said.

Derri turned and smiled at them both. Then her face fell as she realised that they were looking serious.

"What's wrong?" she asked. Jed sat down on one of the dining chairs. Derri and Martin sat down opposite, Martin wiping his hands on a clean tea towel. Kitty stood behind Jed.

"I want to...we want to go home to Devon" Jed stated simply. "I want to show Kitty where my mum is scattered, and I, we want to see if we can live in Exeter, perhaps the old squat, or another one."

Derri regarded her son calmly.

"Why now?" she asked

"Homesick" replied Kitty.

Derri looked at the girl. "You came from there? from Devon?

"From all over," Kitty said, "But I want to be with Jed, so where ever we are is home".

Derri looked at Martin who had an expression of sorrow on his face. Derri knew that she did too.

"Well neither Martin nor I are your parents, but we hope that you will come back to see us?"

Jed launched himself at Derri who had become his protector. He buried his face in her neck mumbling

"Course we will"

Derri hugged him back but wasn't as sure. She turned to Kitty who was looking mute. "Come here love," she said opening her arms to allow Kitty to snuggle in with Jed. They formed a three-way hug, while Martin looked on sadly. "You too," Derri said holding out her free arm. Martin joined the hug. He looked over at his wife and knew she was trying not to cry.

* * *

22

A new life

Jed and Kitty set off on their new adventures three weeks later. Billy had thrown them a "going away" party which had gone on till the early hours. Kitty had gifted her remaining art to Billy and the others. She had explained that she could recreate the same when they found their new home. Billy was especially touched with a drawing in charcoal of him which he hadn't realised Kitty had been working on. She had captured his features, especially the laughter lines around his eyes.

Jed had been relieved that Charlie had not appeared either at the shop or hanging around the squat. There were only so many entrances to the place, and Jed was sick of being paranoid about Charlie.

On a bright sunny morning, they said their final goodbyes to everyone and set off for the station, their rucksacks heavy with their possessions. Kitty had strapped her beloved guitar in its case and was carrying it in one hand, whilst holding Jed's hand with the other one.

Mr Singh had offered them a cheap way to get to the South West coast. He explained that his fish delivery driver came from Brixham Devon every day, and for a small contribution, he would be willing to give them a lift nearly all the way. They arrived at the shop to see Mr Singh and a young man standing by a transit van marked "Devon(ish) Fish".

"Ah here they are, just on time," said Mr Singh with a grin. "This is Jimmy, he's going to give you a lift".

The young man nodded. "Stash your bags in the back". Jed and Kitty walked to the back of the van which was open. Inside were stacks of white polystyrene boxes. There was a faint odour of fish but not as much as Jed had been expecting.

Jimmy came to join them. He noticed Jed's expression.

"Fish doesn't smell unless it's off," he said "Our stuff was doing the breaststroke until about 2 am this morning"

Jed and Kitty put their bags into the back wedging them so they didn't move. Kitty kept hold of her guitar. She wasn't going to risk her precious possession getting bashed. They then came back to the shop doorway where Mr Singh was waiting with another couple of large carrier bags.

"Tin's and stuff," he said with a smile handing over the bags. "Should get you both started right"

Jed hugged the small man. "Thank you for everything," he said simply. Kitty stood by as Mr Singh replied "Have a good life Jed, you and your lady, and come back to see us". Kitty shook Mr Singh's hand. He pulled her into a hug which she accepted.

Jimmy then said, "Better get going, the motorway is a nightmare if we leave it too long". Jed stashed the carrier bags next to his bag and then shut the back doors. He then got into the passenger side of the van which was big enough for him and Kitty to sit comfortably. "Seatbelts on," Jimmy said. "Don't want to get pulled over by the fuzz".

They complied and then as Jimmy started the van, Jed wound down the window to wave to Mr Singh who was still by his shop door. They waved as they departed and Jed saw in the wing mirror Mr Singh was waving back until they finally turned onto the main road. Jed wound up the window and settled back.

Jimmy was a good driver but he didn't talk much. As they made their way through the suburbs of London Jed looked out the window at the passing traffic and commuters all heading off for another day of work. Kitty was content as well, Jed knew. She sat relaxed in the seat between Jed and Jimmy. Her eyes were occasionally shut but he knew she wasn't sleeping. After an hour they were on the motorway speeding west towards their new home.

* * *

Jimmy stopped twice on the journey. He pulled into a service station just outside Swindon and filled up the tank of the van. Jed got out as Jimmy was filling up and offered to buy coffee and snacks.

"Coffee and a Mars Bar please," said Jimmy in reply.

Kitty declined. She didn't like too much caffeine. Jed bought two coffees and two Mars bars and returned to the van. Jimmy went into the kiosk to pay and then moved the van to a spare parking spot. Jed and Jimmy happily munched on their food whilst Kitty got out and walked to the service station toilets at the other end of the car park.

As she walked off Jimmy asked "Your lady?"

"Yep" replied Jed trying not to choke on a mouthful of Mars bar.

"Nice" replied Jimmy.

Jed wasn't offended in the least. He knew that Kitty was more than he could have hoped for. Billy had described it once as "punching above your weight" which had confused Jed until he had explained. Kitty returned to the van and Jimmy and Jed then went off for their comfort break. When they returned ten minutes later Kitty was asleep. Jed carefully got into the van and buckled Kitty up before fastening his own seatbelt. Jimmy then pulled the van back out into the slip road before joining the motorway again.

They stopped again for a meal just outside Taunton at a cafe on the A38. Kitty had woken a few minutes earlier. She had eventually slept in the crook of Jed's arm which was now nearly numb. He hadn't wanted to move in case she had been disturbed. Jimmy pulled into the car park of the cafe which looked busy. Several HGV trucks were parked at the far end of the car park, and Jimmy pulled up a few spaces further down.

"Food?" asked Jimmy

"Starving" replied Kitty with a grin.

"Me too," said Jed "That Mars bar left me ages ago" which made Kitty nudge him playfully. Jimmy locked the van and they made their way to the cafe entrance. The smell of bacon and eggs wafted in the air. As they walked in, the smells got stronger. At the entrance was a small counter.

"Take a seat, the menu's on the table," said a man behind the counter who was flipping eggs expertly "Janice will be along to take your order in a bit".

They decided on a booth near the long floor-to-ceiling window. "Keeping an eye on our transport," said Jimmy as he slid onto the seat on one side. Jed and Kitty took the other side. They each picked up a menu which was printed and laminated.

After a few minutes, a small dark-haired woman came out of a side door and made her way over to them.

"What can I get you all?" she asked holding a pen and notepad. They all plumped for the biggest breakfast

"Three Giants," said Jed with a smile.

"Coffee please too" added Kitty. The others agreed

"Three Giants and coffee's, be about ten minutes" she turned and slapped the order down on the counter. A few minutes later she returned with three steaming mugs of coffee on a tray with sugar and milk. They all sipped their drinks for a while.

"Why are you leaving London,?" Jimmy asked "Mr Singh didn't say anything" he added looking at Kitty whose expression had changed from a smile to a frown. Jed smiled back.

"It's no secret, but we come from Devon and think it is time to go back"

Kitty didn't add anything further so Jed changed the subject

"Do you like delivering fish?"

"It's a good job" admitted Jimmy. "I was rubbish at school, didn't do my exams, but Mr Slater realised that I was a careful driver. He took me on as a trainee. Been driving the London route for nearly a year".

As Jed was about to ask another question their food arrived. As described each plate was heaving with sausages, bacon, and fried eggs plus a plate each of white bread and butter. They tucked into the food and after ten minutes Kitty sighed happily.

"That was amazing," she said leaning back against the booth headrest. "I'll sleep for a month now".

Jimmy laughed "Good job you aren't driving then".

They all finished their drinks and Jed went up to pay the bill. Kitty had suggested it as an additional thank you for Jimmy giving them a lift. They all visited the facilities before going back to the van which was now sitting on its own. All of the surrounding HGVs had already departed. As they set back off on the road Jimmy commented.

"We've made good time so I can drop you off in Exeter"

"Oh thanks," said Jed. He and Kitty had been expecting to thumb a lift on the final stage of their journey. As they arrived in the city, Jed was filled with a mixture of happiness and fear. He knew that the authorities had stopped looking for him now, and he was nothing like the scared little boy escaping nearly five years ago. He had grown nearly a foot in the last eighteen months, and all the work in the squat had given him a lean and toned body. However, he also was aware that Charlie was still looking. Kitty had not lived in Exeter and she was impressed by the buildings and the people.

Jimmy dropped them off near the bus station and protested as Jed handed him a bundle of notes.

"Too much man".

Jed insisted "You've saved us hours and a pile of cash, better you have it than the railways".

Jimmy tucked the notes into his pocket. "Good luck," He said simply as he opened the van and passed them their bags. They hefted them onto their backs. Kitty took a step forward and gave Jimmy a quick hug before standing back again. Jed shook Jimmy's hand and then they both turned and walked away toward the city centre.

"What's the plan,?" asked Kitty as they walked along.

Jed thought about her question.

"Find Big Mike" he replied. Kitty had learned all about the people Jed had looked up to in the squat he had lived in with his mum. "He hangs about in a couple of pubs, so if we can find him, we can find out what digs are available.".

They started in the most likely location, The Ship Inn. This pub was one of Big Mike's favourites. When he could get labouring work, he would spend most of his earnings propping up the bar in the evenings. Kitty volunteered to go and see if she could find him. Jed still looked younger than 18 and was certain he would be removed quickly from the pub, whereas Kitty could be any age, due to her way of dressing and her confident manner. After a few minutes of waiting, Kitty returned.

"Couldn't see him?" she said "Just a really old couple of guys sipping on Guinness".

Jed thought on the matter. "He might be along later" he mused. They gathered their bags and started walking down the road into the city centre. "I can show you a few places whilst we wait" Jed suggested. "The old squat, and some of the other places I used to go".

"The school?" asked Kitty.

"No, no not yet" replied Jed solemnly. "Don't want to risk it just yet. We need to get settled somewhere first". They walked to the other end of the main shopping area and then turned into a quieter street. At the top end was a large cleared space behind sectioned metal fencing. Jed stopped and looked at the fence. They could see into the area beyond.

"They haven't even started building yet," Jed said bleakly. "They got us all out, telling us the land was going to be developed and it's just sitting here. No shiny new offices, or homes," he said down on the pavement heavily. "That was the last place I was with my mum". Jed felt despair.

Kitty sat down beside him and asked. "Tell me about her, about this place." Jed wasn't sure he could talk, but Kitty laid her hand on his arm and said "Tell me" in such an earnest way Jed realised, that she gave him the strength that he could.

331

He started to talk, telling her about his mum, about Big Mike and the others. How this place had been a real community for him growing up. He had people to care for him, not just his mum, others would help with his schoolwork, read to him and watch over him and the other children in the squat. Eventually, he ran out of words and they just sat on the pavement. The road was quiet, and the sounds of the traffic were distant to this place.

* * *

After a couple of hours, they returned to the Cathedral Square. The sun was still warm, and people were sitting on benches, or on the grass. They found a small area and dropped their bags.

"I need food," declared Kitty. "It's been ages since that breakfast".

Jed looked around the square, spotting a kiosk in the corner.

"Sandwich?"

"Sausage and Bacon" confirmed Kitty happily

"with tomato ketchup?" asked Jed with a grin

"Absolutely" replied Kitty.

Jed stood up and checked their funds. "We've got enough for a few days but will need to find Big Mike after this food, otherwise we are bunking down in the town". They ate their sandwiches watching the tourists milling around the cathedral.

"Do you believe in all that? God and stuff?" Kitty indicated the grand building with her sandwich.

Jed thought about the question as he ate. Finally, after he had swallowed his mouthful he said quietly.

"I think there is "something" more Kitty. I hope so. That's what kept me going when my mum died, believing I was going to see her again one day. But I don't really know for sure. The school, the church school gave us their point of view. I suppose it's up to each of us to decide in the end".

"Where to now?" asked Kitty.

"I spotted a building site from the car on the way in," Jed said, indicating a path to the far side of the cathedral grounds. "Worth seeing if anyone knows Big Mike. He told me he used to work all over the place".

They picked up their bags and headed for the path Jed had indicated. They walked down an alleyway at the top of the path, which brought them out onto an area which had several buildings in repair or construction. Jed scanned the area and spotted a couple of men sitting in a white transit van near one of the buildings. They were eating their lunch and one was also reading a newspaper. Jed dropped his bags next to Kitty and said.

"Wait here"

She dropped her bags and watched as Jed walked over to the van.

"Hi, I'm looking for Big Mike?"

The driver of the van looked over at him curiously "Big Mike?"

Jed replied, "Six foot seven, bushy red beard, looks like a Viking? Works construction, or at least he did a few years ago".

The other man laughed

"Ah Mike Higgins" The driver looked at his mate and then smiled recognising whom Jed was talking about. "Yeah he's still around, but he's not been working construction for a while. He had an accident a few weeks back, been working in his mate's garage over on Alphin Brook Rd, that way" the man indicated the main road behind Jed. "About a mile on the right-hand side. Can't miss it."

Jed thanked the man and returned to where Kitty was standing.

"They knew him, or at least one did. Got a location too" Jed smiled as he hoisted up his bags "Come on"

Kitty grumbled but she also took up her bags and followed Jed back the way they had come. Jed led the way further down the main road until they came to a garage with a courtyard full of spare parts. It was a busy place, with customers waiting in a small room just off the workshop. Jed looked around but couldn't see his friend anywhere.

"Can I help you?" said a voice behind him. Jed turned to see a man who must have been the boss, though his overalls were as oil streaked as the others.

"I'm...we're looking for Big Mike," Jed said. "Some guys over at the building site near the cathedral said he was working here?"

The man smiled. "You know Mike?"

Jed nodded "Yes he is a friend, was a friend of my mum too".

The man turned and yelled

"Mike get out from under there, you have visitors"

Jed looked over to where a large transit van was sitting. Suddenly an orange rolling trolley appeared from under the front, and on it, was Mike. He too was wearing a set of overalls but his were far too short and looked uncomfortable in the crotch area.

"Who wants me now" he grumbled before sitting up and staring at Jed. His face lit up

"Jed! My lad where have you come from?" Mike struggled to stand but eventually, he did. As he came upright Jed launched himself at his friend nearly toppling them back onto the trolley

"Steady lad, it is OK," Mike said returning the hug back. "When did you get back?"

Jed couldn't speak for a few minutes. He didn't care that other people were looking over at the strange sight of a huge man being hugged to death by a slip of a lad. Kitty smiled as she watched the reunion. She knew from the many hours Jed had talked how much Mike meant to him.

"Can I take a break for a bit, Jim?" Mike asked the man Jed had first spoken to.

"Go on with you" he replied.

Mike extracted himself from Jed's hug and held him at arm's length.

"Come on Jed, let's go get a cuppa".

Jed suddenly remembered Kitty and turned to her. She was still smiling.

"Mike, this is my girlfriend Kitty" Mike held out one beefy and rather oil-stained hand enveloping her smaller one. Kitty didn't care and took it happily.

"Pleased to meet you, Mike," she said. Mike guided them outside. He realised as they came out onto the courtyard that Jed and Kitty had bags.

"You coming back to Exeter?" Mike asked.

"Coming home" Jed confirmed.

* * *

Mike arranged for their bags to be left in the staff
changing room, but Kitty refused to leave her guitar.
Mike led them to the end of the road where a bright
and colourful cafe now stood.

"Used to be the butchers if you remember Jed?, Mr
Hughes ran it for nearly thirty years but he had a heart
attack and the shop closed a while ago".

The cafe was a new one and was busy, steam covered
the windows as they entered. The tables were nearly
all taken, but Mike spotted one near the back of the
room.

"Go and grab that table, Jed, coffee OK?" Jed nodded.
"Kitty, you come with me, love" Mike said.

Kitty handed over her guitar to Jed who carefully placed it behind her seat. Jed watched as Mike ordered for them, and spotted he had also added a side of scones to the order. Jed realised he was starving again. Kitty was chatting to Mike as they waited for their order to be ready. Eventually, both Kitty and Mike came back with a tray each.

"Kitty said you were hungry," Mike said with a chuckle. Mike's tray was covered with a selection of sandwiches and the scones Jed had spotted. Kitty's tray held the teas and coffee. They sat down and after taking a big gulp of tea Mike said

"So you need somewhere to live?". Jed nodded. "I'm sorry Jed," Mike said with a frown. I'm living straight now". Kitty looked puzzled until Jed spotted her look and translated.

"Not squatting, living in a proper home"

"I had an accident a while ago, and when I was in hospital I got friendly with one of the nurses looking after me. Her name is Cathy and well..." Mike blushed hard "We're living together in her flat". Jed looked at his friend

"Congratulations," he said, and although he meant it, this was going to cause Kitty and him some problems. "Any idea on where we might go?".

Mike picked up a scone and studied it carefully as if the answer to Jed's question might lie in its crumbly texture. He placed it back down again and nodded.

"I can tell you that several squats are still around, but there is a guy who is buying the buildings up, and he is bad news, Jed. His name is Mr C , he's Turkish. Came to Exeter last year, and since he's been around, a few squats have mysteriously been cleared randomly and out of the blue. Established communities all of them, no hassle from the police, they all just up and went and left Exeter too. Then this Mr C starts to turn them all into blocks of flats, posh upmarket ones. You need to stay away from the centre of town, but there is a place I can take you to. Off Cowley Bridge Road, there's a place with some people I know, a guy called Keith runs it. He's a fair guy. It's far enough out not to be on Mr C's radar but it's also clean and the people are nice and if you like trains..."

Jed and Kitty looked confused.

Mike laughed kindly. "Only downside, it's next to the railway line". They both smiled. Neither of them minded the noise of trains and having lived in London for a few years they were looking forward to some noise.

"It could be a good busking spot then?" Kitty indicated her guitar.

"Yeah, lots of commuters, it's behind the car park" confirmed Mike as he took a scone and buttered it. They ate and Jed told Mike the story of how he managed to get away finally from the children's home to London.

"Brave lad," Mike said admiringly when Jed had run out of news. Mike confirmed the Methodist Children's Home was still going strong.

"Horrible place" Mike shuddered. "See the kids going in there sometimes when I am delivering cars back to customers down that road. They never look happy any of them".

When they finished their meal, Mike stood up and said. "Your stuff will be safe in our changing room. I get off at five pm, so why don't you go for a wander and I'll see you back at the garage. I can then take you down to the squat in the garage loaner and get you settled with Keith and the others.".

Jed and Kitty agreed, and on leaving the cafe, Kitty hugged Mike handing him her precious guitar with a promise not to get it damaged before they went off towards the city centre again. Free of their heavy bags, they wandered the city, with Jed as a tour guide for Kitty. Kitty had visited Exeter before but Jed knew a lot of history about the city. Kitty loved to hear Jed speak of places almost as if he was living in those past times.

By five pm they were back at the garage where Mike was moving a small car to the front of the garage forecourt. He got out and said,

"Ah good timing. Your stuff is in the boot of the car, but I haven't moved your guitar Kitty and the lads were told not to go near it on pain of death from me".

Kitty giggled at the chivalrous gesture and went to retrieve her beloved instrument. Jed was already in the passenger seat so Kitty slid into the back seat.

"Belt up," said Mike. They complied, Kitty also fitting a seatbelt around the guitar case.

"My driving is not that bad!" Mike laughed as he spotted Kitty's action in the mirror.

"Better safe than sorry" she replied sitting back satisfied her beloved instrument was strapped in.

Mike started the car and they set off. The roads were busy with evening commuters but after a short ride, Mike turned into an industrial estate which as he had mentioned was right next door to the railway station. He turned left then right ending up in a small cul de sac. Ahead was a run-down warehouse, but Jed spotted signs of habitation. The parking area was clean and litter-free unlike the other parts of the estate.

As Mike pulled up into one of the parking spaces, a side door opened and a small man looked out, then smiled when he recognised Mike in the car, he came outside and left the door slightly ajar.

Mike got out followed by Kitty and Jed. He stretched and winced commenting "Bloody back!"

"Ah, Mike my friend" Jed looked over at the man he knew to be Keith. He had a strong Scottish accent and several missing teeth. He also had a limp on his left side.

"Hi Keith, these are the two I mentioned Jed and Kitty. Do you have a spare room for them?"

" Plenty of spare rooms" Keith laughed. "Only got five rooms occupied at the moment, still the school holidays. Students will be back in a few weeks' time".

Keith spotted Jed & Kitty looking puzzled and explained.

"Lots of students studying here can't afford the price of living in the city, so we help them out. At peak times we have a full house, but luckily I know a couple of students who have already given up on their studies, so you can have their room. Follow me".

Keith led the way back into the building via the door he had just come out of. Mike came along to see where they would be staying. Keith led them into a large cleared warehouse space.

On one side was a basic kitchen area and a couple of large comfortable sofas. Keith turned to the back of the space, where several partitions had been erected turning the back of the space into individual rooms. Keith walked past the first few spaces, which as they passed they could see were occupied with bags and in one space a young man asleep on a raised mattress. Keith turned to them

"The last one on the left is yours if you want it, it's near the back door, and there is a window too".

Jed and Kitty walked to the space indicated. Each of the areas had plenty of storage space and a clean mattress which had been lifted onto a bed of pallets but the one they had been allocated also had a view over the back of the warehouse towards the railway line. Mike joined them

"Is this OK for you both?"

"It's great," said Jed, turning to Kitty who also nodded happily. They walked back to Keith

"OK then? Right here are a couple of rules, nothing too heavy. 1. clean up after yourself in the kitchen and 2. absolutely no drugs. We've had issues in other squats with a nasty gang using some of the residents to stash drugs for him. That's why we moved out here, they seem to be just in the centre of the city for now."

Keith looked at his watch

"The others will be back in a bit, there's Hugh - he's an NHS carer, Kim, she works in the council offices, Thomas, he works in the local school".

Jed looked up at this

"Not the Methodist School?"

"Yeah, that's right, why?"

Mike chuckled

"Jed was in the adjacent children's home for a few years"

Keith smiled. "Yeah, Thomas told us about that place, expecting more waifs and strays before too long. Right where was I? Hugh, Kim, Thomas, me, oh yeah forgot about Liam. Liam is a barman in the city, he's the chap spark out on the bed. He'd sleep through Armageddon !"

Keith smiled as he finished his resident call. Mike looked at Jed.

"OK then you two, I'll leave you to settle in" Mike accepted another hug from Jed and Kitty, and then he walked back to the car. "I'll expect to see more of you both," he said with a parting wave. Jed and Kitty unpacked their belongings for the rest of the evening. They decided to donate some of the food Mr Singh had given them.

"There's far too much for us" Jed reasoned as he unpacked bags of long-life groceries. Keith was delighted to accept these into the squats store cupboard.

"Don't expect either of you can cook can you?" he asked hopefully as he examined a large tin of tomatoes,

Jed laughed. "I learned a bit". Jed had a look in the rest of the cupboard and realised he could make a good vegetable curry. He roped in Kitty for peeling and dicing the vegetables he located in the back of the cupboard. By 8 pm the smell of cooking had attracted the rest of the residents including Liam, who looked surprised at being awake for food. Keith introduced them all to Jed and Kitty, and they sat around eating bowlfuls of the delicious curry. Liam left for work at 9 pm, but the rest were happy to sit and chat.

Jed explained to Thomas about his background. He liked Thomas. He listened without interruption as Jed told him about being forced to go to the children's home, and how after Simon Thomas had arrived, things had got very bad for him.

"He's still there," said Thomas.

"Who is?"

"Charlie Gibbons. Yeah, he's even worse now. We've got the social services involved in a case, can't discuss the details but suffice to say, one of the kids who were there is not going to be going back"

"Can't they just sack him?" Jed looked appalled at the news, though he hoped it wasn't one of his friends.

"He's too clever, but, we live in hope". He stood up. "Thanks for the food Jed, I need to get my head down, I have a long day in the classroom tomorrow".

Kim picked up the dishes and took them to the sink, where Kitty was washing the pans. Kitty had got on well with Kim during the meal. Kim shared Kitty's love of art and had promised to take her to a local gallery the following weekend.

Jed was delighted to see Kitty getting on with life in a squat. He wasn't sure she would be happy living in a slightly run-down place, but he realised that she had spent many months living on the floor of a flat, so having her own bed that didn't need to be packed up, would be in her eyes a luxury.

Jed helped with the drying of the pots and dishes before they said goodnight to Keith, Hugh and Kim and retired to their space.

* * *

Kitty sat on their mattress and smiled up at him. Jed gulped noisily as he realised that their relationship was moving into a new phase. Neither of them had pushed sex as a thing, content to neck and physically sleep together. Jed often awoke to find Kitty cured up into his shoulder. She often had bad dreams but didn't wake from those. He would gently stroke her dreadlocks and she would quieten down and fall back asleep.

"Come here". Jed sat down. "Whatever comes next, is fine with me" she added.

He stroked her face. He loved this girl so much. They kissed gently at first, before falling backwards onto the mattress shedding clothes, trying to be quiet as they knew sound carried. Jed's head was full of thoughts of 'am I doing this right ... will I last?' but the smell and the feel of his girl overwhelmed him to just relax and enjoy the moment. He grabbed his wash bag and took out a condom. Kitty took it from him and put it on, smiling at him knowing he was getting overexcited. She whispered

"I love you" as they came together in love.

Afterwards, Jed and Kitty lay together sated. Jed had thought he couldn't be happier than at this moment. Kitty's soft body lay curled around him, her leg draped around his. He looked down at her, her face now soft in sleep. She was his girl and he would fight demons to protect her.

* * *

23

Old friends new enemies

Kitty found a busking spot the following day. She rose early giving Jed a wink as she got dressed.

"Suppose you think that's gonna be a nightly occurrence?" she laughed noticing his hard-on under the blanket. Jed blushed but didn't reply. "Well one of us will have to get protection, I'll speak to Kim about getting the pill. Shouldn't be an issue if we can get registered with a GP."

Jed realised that Kitty was far more practical than he was. That was a good thing he learned.

"What are your plans for today?" she asked pulling on her jeans.

"Look for the others," he said. "Thomas confirmed that Katy Sam and Ben are all registered at the Methodist School. I'm going to try and wait for them all this afternoon. How about you?"

"Gonna go and earn us some money," she said hooking her guitar over her shoulder. "Fancy being my wingman?"

Jed laughed but realised that he wanted to see his girl play again. "Alright then" he grumbled getting out of bed and pulling on his tee-shirt and jeans.

They made their way out of the squat, Keith was sitting in the sunshine drinking a cup of coffee.

"Off to work then?" he asked

"Yeah, gonna see what Exeter commuters pay a guitar maestro" Kitty laughed as they made their way to the road. They followed the road around until they got to the main entrance of the station. Kitty appraised the building.

"Over here" she pointed towards the right-hand side of the building "Car Park is over there, so commuters will need to walk past us". She walked towards the spot she had picked out. Already several cars were turning into the car park, and Kitty set up close to the ticket machine.

"No chance of missing us here" she winked at Jed as she placed her guitar case on the ground and opened it up. Kitty had a hand-painted sign she carried in the case which read

'Struggling artist - grateful for your change - thanks'. She had added a smiley face at the bottom of it.

Kitty took out her beloved guitar and spent a couple of minutes fine-tuning it. Her concentration was intense, but finally just as the first commuter came over to the ticket machine she launched into her first song. She had a range of different songs but chose an upbeat one for her debut here in the car park. Jed sat on a nearby wall off to one side, keeping out of the way of the commuters and watching Kitty as she strummed and sang.

Most of the commuters that passed were friendly, some dropping coins into her case as they passed onward to the station. A couple of grumpy men in suits muttered as they passed, and one commented about "Bloody noise" as he walked stiffly across the road to the station. After about an hour Kitty turned to Jed and said in a theatrical hoarse whisper

"Need a coffee, throat parched".

Jed laughed and stood up "Milk two sugars?"

"Thanks" Kitty stooped to gather some coins from her guitar case. "Sticky bun too please" as she handed the small pile to Jed. "Treat yourself to one too, as you're my roadie/wingman/bodyguard".

She kissed him and then started another tune spotting a small group coming towards the ticket machine. Jed walked to the station entrance and found the cafe near the back. He picked out an enormous iced bun with a glazed cherry for Kitty and a buttered scone for himself. As he was waiting for the coffees, the counter clerk, a young woman wearing an apron and her hair in a net asked

"Is that your girlfriend outside busking?". Jed was surprised but replied,

355

"Yes that's right. I'm on a coffee and cake run".

"She's good, I heard her from the service yard out the back whilst I was having a smoke earlier".

"Thanks, I'll tell her you to appreciate her songs". The woman put her hand into her pocket and handed Jed a small business card.

"My boyfriend is a pub booker in Exeter, give him a ring, he might be able to arrange some work for her". Jed took the card and looked at it

'Sly Cetin, Agent to the Stars '.

He looked at it and back at the woman "Agent to the Stars?"

She laughed dryly. "Yeah, it's a bit much for Exeter but he also works in London and they seem to like it. He told me once, that if you don't make big claims you will never get on. His brother Emir runs a club and a casino here in the city."

Jed slipped the card into his jeans pocket and picked up the coffees and bag containing the cakes.

"Cheers, I'll pass it on".

He carefully made his way back out into the station concourse and was just about to walk outside when a voice behind him said in a stern voice

"You can't beg here". Jed turned carefully so as not to spill the coffees.

A tall stern man in a GWR uniform stood in front of him. He had a shiny badge on his lapel 'Roger Kingston, Station Master'

Jed smiled "Not begging mate, just buying coffee and cake".

The man pointed across to where Kitty had attracted an audience including a family with a small girl who was swaying to the beat of Kitty's guitar.

"Her, she's begging for money".

Jed smiled more broadly

"Nope, she's singing, and people are appreciating her talents with money, not begging, providing a light-hearted service before they come into the pits of despair here"

Jed turned again and walked out pleased to hear the man splutter but not comment further. Jed walked over to where Kitty was accepting a round of applause from the family. The father of the group dropped a pile of coins into the case. Jed realised from their accents they were American.

"Oh honey you are so good," said the mum "But we'd better scoot otherwise we won't catch our train to London, come on Pam" The little girl looked annoyed but took her mum's hand, turning to wave to Kitty.

Jed sat down on the wall again, and Kitty joined him, accepting the enormous bun with a smile.

"Come here my ginormous sugary treat" she cooed as she broke off pieces and chewed.

Jed sipped his coffee and watched the trains arriving and departing the station.

"Station Master was inside, thinks you are begging".

Kitty looked over and said "Him?"

Jed followed her gaze. Roger Kingston was standing in the entranceway looking over at them. He did not look happy. Kitty waved to him with her hand still clutching her bun.

"Lovely chap, wonder if he wants a dedication?" She pointed to the sign next to the ticket machine "This land isn't part of the station - owned by a car parking company, so he can't throw us off. Been through that shit in London a couple of times, I always check the area and make sure" she pointed at Roger Kingston again" people like him can't stop me"

They ate their cakes and Kitty accepted her coffee gratefully. After a few minutes, the car park started filling up again.

"My audience awaits," Kitty said handing Jed her coffee cup.

He took both cups and the paper bag the cakes were in, over to the bin outside the station. Roger Kingston was still standing in the same place and glared at Jed as he deliberately placed the rubbish carefully in the bin. Jed knew that any infringement would be acted on, and he took great pleasure in making sure the rubbish wouldn't be leaping out of the bin to give Roger something else to moan about.

Jed walked back to Kitty who now had a bigger audience than before. Most of the audience seem to be tourists, one couple who appeared to be Japanese was taking photos of Kitty as she sang.

One for the holiday album

Jed thought as he sat back down on the wall. After another two hours, the car park traffic had died down. Jed stood up as Kitty stopped and put her guitar carefully on the floor. She bent down and scooped up the coins and notes in the case, placing them into her jacket pocket.

"Always count the money later," she said winking putting her guitar back in her case. She stood up again and stretched upwards with a groan.

"Right back to the squat for a quick nap, you going off to try and find your friends now?"

"I'll walk back with you, it's on my way". Kitty slipped her free hand into his and picked up her guitar. Roger Kingston was still standing at the entrance watching them.

"Oh he's a love," Kitty said blowing a kiss towards the man. They walked off back towards their new home.

* * *

As Kitty was counting the takings sitting on their bed, Jed suddenly remembered the conversation with the woman in the cafe. He explained the card and passed it to her. She studied it carefully

"What do you think? Worth calling?"

Jed wasn't sure but he could see Kitty was excited

"Go on then"

"Let's see how much my adoring audience loved me first". Kitty totted up the piles of coins and a few notes and announced with a drum roll on their bedside table

"aaannd the total is £16.89. That's not bad for a few hours". Jed stood up and stretched.

"Right I'm off to go and see if I can find my friends. Is it OK if I bring them back here I do if they want to come here?"

Kitty stretched back onto the bed grabbing a pillow

"Sure, I'm just going to recharge now, I'll call that guy later when you are back". Jed kissed her and left her to her slumbers.

* * *

Jed glanced at the clock tower above the school hall. Half past three. He had found a good spot, just up the road in the other direction from the Methodist Children's Home. He sat on a low wall dividing some communal gardens and waited.

Five minutes later the bell tolled and the children started to leave the grounds. Groups of boys and girls left through the main gate Jed was watching. He scanned the groups looking for Katy, Sam or Ben.

He was starting to think that perhaps he had missed them when he spotted Ben swinging his bag and talking to another boy. Behind him Katy and Sam were earnestly chatting, Sam had got taller, Ben also - his chubby features now lean and tanned. Katy though had blossomed, her hair now longer and blonder than it had ever been. Jed stood up and walked towards the group who were turned away from him and stood just outside the gate.

"Maths isn't great," said Katy pointing a finger at Sam who had spotted Jed and was gasping. Katy continued "It's pointless, and I will not be using algebra when I am a famous author".

She realised that Sam and Ben were not paying attention to her and turned. She also gawped realising who the strange tall boy was.

"Hello," said Jed. He didn't manage to get any more out.

"Jed!" said Sam "my man, you aren't dead in a ditch". Katy snorted loudly beside Sam but Jed could tell she was happy to see him. "See Katy, Jed survives".

Sam grabbed Jed and bear-hugged him until Jed begged for mercy. Ben added to the hug - the three boys all tangled limbs and voices raised. Finally, Jed released himself from their grasp and turned to Katy.

363

"I'm sorry alright. I couldn't stay. Simon, Charlie, a total nightmare. I had to leave". Katy looked mute but didn't comment.

Jed continued. "I went to London, found friends in a squat, but eventually this place" Jed indicated the buildings "Exeter, you all, I had to come back and see if I could live here again". He looked at his friends. "I'm back, I've found a place near the railway station, and I want to be in your lives again."

Sam and Ben gave their acceptance with another bear hug and then released Jed to the appraisal of Katy.

"You need a good meal" she commented. Jed understood Katy and nodded. She was going to take time to understand his reasons.

Suddenly Ben looked stricken.

"Charlie's down there...run!".

They all took off in the opposite direction, glancing back Jed saw Charlie, older and much fatter than he had been starting to trot after them. As they rounded the corner onto the main road, Sam speeded up and headed for a row of shops. At the end was a cafe, its windows tinted against the strong sunlight.

"In here," said Sam as he hurtled towards the front door. They all piled inside standing against the back wall waiting to see if Charlie would spot them. After a couple of minutes, they relaxed.

"He's not as fit as he used to be," said, Ben

"Right old porker" added Katy with a grin. They turned to the counter where an assistant was looking at them curiously.

"Hiding from someone?"

"Nah" replied Ben with a cheeky grin "Four coffees and four sticky buns please Ruth".

"Go sit yourselves down then, I'll bring them over in a bit".

Ben pointed to a table near the back.

"That one," he said indicating the corridor beyond. "Leads to the back yard, in case we need to make our escape if fatty finds us".

They all sat down, piling school bags on one side of the table. The coffees and buns arrived and Ben handed over a £10 note. Ruth blushed as she counted out change from her apron pocket.

"So tell me what's been going on then? Simon? still a fart arse bully? Charlie - tummy of the year"

Ben spluttered on his coffee, and Katy patted his back until he recovered.

They talked for the next two hours. Jed found out that Charlie had been suspended after his escape and was now nastier than ever.

"More kids arrive every month now, the place is rammed full of eight and nine-year-olds, which does Charlie's nut in," said Ben with a nasty grin "One of them superglued his chair, and the fire brigade had to come and release him"

"Simon's now living with an elderly relative up in Leeds" added Katy "His dad got twenty-four years for the attempted murder of his mum. She died......lasted about a year on a ventilator... now what's your news?".

Jed brought the others up to date on his adventures.

"How exciting," said Sam "Living in London"

Jed shook his head "Not really, I was lucky I found Billy otherwise I could have been in trouble. Lots of gangs, lots of nasty people there"

"Same here," said Ben. "There's been a spate of kids overdosing on drugs in the local park. Not sure where it's all coming from but John in the 4th Form, his big brother died last month"

"Got a girlfriend?" asked Sam with a grin

"Or a boyfriend" added Ben. Jed looked over at Katy and realised she wasn't adding to the joshing. He couldn't read her expression. Jed said looking back at Katy

"Actually yeah I do. She came down here with me, I met her in London. Her name is Kitty"

"Kitty? as in Kitty Cat?" replied Ben.

Katy's expression hadn't changed, it was like she was made of stone or something. Then her expression changed and she said loudly

"I'm dating Henry from the 5th year. He's a rugby star" Ben looked at Katy, and Jed caught the expression on Katy's face. He knew it well.

Don't bust me!

He let it go and just asked politely if she was happy. Before she could answer

"Oh, ecstatic" added Sam who was also in on the ruse. "They'll be King and Queen at the year-end ball next month if Phobe and Tim don't beat them to the thrones."

Sam explained that the school had gone 'all Yankee' in the last couple of years.

"Full on Prom for leavers and Sixth formers. All the rich kids turning up in their family's posh cars, prom dresses, hair and makeup"

Jed was bemused. "What about the other kids?"

"Nag their parents, get them to spend money they don't have to fit in" Sam replied. "No chance for us, not with Charlie holding the purse strings so tightly, his hand nearly came off. Katy's sorted though".

Katy blushed and nodded " Saw Miss Goodwin in the city a few weeks ago, she offered to make me a dress. My first fitting is tonight at the home" Katy glanced at her watch "Oh god, I'm gonna be late". She got up quickly, kissed Jed on the cheek and dashed off out the cafe door.

"She's really worried about the Ball," said Sam looking over at Jed. "She wants to look"

"Like a beautiful Princesssss" added Ben getting up and performing a convincing twirl across the cafe before returning and slumping back into his seat. "If anyone can pull it off, Miss Goodwin can"

* * *

Jed Ben and Sam stayed in the cafe catching up on their missed times. Jed was glad to see his two friends didn't resent him leaving, that they understood that he couldn't stay, being bullied at home and school.

"Simon got his comeuppance in the end," said Sam "Living with his great auntie in Leeds. Charlie told us she's in her seventies and never liked Simon's father, but as a 'Christian' she was obligated to give Simon a home. I give it six more months before he's back at the home". They finished their drinks and made plans for Katy, Sam and Ben to visit Jed and Kitty the following weekend.

"We have a bit more freedom at the weekends" Sam commented as they walked out of the cafe "As long as Charlie sees our homework is finished, our chores done, we can pretty much leave and not come back until dinner time". Jed hugged his friends goodbye and set off back towards the squat.

* * *

When he arrived back at the squat Kitty was sitting on the wall outside. She squealed when she saw Jed turn the corner and dashed over to him.

"He wants me!" she yelled

"Who does?" Jed had forgotten the card he had passed over earlier

"That agent, 'Sly Cetin, Agent to the Stars'. I woke up and decided to call him from the phone box, his girlfriend had already mentioned me, and he wants me to come and audition tomorrow at his brother's club. Isn't that fabulous?"

Jed paused for a moment "Yeah that's great news, but I should come with you, roadie/wingman/bodyguard remember? We don't know this guy".

Kitty looked both annoyed and deflated."You don't trust me?"

"Of course I trust you, but I don't know this man, and I want to make sure he doesn't rip you off for work. He could offer you a crap rate, and you are worth a lot more than that". Jed tried to look appeasing but inside he was worried about the reaction of a stranger to his girlfriend. "Right, so what are you going to sing, what are you wearing?"

The distraction worked. Kitty happily chatted about the songs she was planning on trying at the audition, but as she talked Jed was distracted by a feeling he had not had for many years. Not since his mum left him in the care of the council. He realised it was fear.

* * *

Later in the kitchen, Jed approached Keith with his worries.

"What's the geezer's name?" asked Keith

"Sly Cetin. His girlfriend was working in the cafe at the railway station and gave me his card"

371

"Doesn't sound familiar" replied Keith "but let me ask around. When is Kitty's audition?"

"2 pm today at the casino in North Street" "And you are going with her?"

"Yes, she wasn't thrilled about it, but it's worrying me a bit. Starting to wish I had thrown that bloody card away"

"Well it's done now"

Jed felt a little better after discussing with Keith, but as they walked into the foyer of the Casino, Jed felt a little sick. Kitty however was buzzing. She had worn her favourite cotton dress, her dreadlocks were glinting with some jewels she had woven through them, and her guitar was tuned to perfection.

Inside the foyer was a desk to one side. Sitting at the desk was a glamorous lady wearing an evening gown, which was slightly over the top for a Wednesday afternoon. She gave them both a dazzling smile

"And you must be Kitty?" She held out her hand, and Kitty shook it. "and you are?" She held her hand out to Jed

372

"I'm Jed, Kitty's manager" Kitty looked surprised but managed to keep a straight face.

"Ah OK" replied the lady "I'm Kim, Sly and Emir's, right-hand woman. I look after their club and casino" She indicated the door behind her

"Sly's waiting for you in there" Kitty moved towards the door, and Jed started to follow

"Just her sweetie, you can wait here with me" Kim smiled beguilingly "Now how old are you gorgeous?"

Jed didn't reply at first watching as Kitty waved to him as she opened the door to the room. As the door closed, Kim indicated the chair next to her

"She'll be fine sweetie. Now tell me all about you?". After a few minutes, Jed heard the first of Kitty's songs faintly behind the door. He wasn't happy but Kim continued to ask him questions which he eventually answered.

After about ten minutes the door opened again. Kitty came out, looking happy followed by a man with tanned skin, plenty of gold jewellery and a crisp white shirt opened to the waist. He sported a lot of chest hair, some turning grey. His trousers looked tight, and he wore soft leather loafers on his feet. Kim stood up and looked over at the man who nodded, then turned and went back inside the room.

"Kitty darling, come with me into my office, we can get you booked in for your first gig" Kim swept Kitty along towards a door at the back of the foyer. Jed sat back down again on the chair and looked around. There were statues and gold-coloured decorations all around him, and the light made his eyes sore. Kim walked back into the foyer

"Now don't forget, Sly won't tolerate lateness, or not being professional. You've got a good chance of a regular slot here, you just have to behave".

Kim came over to Jed, "She's booked in for Friday night" She handed Jed a piece of paper. "Here's her contract, four slots, then we review. £50 a night for three hours, you deal with the tax man OK?"

Jed nodded and looked at the piece of paper. It was typed and full of legal jargon. At the bottom were two signatures. Jed recognised Kitty's signature, big and looping, and the other must be Kim's. He studied it for a moment and tried to look like he had dealt with professionals all his life. He failed, but as he started to ask a question Kim interrupted him.

"Don't worry, we won't be putting her costs through on the books, so no tax, and as she is underage, we have to be careful not to overwork her. ".

Jed looked immediately relieved, then a little disconcerted that Kim, and presumably Sly had realised they were both under aged.

"OK then, see you Friday Kitty, and remember, wear something sparkly". Jed and Kitty left the foyer and blinked in the bright light outside. Being in the casino, even the foyer gave them a sense of lost time.

"How was it?" asked Jed as they walked back along to the squat

"Good I think," Kitty said with a frown. "Sly was a bit of a creep, but once I started singing, he listened, and gave me a couple of good tips". Kitty continued to update Jed with the details of her audition. "He said, that if I was any good, he might put me on more slots. We could do with the money, busking won't bring in the big bucks"

Jed frowned. "I could get a job. Help out. Maybe Big Mike might know of something?"

"Until I hit the big time then". She held out her hand and Jed took it before she took off down the road dragging him behind her singing 'superstar, where you are' giggling as Jed tried to add his voice to the tune.

* * *

Three days later at 5 pm Kitty and Jed arrived at the casino door. It was locked but Jed saw that Kim was inside. She was wearing a different dress than the previous time they had seen her, this one a rich green velvet that hugged her figure and sparkled with green jewels in the light. Kim opened the door

"Come in, my dears. I should have warned you that most of our staff come in the stage door off Fore Street. Never mind though, come in"

She opened the door further so Kitty and Jed could slip inside.

"You can't be inside the casino Jed, sorry but you'd not pass our age checks. You, however"

Kim appraised Kitty who was wearing a shimmery flowing top and black fitted jeans with cowboy boots. She had also piled her dreadlocks up so they almost floated around her head

"You would get through the age checks but if any punters ask you, you are eighteen OK?".

Kitty turned to Jed and said "Come get me at 9 pm, I'll wait here for you"

She kissed him on the cheek and turned to Kim who said "OK then" as she opened the door again for Jed to go outside.

Jed hadn't been surprised he wasn't allowed in the casino but he had hoped he could have waited maybe in an office somewhere. He pondered on his options. No bar would allow him inside, most of them had door security to prevent underage kids from getting in. He decided to go and get a coffee from one of the cafes near to the casino and then wait for Kitty on a bench he had spotted opposite the casino.

* * *

Jed was sitting on the bench, his coffee long gone as the casino doors opened and closed. People came and went, groups of housewives, friends and even a large group of mostly male students entered, laughing and joking as they submitted to pat downs from the two burly security guards.

Eventually, he spotted Kitty coming out of the casino. She was talking to Kim who was laughing at something Kitty was saying to her. Jed was too far away to hear the conversation, but as he stood up, he spotted the man Kim had referred to as Sly Cetin. He was behind Kim and Kitty talking to another man, who looked very much like him.

The brother, the casino owner Emir?

Jed didn't like the way Emir and Sly were looking at Kitty. She was oblivious chatting to Kim, who also had spotted Jed who had moved to the front door, just in front of where one of the security guards was looking at him.

"Picking up my girlfriend," said Jed pointing at Kitty. The guard sniggered but didn't reply. Kitty finally turned and spotted Jed. She waved goodbye to the group, Kim had now been joined by Sly and his brother Emir who had kind smiles plastered on their faces until Kitty turned away. Emir nudged his brother and said something into his ear which made Sly snigger. Kim spotted Jed looking over at them and added her low comment which stopped the sniggering. Kitty came out onto the street with her guitar case hooked over her shoulder.

"God I'm knackered, but buzzed," she said as she kissed Jed on the cheek. He looked over at the security guard who was watching them and smiled broadly. The guard nodded and looked back at the door where a group of women were about to enter.

Kitty and Jed set off down the street. "Shall we get a coffee or do you want to go home? " Jed asked looking at Kitty.

"Home," she said "I need some sleep, but I have so much to tell you" Jed held Kitty's hand as she talked.

"Kim was pleased with my songs. She asked if I could try some more upbeat ones earlier in the set, so it gets the punters spending. Oh and I have a tab at the bar now"

"Why? you aren't old enough to drink?"

"Kim said it would be weird for me not to have a drink next to me, she arranged for a soda and lime, but to tell any punters that want to buy me a drink, it's vodka lime and soda. It worked. Six fans 'bought' me a drink, Kim got the bartender to bring my drinks over, only soda and lime. Kim's splitting the costs and she gave me" Kitty reached out into her pocket "Fifteen extra pounds, so that's £65 I have earned tonight" Kitty looked at Jed who looked startled and a little disconcerted at the supposedly easy money Kitty had made.

"So what are they charging the punters for a drink if you get £15 for six drinks then?" Kitty laughed as she replaced the money in her pocket.

"No idea but the punters loved me. I'm back on Sunday afternoon for another session. It's a pensioner special. They get a hot Sunday buffet and access to the casino for £5 a person"

Jed listened to Kitty but his tummy felt tight. He was worried about the looks that the two owners had given Kitty, and not being able to be there worried him more.

"How was the agent?"

"Sly? Oh, he's a pussy cat. Don't even know why I was worried, he told me if any punters 'tried it on' he would deal with them. They put me on a small stage to one side of the roulette wheel, proper mike and amplifier and everything. Good job too, because the noise is tremendous in there. I would have lost my voice without some amplification" Kitty laughed. "Show business, well sort of".

"And the brother Emil? was that him with Sly as you came out?"

"Yes, he didn't speak much to me. Only to say he was glad I was working for him now" Jed's tummy turned as he realised the hard truth of Kitty's comments. He knew that this was not a good idea. He wished again that he had thrown the business card away

she's so excited to be playing for proper money, and Sly could see her talents. He wouldn't want to taint that, would he?

Back at the squat Kitty continued to talk quietly about her first night singing as they got ready for bed. Jed tried to look happy for her, but Kitty spotted he was quieter than normal.

"It's a good job Jed, proper money, not busking for hours for a few quid. The winter's coming and this is a warm, dry and safe place." She held his face in her hands as she talked.

Jed looked back at her "I don't like them, the brothers. They look mean. If anything happens walk away. Promise me?"

"I promise" Kitty replied solemnly. She snuggled into Jed's arms and was asleep in minutes. Jed however lay awake for a long time remembering the looks on the Cetin brother's faces.

* * *

The following morning Jed rose early and was careful not to disturb Kitty. He found Keith outside having a smoke and a coffee.

"Did you ask around about those brothers?"

"Oh yeah," Keith turned his cup upside down and put it on the wall

"They are well known in the city. The older brother Emil, he's got a bit of a reputation. He's been in prison a couple of times when he was younger, but in the last few years, he seems to have turned himself around a bit. The younger one Sly, who spent a few years living in London seemed to have got himself on the wrong side of a gang and was brought back to Exeter by Emil last year. Got set up as a promoter and is now working for his brother. How did Kitty get on?"

"She was a hit," said Jed glumly "However they have her on some sort of con getting bought drinks by punters"

"They're giving her booze?" said Keith who looked startled

"No, no. It's cleverer than that. They get told she's having vodka lime and soda, and they pay the inflated price for that. However, the barman brings her a soda and lime. They look the same, but obviously, the casino gets a massive profit. She made an extra £15 last night for six drinks. On top of her fee, that's £65 in three hours."

"That's tempting for sure" replied Keith. "I make a measly £40 a day grafting on a building site and no free drinks for me. Speaking of which, I need to get off to site otherwise I might not have my job."

Jed nodded and went inside. He was too wired to go back to bed, tempting though the thought of Kitty was. He tip-toed back to their cubicle and retrieved his memory book and a pen. He sat down at the dining table and selected a fresh page at the back of the book. He thought for a moment and then headed it 'The Cetin's' he wrote down everything Keith had told him, plus everything that Kitty had told him about the evening. By the time Kitty made her appearance, dishevelled he had written a full page about the two men. Kitty sat down and looked over at his book.

"What are you writing? she asked curiously.

Jed turned the book around so she could read. She sat still and read the page before looking up at him.

"You're really worried about them aren't you?"

Jed nodded.

Kitty grabbed Jed's hand and said earnestly "I promise you, any funny business, anything illegal and I am out of there. I can busk in the cold, just might have to jig around a bit more"

* * *

24

A slippery slope

Jed found work on the same building site as Keith as a
runner and over the winter, he grew taller and leaner.
Kitty started regular shifts as the casino's
entertainment and by the end of the year, she was
earning considerably more than Jed was.

Jed would always collect Kitty from her gigs and
occasionally spotted either Emir or Sly in their office to
one side of the foyer. They both mostly ignored him,
except when Kitty would greet him with a kiss. Then
they both paid attention. Jed didn't like them at all but
he couldn't argue that they had provided a steady
source of income for Kitty. He tried to ignore their
stares at his girlfriend but as time went on he found it
more and more difficult.

As the winter moved into spring, Kitty brought up the thought of them moving out of the squat into their own place.

"I earn enough now for a place" she urged one evening as they were preparing their dinner. "You bring in a good wage too". Jed wasn't sure. He liked the community spirit of the squat. It was the thing he knew best but he could see Kitty needed her own proper space again.

"OK, we can look, but how are we going to get a deposit together? Most of the landlords want two months upfront"

Kitty smiled "That's easy. Kim told me that Emil converted one of the large houses in Athelstan Rd and is looking for tenants. Self-contained apartments fully furnished and she reckons he would do a deal for his workers. She's thinking of moving there herself."

Jed was startled to realise that Kitty had not only been thinking about this, but she had also talked to others about it before him.

"Sounds like you have it all sorted then? "

"Don't be sulky on me" she replied tersely. Jed was frustrated by Kitty's inability to see what Emil and Sly were really like.

"They offered you a job as well."

"What! when?"

"Last week. Kim had mentioned to Sly we were still living here. He is about to start a courier bike service and he needs people to work the rounds. He mentioned that he thought you look like you would be good at the job, you've lived here for years. I said I would mention it, but you've been off with my friends at work for a while, so I decided to wait."

Kitty sat down heavily on one of the chairs.

"I like the people I work for, they pay well, they look after me. The bouncers keep away the creeps, and it's easy Jed. Sing for my supper, and why shouldn't I want a little bit more than all this" Kitty indicated the surroundings. "I want a nice home, all to ourselves, don't you?"

Jed sat down on the other chair. "I think so," he said carefully but can you see why I am worried about them, the brothers? They seem too good to be true, that's all."

"Give them a chance, take the job. You can still work the building sites, just having a bit more money" She leaned over and squeezed his tummy "and you'll get rid of this belly"

Jed laughed "Nothing to it" he replied relieved that Kitty had changed the subject. Inside he was still not sure "OK then, ask your boss if we can come and view one of these swanky apartments"

Kitty squealed and jumped up and down singing

"We're gonna have a love nest"

Keith poked his head around the door and replied dryly "Don't you already have one here?"

Kitty blushed and stopped jumping. "Sorry. Keith"

"That's OK" he replied with a smile "Young love"

Jed laughed but he decided for now not to speak to Keith about leaving. He wanted to be really sure of this new place before he gave up their space at the squat. He knew from chatting to Keith, that there was now a waiting list at the squat. The cost of living in the city was driving more and more people towards their place. All of the spaces were filled with a mixture of students desperate to make their allowances go further, through to professionals unable to afford their own place, or the costs of commuting.

* * *

Things moved fast after the conversation. The following evening as Jed arrived to collect Kitty, she beckoned him over to where she was chatting with Sly.

Mr Cetin, this is Jed" Kitty announced proudly

"Nice to meet you at last Jed, I meant to come and say hello before, but it's manic around here at times," said Sly with a broad grin on his face. "Kitty has turned our entertainment around. We had a pub singer in here before. Most punters couldn't get out fast enough, her voice makes them stay and play. Now Kitty tells me you might be interested in one of my courier jobs?"

"Yes possibly" replied Jed uncertainly "Can you give me some information?"

" I can do better than that" Sly replied with a broader grin. "Come and see me tomorrow at 9 am, I'll pay you £50 a day, fifteen drops in the city, mostly offices, business papers and the like you get a brand new bike, all the kit, if you don't like it, then no harm no foul, you still get the £50"

Jed was surprised at the offer but out of the corner of his eye, he could see Kitty watching to see what he would do.

"OK, that sounds good" he replied. Sly held out his hand and shook Jed's. Sly's hand was huge and very sweaty. Jed resisted the temptation to wipe his hand down his trousers. Kitty took his other hand

"See you in the morning, Jed," said Sly smiling.

* * *

Jed arrived at the casino and was surprised to see a queue of other people. Mostly young men like him, but a couple of girls as well. As they waited some of them chatted softly.

From the conversations, Jed gleaned that several were students at the university. He also realised that Sly had been canvassing the University bars looking for workers, several of the students also had one of Sly's business cards. He wasn't sure if this was a good thing or not.

Eventually, the doors to the casino opened and Kim was standing there, this time not in a dress but a business suit in dark blue pinstripe, trousers and red high heels. She looked very glamorous compared to the group of people waiting for her.

Hello, all you lovely people," she said in a loud and clear voice." Please be patient with us, we need to get each of you registered on our database. If you do not have an ID, please step out of the queue and go and get it. We cannot register you without one form of ID."

Jed looked worried at this, he had not been told. As he was about to step out of the queue, Kim spotted him and mouthed "Not you" with a broad wink.

Jed remained and waited. Things moved swiftly after that. The five people ahead of him, each went into the foyer where Kim Emil and Sly were waiting. Kim was standing by the photocopier which had been brought out from the office and was taking a copy of the ID as Emil quickly wrote down the information each person provided.

As they finished each person moved over to Sly who provided them with a bag similar to a paperboy one plus a street map of the city. The bags each had a bright blue logo on them which read 'Cetin Couriers'.

Just as Jed was wondering where the bikes were, Sly moved over to the back of the room and opened another door. Inside were a bunch of brand new mountain bikes also in bright blue with the logo marked on the front and rear mudguards.

"Now look after these with your life," said Sly who didn't look like he was joking. "If you lose this, you are out of a job. No leaving them unlocked either." He lifted a large bike lock. "NO excuses".

The room went quiet until Kim said "Next" Jed walked up to the desk. Kim looked at him then Emil started to write down Jed's details. The student behind Jed noticed that Jed hadn't provided an ID.

"Hey, why doesn't he have ID? I had to go back to my digs to get mine"

Kim looked sweetly at him and said "He's family darling, you can go now"

The student looked mute but spotting Sly coming over he shuffled out of the line, and left.

"Now then, where were we?" asked Kim giving Jed a wink. Ten minutes later Jed wheeled out his first ever bike.

Sly had finished the interviews by confirming that each rider should attend daily, and if there were drop-offs, they would be given these on arrival. They would receive £10 a day just for being available at the offices, some of the students liked this, they could work on their course work and also earn some money.

Sly implied that most of the couriers would be working hard. Jed didn't mind hard work. The building site had been a good start to his working life. He rode the bike down to the squat and decided not to lock it up outside.

He wheeled the bike inside, where Thomas was standing talking to Hugh.

"Nice bike man!" said Thomas who then spotted the bag across Jed's thin shoulders. "Got a job then?" Thomas swung Jed around so he could read the logo

"Cetin Couriers" Jed explained that the blokes Kitty worked for in the casino were branching out.

"Wouldn't have thought there was much business in the city, hope it's legit?" remarked Hugh.

Jed had the same thoughts, but he remained silent.

"I wasn't going to leave the bike outside. Is it OK to leave it in the storeroom out back?"

"Yeah, that's fine" replied Hugh. "Just make sure it's out of the way so Thomas doesn't trip over it on his midnight feast hunts". He received a light punch in the arm from Thomas as he failed to duck out of the way.

Jed walked the bike into the store room and parked it up against the far wall. He liked the camaraderie of the group, but Hugh had raised a good point. Jed knew each of the bikes was expensive, plus the rest of the equipment, helmets, locks and fancy bags. He locked the bike to one of the metal racks fixed to the wall and placed the bag on top. He would see what happened in the morning.

* * *

25

Courier life

Jed rose early the next day. He wanted to be the first person arriving at the office, and he wanted to earn as much as Kitty. He felt terrible that she was working so hard, to make money for them both. She hadn't mentioned the apartment again since, but Jed could tell she was keen to move away. Jed had decided that he would try out the job, and if it weren't for him, he would return to the building site.

Mike had gone back to working as a builder again as his back issues had gotten less painful. The last time Jed saw Mike, he had confirmed that working in the garage had started to give him callouses on his knees from all the kneeling to work on cars.

Jed arrived at 8.30 am and was pleased to see he was the first in line. He waited, his bike leaning against the wall and watched the traffic and the commuters for a while. The next person arrived about ten minutes later, a young female student Jed had been standing in front of the previous day.

"Hi," she said, shifting her bag to her other shoulder. "Great minds eh?" indicating the lack of other people.

"Need the money?" asked Jed curiously.

"God yeah" she replied, parking her bike up against the wall. I only got a limited grant this year, and books are so expensive."

"What are you studying?"

"Politics" she replied "I'm Greta"

Jed stuck out his hand "I'm Jed"

Greta looked curiously back at Jed. "You're young to be doing this. How old are you?"

"Seventeen" replied Jed "Yeah and I am the Queen," Greta said with a giggle and a twirl, nearly knocking Jed out with her bag

"Sorry," she said, "Got my books in there in case I get a chance to study". Jed looked back at the door. Kim was unlocking the top bolts. She was wearing a bottle green version of the suit from the previous day.

"How do you know them?" asked Greta under her breath.

"My girlfriend is the casino singer" replied Jed quickly just as Kim opened the door.

"Welcome, welcome," Kim said "Come in, you can park your bikes over there behind the screen "

Kim indicated a plush floor-to-ceiling velvet screen, Behind it was a large metal bike rack similar to those he had seen outside the railway station. It hadn't been there the previous day. Jed wondered who had manhandled the rack inside the casino. It looked very heavy indeed. Once their bikes were locked, Kim lead them into the corridor to one side of the main casino doors, stopping at the top, and opening the door to the far right.

"This is your room," Kim said as Greta and Jed followed her inside. The room was large and bright, with a vending machine on one wall, and three large sofas set around a small coffee table.

"If you are on-site, you get £10 a day 9 am to 5 pm, if you leave before then, nothing. Any jobs are paid on top of the £10 cash in hand." Kim winked. "No need to bother the tax man OK?"

Jed and Greta nodded.

"OK, then, the loo is the next door on the left."

Kim smiled at them and then left, closing the door behind her.

"Wow, this is nicer than the university study rooms," remarked Greta sinking down into one of the sofas. She opened her courier bag and laid out her books on the coffee table. There were several large books, plus notepads, and a fluffy pencil case. Jed sat down beside her. He had forgotten to bring a book with him. One of the ones Greta had laid out interested Jed. The book had an interesting man posing on the front, which looked like a painting.

"May I?" asked Jed pointing to the book.

"Ah good choice!" replied Greta "The Prince by Machiavelli, I read that in the sixth form. That gives you a good grounding if you want to work in politics in the major political parties."

"What's it about?"

"Basically you can do what you want in order to hold onto power, including murder and betrayal" Greta laughed at Jed's expression of horror. "Not in current times, but it was written in the 16th century for the Florentine rule of Lorenzo de Medici. Very unpopular chap, Catholic Church despised him. Even ended up with his own phraseology "Machiavellian tendencies" referring to current-day politicians who use some of his betrayal ideas. You can borrow it if you like to read it here, but I need it back for an essay in a few week's time"

Jed opened the book and started reading. Some of the phraseology was complicated but Greta was happy to explain it. The room started to fill up with some of the other students who also bagged space to start their homework or revision. After about an hour Kim came into the room and pointed at Jed, Greta and one of the other students called Mat.

"You three, have a round of drop-offs" Greta closed her books but left them on the table

"Who'd want those old dusty volumes" she laughed as she followed Jed & Mat out into the foyer. Sly was waiting for them - an additional table had been set out next to the screen. There were three piles of envelopes & small packets. Kim stood next to the table and pointed at Greta first

"You dear" she handed her a piece of paper on a clipboard "Eleven drops off, mostly in the EX2 area" Greta opened her bag and Kim placed the packets and envelopes inside. "Do them in order, it has been planned out so you are back sooner and DO not give over your parcel or packet without getting a signature"

Greta nodded and winked at Jed

"See you later for more tuition"

before grabbing her bike and wheeling it out of the door. Jed watched as she consulted her paper before shoving it back into the bag and cycling off. Mat was next

"EX3 and EX4," said Kim, "Will take you a little longer, so there are a few less for you to deliver to make it fair". Mat didn't reply but just grabbed his bike and set off.

Finally, it was Jed's turn

"No favouritism," said Kim with a wink indicating it was just that "You get EX1 today and there are nine drop-offs but expect you to be back first OK?"

Jed nodded and took the piece of paper. There were nine addresses, three of which were for specific people in office locations, and the other six appeared to be home addresses. He saw that the first location was only two streets away.

He wheeled his bike out to the road, fastened his helmet, and swung the bag across his body before peddling off. The weather was pleasant to cycle in, with a light breeze, and there were not too many tourists who had a tendency to step off in front of traffic.

Jed pulled up outside the first location and secured his bike with the lock to a nearby lamppost. He took out his paper and saw that the drop-off was on the first floor. 'Johnny McKee, Hubert and Taylor Solicitors'.

Jed walked to the door which had a selection of doorbells for each of the businesses on the block. Jed pressed the bell and heard a voice ask

"Who is it?" in a posh and rather haughty voice

"Cetin Courier, have a delivery for Johnny McKee"

"Oh thank God" replied the voice.

A buzzer sounded and the door clicked. Jed was a little surprised at the change of tone, but he opened the door and started up the stairs. Standing on the first-floor landing was a rather dishevelled man wearing a suit, but the tie was undone, and the shirt was slightly unbuttoned.

"Come on, come on," said the man, whom Jed assumed to be Johnny McKee.

Jed opened the bag up and fished out the right envelope. It was heavy and sealed with a lot of packing tape. He handed it over to Johnny who finally smiled at him. Jed handed him the clipboard and watched as Johnny scrawled a signature next to the entry for his parcel.

"You can go now" Johnny turned and walked back into the room. Jed shrugged and turned back to the stairs. Jed unlocked his bike and took out the paper again, the next delivery was a private house by the look of it. He knew the road Temple Road, which was just down from the street Kitty had said Emil had been renovating. Jed decided he would take a slight detour after this drop-off to have a look at the place. No harm in dreaming.

Jed parked his bike at the next drop-off next to a hedge. He didn't bother locking it here, there was only an old man walking his dog, Jed didn't think he would be pinching his bike. The house for the drop-off looked very battered. The porch looked like it might crumble at any moment, and there was a large rusty car on bricks next to the house.

Jed rang the bell and fished out the envelope for this address. It took an age but eventually, the door opened slightly to reveal a bearded man that looked as battered as the house he was in. He had a large bruise on his right cheek, was unshaven, and his hair looked grubby and unwashed.

"Yeah, what do ya want?" the man said in a very strong Scottish accent. Jed held out the envelope and said brightly

"Cetin Couriers, delivery for you" The man blinked slowly then comprehension dawned.

"Oh yeah, thanks" he grabbed the envelope and dropped it behind him.

"I need a signature" Jed said.

The man grabbed the clipboard in Jed's hands and scribbled on the page. Jed looked at the signature. It could have been done by a monkey he thought. Jed waited for a second but the man closed the door without another word. Jed turned back to the road. The man with his dog was standing looking at him.

"Weirdo's in there," he said then walked on with his dog. Jed couldn't disagree.

Jed delivered the rest of his round in the next two hours, managing to stop off to look at the redeveloped house Kitty had mentioned. He could see why she was impressed. It had been painted and cleaned compared to the ones on either side of it. He wondered how many months of delivering parcels would get them access to this place.

* * *

Over the next few weeks, Jed and Kitty's life became more routine. Kitty became the regular entertainer at the casino which meant that she was rarely awake when Jed crept out each morning to go and wait for a courier round at the casino.

Jed became good friends with Greta who true to her word allowed him to finish The Prince. He found the book quite hard going but Greta was patient with him and explained the complex bits. Jed was now sixteen and he decided that he wanted to go to college and do his exams.

Jed spoke to Thomas one night about his plans.

"Gonna be tricky Jed without getting social services involved"

Thomas suddenly brightened up

"What about your mate Mike ? that's his name isn't it? Could we do something like pretend he's your stepdad or something? If you had a parent or guardian, it's a lot simpler to get you back into education, especially if it's suggested you live with him."

Jed wasn't sure whether Mike would want to be involved like that with him.

"Worth asking I suppose. What would he have to do?"

Thomas wrote down what was needed, thrust the paper towards him and said

"I think from what Keith said, he has a soft spot for you".

* * *

The following day on his courier round, Jed pulled up at the building site where Mike was working. He spotted him sitting outside a Portakabin drinking a cup of tea.

"Blimey, where did you get that bike, Jed?" Mike asked astonished. Jed turned so his bag was visible. "You've got a job? Well done lad!". Spotting the expression on Jed's face "What's wrong?".

Jed took out the piece of paper Thomas had written out and explained that he wanted to finish his exams and go to college, but he needed Mike's help to do it. Mike studied the piece of paper carefully then looked down at Jed whose expression was wretched.

"I never did my exams at school Jed, and I regretted it , then and now. From what I remember you always were a good pupil, and from what I can see, you would do well, so yes I will help you". Mike sat down again on the seat and patted the one next to him.

"Right, we need to get our stories straight OK?" Jed and Mike spent a while discussing and writing down the story that they would tell social services.

"I'll make an appointment to see the Education department next week with you. We'll see where that leads us. You'll have to move in for a while, I'll square it with Cathy. We've just moved into a bigger flat with a spare box room. Once social services are sorted, you can go back to the squat."

Jed suddenly realised that he hadn't spoken to Kitty about the idea. Mike noticed his expression.

"You've not told Kitty, have you? You need to get that sorted first. Tell you what, sort out with Kitty first, but if it's OK, then we go to Operation Jed Education!"

Jed laughed. Mike had a way of sorting things out logically but he also wondered what Kitty would make of his idea.

* * *

Jed got back to the squat at about 2 pm. Kitty was sitting in the kitchen yawning and drinking a cup of coffee.

"Hello, gorgeous!" Kitty slid out of her chair and wrapped her gown around him. Jed was trying not to be distracted by her but kissed her before stepping away.

"What's wrong?" Kitty asked sitting back down. Jed sat down on one of the other chairs and sighed.

"I want to do my exams, and maybe go to college one day. I've been reading a book another student had loaned me, and it's given me a taste for more."

Kitty frowned. "But what about our plans for getting out of here? I thought you wanted to work?"

"I can do both, studying while I am waiting for work at the couriers, and studying here in the evenings when you are working. But of course, first I have to go my GCSE's which means a change for a while."

Jed explained that plan, that he would go and live with Mike for a few weeks until social services had enrolled him at the local college to do his exams.

"Once I am enrolled I just come back here."

Kitty stood up her face a mask of fury

"And what if I am not here when you get back from your great educational adventure? Do you assume I don't have plans of my own? What if I am living over in the nice apartment in Athelstan Rd?"

Jed was startled. Kitty had always been supportive of his education in the past. She had often urged him to purchase new books for his collection from charity shops. Now things had changed and he was more confused than ever.

"Would you want me to live with you there, or is this a way for you to move on without me?" Jed asked softly. "I want to earn more money than some courier round, real money for us but no one will employ me other than for labouring. I need to do my exams, and in order to do that, I need a permanent address. Mike wants to help, and I hoped you might too?"

Jed was distraught. This was their first big row, and he felt sick. All his plans, his hopes of learning looked like they were washing away before his eyes. Kitty sat down again. She was still looking furious but her face had softened a little.

"I'm annoyed you hadn't spoken to me first, before Mike and Thomas. I thought we were a team, Jed? And yes of course you silly, I want you to live with me in the new place. Can we agree that's a plan for the future, alongside your education?" Jed nodded. They embraced.

"Now what were you showing me?" Jed asked playfully making a grab for Kitty's robe. She stood squealing and trying to avoid his grasping hands.

* * *

26

Problems

Mike called in at the squat the following evening. Jed was apprehensive as he wasn't sure whether Cathy Mike's new girlfriend would be up for the plan of pretending that Jed was part of her new boyfriend's family. However, as Mike got out of his car, he was grinning.

"Kitty all sorted?" Mike asked.

Jed nodded "Yeah, she was pissed I hadn't spoken to her first before you, but yeah, she's cool with it. Think she quite likes the idea of me being educated a bit more. She's at work at the moment"

Cathy's cool with it too" Mike replied. "She's quite looking forward to having another person to fuss over for a while. I'll come back tomorrow and help you get your things all moved over to ours, and I'll call social services on Wednesday to make an appointment to get you registered back in the education system. We can get our stories straight on Tuesday night.".

* * *

The following evening Jed and Mike got his possessions moved into the new box room. Jed instantly liked Cathy and knew she was good for Mike. Over a homemade curry, Jed and Mike worked out a plausible story for their relationship.

"Makes sense that you found me after moving back from London" Mike commented as they worked out a plan. "And I can prove I knew you back in the old squat before you got taken into care.". Mike called the local office for social services the following morning. Jed was eating toast in the kitchen with Cathy when Mike came in, a pad of paper and a pen in his hand.

"All sorted mate, we are seeing Mr Barker at 2 pm today"

"Not Mrs Hilston?" Jed asked. He was looking forward to seeing her again

"No, the person I spoke to initially said she had left the department last year."

Jed was disappointed, but at least things were starting to happen. He rose from the table and placed his plate on the sideboard

"Leave that Jed, I'll clear up in a minute," said Cathy, "Don't you have to get off to work now?" she asked Mike.

"Yeah, I'll come back and collect you at 1.30 pm from here Jed OK?"

Jed agreed with a nod. "I'd better get off to the couriers, should get a round in before then". Jed spent the quiet times talking to Greta about his plans for the future.

"That's great news Jed, might see you at lectures one day perhaps?"

"GSCE's first" Jed agreed with a laugh. He had spoken to Kim about his plans earlier as well.

"Good to see you are ambitious" Kim replied "I left school at sixteen without an O Level or CSE to my name, but I never regretted it. Got working at fourteen on a paper round, and started working for Emil when I turned seventeen. Now I am in charge of all you lot"

Kim laughed as none of the other couriers even looked up or acknowledged her. Most were furiously working on assignments or reading large volumes. Jed had done a large round by noon, so Kim agreed he could get off early. As well as the money for the round, she also slipped him an additional £50 in his wage packet.

When he started to protest she silenced him with

"You're my best courier, discreet and hard-working, call this a little bonus"

Jed was delighted with the extra money. Things were starting to look up.

* * *

Mike and Jed walked into the council offices early.
Mike spoke to the receptionist who indicated a seating
area and asked them to wait there. Jed was fascinated
that the offices hadn't really changed since his mum
had given him up years earlier. There was a new shiny
logo behind the reception desks now, and the stairs
looked more polished than before.

Sitting there brought back memories of his last time
with his mum outside the offices.

"The trolley" Jed exclaimed loudly.

Mike looked startled "Trolley, what trolley?" he
whispered.

"When my mum went to hospital, we left our
possessions with the council. Do you think they might
still have them?" Mike shrugged.

Jed vowed to ask.

After a couple of minutes, a man descended the stairs
and came over to them

"Mr Higgins ?" the man asked

"Yep, that's me," said Mike standing and shaking the
hand offered to him "This is Jed, my stepson".

417

"Hello Jed, I'm Mr Barker. I understand from my notes, that your social worker used to be Mrs Hilston?"

"Yes is she OK?"

"She's fine" Mr Barker smiled "She decided to move into the charity sector, over in Hampshire. She's working there as a care officer for a local charity, loving it apparently. Come with me please"

Mr Barker led the way back up the stairs, and down a corridor before stopping at a door at the end. He opened the door and indicated two chairs on one side of a polished table.

"Have a seat, I'll just go and get your notes, Jed".

They both sat down. The room was quite spartan, but there was a small window overlooking the car park and the cathedral square beyond that.

Mr Barker came back into the room, holding a large box file. Jed could see his name printed on the edge of it. Mr Barker dropped the file onto the table in front of him, and then sat down. He took out a pad of paper and a pen from the box file and sat back.

Mike coughed. "Before we get started, my stepson was wondering if his mum's possessions might still be here?" Mr Barker looked as confused as Mike had been.

"My mum's possessions were being stored here six years ago when she went to hospital and I was sent to the children's home" Jed explained " In a shopping trolley, were they kept?"

Mr Barker looked at his notes.

"It says here that the storage area was being renovated a couple of years and a Mr Gibbons was asked if he wanted the items. He did not, so they were disposed of. "

Jed was devastated He knew the items were mostly his mum's clothes. He fervently wished that he had taken something of his mum's, just to keep her close. Jed kept his face looking down to the floor. He knew if he looked up he would cry. He wasn't going to let Charlie beat him at the last hurdle back to education.

"So Mr Higgins, you mentioned to my colleague that Jed found you last week, having left London where he had been living" he consulted his pad "since running away from the Methodist Children's Home when he was eleven?"

Mike nodded "I was with Jed's mum in a relationship before she died, and Jed had been like a son to me all those years. I wasn't able to take him in, on account of my living conditions at the time, but I'm settled now in a flat, and I have a good income from labouring" Mr Barker made notes on his pad as Mike talked.

"And Jed, you are now wanting to finish your schooling, and possibly go onto college, is that correct?" Jed confirmed it was "But you haven't been at school since the age of eleven, so what made you decide now to do this?" Jed decided to stay close to the truth.

"Someone I know is at University, studying politics. They loaned me a book, and I loved it and wanted to know more. I know I have to do my school exams first, but I am really keen on this, honest". Mr Barker nodded.

"Well this is slightly unusual" he put down the pen "I am more often trying to persuade truants to return to education rather than being persuaded to get someone back into education, but it's a refreshing change for sure. First of all, though, I need to come and do a home visit, to make sure you are being well looked after. Shall we say tomorrow evening at 7 pm?"

The meeting was agreed, and as Mike and Jed left, Mr Barker addressed Mike

"It's nice to see a parent take up their responsibilities"

Jed saw Mike was trying not to blush as he mumbled

"Thanks"

"He's the best!" which made Mike go even pinker.

As they left the building Mike turned to Jed

"What do you think? He believed us?" Mike stopped and said "I'm sorry about your mum's things. That Mr Gibbons, that's your old manager at the home right?"

Jed nodded, still unable to utter his name.

"Well if he walks by my site, I'll be sure to drop a brick or two on his head" Mike suddenly stopped and smiled briefly

Jed was pretty sure that it had gone well but there was a long way to go before he would be back in school. The following evening Mr Barker arrived at Mike and Cathy's flat. Cathy had made sure that there were plenty of foods a sixteen-year-old would enjoy.

Mr Barker examined the flat briefly before talking to Cathy separately from Mike. Mike and Jed had briefed her on the story, so there were no unpleasant surprises when Cathy and Mr Barker joined them in the living room. They all sat down before Mr Barker commented

"OK Jed, I'm satisfied you have suitable adult guardians here." He took out a form from a briefcase and a pen and started to fill out the information before getting both Jed and Mike to sign it.

"This will get you into the local college for your GCSEs next week, as you are sixteen nearly seventeen, It's quite handy as it's the start of the autumn term." he handed Jed a copy "You need to report to the college at 9 am on Monday next week, you will be assigned a tutor who will give you an exam to see where you are at on the curriculum. Classes will be held both in the day and the evening, depending on your abilities, but hopefully, you will be able to take your first exams in January. And good luck"

Mr Barker stood and shook Jed's hand. Cathy showed him out, before coming back into the room to see Mike and Jed hugging.

"Went well then?" she said

"Very well" replied Jed who started to dance around the living room. Mike released himself from Jed's grip and walked over to a small drawer in the corner of the room. Jed was puzzled until Mike turned with his hands clasped behind his back.

"Close your eyes Jed" he said. Jed complied confused and a little dizzy from all the twirling. "Open them"

Jed opened his eyes and saw Mike holding out a small pale blue box. Jed recognised it immediately

"Mum's perfume" he exclaimed. "Is it hers?"

Mike shook his head sadly "No, but whilst we were sitting in the council offices yesterday, I remembered its name. They still make it - Angel it's called, so I bought you a small bottle, you can open and sniff it when you want to." Mike held out a small embroidered handkerchief "or you can spray it on this?" Jed took the handkerchief and bottle and sat down on the sofa.

"Thanks Mike" he said simply

* * *

Later that evening Jed slipped out of the flat and went to the squat to see Kitty before she went to work. He arrived to find that Thomas was also there. He briefly brought him up to date on the success of Operation Jed education, before heading off to their space. Kitty was applying makeup as he arrived, and squealed as Jed snuck up behind her grabbing her arms and spinning her around.

"I've got to get to work in a bit" she yelped.

"I'm in," Jed said looking at her.

Kitty replied distractingly "That's great, when do you start? as she picked up her lipstick and carried on with her preparations.

"Next week, I'm going to have to jiggle my shifts at the courier company with lessons"

Jed sat heavily on the bed. Kitty sniffed the air. "Are you wearing perfume?" she asked getting closer and closer.

Jed took out the handkerchief which Cathy had expertly sprayed with the perfume earlier in the day.

Cathy had commented as she did it

"You'll only need a small bit" she said "This one was a strong perfume even back in the 1990's"

Jed explained about the shopping trolley and how Charlie had caused more grief for Jed, even whilst Jed was in London.

Kitty smiled briefly "Well glad it's your mums and not some other birds. That's great news babe re your courses, but I've got to go"

"Do you want me to walk you?"

"No need, Sly's picking me up, he's dropping someone off at the train station, offered me a lift yesterday"

Jed was dismayed to hear that news. He didn't like either of the brothers, but especially found Sly a bit of a ladies' man.

Jed walked Kitty out to the road where Sly's sleek Jag was already waiting. Sly got out and came around to open the passenger door for Kitty,

"My lady," he said with a chuckle bowing. He winked at Jed who immediately hated him even more.

Jed tried not to show how annoyed he was. Kitty kissed him on the cheek before sliding into the car. Sly then got back into the driver's side, and roared off up the road. Dejected at Kitty's lack of enthusiasm for his news, Jed walked back inside where Keith and Thomas were drinking coffee. They were both thrilled for him, Thomas commented

"I do some night classes at the college, you might even get me if you are lucky".

Jed felt better after talking to them. Kitty was just busy.

* * *

Jed spent the rest of the week doing as many rounds at the courier company as he could. The recipients of the parcels and envelopes he delivered seemed to him to fall into two categories.

The first was the 'normals'. Business envelopes, often delivered to solicitors and accountants, were handed over to bored and annoyed receptionists as quickly as possible.

The second category was the 'weirdos' as he had come to call them. The same small group of people repeatedly being handed small light parcels, or envelopes marked "Private and Confidential" including the man in the battered house and just recently a few on the new executive estate near the harbour area.

One recipient he remembered was waiting for him outside a very luxurious house with large steel gates. It was a young woman, who looked like she had been out all night partying. She was wearing a mini dress and had no shoes on. Her eyes were bloodshot and she was shaking visibly. Jed rode up and her face lit up.

It was a disturbing sight, which reminded Jed of one of the drug addicts he had seen in the squat he had lived in with his mum. That person was an older woman, called Issey, and his mum had warned Jed not to give her any money.

"She'll spend it on smack" Clare had said.

"What's smack?" asked Jed, confused because he only knew the word for a slap on the legs.

"Nasty stuff, drugs it is" replied Clare. "Drags you down into the pits of hell".

Since that time Jed had been aware of drugs but seeing this girl and the expression of joy on her face at seeing him ride up, Jed was reminded of Issey. He stopped and fished in the bag for the right parcel.

"Oh man, been waiting a while. What took you so long?" she said as Jed handed her the parcel and held out the clipboard for her signature. She scribbled briefly on the page. She cradled the packet in the crook of her left arm, almost cooing at it like a child.

Jed was even more disturbed. She looked at him briefly then turned and opened the gate without another word. Jed looked at her as she walked down the long gravel driveway, without shoes which should have hurt her feet. He knew if he had walked barefoot for that long, he would be hobbling and stepping off the driveway. This girl however just seemed to glide away before letting herself into the house. Jed mused on this as he rode back to the casino.

As he arrived, he was annoyed to see that Kim was in the office talking intensely to Sly who was gesturing back at her.

Jed parked his bike back on the rack and walked into the courier room. It was nearly empty, but several piles of books and bags suggested that a few of his fellow couriers were currently out on their rounds. Jed sunk into the sofa nearest the door. He was knackered, but he also wanted to speak to Kim. He leaned back and closed his eyes.

Jed jerked awake. He had fallen asleep but a noise outside the room had woken him up.

"We CANT increase the rounds, it's too risky, you know that!"

Jed recognised the voice of Kim but she sounded very angry. The other voice was lower, Jed strained but couldn't hear what they were saying.

The voices moved further away, Kim's voice was still much louder. Jed crept to the door and opened it a crack. He could see Kim, and the people she was shouting at were Emil and Sly.

Sly grabbed Kim's arm and pushed her into the office in the lobby, then nodded at Emil before going in himself. Jed shut the courier door and sat back down.

What on earth was going on?

429

He sat there thinking about the conversation he had heard.

Kim was angry because Sly and Emil had more work. Surely that was a good thing for the business? More work would also be good for the couriers like him, more rounds. But she was angry because it was risky. Why would more work be risky? And then suddenly he thought about the two types of customers he had been dealing with. The weirdos. The second category of parcels and envelopes must be drugs or something like drugs. All of the people in the second category were receiving drugs and he was part of it.

Jed sat back and realised how much trouble he could be in. As he was working through the events and consequences Greta arrived back from her round.

"Hiya!" she greeted Jed before realising he was looking very solemn. "What's up?" she asked sitting down beside him.

Jed waited, listening to hear if anyone else was coming in. He stood up and beckoned her over to where the tea and coffee supplies were.

"Have you had any weirdo customers on your rounds?"

Greta laughed. "I got eyed up by one of the local solicitor's clerks, who asked me out on a date last week".

"No, No, not perverts, weirdos, like they were waiting for you to arrive like it was the most important thing in their lives?"

Greta looked puzzled. "No, I don't think so, just businesses and a few private homes, mostly legal stuff. Why? have you?"

Jed leaned back against the counter "Yeah a few. Never mind".

He was even more worried now, but he tried to forget the conversation and chat to Greta about his upcoming reentry into the world of books, as she called it.

Later that afternoon, he spotted Kim, who looked like she had been crying. He was tempted to go and speak to her, but Emil was nearby and he realised he would have to be even more careful. He decided to keep his suspicions to himself for the time being, but he also decided to be more aware of what was going on.

* * *

27

The world of books

Mike and Cathy waved Jed off on Monday morning. Cathy had presented Jed with a full set of stationary in a subtle grey print, and a new rucksack. She had also prepared him a packed lunch. Jed hugged both of them and set off for the college.

On arrival, the place was buzzing with new students, and groups of tutors who were directing people to different parts of the campus. Jed waited in line at the entrance to the main hall and pulled out the paperwork Mr Barker had given him. There were people of all ages there, from teenagers like him to older people whom he assumed were doing evening classes.

"Next!" said one of the people manning the first set of tables. Jed walked over and passed his paperwork to the young man who looked through it.

"Right GCSEs, you need to go to that table over there" the man pointed to a table on the right "The blue one" he handed back the paperwork and Jed walked over to the blue table.

The blue table had three people looking through paperwork and handing out clipboards and pens to the people coming to see them. Jed smiled as he handed over his paperwork to a bearded man.

"Hello, welcome to Exeter Community College..." he looked at Jed's paperwork "Jed. I'm Mr Wright, I will be your form tutor for your first set of exams. You need to fill out these forms, there is a pen" Mr Wright passed Jed a clipboard and pen. "You can sit over there, come and see me again when you've filled them out".

Jed walked over and sat down. There were four other students also busy filling out the forms. When he had finished, Jed walked back over and passed the clipboard and pen to Mr Wright.

"OK then" Mr Wright glanced through the forms, then looked back at Jed.

"Come with me" he stood up, and Jed followed him out of the hall and into one of the corridors. The place was noisy, the sounds of classes followed him as he walked behind Mr Wright who stopped at one of the last doors on the right. Jed followed Mr Wright into a classroom, where another young man was sitting waiting.

"Jed this is Joseph, he's from Poland. He and his family have just moved to England. You both will be taking an exam today, to see where you come on the grading for the GCSEs you will be both taking this year."

Jed nodded at Joseph who smiled back.

"Sit down, anywhere. Make yourself comfortable. Do you have a pen?" Jed confirmed he did. He sat down and took out his brand new pencil case fishing out a pen. Mr Wright walked to the front of the room and picked up some paper packs before passing one each to Jed and Joseph.

"General knowledge, maths and science. It's a bit of a mishmash but it will help us to grade you accordingly. Do your best, and write your name at the top. Time starts....now".

Jed wrote his name at the top of the paper and then started to read. He knew from his school days that you always read the paper before deciding how to answer the questions.

He realised that he could answer most of them, so after glancing at the rest of the paper, he made a start. He concentrated on answering the questions so hard, that the time flew by, and suddenly he heard Mr Wright say

"Time's up"

Jed glanced at the clock behind Mr Wright. It was noon. Three hours had gone by in a flash. Mr Wright took their papers and placed them both back on the front desk.

"Right, lunchtime now, if you can come back here to room 601 at 1 pm, there is one more paper to do. I'll show you where the canteen is."

Jed and Joseph followed Mr Wright back out into the corridor which was quieter than earlier. Mr Wright walked back into the main hall and then took a right into a corridor where there were two lines of people.

"If you've brought a packed lunch you can go right in, there are tables on the right. If you haven't the queue is here on the left for cold food, and on the right for hot food".

Jed was glad that Cathy had packed him a lunch. The people waiting for food looked hungry and bored. Joseph joined the right-hand line. Jed walked into the hall which was packed with students and staff. He found the tables that Mr Wright had mentioned, quite a few students were sitting eating packed lunches from boxes and bags. Jed found a chair on the last table and sat down. He opened his packed lunch box and pulled out a packet of ham and coleslaw sandwiches.

There was also a packet of crisps, a can of soft drink and a piece of malt loaf. He realised he was starving. All that concentration on the paper had made him very hungry. He watched the people in the hot and cold queues as he ate. Joseph eventually managed to get to the head of the line and took a portion of what looked like a stew. As he moved away from the till Joseph spotted Jed who nodded to the seat on the other side of the table.

"Thanks," said Joseph as he sat down. He examined his stew with a fork. "What is this?"

"No idea!" laughed Jed looking at both the stew and the expression on Joseph's face. "What did it say on the label?"

"Beef Stew, but I was hoping it might be Bigos, you know hunters stew?"

"Sorry I don't know that," said Jed munching on his second sandwich.

Joseph picked up his knife and started to eat.

"Nicer than it looks" he commented. They ate in relative silence until Joseph asked "Why are you taking your school exams at college?"

Jed had prepared a basic answer to these types of questions with Mike. They both knew people would be curious, and it was better to give an answer rather than none. Jed explained that his mum had died when he was young, and he had been living on 'the streets' until Mike his stepdad had gotten in touch via an old friend. Jed had come back to Exeter to live with Mike and his girlfriend. Joseph listened carefully.

"That's tough, I'm sorry about your mum" Jed nodded and opened his crisps. He offered Joseph one, but he declined. "I'm getting used to the taste of this" he indicated his stew which was almost gone.

437

"What about you? Your family moved to Exeter?"

"A few months ago, mum got a job working in the hospital. She's a nurse for children. She brought me and my little sister. My sister is in the local school, she enrolled last week, but I am now seventeen, so I cannot go to school. I want to be a man of business - are that the right words? To run my own business., but also to be in a world of books, like here. Learning about stuff"

"What sort of business?" asked Jed who was intrigued by the passion Joseph was expressing

"A Polish shop, selling Polish foods and other things. I have seen many Poles in this city, and when I talked to one of them at the bus stop, they were moaning about having to send home to get hold of the ingredients for meals from Poland"

Jed was impressed with Joseph's idea but he didn't know if that sort of shop would do well in Exeter. Once they finished their food, Joseph took his tray and stacked it carefully on the trolley. Jed and Joseph then made their way outside into the car park and sat down on a wall. Joseph looked at his watch

"Five minutes," he said "For the digestion. My mum said we should let our food go down"

Jed sat looking at the groups of students around the car park. Just like at school there were the rich kids, the popular ones, and in one corner the geeks and the nerds.

Joseph wasn't paying too much attention to the groups but after five minutes he stood up and stretched. Jed followed him back into the college and was amazed he was able to find room 601 without asking anyone for directions. When Jed asked Joseph just shrugged and said

"photograph memory"

"You have a photographic memory? Really? that's amazing"

Jed was very impressed. He only knew one other person with that ability, Sid from the Exeter squat. Sid was able to play magic tricks in the local pub, which got him free beers on bets, he would be able to remember the sequence of playing cards being dealt. He always won, and eventually had to change his local, as the regulars would spoil his game by telling the gullible punter he had "special abilities".

Mr Wright came into the room and smiled at both of them.

"Nice break?" he asked as he passed both Jed and Joseph their final paper for the day

"The stew was interesting" replied Joseph which got Jed giggling. They waited for Mr Wright to get back to the front desk before he then said

"You may start". Jed turned over his paper and started to read. It was an English exam, English literature.

Describe your favourite book and explain how it shaped your life

Jed smiled. He knew exactly which book he would be choosing. Islands in the Sky. He started to plan his essay. He looked over at Joseph who was looking puzzled.

"Describe your favourite book and why you like it" he whispered. Joseph smiled and winked. Jed wrote without pause until Mr Wright finally announced

"Time's up". He walked over and collected their papers, Jed had written his best work, he knew. He smiled and sat back in the chair.

"OK, you will get your results tomorrow from the front desk in reception. They will give you both your timetables and classes. Good luck".

Jed and Joseph left the classroom into the hallways which were mostly quiet.

From the corridor, Jed could hear classes going on around him. He was looking forward to being part of this life again. Jed walked home after saying goodbye to Joseph who headed toward the hospital

"My mum finishes her shift in half an hour," Joseph said "She'll want to hear all about my day"

Jed was briefly jealous of his new friend. He also wanted to tell his mum about his good day, but he realised that both Mike and Cathy would also be interested. He wondered about stopping off at the squat on the way home, but after checking his watch he knew that Kitty would be on her way to the casino for her afternoon shift. He could tell her tomorrow.

* * *

Cathy had arranged a "student dinner" for Jed and Mike that evening which was mostly fried chicken, onion rings & chips plus ice cream for dessert. Mike had been thrilled to hear that Jed had enjoyed his first day back in education despite it being an exam day.

"You'll do great" Mike said helping himself to another piece of fried chicken. Jed suddenly remembered Joseph's mum

"Do you know a Krystyna Wojcik works in the children's ward as a nurse?" Jed asked Cathy "She's from Poland"

Cathy picked up an onion ring

"I think I might know her - why?"

"Her son was doing his GCSE assessment with me. He's called Joseph".

"Small world," said Mike.

Jed put down his piece of chicken "I was jealous of him"

"Why?" asked Cathy

"Because he could go to her place of work and tell her all about his day. I miss that with mum".

Mike looked at Jed "So why don't we go and tell her tomorrow then?"

"How, where?"

"Cherrywood Farm," Mike said simply "Go tell her you are home and good, and doing well".

Jed realised he really wanted this, and looking at Mike he knew that Mike wanted this for him. For Mike taking on Jed was a big step up in his life, despite living with Cathy, Mike was a nomad at heart and his first love Jed realised had been his mum.

"OK then, yes please" Jed replied, "Can we go via the college first though, I want to see whether I have enough" Jed knocked his head "to be able to take my GSCEs".

"Course," said Mike taking another onion ring with a grin, "want to see how clever you are"

* * *

28

The end of Cherrywood Farm

Mike dropped Jed off outside the college gates.

"I'll wait in the car, too many traffic wardens around. If I'm not here when you get back I'll be doing a loop round the city, just wait for me"

Jed nodded and shut the passenger door. He made his way through to the front desk where a large group of students were chatting nearby. Jed waited for a receptionist to be free before asking for his results.

"Name, and course," said the bored-looking young receptionist whose name badge said 'Jinny'

"Jed Long" replied Jed.

Jinny leaned over and started to rummage through a large box on the desk in front of her. "Here you go," she said thrusting an envelope into his hand.

Jed looked at the envelope which was sealed. On the front, it said 'Jed Long '. He walked back to the gate where Mike was still waiting.

"Get in" Mike urged "Warden at six o clock"

Jed looked back down the road where indeed a male traffic warden was headed their way. He got into the passenger side quickly and Mike roared up the road even before Jed got his seatbelt on. Jed looked at the envelope

"I don't want to open it until we get to the farm, is that OK?"

"Course it is" replied Mike "It's only fair".

Mike concentrated on the road ahead whilst Jed kept looking at the envelope wondering if it was good news. They drove in silence for the rest of the way. Mike had planned a route to the farm the previous night, using his battered AA Road map. Jed looked out at the changing landscape from city to countryside.

Eventually, after negotiating their way through a traffic jam caused by some loose sheep on the road, they arrived in the lane where Cherrywood farm was. Jed looked at the rolling hill behind the farm and he could see the cherry trees at the top. The sign was still in the same place, a little more battered than the last time he had been here. There was also another sign next to it, this one shiny and new

'For sale by Stags Auctioneers'

Jed was dismayed "They're selling up?" he wailed "They can't sell, my mum is here".

"Calm down" replied Mike but Jed could see he was also disturbed by the sign. "Let's see what they have to say before we lose it OK?".

Mike turned left and parked behind a battered Land Rover Jed didn't recognise. Mr & Mrs Goodwin had a Volvo which Mr Goodwin had described as being held together by the rust. As Mike switched off the engine and they both got out, a door at the far end of the building opened and a man dressed in an olive green coat came outside. Jed didn't recognise him either.

"Hello, can I help you?" the man asked "Are Mr & Mrs Goodwin around please?" asked Jed politely. The man stopped and looked at Jed.

"No, I'm sorry who are you?" Mike stepped forward and put out his hand "Mike Higgins"

The man shook his hand

"John Kingsley, I'm in charge of selling, and you are here because? You don't look like someone who is looking to buy this farm"

Mike replied

"We're not. My son here" he indicated to Jed "He was cared for by Mr & Mrs Goodwin and their daughter Hilda a while back, they were very kind to him, and he's back in Exeter now, wanted to see them".

John Kingsley's expression softened a little bit.

"Oh right, OK, well..." he trailed off still looking at Jed. He then looked back at Mike again. "There's no easy way to say this, but Mr and Mrs Goodwin died a few weeks back in a car crash near Exminster. Their daughter wasn't with them, but as she is the sole beneficiary, she has decided to put the farm up for sale."

Jed heard the words but the meaning of them made his head swim. He stepped back and collapsed on the ground. The next thing he knew Mike's face was above him looking frantic.

"OK...I'm OK" Jed mumbled.

"Stay still," said Mike with tears in his eyes. "I'm so sorry Jed"

He wrapped his arms around Jed who started to sob. John Kingsley stood off to one side looking embarrassed. Jed eventually indicated he wanted to stand up. His eyes were full of tears but he asked

"Miss Goodwin, is she here?"

John Kingsley shook his head.

"No, she is living in the city for now. She was talking to me about moving to another part of the UK in a few months' time once all the paperwork is sorted."

Mike took hold of Jed's arm and said "You have a seat in the car, I want to talk to Mr Kingsley OK?"

Jed allowed himself to be led back to the car. He realised he still clutched the envelope in his hand. His head swam still, with thoughts of the couple who had given him nothing but kindness. Dead, both dead, and Miss Goodwin is now an orphan. Jed wondered if old people could be orphans. He supposed they could. He thought of the times he had spent here, warm and cosy in homemade socks drinking warm milk straight from the cow. Tears continued to slide down his face. He could see Mike and Mr Kingsley talking earnestly to one side of the door Mr Kingsley had come out from.

After a few minutes, Mike shook Mr Kingsley's hand and came back to the car and opened the door. "Mr Kingsley is going to call Miss Goodwin. Can you wait for a bit longer?"

Jed nodded. "What did you say?"

"Told him that you wanted to tell your mum about your exams, your college course, and wanted to see Miss Goodwin, if she wanted to see you" Mr Kingsley came back outside and this time he was smiling.

"She's on her way," he said simply. "Now can I offer you a cup of tea while we wait for her to get here ?" Jed and Mike followed Mr Kingsley

* * *

Jed sat in the kitchen drinking a cup of tea. It wasn't the same as before, the milk came from a carton Mr Kingsley had fished out of the fridge. Jed saw there were no piles of cheese, ham and sausages in the large fridge any longer. The house felt sad and empty. Mike made small talk with Mr Kingsley who didn't mention the Goodwins but asked Mike about his work with cars.

Eventually, they heard a car pull up outside. Jed stood and walked to the door. Miss Goodwin was getting out of her car Yogi. Jed was glad something had stayed familiar to him. The car looked a little more battered than he remembered. Miss Goodwin looked over at Jed and her face crumpled. She held out her arms and Jed ran into them.

"Oh my boy," she said softly into his hair. Jed felt her tears run into his hair but he knew he too was crying. "You've grown so tall" They stood in the yard holding each other until eventually, Jed heard Mike say

"It's nice to see you again Hilda, but I am so sorry about your parents".

Miss Goodwin pulled away from Jed holding him at arm's length. "Tall and handsome too. Hello Mike, thank you, it is lovely to see you. Thank you for bringing Jed, I'm so sorry it's not what you hoped for".

Mike shrugged. "Did you hear why we came?"

Miss Goodwin brushed a tear away. "Yes, John explained. He's here to value the property for sale, there is an auction next month." Miss Goodwin looked down at Jed "I couldn't find a farmer husband Jed, I did try". She smiled wanly.

"Where are the animals?" asked Jed "The piggies and the sheep?"

"Sold" replied Miss Goodwin "All gone now, but most to a sanctuary who will care for them, they won't go for meat". Jed was relieved at that news. "And the orchard, will that stay?"

Miss Goodwin glanced at John Kingsley and Jed saw that her expression was strained,

"I hope so" she replied simply "The cherry trees do take a lot of work, I'm discussing putting a covenant on the property"

"What's that?" asked Jed puzzled.

"It's a sort of legal promise," Miss Goodwin said "Whoever comes to live here, must promise not to tear down the orchard, but John has objections to that."

She glanced at John Kingsley who was looking uncomfortable at the conversation.

"I simply pointed out that any legal ties or promises do reduce the market for this lovely farm"

"But my Mum is there, buried"

John Kingsley looked startled at this news "A body?"

Miss Goodwin laughed

"No, no John, Jed's mum's ashes were scattered at the end of the orchard, but the container was buried beneath the last tree at the very top." She turned to Jed and winked "Mum and Dad will be keeping her company next week. Can you both come to the funeral? I don't have many friends and it would be nice to have you there"

Jed turned to Mike "Can we?"

"Of course, we will be there". Miss Goodwin turned and pulled open the boot of the car. "These are the details" she handed Mike a piece of paper which had been folded in half. "It's Wednesday morning at 10 am, at the crematorium"

"Can I bring my girlfriend?" asked Jed, thinking of Kitty

"Of course, the more the merrier, a girlfriend eh?" Miss Goodwin smiled. "Now, let's go and tell your mum about your news".

She took Jed's hand and beckoned Mike to follow them. John Kingsley stood in the yard as they made their way up to the orchard. As they arrived Jed could see how much the trees had grown since he was last there.

"They got big," he remarked.

"They sure did" Miss Goodwin agreed. "Mum and Dad were always convinced you would come back one day. They knew though that the bullying at the home drove you away." Miss Goodwin stopped "Can I tell you something in confidence?" Jed nodded. "I punched him" she whispered "Charlie, I punched him on the nose when I found out you had gone"

Jed laughed "Really, wish I had seen that"

Miss Goodwin smiled "Yeah he wished he'd seen it coming too". She walked to the end of the trees "That one, remember?". Jed nodded. The ground now was covered in grass, but he could see the spot where his Mum's urn had been buried. He stopped startled. On the ground next to the spot was a beautiful cross made of cherry wood with a small plaque on it in a lighter wood. Jed dropped to the ground to read it.

Miss Goodwin smiled. "Dad made that the following month, he said that it was wrong to not mark the spot where a soul lay".

Jed read aloud "Clare Long, born 1st September 1971, died 15th November 1999 aged 28 years and 82 days A soul in heaven watching over Jed" Jed looked up at Miss Goodwin. "He calculated it? how old she was?"

Miss Goodwin nodded "Dad loved to be precise." She stroked the wood of the cross "I would love to have two more made for Mum and Dad for when they come here."

Mike coughed "I know someone"

Miss Goodwin smiled "Really?"

Mike shuffled his feet and started to blush "I like making stuff, my mate has a workshop in his back garden, he could help me"

"Well that is sorted then, come up any time to get some wood, the dried stuff is behind the pig pen. I'll show you, Jed are you OK chatting to your mum whilst I show Mike where the cherry wood is?"

Jed nodded. He watched as Miss Goodwin and Mike started back down the hill. He sat for a while watching the sun dapple through the cherry trees. Then he started to talk whilst opening his envelope.

* * *

Jed joined Mike and Miss Goodwin back in the yard after his 'talk' with his mum. He knew she wasn't really there in the ground, just the urn that held her for a while, but it comforted him to talk to something, and now he had the beautiful cross.

"All OK?" Mike asked.

Jed smiled "All good". He hugged Miss Goodwin hard. He fished the envelope out of his pocket and waved it at them both "I passed the entry qualifications, next step is a year at college to do my GCSE's"

"I expect you've grown out of that suit you wore for your mum's funeral?" she asked with a smile. "No need for suits for Mum and Dad's funeral. I've asked people to wear something pink for the cherry blossom, just a flower, or a handkerchief. I'll see you all next Wednesday. I'm looking forward to meeting the girl who stole your heart"

* * *

Jed asked Mike to drop him off near the station on the drive back to the city. Mike pulled over near the entrance, before turning to Jed

456

"I'm sorry about the Goodwin's Jed, I'll see you later at home for dinner, Cathy's making lasagne"

Jed walked to the squat, mulling over the changes happening in his life, good things including new education, the return of Mike into his life, steady work as a courier, but the loss of Mr & Mrs Goodwin, whom Jed had loved dearly through the toughest times of his life. Miss Goodwin too had changed. She had a sadness about her like a gossamer cloak which she tried desperately not to show. Jed knew though, that the loss of a parent, two in her case, meant fundamental changes in her life.

Kitty was getting dressed as Jed arrived back. Her skin was damp from the shower Keith had rigged up in one of the old toilet rooms. She was distracted Jed could see, slightly twitchy as she dried herself off.

"Hello Sexy" Kitty turned startled

"Jed, you frightened me" she laughed shakily wrapping the towel around herself more.

"What's that?" Jed pointed at Kitty's wrist. There was a mark, like a bruise.

"Nothing, nothing," she said, but her eyes didn't meet his

"Has someone hurt you?"

"It was a punter in the club last night, some drunk who had lost at the tables grabbed my wrist as I was leaving the stage, Sly sorted him out."

Jed was distressed to hear that what should have been an easy gig for Kitty was turning out to be something more sinister.

"How?"

"How what?" Kitty replied as she sat on the bed fastening her bra.

"How did Sly sort out the person who grabbed you" Jed was starting to get annoyed.

"He took him out the back and beat him up" Kitty looked defiant as she looked up at Jed. "Sly also banned him from the casino for life, and gave me this" Kitty pulled out a wad of notes "to keep stum in case the punter complained to the police".

Jed was more concerned by Kitty's tone of voice. She sounded hardened, not the girl he had fallen in love with.

"And you are OK with that, how Sly does do business? How he deals with people like that?"

Kitty's expression changed to one of rage "He keeps me safe Jed when I am working. I earned this money, the cat calls, the 'does she do after shows' comments. It's good money, I'm not walking the streets, and yes, I am OK with that. Now did you want something, otherwise I have an hour before I need to be at the club again."

Jed sat down on the bed. He felt deflated and sadder than he thought he could be.

"I went to Cherrywood today, to talk to mum. Mr and Mrs Goodwin died a few weeks back in a car crash. Their funeral is Wednesday, I'd like to take you".

Kitty sank down in front of him, and her rage dissipated.

"Oh Jed I'm so sorry." she wrapped her arms around him.

Jed sank his head onto her shoulder and wept.

* * *

Jed returned to Mike's house after walking Kitty to the club. She had promised to make the funeral and Jed had put his fears to the back of his mind, as she held his hand. He still felt saddened that she had been assaulted at the club, but he was also comforted that Sly seemed to be in control. He kissed her as they arrived, Sly was waiting inside talking to Kim. Jed nodded to Sly as Kitty opened the casino door and walked inside. He turned and made his way back to Mike and Cathy's place.

* * *

The day of Gary and Millie Goodwin's joint funeral was a grey and windy one. Jed had borrowed a pink scarf from Cathy which she expertly turned into a cravat and tucked into Jed's brand new white shirt. Jed wore his best trousers, grey pinstriped ones and had spent ages with Mike learning how to polish shoes the previous evening. Mike also wore a white shirt, but he had a pink handkerchief in his chest pocket.

"Come on, get your anorak we'd better go, we need to pick Kitty up and traffic on the Topsham Road is bad this week"

Mike urged Jed out of the door blowing Cathy a kiss as they left. Cathy had also been invited by Miss Goodwin, but she had a shift at the hospital which she wasn't able to change.

Mike and Jed drove to the squat and Jed was relieved to see Kitty waiting at the side of the road. She wore a pale blue dress with a pink carnation pinned to one shoulder. Her dreadlocks were tied back with a pink ribbon. She also carried a small pink bag that Jed had not seen before. As Kitty got in the back of the car she said

"Morning Mike, morning Hun, blimey it's not warm out is it?"

She shivered a bit dramatically. Mike pulled away and rejoined the traffic. The radio played a classical music station which Jed appreciated. He liked all sorts of music but today was not the day for upbeat pop. As Mike had already indicated the traffic on their route was heavier than expected. Jed spotted Greta out delivering her parcels, but she didn't see him. The rain had started as they drove which made Jed feel more depressed. He wondered if Miss Goodwin felt the same.

Eventually, they arrived at the crematorium and parked in one of the spaces. Around them other people were getting out of a range of cars, and very old land rovers, most of which looked like they had driven over fields to get there.

One particular mud-splatted car caught Jed's attention. A young man, ruddy-faced got out and looked around before heading off towards the entrance of the building. As he walked Jed spotted Miss Goodwin talking to a group of people who mostly looked like farmers. The young man joined the group and kissed Miss Goodwin on the cheek. Jed realised that she had blushed. He hoped fervently that this was someone who might be Miss Goodwin's much-longed-for farmer.

Jed, Kitty and Mike got out of the car and dashed over to the group. The rain started to get heavier and the group moved inside. The celebrant Jane, who had conducted Jed's mum's funeral was waiting for them.

"Hilda, welcome," she said with a polite smile and a handshake. Miss Goodwin shook Jane's hand and then started to introduce the people around her. As Jed had suspected, most of those attending were neighbours and friends of Gary and Millie.

"And this is Michael," said Miss Goodwin with a blush "He's a friend, his father owns most of Sussex".

462

"Not true" replied Michael with a genuine laugh "He's got a few acres to be sure"

One of the ladies Jed stood next to whispered to her husband "Earl of Stockton".

Jed decided he liked Michael. He seemed genuinely happy to be with Miss Goodwin, and she obviously liked him too. Miss Goodwin continued the introductions "and you know Jed, you conducted his mum's funeral"

Jane smiled warmly at Jed. "My you have grown since I last saw you," she remarked. "Lovely to see you, even under these circumstances." Jane turned to the group and said "The hearses are just arriving outside, can I ask that we go out and form two lines to see Gary and Millie in?"

The group moved outside and formed two lines on either side of the path. Several of the farmers removed their flat caps or hats, and the group waited as the two coffins were removed from the hearses and carried by the funeral team into the chapel.

Miss Goodwin then followed them in, each line, in turn, followed her, and began to take their seats. The two coffins were placed at the top of the room, flowers arranged in two vases nearby.

The funeral service was very similar in nature to the one Jed remembered from his mum's. Jed realised that Jane was very good at making these things personal. She had obviously spoken at length to both Miss Goodwin and others to get a very unique and uplifting picture of both Gary and Millie. Michael sat to one side of Miss Goodwin on the front row, and Jed realised that he was holding one of her hands, and passing her tissues when it was needed.

* * *

Miss Goodwin and Michael stood at the doorway saying personal goodbyes to each person who attended.

"There's a wake at Cherrywood, please come along if you can,"

Miss Goodwin said this to each person as she shook their hands or hugged them. Many of them nodded in agreement. As the last of the other people left, Jed, Kitty and Mike were left.

"And you three definitely need to come to Cherrywood for the wake. Hello Kitty it's lovely to meet you" said Miss Goodwin with a genuine smile as she held out her hand.

Jed noticed that Kitty was reluctant to shake hands, her bruise more defined than it had been the previous day. Miss Goodwin had also noticed her bruise but was polite to not comment on it. She did give Jed a concerned look which he tried not to notice. Mike and Jed shook hands with Michael. Jed noticed that Michael's hands were rough like Gary Goodwin's had been. Jed smiled, Miss Goodwin had found her farmer.

* * *

Back at Cherrywood the yard and the field adjacent were full of vehicles. Jed, Kitty and Mike walked into the kitchen which was a hive of activity. It looked like Miss Goodwin had rallied an army of farmers' wives and daughters to give her parents a great send-off. The kitchen was warm and cosy, with a range of tables set out with dishes of hot food, sandwiches, and crisps and one table in the corner almost bowed with a range of beer kegs, bottles of wine, soft drinks and glasses. The house was mostly empty, so people had brought their own picnic chairs which added to the atmosphere of a good party.

"We should have brought something" Jed exclaimed out loud,

"Nah lad " replied a tall woman who was carrying a platter of sausage rolls into the living room "The lasses have worked hard to send Gary and Millie off, you sit down over there and help yourselves. They won't want anything left, so make sure you get a box to take home".

Jed, Kitty and Mike sat down on chairs near the fire.
The rain had mostly stopped and the sunshine dappled
the net curtains in the window. The fire cracked in the
hearth, and the noise around them comforted Jed. He
knew this was likely the last time he would ever sit in
this farmhouse. Maybe the last time he would ever be
able to go and chat with his mum. Kitty was examining
a sandwich she had been offered before she shrugged
and started to eat it. Jed couldn't eat though. He
walked out to the kitchen where Miss Goodwin was
chatting with two of the ladies manning the Aga.

"Miss Goodwin, can I ask you something?" She turned
and saw the expression on his face

"Come on, Jed, let's go outside." Jed followed her. He
hated to be selfish but he needed to know. As they
walked to the old pig barn, Jed stopped.

"Will I be able to come back and see my mum?"

Miss Goodwin stopped too and looked at him. "The
farm is sold Jed, I couldn't save it. Mike Higgins didn't
want me to, but I insisted that the cherry orchard is not
disturbed, and the buyers have agreed to it"

Miss Goodwin looked up at the hill where the trees
were moving in the breeze.

"But this land will not be a farm, I'm sorry. The buyers want to build some nice houses, and it looks like the council will allow it. Mum and Dad's ashes will join your mum soon." Miss Goodwin sighed.

"But you have your farmer, don't you? Michael? Can't you continue?"

Miss Goodwin smiled. "Michael and I are together, but he's going to be inheriting a large estate when his dad dies. He won't be able to look after Cherrywood, I'm sorry Jed, really sorry". Miss Goodwin smiled "But the orchard survives, Jed, that is certain."

* * *

Jed and Miss Goodwin walked back into the kitchen. In the corner, by the aga, a young man was plucking a guitar. Kitty sat next to him, and whispered in his ear, he nodded and started to play a song Jed knew really well. Kitty sang one of her favourite tunes, 'Love That Will Never Grow Old'. Jed admired her voice, which he realised had got much huskier since they moved back to Exeter.

The farmers and their wives all stopped and listened to the lyrics which were appropriate for the couple they were all mourning. Jed realised that Gary and Millie were another mum and dad to him. They had treated him with kindness, he missed them terribly. Jed along with many others standing in the warm kitchen of Cherrywood Farm wept openly as Kitty's voice echoed around the room.

* * *

The wake went on till the early hours of the morning. Mike, Jed and Kitty finally left with boxes of food presented by one of Miss Goodwin's neighbours Tilly. Jed had talked to many of the people there, most of which knew him, through the Goodwins. Jed learned that Gary and Millie had often spoken of Jed to their friends, and he was glad to hear their stories.

"Got enough here to feed an army," Mike remarked as he loaded boxes into his car. Kitty was quiet again. She hadn't eaten much during the wake but had spoken to Miss Goodwin for a while.

"Thank you for coming, both of you," Jed said as he got into the car.

"Remarkable people" replied Mike. "my mate Simon and I have a lot to live up to making Gary and Millie's memorial crosses, but I reckon we can do them both proud. Your Miss Goodwin is lovely too. I can see why you care for her - eh Kitty?"

Kitty nodded but didn't reply. Jed looked at her, but she was staring out of the window. He didn't want to fight again, but he could see something wasn't right. Mike started the car, and carefully drove down the lane towards the road. Jed strained his head back to watch the hill and the trees.

"Back soon mum" he whispered.

* * *

Jed arranged to meet up with Katy, Sam and Ben the following day. As before he waited at the top of the road and when they left the school yard, they spotted him and managed to disappear before Charlie came out of the home's yard to wait for them. They sat in the same cafe catching up on the news.

"Ben's going to the sixth form," said Katy smiling "Maths and Physics, he wants to be a lab bunny" she mimicked a rabbit eating a carrot.

Ben groaned "Come on, I want to be a scientist" he added sipping his coke. "What about you both?" asked Jed indicating Sam and Katy.

"Katy's going to be a trainee office worker, filing paper clips and answering phones with Heloooooooo" Sam giggled as he imitated a posh voice.

Katy blushed. "I'm going to work in the planning office, one of my teachers knows the head of the department there"

"And I am going to be an apprentice mechanic in the local garage round the corner" announced Sam "One day a week at college, and I get paid too"

"Yeah, we will all need it when we are eighteen," Ben said gloomily

"Why? what happens at eighteen?" asked Jed.

"Charlie kicks us out," said Sam. "Council don't have to look after us anymore."

Jed was appalled "They can't DO that?"

471

Katy nodded sadly "They can, Mr Cooper came to see us all last week. We can get some benefits to help us find digs, but Exeter is expensive, so unless we can find cheap rooms, we all might have to move further out of the city".

Jed suddenly had an idea "Why don't you come and live in the squat when Charlie throws you out? It's warm enough, and it's right by the railway station."

Katy wrinkled her nose, but Jed could see the idea was starting to appeal to the others.

"Kitty and I will be moving out soon enough, so there will be plenty of room. Your teacher lives there too Thomas, Mr Matthews"

"Mr Matthews lives in the squat!?" said Sam almost choking on his drink.

"We'll think about it," said Katy, but he could tell she wasn't interested.

* * *

29

Scattered

Mike and his friend took over three weeks to make the memorial crosses for Gary and Millie. Jed occasionally asked after progress but Mike remained tight-lipped. "Soon lad, soon" he replied.

Finally, at breakfast, one morning Mike announced that the following day they would be going back to Cherrywood.

"Called Hilda last night," Mike said as he buttered a piece of toast " She's had her parent's urns back, and we are going back tomorrow afternoon. Simon and I finished the crosses late last night. Right proud of them, best work we've ever done".

Jed nodded then remembered "Kitty's working tomorrow".

Mike looked at Jed steadily "Hilda asked that just you and I come along"

"Why?" Jed asked worried "Doesn't she like Kitty?"

Jed remembered how quiet Kitty had been at the end of the wake. Kitty hadn't commented on the wake afterwards, but Jed knew something was wrong.

Mike shrugged "I think she just wants you there, and me because I helped make the crosses, sorry I don't know anything more".

Jed mused on the news all day, but he realised that he would have to speak to Miss Goodwin to find out. He decided to leave it, Miss Goodwin wanted him and Mike there, so that's what would happen.

* * *

Kitty didn't comment on Jed's news about the scattering when he saw her later. She had been quieter than normal, but Jed also knew she was missing him.

He had decided that from the following week he would move out of Mike and Cathy's flat back into the squat. There had been no further inspections from the council since the original visit, and Jed was now enrolled in the system. He would leave Mike's flat as his contact details, Mike had agreed to keep any mail for him.

Jed sat on the bed watching Kitty get dressed for her shift. The bruise on her wrist was fading now, but Jed realised she was also looking more tired.

"We should have enough for a deposit on a flat soon," he remarked. Kitty glanced at him and replied.

"One of the Athelstan Road ones is vacant. Sly had to evict a tenant for non-payment last week."

Jed didn't like the sound of that. "How did he evict them?"

"Legally" Kitty replied hotly "He didn't send the boys round, he got his solicitor to get possession through the courts. He's not stupid Jed"

Jed was concerned to hear Kitty defend her boss so forcefully

"OK, OK," he said putting up his hands in mock surrender "Just that every dodgy thing that happens in that club, Sly or his brother seem to be behind it".

Jed knew that this was a job he needed, he wouldn't be able to be at college with any other job, and not finishing his education meant even less choice. Jed was worried though. Jobs were one thing but also making your boss your landlord. It reminded him of a saying his mum had often used, about not putting all your eggs in one basket.

At the time, Jed had not realised what this meant, but now he realised that having both their jobs and their living arrangements through Sly and his brother, might not be a good idea. Still, he reasoned if things went wrong they could always move back to the squat again. Jed and Keith had become good friends since they had lived there. Jed sighed and replied

"OK then, can you ask Sly if we can look around the vacant apartment?" Kitty squealed in excitement and jumped onto the bed. Jed smiled back at her, but the niggling fear didn't leave him.

* * *

Mike picked Jed up the following day. It was another bright and cold day, the clouds rushing across the sky. Kitty had kissed Jed deeply and promised to ask Sly for a viewing of the apartment as soon as possible as he left.

Kitty's mood had improved since he had agreed to move out of the squat. He knew she didn't really like squat living, too many other people in the space and a limited amount of privacy and with him living with Mike, she was lonely he reasoned.

Jed leaned back and looked at the crosses carefully placed on the back seat of Mike's car. They were wrapped in bubble wrap but Jed could tell these were works of art in wood form.

"They look amazing," Jed remarked as he buckled up his seatbelt.

"Aye, they were a project alright" replied Mike "My mate did all the complicated bits but it was good to do something with my hands again. Hope Hilda likes them"

"Sure she will" Jed was certain that this was the truth. Miss Goodwin was waiting in the yard when they arrived. Her car Yogi was parked with mud splattered at one end.

"Hello," she said as they both got out. She held a spade in one hand. "Mum and Dad's urns are in the house"

"Hello Hilda," said Mike. He lifted out the bubble-wrapped crosses carefully and carried them into the farmhouse. Inside the kitchen, on the table, two large urns sat. There were no other pieces of furniture so the room seemed even bigger than before. Mike placed the crosses on the table at the other end to the urns. He nodded to the urns murmuring

"Gary" and

"Millie"

as he placed his hand over his heart. Jed noticed as did Miss Goodwin but neither remarked on it. Jed noticed Miss Goodwin looked like she had been crying.

Miss Goodwin carefully unwrapped the crosses. These were slightly different to the one her father had made for Jed's mum but Mike and his friend had also inscribed across the face.

Gary Charles Goodwin, born 3rd October 1944, died 18th October 2006 aged 62 years, together with his love always watching over Hilda

Millie Jessica Goodwin, born 12th September 1945, died 18th October 2006 aged 61 years, together with her love always watching over Hilda

Miss Goodwin touched the crosses and the beautiful script across each of them.

"Pops" she murmured and "Mamma". Her eyes filled with tears but as she looked up at Mike her smile was radiant. "They are simply perfect," she said. Mike blushed and Jed could tell he was also close to tears. "Thank you, and thank you to your friend."

* * *

They climbed the hill, Jed holding onto one of the crosses and Miss Goodwin holding onto the urns. Mike held the other cross in one hand, and the spade in the other hand. Miss Goodwin led them to the back of the orchard. Jed could see his mum's cross at the base of the cherry tree her urn was buried in. She stopped and carefully placed the urns on the ground.

"Here," she said pointing to the tree ahead of her "This is the best view of the valley, they can watch over the land" she turned to Jed "and be with your mum, is that OK?"

479

Jed nodded. He liked the idea of his mum having company, silly though it sounded. He knew his mum wasn't really there, like Gary and Millie, but their souls were linked to this beautiful place. Mike placed the cross on the ground, and Jed laid the other one next to it. Miss Goodwin handed Mike the spade

"One hole please, big enough for both of them" Mike started to dig through the turf at the bottom of the tree. He had started the hole not too close to the truck so the roots wouldn't be disturbed. After a short while, Miss Goodwin took up the spade and carried on. Jed watched as the hole became bigger and eventually Miss Goodwin stopped

"OK, that's big enough I think" She placed the spade on the floor. She then licked her finger and held it up "Wind from the south, stand back".

Mike and Jed complied moving behind her. Picking up the first of the urns, her fathers, carefully opened the lid and turned it slightly downwards. The silver-white ashes tumbled out of the urn and like Jed's mum's years before sparkled and moved in the breeze before landing on the tree.

"Bye Pops," she said softly. She turned and offered the urn to Jed. He took it and carefully shook it as more ashes came out

"Thank you for everything," he said. The ceremony made him sad and yet also contented. Mike had told Jed the previous night about rituals.

"Humans need them, it's more for those that are left than those who are gone. To say this person mattered".

Jed knew this to be true. Most people, not in the squat community wouldn't have known Jed's mum, but he remembered the more than twenty-eleven who came to say goodbye to his mum at the time. He remembered being happy so many people were there He handed the urn back to Miss Goodwin who passed it to Mike..

"You too Mike, they would have liked you a lot". Mike blushed but accepted the urn. He repeated the action Jed and Miss Goodwin had done, his scattering landing partly in the hole as the wind had started to fade.

"Hope you like the view Gary, thank you for being kind to Jed"

Jed could see tears on Mike's face as he turned back.

Jed and Miss Goodwin too were crying but it was more acceptance of the ritual. Once empty the first urn was placed in the hole. Miss Goodwin picked up the second urn, opened the lid and started to scatter the ashes of her mum.

Jed couldn't hear the words but he knew she was saying a difficult goodbye. He knew how much Miss Goodwin adored her parents, and her relationship with her mum had been especially warm and comforting to both of them. Miss Goodwin turned and handed Jed the urn. She took out a handkerchief and patted her eyes without comment. Jed walked forward and jerked the urn

"Thank you for the socks, hat and scarf and for the lovely welcome"

Jed heard a sob behind him. Mike had wrapped his arms around Miss Goodwin who was freely sobbing on his shoulder. Mike nodded to Jed to continue. He jerked the urn upwards and more ashes fell out onto the ground and the tree. He didn't feel the need to say anything more. He stood there with the urn for a while until he heard Mike behind him. Mike took the urn and finished the job.

He then placed the second urn into the hole. The size was perfect. Miss Goodwin stood, and Mike took up the spade again, starting to fill the hole with the dirt they had taken out. Miss Goodwin and Jed watched as the hole filled.

Eventually, the soil was in place. Miss Goodwin kneeled down and touched the soil "Bye Mum and Dad, I will miss you".

Mike picked up the first of the crosses and carefully set it just behind the hole, using the spade to drive it into the softened soil. He repeated the same action with the second one. Now the hole was filled, and the crosses in place, Jed knew that this place would always be something special to him, Three of the people in his life were here now. They were together but as they walked down the hill Miss Goodwin was actually the one who was scattered. She would not live here again. This troubled Jed so much

"Where are you going to live now?" Miss Goodwin smiled as they walked down to the yard

"Michael has got a lovely cottage not far from the city".

"Will you marry him?" Jed asked. It seemed important to know

"Jed, that's rude to ask a lady," said Mike who was walking in front of them

"It's OK" replied Miss Goodwin. She turned and took Jed's shoulders "I think he wants to, and if he asks I will say yes. My parents met him a couple of times, and mum, in particular, was very fond of him"

Jed was relieved to hear that Mr and Mrs Goodwin had approved of Miss Goodwin's man. He trusted their judgement and smiled.

"I hope he does soon" as they continued to walk down to the yard. She kissed Mike and Jed on the cheeks as they got back into the car. She had passed Mike her telephone number and he had done the same.

"Now make sure you pass your exams!" she added as Jed wound down the window to wave to her.

Jed watched as Miss Goodwin continued to wave as the car left the yard and wound its way down to the road. She looked smaller than he remembered last time. The weight of losing her parents in such an awful way. Jed watched the landscape change as they made their way back to the city. As Mike drove, Jed brought up the subject of the Athelstan Road apartment.

"Thought you were moving back to the squat?" Mike commented

"I was, but Kitty wants to move into a proper home, have a bathroom to herself, not be cold at night" Jed replied. "But the landlord is Sly Cetin"

"Your boss at the courier company?"

"Yeah"

"Is that a good idea?"

"That's my problem, Kitty can't see they are dodgy"

Jed had not mentioned the special deliveries to Mike, he knew as soon as he did, Mike would stop him working there, though he also knew that Kitty was becoming addicted to the easy money working in the casino as entertainment. Mike would have no influence on Kitty, she had not warmed to Mike as much as Jed had hoped for.

He knew that Mike knew about Sly and Emir, he worked in the building industry and a few of his acquaintances in the pub had come off worst when they had done work for the brothers on their new properties, then chased for months for payment.

One night Mike had told Jed that a friend was over six thousand pounds down for a job that had taken several weeks. Eventually, the friend gathered a few mates and made a stand in the casino one night. Mike said that the look that Sly had given his friend as he reluctantly took the cash out of his safe had made him realise that the Cetin brothers were bad news.

"Len said, there were piles of cash in the safe, I know casinos have a lot of cash, but that was a LOT of cash"

Jed hadn't replied but in his mind, he knew how much worse Sly and Emir actually were.

"Well, you will always have a place at ours, and I am sure that Keith could find you a bed if you were stuck. He really likes you, Jed" Jed was reassured to hear Mike confirm his hopes.

"We taking your stuff to the squat now?"

"Please" replied Jed.

"And I expect you need a hand getting yours and Kitty's stuff in your new place when it's ready?" Mike smiled. "I'll borrow my mate's van, just let me know when you want it done?" Cathy was waiting at the flat when Mike and Jed arrived home.

"I've made you dinner Jed, a final meal, hope that's OK?"

"Oh love, it smells wonderful" replied Mike "Your special dinner - chicken wrappies?"

Cathy nodded and smiled. Mike strode over to her and twirled her around making her giggle. Jed knew what this dinner was - Chicken Fajitas but he also knew that Mike couldn't remember that name, so Chicken wrappies became its new name.

Jed loved that Mike and Cathy had their own language, like Mr and Mrs Goodwin, easy companionship bonded with love. As they sat down and started to prepare their own meals from the bowls and dishes Cathy had set out, Jed and Mike told Cathy about the day.

"It sounds to me a perfect goodbye" Cathy remarked as she added sour cream to her fajita. Jed thought for a moment, his fajita almost full to bursting then replied

"Yes, it really was. Mike's crosses were perfect." Cathy smiled at Mike

"Not just a pretty face then, you fix cars, make lovely wooden crosses, oh and sometimes you take your turn with the washing up".

"Is that a hint" laughed Mike as he helped himself to another wrap.

"I'll help," said Jed.

"Good man" laughed Mike, you can scrub the frying pan, Cathy always leaves it in a mess" Cathy laughed and pretended to throw her fajita at him before chowing down on it instead

"Can't waste good food?" she remarked. They finished the meal with more banter before Jed and Mike took the dishes into the small kitchen.

"Thank you," Jed said "for everything"

"Aww lad, you know I'm always there for you, Cathy too. If things don't work out, you can always come back here"

"I know, but Kitty and I need our own space now, a proper home, like yours"

* * *

30

Athelstan Road

Things moved quickly once Kitty told Sly they were interested in the apartment. Keith was cooking a curry, and Jed was helping cut up the onions. Keith shot Jed a bemused look as Kitty grabbed Jed by the hand and led him outside, her eyes shining.

"We can move in next week, Sly said our deposit was enough, that he trusts us not to muck the place over" Jed was surprised, but he knew this was the next logical step for them.

"Mike's offered to move our stuff, shall we say Saturday, we can get most of the stuff moved before your afternoon shift at the casino?" Kitty nodded at the door, Keith was standing there with a tea towel in his hands

"You are helping mate? " asked Keith wiping his hands but he was smiling.

"Sorry Keith, we've just had word our flat will be ready next week" Jed replied "We're out of here next weekend"

Keith nodded then added "Onions need more chopping" as he returned to the kitchen.

Jed laughed and then followed Keith back inside the kitchen. Kitty's mood was lifted for the next few days. She spent time looking through their possessions and finding household items in the local charity shops during her free time. Their area of the squat started to look like a charity shop by the weekend. Keith found some spare plates, cutlery, and cups for them.

"Only fair, you gave us all that food when you arrived," he remarked. Jed wondered about Mr Singh and his little shop and the others in the London squat. He had written to Mr Singh a few weeks after they had arrived back in Exeter, telling him all their news. He had received a long reply back, including the comment that Charlie had revisited Mr Singh's shop only to be escorted out by Mr Singh's young grandson 'who had been a kick-boxer for years'. Jed had laughed out loud to hear Charlie being put in his place. Jed decided there was enough news including the sad ending to Cherrywood for another letter. There was good news too, including Jed now taking his GCSEs at college.

Jed's first evening classes happened a few days before their move to Athelstan Road. Jed was going to be studying or at classes for most of the week, coinciding with Kitty's shifts at the casino.

Mike had helped out with the costs as Jed was still only managing a few courier shifts each week, though thankfully none of the special deliveries seem to happen during these. Mr Barker had spoken to his colleagues in the DHSS and was in the process of arranging a limited grant to assist him with college expenses.

Kitty seemed distracted as Jed was packing up his textbooks and finding enough snacks in their cupboard in the kitchen area to tide him over for the evening.

"Wish me luck?" Jed asked hopefully. Kitty looked up from her mirror, she looked more beautiful without makeup, but Jed had learned not to comment on this.

"Good luck," she said standing up to kiss him "Go get them tiger" she added.

Jed smiled and hefted his rucksack onto one shoulder.

* * *

Joseph was waiting in the foyer of the college looking at a pinboard as Jed arrived. He turned and smiled at Jed broadly

"Hey man!" said Joseph "You passed too" He turned to the pinboard and said, "We're in the same classes room 6A top floor I think".

Jed checked the pinboard, and yes the classroom was 6A.

"Better follow you I think" Jed commented with a grin. Joseph laughed but Jed was right, Joseph led them to the correct room after a brief glance at the college room map on the pinboard. The room was bright and well-lit, and there were five other students waiting. The desks had been arranged not in the traditional rows Jed remembered from school, but in a semi-circle facing the blackboard. Standing next to the blackboard was a familiar face

"Thomas" Jed exclaimed laughing. "You teaching evening classes?"

Thomas smiled and walked over to Jed. "Didn't want to say just in case you weren't in my class but yes, don't get enough of teaching kids in the day." Thomas turned to the rest of the class. "This is a friend from our digs Jed Long, and..."

Joseph announced "Joseph Wojcik".

Thomas then pointed at the rest of the group,

"Now the rest of you, please introduce yourselves. "

The rest of the group shuffled their feet under their desks but eventually, a dark-haired girl started with

"I'm Mandy Willis" she blushed hard and then looked at the blond girl next to her "Sarah Philips"

The rest of the group were Kenny Young a stout youth who smelled of tobacco, Laura Inges who smiled at Joseph constantly and Gary Hill who had a pair of crutches beside him and a cast on one foot "Broke my ankle tripped down a curb running for the bus" he added as an intro. "Wanted to say I was skydiving but it was more embarrassing than that".

"Right that's the ice breaker, now comes the work. All of you are here to get your GCSEs, some of you didn't do so well at school, but here, that doesn't matter. You are all taking four exams by the end of next year."

Kenny groaned "I didn't know that"

Thomas smiled and continued

"The first ones will happen next June, so we have just over eight months of work before these happen. You will find some of the work difficult, but I am here to explain and ensure you get what you came for. I do expect homework to be done, some of the exams are partly marked on coursework English Language, and 40% of the end grade comes from the coursework you will complete"

Thomas stood and picked up some sheets of paper from the desk and handed them out.

"This is your timetable, you will be here three evenings a week, Monday, Wednesday, and Thursday. Monday is English Language, Tuesday will be Maths, and Thursday will be English Literature. Any questions?"

No one replied, all were looking at the timetables.

"Right then, English Language books and course books out please"

* * *

Jed felt quite exhausted by the end of the first lesson which lasted an hour. He realized that his grasp of the English Language was not great, but he could see Joseph was dealing with the work and Jed felt that he should try.

The first part of the course dealt with creative writing. The first lesson dealt with the construction of a story, Thomas explained the basics, and at the end of the lesson, he announced.

"Your homework for next week is to prepare a short story about a place you have explored, it must have a beginning, middle, and an end, and needs to be constructed as we discussed, I will see you back here on Wednesday evening for English Literature. Tomorrow you will have maths with my colleague Rachel. She is an accountant but has been teaching maths at evening classes for a while"

Jed and Joseph walked out of the room together. "What are you going to write about?" asked Joseph.

"Not sure, probably the twenty eleven" replied Jed who then realized Joseph had stopped.

"Twenty-eleven, what is this?" asked Joseph puzzled.

Jed explained about the twenty-eleven as they made their way down to the lobby where the caretaker was waiting to close the building.

"And you lived in there, a big squat?"

"I still do, for now, a different one, but my girlfriend doesn't really like it, she wanted us to have our own place, so we are moving to Athelstan Road next weekend"

"It sounds amazing" replied Joseph, "Mum makes me help her with chores before I can use my computer".

Jed laughed "You've got it, good mate, you often have to wear multiple layers and a coat, and hat and scarf in the squat, any heating limited, food, well you have to earn money to buy it."

"and you work as a courier?" Joseph asked, "What's that like? Have they got any vacancies?"

Jed stopped suddenly "I can't recommend them, Joseph, they are not good people. I'm only working there because my girlfriend is their singer in the casino, and it helps me to keep a good eye on them, they are gangsters, criminals - do you understand?"

"Gangsterzy, przestępcy, gangsters, criminals, yes I know those words" Joseph replied solemnly.

"I need to get my qualifications, so I can get a better job, and get Kitty away from them, that's my plan" Jed added.

* * *

The day of their move to Athelstan Road dawned bright and cold. Jed was busy in the kitchen packing up the last of their things whilst Kitty located their laundry

"Hello"

Jed turned around to see Mike & Cathy

"Thought you could use an extra pair of hands,?" said Cathy who was wearing one of Mike's work overalls "Think I rock these better than he does" Mike laughed

"You all sorted?" "Nearly" replied Jed "Kitty's in the laundry room, she's looking for my odd socks"

Kitty walked in with a limp black sock in her hand

"Found this behind the washing machine, there's a pair of Thomas's boxers down there too" she shuddered "I put those back in the washing machine pronto" Kitty smiled at Mike and Cathy "Thanks for helping, it is a pain when you don't have a driving license for this sort of thing"

Mike smiled back but Jed noticed Cathy appraising Kitty carefully. Cathy caught Jed's eye and smiled but her eyes were not smiling. Jed made a note to ask Cathy what was wrong when they were all done.

The move took a few hours, Kitty was stationed at the new flat, whilst Jed, Mike, and Cathy brought boxes and other possessions from the squat to the new place in the borrowed van.

When all their items were in the new place, Mike offered to go and get fish and chips. Cathy went with him, which gave Jed a chance to sit down on one of their chairs. Kitty had found the table and chairs in one of her 'charity shop raids' The chairs were battered but useable and the table only needed cleaning to make it look good.

Kitty rummaged in a box picking out their second-hand kettle, cups, and tea bags, before setting them out on the kitchen counter. She waved the tea bag jar at him "Brew?"

Jed groaned "I forgot, didn't get any milk this morning"

Kitty smiled and plucked a small container from the same box "Got some this morning, whilst you were still sleeping"

Jed laughed "Up early? you?"

Kitty turned back to the counter

"Couldn't sleep, still buzzing from last night"

Jed knew that Kitty couldn't sleep well on her working nights. She had explained that working in the casino, with all the noise, and lights meant she struggled to fall asleep afterward. Jed had gotten used to Kitty getting up in the night and not coming back to bed for hours. Once he got up himself wanting a drink of water, he found her reading in the kitchen, the harsh overhead light highlighting her features. She had developed dark circles under her eyes and had taken to applying even more makeup to disguise them.

When Mike and Cathy returned with the meal, it reminded Jed of how he had first found Kitty in London. The smell of the chips, hot and oily with salt and vinegar in the paper made his mouth water. He hadn't realized how hungry he was. They ate out of the paper, in companionable silence.

"Can't beat a good brew" announced Mike as he picked up his mug of tea. "Cheers to you both, may you make happy memories here"

Cathy, Jed, and Kitty raised their mugs and clinked them together like champagne glasses. Jed silently hoped this would be the case.

* * *

Mike and Cathy left them after the food. Jed looked at the boxes surrounding them with dismay.

"Tell you what, why don't you go and have a lie-down, and I'll get started on some of these?" Kitty said with a wink.

Jed decided that this was a good idea. The flat came with a basic sofa and bed included in the rental. He wandered into the small bedroom, noticing that Kitty had made the bed up, their pillows and duvet looked inviting. He sank back onto the bed and sighed happily. He closed his eyes and was asleep in moments.

Kitty waited for a while, making a small amount of noise but not enough to disturb Jed. When she was sure he was asleep, she carefully picked up her purse, and coat and left the flat. As she walked down the communal stairs and out into the street, she put on her coat and walked down towards the city centre.

* * *

Mike dropped Cathy off at the hospital after leaving Jed. "Thanks for helping, especially before your shift," said Mike kissing Cathy before she left the van.

"My pleasure, Jed's a lovely lad, now scoot before the traffic warden spots you" she replied before closing the passenger side door and waving him off. She turned and was about to go into the main door of the hospital but spotted Kitty on the other side of the busy road. She had not seen them arriving, and was walking swiftly.

Cathy watched as Kitty crossed the junction and was standing near the bus stop further up the road. As Cathy watched a sleek Jaguar car pulled up next to Kitty and beeped its horn. Cathy saw Kitty smile and get into the car. Cathy wondered what was going on, but she realized she would have to leave this for later, otherwise, she was going to be late for her shift.

* * *

31

Protection

Cathy decided to tell Mike about her spotting Kitty getting into a car shortly after they had left the Athelstan Road apartment. Cathy was pragmatic but this strange behaviour of Kitty's was starting to disturb her. Although Jed wasn't truly her son, she like Mike had come to love and protect him. Mike had picked her up after her shift ended, and as he drove them through the traffic she explained the strange sighting.

"And she got into the car?"

Cathy nodded. "I recognised the driver too, it's that casino owner Sly, the one that Kitty and Jed both work for. My friend occasionally works in A & E and a few times punters from the casino end up in there. One of them, an American was shouting about some 'Turkish tosser' who had bodily thrown him out of the club."

Mike was disturbed to hear about Jed's boss. Like many of his friends he had been aware of the Cetin brothers and their activities. Once of Mike's friends had also been thrown out of the casino a few years ago.

"We're going to have to keep an eye on Jed, you know that right Cathy?"

Cathy nodded. "He's nearly an adult Mike, but I agree, these people are bad news and I'm not convinced of Kitty any more. She's changed, she's got harder, since they first got back"

* * *

Jed was blissfully unaware of Kitty's strange behaviour for a couple of days. All Jed could see was how happy Kitty was now she had her own space. Kitty spent a lot of time setting out her purchases from the charity shops, moving the chairs and table around until she was happy. Jed spent his time at home studying for his exams sat at the table with his books around him.

Jed had hoped the privacy of their own space might revive their romance again, but Kitty made excuses first being tired from her shifts, then her period, then in the end Jed stopped asking. She was still affectionate with him, kissing his head on waking up after her afternoon naps, but the romance was dwindling. Jed was puzzled but he hoped things would get better.

On the second evening after they moved into the apartment Jed had arranged for Joseph to come and visit to have an evening of revision. Jed had mentioned it to Kitty who had shrugged and said

"I'm at work this evening, knock yourself out"

Jed was hurt at her tone. He knew she was working but thought she might have been interested in knowing Joseph was coming over.

"Your attitude stinks!" he said angrily" You wanted this place, a space for us, and you spend barely any time here bar sleeping."

Kitty looked mute, but Jed was furious.

"What's going on with you?" Jed grabbed Kitty's arm but she twisted away from him. Suddenly Jed realised that Kitty had been wearing long sleeved tops again. He grabbed her arm again and pushed the fabric up her arm before she could stop him

"Let me go!" she yelled trying to get away. Jed stared at her arm. In the crook of the elbow was a yellowing bruise. He realised that he could make out parts of the bruise which looked like finger marks , suddenly he realised someone had wrenched Kitty's arm.

"Who did this?" Jed was stunned. "Another punter?".

Kitty started to weep and collapsed on the nearest chair. Jed was mortified at his actions but he realised something very bad was going on.

"Tell me" he said softly. Kitty continued to weep not looking at him, her dreadlocks almost covering her face.

"It's not important" she sobbed.

"It is, who hurt you Kitty?"

Kitty didn't reply for a long while but eventually she looked up at him. Her face was pale and her eyes were red from crying. She carefully pulled down her sleeve over the bruise.

"It was Sly"

"He hurt you? The bastard. Why? Tell me or I am going round there?" Kitty looked frightened. Jed realised that this was serious.

"Why did he hurt you?"

The story Kitty told made Jed go cold with fear. Kitty had been working her normal shift and was on a break. She kept her bag in the main office where Kim was normally working and needed to grab a headache tablet. She had popped out of the main casino room and knocked on the office door. No one replied.

She opened the door to find Sly slumped in a chair and his brother Emir hunched over the desk. Emir was snorting cocaine from a line laid out on the desk. Kitty had tried to reverse back out but Emir spotted her

"Oh come in my child" he said. Kitty shook her head

"Just here to grab my bag, got a headache" Sly then looked up and swiftly grabbed Kitty's arm before she could get to her bag and get out.

"Got something much better than paracetamol for you. Makes you fly chickie"

"I said no thanks" Kitty continued. "Emir was looking like he wanted a fight.. I saw my bag behind the chair Sly was slumped in, then just grabbed it and ran. Kim was coming out of the ladies, so I told her. She said not to mention it to anyone but she looked scared too. She let me go early, and gave me this" Kitty pulled out a wad of cash from her pocket. "£300, told me not to talk. I just never knew they were on drugs"

"I did" Jed replied. "Not that they were taking them, but their courier business. It's a front for drug distribution"

"How?"

Jed sighed. "We need to have a talk". Jed brought Kitty up to speed on what he knew about Sly and Emir. "Kim's in on it too, but she isn't happy about the risks the brothers are taking."

"I think they are selling in the casino too" Kitty said
"There's a private room at the back of the main casino.
I've seen some of the high rollers head back there.
Emir never let any of the wait staff go in, they would
have to leave the drinks outside on a table. I was
walking by one time, and the door was slightly ajar, I
could see two of the punters got handed a small packet
by Sly. The door closed before I could see any more."

Jed was more scared than he had ever been before.

"We're in deep shit" he said "We both work for them,
they are our landlords too. Why were you so keen to
move here, knowing what you did?"

"I thought they would be kind to us, Sly gave over a
protective air, said he didn't want his singing star to be
in a slum, as he called it but this" Kitty indicated her
arm "told me that we know more than they want us to
and that makes us dangerous to them. I can't see a way
out"

Kitty started to sob again. Jed pulled her up and into
his arms, stroking her dreadlocks softly.

"We can beat them"

"How?"

"Evidence. We keep a record of what's going on, then hide it away. If they cause us trouble we tell them the authorities will have it. "

"Blackmail?" Kitty looked more scared.

"Protection for us" Jed replied. "But we can't tell anyone. We have to make a plan and quickly". Kitty was reluctant to go to work that evening, but Jed explained that they had to behave normally.

"What's normal about this?"

Jed nodded "I know Kitty but you have to try. They would expect you to be nervous and will likely try and reassure you. Keep Kim close and make sure that you aren't alone with them" Jed reached into his pocket "This is my locker key for the courier room, use that to keep your bag in for the time being. There are loads of people around in that area since Sly increased the shifts for the couriers so you should be OK"

Kitty took the locker key which had the number 6 marked on a tag attached. She put it into her jeans pocket.

"OK, then tomorrow when I wake, we can start to plan our protection?"

Jed smiled and nodded.

"I love you, and we can beat them".

Jed drew Kitty close. He wasn't so sure but he knew he had to try.

* * *

Joseph arrived at the apartment on time, bringing crisps and other snacks.

"Food for the brain" he announced as he waved the packets at Jed as he opened the door.

Jed tried to behave normally but Joseph realised that something was up. Jed didn't want to involve anyone else in this especially his friends or Mike and Cathy, so he just shrugged and said

"Women trouble" which sufficed. Joseph had also been having girlfriend troubles and like many young men of their generation, they didn't share their feelings with each other. Joseph was impressed with the apartment.

"Wow this is cool" he remarked as he looked out of their window, the view over the city impressing him enormously.

Jed tried to be enthusiastic but his mind was distracted by wondering whether he and Kitty would be here in a few months time.

The rest of the evening passed quickly. Joseph had a better grasp of Maths than Jed did, and Jed had a better understanding of both English Language and Literature, so each was able to assist the other.

By the end of the evening Jed realised that the work had distracted him from worrying about Kitty. He decided he would collect her from her shift each evening so Emir and Sly could see she wouldn't be walking home alone.

"Sorry mate, I have to go and collect Kitty from her shift, can we do this again on the weekend?"

They made plans for Joseph to come over again on Saturday afternoon. Joseph and his mum lived in a tiny flat which didn't have as much room. Joseph collected his coat and waited for Jed to find his keys and coat before they walked out onto the landing. Jed locked the front door and then walked down with his friend onto the street. Joseph set off towards his home, and Jed walked the other way to the casino. He glanced at his watch, as he walked.

Plenty of time.

* * *

Jed arrived at the front door of the casino as a group of men were leaving. A couple of them were drunk and unsteady on their feet, being supported by some of the more sober ones. Jed could see Kim and Sly standing in the foyer watching them leave. Jed knew he couldn't enter on the evenings as this would attract too much attention. He still looked younger than his age, though he would soon be seventeen, and he was starting to get taller at last.

Jed caught Kim's eye and waved to her. She nodded back but Jed realised that she still looked scared. He wasn't surprised, working for the two brothers must put her in jeopardy every day, and their extravagant plans for the drugs business must be putting them in the authorities radar too, surely?

Just as this thought crossed his mind, he saw another group leave the casino room. These people however got the full charm treatment from Sly and Kim. There were three men all dressed in suits, though their ties were adrift and their shirts had several buttons undone. As the door opened for others to leave Jed heard Sly say to the tallest man

"Chief Constable Matthews , it is wonderful you could join us for the evening, I hope our tables were fair to you and your colleagues?"

The man seemed slightly embarrassed by Sly's booming voice which was attracting attention, but he smiled politely.

Sly then showed them out of the foyer just as Kitty appeared from the courier room. She had her bag with her, which meant that she had used Jed's key. Kim had also noticed Kitty's arrival from the courier room but didn't comment as there were more people to speak to.

514

Jed suddenly realised than the man Sly was fawning over was the head of the police for the county. Jed had seen his photo in the local papers that summer during a hearing into a corruption scandal involving officers across the county.

Sly had the police in his pocket, or certainly was giving out favours to the head people in the police. Kitty followed the Chief Constable out of the foyer and was delighted to see Jed waiting for her. Smiling she came over and hugged him fiercely. Just as they were about to leave Sly said in a loud voice

"See you tomorrow Kitty!"

Kitty turned and managed a wide innocent smile and wave before she grabbed Jed's arm and hissed "Get me out of here"

Jed obliged also turning and adding a wave and a smile to Sly as he went.

* * *

32

The Plan

As promised the following afternoon Kitty awoke and after she had finished her toast and tea, Jed cleared the table and they started to plan. Jed had plenty of notebooks thanks to the grant organised by Mr Barker and the council. He decided to lay out what they knew of the network first on a large sheet of paper.

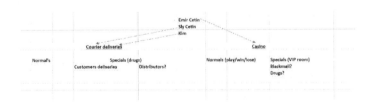

Kitty appraised the sheet.

"Blackmail?"

Jed pointed at the sheet

"Anyone going in that VIP room, I think is being lined up for doing favours for the brothers. They had the Chief Constable in there yesterday along with a load of his mates, possibly not police but I bet influential. I could see Emir and Sly perhaps videoing bad behaviour, drug taking, groping the staff etc.. and then being asked to 'do a favour' with the threat of these being made public. You've told me already that there are drugs being sold or even given away in that room."

"And the courier side, you know that better than I do"

"Exactly, I've thought about it, Kim's definitely involved though I think she is also under threat as well. She's been looking more and more stressed as time has gone on, but I don't think we can excuse her either."

"How are the specials split?"

"By size mostly I think. Some of the packets are more like small but well packed envelopes. The other factor is how keen the customer is to see me. The ones like the girl I mentioned, who walked out in bare feet hardly wearing any clothes and was almost beatific when she saw the packet I pulled out of my bag. However the guy in Temple Road, think he was a distributor. He was less frantic about the delivery but it obviously meant more to him than some random legal papers, as Kim was trying to tell me it was"

Kitty sat back in the chair.

"Right onto the detail then".

Using another sheet of paper they plotted the timeline of things they had observed, and then made detailed notes in two separate notebooks. They then made another copy of the network onto a new sheet of paper.

"I can keep one of these in my locker at the college, and update them both as we find more evidence. If Sly or Emir find one, we still have the other one."

"I know where we can put the other one" Kitty said as she stood up. In the corner of the room was a large Swiss cheese plant. Jed had laughed at Kitty when she brought it home but he was intrigued as she pulled up the plant.

"It's plastic!" she announced. "But it looks real with soil on it."

Beneath the plant inside the pot was a large brown wooden box sitting on top of the rest of the soil.

"I thought this might be good to hide money and stuff but" she picked up one of the notebooks and placed it into the box "this is a much use for it".

She put the plant back down and rearranged the soil.

"Ta dah!" Jed was impressed. He looked at the pot. There was no sign that anything other than a plant was inside it.

* * *

Each week both Jed and Kitty added information to the notebook hidden inside the plant pot. Jed then took the notebook with him to college and updated it in his break times during his evening classes. Joseph had been keen to know what Jed was doing but he managed to avoid any conversations after Jed mentioned it was a notebook about memories of his mum. Jed hated to lie to Joseph who was becoming a good friend, but he didn't want to drag anyone else into this mess.

Jed and Kitty were well aware that Sly had a key to their apartment and as the landlord he had previously told them he did 'spot inspections' to make sure the place wasn't being trashed. Kitty was sure that Sly had been in their apartment on at least two occasions over the months they had been living there though she and Jed were out at the time.

Kitty had draped a scarf casually over the plant which had not been disturbed. She had also left a coat on a nearby chair so the scarf just looked like a casual draping rather than a deliberate bid to see if the plant and its content was discovered.

* * *

33

Discovered

Jed's worst nightmare started on a beautiful day. He was studying in the courier room whilst waiting for his next round. Greta had just left for her second round, and there was only one other courier in the room. Kim came into the room, she looked both scared and angry.

"Can you come into the office please Jed?"

Jed looked at her and realised that something was very wrong indeed. He shrugged and got up, leaving a piece of paper in the book he was reading. As he followed her back into the courier Kim hissed

"You are a fucking idiot Jed".

Jed didn't have a change to ask her what she meant as he saw Sly and Emir were both standing by the office door. Neither of them looked happy. Jed tried to smile but his face showed his concern, which seemed to please Sly in particular. Jed knew he was a sociopath and a bully. He managed to ask as he was ushered into the office

"What's wrong?"

Kim stayed outside as Sly closed the door after Jed had gone inside. That was another worrying sign. Kim had always been in charge of the couriers so for her not to be involved in whatever this was, was very bad news.

"Sit down Jed" Emir said indicating a chair in front of the desk.

Jed complied. He waited. The experience of being involved with social services had taught Jed not to speak to fill the silence. He placed his hands in his lap and looked at Emir. Emir glanced at Sly then sat down. Jed knew that Sly was standing blocking the door out into the casino.

"What are you up to Jed?"

Jed shrugged "Learning, working, sleeping"

Emir's face got the "chewing wasp" look.

Jed added quickly "What's wrong ? What have I done? Missed a delivery?"

He tried not to panic. He realised that they were suspicious though he couldn't fathom how they could know how he and Kitty were tracking the drug business and other criminal activity they had become aware of.

Emir sighed heavily.

"One of your last deliveries didn't arrive. Temple Road. The recipient said he never got his parcel on Monday. I checked the signature sheet, and you did get a signature for it. Therefore I want to be sure before I go back to the customer to explain his error, that you did hand over the packet to him at" Emir consults a sheet "15.32 pm"

Jed quickly realised that the occupant of Temple Road was trying it on. He tried not to breathe out too quickly but smiled.

"Yes, I did hand it over, he was wearing a grey tee shirt, looked like he had a curry as most of it was down the front of it"

Emir looked over at Sly and nodded. Jed turned to see Sly leaving the office. Kim was outside still. She looked very worried until Sly nodded at her. She glanced in at Jed and tried to smile but it didn't reach her eyes.

"So is that all?" Jed asked Emir.

Emir looked at him for a moment "Yes, thank you Jed. I did tell Sly that you are not a criminal , you have a good work ethic, and that this was a mistake on the part of our customer. Sly is going to explain to him that we are not taking responsibility for this error, and he needs to look in his rather messy home for the parcel he did receive".

Jed's blood went cold at this news. He knew the drug dealer was probably going to be very badly beaten up, possibly killed. He also knew that it was likely that his death or injury would need to go into the notebook at some time.

Jed stood up and left the office. Kim was talking to one of the barmen so Jed managed to avoid her on his return into the courier room. He couldn't concentrate on his books, but needed to give the impression that this event wasn't worrying him. He picked up his book and tried to read.

* * *

Jed was waiting for Kitty after her session that evening. Jed was starting to get paranoid about their apartment now, so he pulled Kitty towards a cafe which was still open just down the road.

"Jed, I'm really tired"

Kitty complained, but when she saw his face she stopped whinging, and followed him down to the back of the cafe. Jed went up to the counter and ordered two coffees, before sitting down again.

"We have more trouble"

He brought her up to speed on the events of the afternoon. Kitty's eyes filled with tears but she managed to keep calm.

"They will kill him" she said softly.

"He's likely to die yes, but it's made me realise just how evil the two of them are. We can only watch and wait, and document it all. The idiot tried to scam them. Either he's trying to skim the delivery or has lost it or had it stolen maybe? Anyway, I need to be certain I get a signature for each and every parcel or packet I deliver, otherwise they might look to me".

Kitty's expression showed her fear, but as their coffees arrived she managed a bright smile and "Thank you" to the cafe assistant who brought them. They waited until the assistant walked back behind the counter.

"Any more from the casino?" Jed asked. Kitty took a sip of her coffee before shaking her head. "Been pretty quiet these last few shifts"

* * *

34

A slippery slide to hell

Jed was asleep when Kitty came into the apartment. Over the previous few days she had been happy to walk home alone. Jed's workload at the courier and his studies had increased dramatically and he was often in bed before she got home.

She had always been careful not to wake him, but this evening he could hear her stumbling around, at one point knocking into the table which Jed heard her grunt in pain. He got out of bed, his tee shirt creased from sleep and opened the bedroom door. Kitty was sitting on the sofa but Jed could see her eyes were not focused. As he got closer he could smell alcohol on her.

"You're drunk!" he said not amused.

Kitty giggled "A teeny tiny one"

"Who gave you that? You're underage. Kim? Sly? A customer?"

Kitty giggled again. "Sly" she said carefully trying to make her words clear "We had a drink after my shift, he wanted me to try a new cocktail he was going to be putting in the bar. He was asking me about my life. He didn't tell me it had" she lifted her hands and put them far apart "This much alcohol in it. He gave me a lift home".

Jed stared at his girlfriend in dismay

"I'm sorry Jed"

Kitty said trying to focus her sight on him. She tried to stand and walk to the bathroom, but her legs gave way under her.

"Gonna be sick" she moaned as she tried to stand again. Jed grabbed her and managed to get her into the bathroom pulling back her dreadlocks so she could vomit down the toilet.

Jed was dismayed at Kitty's behaviour. Jed had been clear that they couldn't relax around the brothers, simply for the risk of letting them know that they were being tracked and watched. And here Kitty was drinking so much that she couldn't stand. He knew Sly was to blame though. Another reason to hate the brothers.

Kitty slept through to the afternoon once she had brought up the toxic alcohol. Jed had put her to bed with a washing up bowl next to her pillow in case she needed to be sick again. Jed had spent the night on the sofa, but he hadn't managed to get any sleep. He realised he need to make more plans than they already had.

* * *

The opportunity came the following day. Jed was at college and he was in Thomas's class. After the lesson Jed stopped behind to talk to his friend.

"What's up Jed" Thomas asked noticing his friends worried expression.

"Can I tell you something in confidence?" Jed asked.

Thomas sat down on the desk and nodded. "Course you can"

"Even though it involves crime?"

Thomas frowned "You're involved in crime?"

Jed shook his head. "No but we know about crimes that are going on, me and my girlfriend. We can't tell the police, once I tell you you will understand why".

Thomas looked at his watch.

"I've got a free period now. Better come and get a coffee and tell me"

Thomas and Jed walked down to the canteen. Most of the students and staff were now gone, it was after nine pm. Thomas pulled some change out of his pocket and asked

"Coffee or tea, actually it's pretty much the same"

Jed opted for coffee. Thomas went to the vending machine in the corner and fed in some coins, returning to the table Jed was sitting at with two plastic cups of drink. Jed sipped his before starting to tell his story. He went to his locker and brought back the note book and chart he had been talking about. He laid out the sheet of paper. Thomas frowned

"This is serious stuff Jed, you could be, in the eyes of the law, a part in all of this"

Jed was dismayed to hear this from Thomas but he had also been thinking the same himself. Kitty was already distressed at how Sly and Emir had changed in the time she had been working at the casino, so Jed decided not to pass this knowledge on. Thomas studied the book.

"This is in your locker here, at the college?" Jed nodded "And you have another one at home hidden" Jed nodded again. "That's wise Jed" Thomas sat back and sipped his coffee. "I can only think of one person in the police I trust completely her name is Kim Turner WPC Turner. She was the one who worked out you had gone to London when you ran away from the home. She hates the Cetin brothers as she has to deal with the fall out of their operation, the people they beat up, and in the past the girlfriends who have complained about Sly. I can show her this and see if she can pass the information up the chain?"

Jed thought for a moment. "She is clean I am sure, but seeing the Chief Constable and his cronies in the casino the other night, I think the Cetin brothers have people on the inside. Actually what I was hoping was if something happened to us, to me and Kitty, you could pass this onto her. It's insurance you see." Jed knew this was the best way.

"If you are in that much danger Jed, you need to tell Kim, she can help you"

"She cant protect us Thomas, we know that. If the brothers think that we have information on them, without you knowing about it, its useless. And they could threaten Mike, Cathy, our friends in the squat. Now that you know where one of the books is, and you can get to it easily" Jed took out his locker key. "The college issued two keys, you have one" Jed plucked off the key and held it out to Thomas.

Thomas looked at Jed. The young boy Thomas had known in the squat was turning into a man. He took the key and waved it

"Any trouble, you get out, get to the squat OK? We can protect you." Jed nodded but he knew it was already too late for that. He knew he couldn't get his friends involved any more with this. Knowing that Thomas could get to the evidence was enough for now. He hoped it was enough.

* * *

Kitty came up with an idea when Jed got back to the apartment. She had rung in sick that afternoon to Kim who was sympathetic and told her to go back to bed with a paracetamol.Kim was also annoyed when Kitty told her why she was feeling so ill, and promised to have a 'word' with Sly about giving underage staff alcohol. Kitty was copying out the information into a third notebook.

"What you doing?" Jed asked as he climbed onto their bed. "You feeling better?" Kitty was concentrating on the notes but smiled and said

"Got another place we can hide the information. Post it to Mr Singh. You regularly send him letters about how we are doing, so we already have a reason why. Send him a copy of the book, and have him as an extra safe place, not all up to date but its information that could start an investigation"

Jed thought about it "It puts him at risk though" he said sadly "He's been so good to us, dealing with Charlie when he turned up all official"

"But he has a grandson who kicked Charlie's arse. I'm sure he can kick the Cetin brothers as well.. Tell you what, lets prepare the copy anyway and give him a call from that call box down the road. If he says no, then no harm done, but I think he will want to help, and all he needs to do is just hold onto it"

* * *

The following day Jed was about to leave for work when the door bell rang twice. Jed and Kitty rarely had visitors and Kitty was sleeping. Jed walked to the front door but before he could open it, the door opened from the other side. Jed was dismayed to find Sly and Kevin, one of Sly's many bouncers standing on their doorstep.

"H..hello" Jed said puzzled. "What's going on?"

"Routine inspection of my property" said Sly, "I did mention it to Kitty the other night. How's she doing?"

"Still recovering from that booze you gave her" Jed said steadily

535

"Yeah Kim did tell me off for that" Sly looked slightly sheepish. Kevin looked impassive and very large standing in the doorway.

"Can you not come back when we are not here?" Jed asked "Kitty's sleeping at the moment"

Sly looked annoyed but he nodded "Yes, we can come back later on". He turned and Kevin followed him back out onto the landing. Jed closed the door, but he felt unsettled about the encounter.

On a whim he looked through the peephole and Sly and Kevin were looking back at their door. Jed was worried. He had a sense of something being wrong. He lived on his instincts and often was proven correct.

He walked over to the plant pot and lifted the fake Swiss cheese plant carefully making sure the soil didn't spill onto the floor. He took out the second and third notebooks they had left there and popped them into his bag. He then had an idea and walked over to the table where some of Kitty's jewellery was out. He took a pair of bright flashy earrings and laid them down in the box before putting the plant carefully back onto the box.

He decided to go to the college on the way into the courier office and deposit them there instead. He looked through the peephole and saw that Sly and Kevin had left.

Jed walked over to the window which looked out over the road, and saw that Kevin had brought Sly's car around. Sly got in, and Kevin roared off along the road nearly sending a cyclist off into a bus shelter. Jed walked back into their bedroom, Kitty was half asleep. He shook her awake and told her what had just happened.

"I left a pair of your earrings inside the box. If they spot the hiding place, hopefully they will just think its for possessions like that"

He also mentioned that the books were now all in his rucksack and he would take them to the college on the way into work.

"Is that a good idea?" she asked her face pinched in anxiety.

"It's the only thing I can think of, if we hadn't been here, I think Sly, or more likely Kevin would have tossed our place over, maybe pretend like it was burglars?" That thought didn't make Kitty any happier but she nodded.

"I trust your judgement" she said sinking back onto the pillow.

"Double lock the door when I go" Jed added. "Don't want you here alone with them OK? And don't answer the door"

Jed kissed her and walked back out to the lounge picking up his rucksack. Kitty followed him out and as Jed closed the front door behind him, he heard Kitty set the double lock. Jed walked down the stairs and out into the lobby.

As he left the building he looked both ways, but he couldn't see Sly's car anywhere nearby. He walked swiftly down the road and headed off to the college. He had plenty of time before his shift and if Sly or someone else was to spot him, he could always say he left a book which he needed.

Jed realised later that the plans he and Kitty had made, gave them a false sense of security and that the meeting earlier had annoyed and upset him almost as much as Kitty. They both had been told by Sly that he could and would inspect his properties, but this visit just seemed off.

He walked into the college foyer and took the corridor down to the lockers. He fished out his single key and opened the door. Inside nothing had been disturbed as far as he could tell. The college had good security on site and there were cameras in all of the corridors. The lockers were a generous size, and Jed had popped the one notebook in a bag of his dirty washing. The smell of unwashed socks would put most people off looking inside. Jed popped the notebooks from his rucksack inside the same bag. He closed and locked the locker door then walked back out into the lobby. No one he knew was around, so he made his way back out onto the street and making his way towards the casino building.

* * *

As he arrived at the casino, Kim was nowhere to be seen. This was also unusual as she was always there to greet the couriers each morning and to give them their rounds for the day. Sly was sitting at Kim's desk. It was obvious he had been looking through the drawers and was startled when Jed came into the office.

"Morning, again" Jed said "No Kim?"

Sly looked up still with a strange expression on his face. "No, she's taking a holiday" he said gruffly "Where are the rotas? Can't find anything in this place"

Jed pointed to a notice board where a clipboard was fixed "Behind you" he said "The clipboard" Sly grunted and stood up plucking the clipboard from the wall.

"Sorry about the early visit" he said "Haven't done your place yet and Emir wants to make sure you are not messing up the place" he added with a laugh Jed knew to be false and hearty.

"Well you know when we aren't there, as we both work here" Jed said "So it would be good if you can do those then" Sly nodded but Jed could see he was distracted by the rotas. Jed walked out and went to the courier room where Greta was already sitting down.

"Did you know Kim was on holiday?" Jed asked

"No, really. Lucky woman" Greta said. She then added "I'm sure she said she would see me in the morning. That's strange"

Jed mused over the events of the morning as he worked, and whilst he was on his rounds. He knew where Kim lived. She rented another one of the brothers places three streets down from Jed and Kitty's place. He decided to check in on her after his round.

* * *

Denmark Road was a similar street to Athelstan Road and several houses had been turned into flats from being single homes years ago. Jed knew Kim lived on the top floor of the end house, opposite the school.

Kim had told him that the sound of the kids playing out in the morning when she had been on a late shift was the only thing that got her out of bed.

"I sleep like the dead otherwise" she had joked with him.

Jed walked up to the front door which like his place had a set of door bells on the nearside wall. Jed pressed the bell for the top flat realising that Kim's last name was Cooper. The intercom cracked but no voice came out so Jed said in a loud voice

"Kim, its Jed. Are you OK? Sly said you were on holiday?"

The intercom crackled again and the front door popped open.

"Come up" said a voice Jed barely recognised.

Jed put his bike inside the front door out of the way and dropped his bag next to it. He then climbed the grand staircase up to the top floor. No one was around.

Kim was standing just inside the door, she was wearing a fleecy bathrobe but Jed wasn't looking at her clothes. Her face was battered and bruised and looked very painful. Her right eye was partly closed and when Jed looked closer, her hand was bandaged up.

"Who did this?" Jed asked pointing at her "Emir or Sly?"

Kim opened the door further and Jed followed her inside. Kim's place was well furnished with a plush sofa and chairs. She sat down on a chair and pointed at the sofa.

"Mercy visit?" she asked though her face injuries made it difficult for Jed to understand her.

"I was worried about you" Jed replied "Greta said you didn't mention a holiday to her yesterday. I can see that it's not" Jed waited for Kim to explain.

"They are dangerous men Jed, I think you know that already. I also think you and Kitty need to be really careful." Jed was surprised at her comment

"Why? The Temple Road thing? Sly sorted that out" Kim laughed loudly but it wasn't a kind laugh

"Oh yes they did that alright" She pointed to a newspaper on the table "Page 13" she said. Jed picked up the local paper and turned to page 13. At the bottom of the page was a small story.

Drug Addict Death
   A body was discovered in the River Exe near Millers Bridge on Tuesday night. It has been identified as Kenny Noland a known drug dealer and addict known to the Devon Police. Police are appealing for witnesses to the incident.

"You cross them, they will destroy you Jed. You stand up to them, then you end up like me!" Kim indicated her face. "They are into things you don't want to know about, and if they think you are going to grass on them, or you steal from them, you end up like poor Kenny, floating around in the river until some poor constable fishes him out" Jed sat back on the sofa

"What did you do then, to get your face all bashed up?"

"Not grassing" Kim replied "I learnt that years ago. No in my case I was trying to protect Kitty."

Jed stood up "Kitty, why what happened?"

"The other night when Sly got her drunk? He wanted to make sure she and you were not aware of their...other businesses. Seems that Kitty before she got too pissed started talking about your studies, or at least that's what she said at first. Something to do with notebooks, but Sly didn't think much of it as you are a student. He thought at first she was complaining about all the mess you might have left around. Like you do in the courier room. However when he asked her about the notebooks a few minutes later she clammed up. That's why he was at your place this morning, his bouncer Kevin put the idea in his head. And that's why I look like this. I told him it's rubbish, that you like all the other students just abandon your books and notebooks once you get a round given out and you are probably a mucky pup the same at home. But there is something isn't there?" she finished looking at Jed who had gone a deathly shade of white.

"I need to go home" Jed said

"Yeah I think you do too" said Kim.

Jed stumbled back out of Kim's flat his mind racing. He grabbed his bike and bag and headed home. As he arrived back at the apartment he could see the front door was slightly ajar. He dropped his bike and bag in the lobby and raced up the stairs. His door was open also.

Jed pushed the door open and was horrified to see Sly, Kevin and Kitty sitting down in the living room. Kitty was slumped in one of the chairs. Her eyes were closed and one of her dressing gown sleeves was ruched up.

"Sly? Kevin? what's happened to Kitty? why are you" Kevin stood up and walked menacingly over to Jed before he could finish his questions. He grabbed his arm roughly which caused Jed to yell out

"What the fuck is going on Sly?"

Sly stood up, he had a dreadful smile plastered across his face. Jed realised that Sly had a syringe in his hand which he hadn't noticed before.

"Things are about to change Jed in yours and Kitty's lives. Now I would like to say for the better, but perhaps not. I think you have been" Sly bonked Jed's nose hard "Putting your noses in where they are not wanted. Spying on me, and my businesses, and now it stops. Hold him"

Sly addressed Kevin who grabbed Jed's other arm so he was facing Sly and not able to wriggle away. Jed was horrified to see Sly slide the needle into his arm. There was nothing he could do about it. Jed looked over at Kitty whose head was now leaning over to one side.

"Just a little truth drug" Sly said smiling more broadly. Jed felt his arms start to tingle and then his brain exploded.

He heard Sly say "Dump him on the sofa" before the world went to black.

* * *

The water gushed over his face. Why was he wet? Jed came around to see Sly looking at him steadily. Kevin held a bucket. That must have been where the water came from.

"Now you have had a little taste of my product, you can tell me where your little grassing notebooks are? Kitty said you took them this morning?"

Jed realised he was lost but knowing that Thomas could get to them made him brave, and possibly a little bit reckless.

"They're gone, posted far far away" Jed said "Poof"

He giggled. Whatever Sly had given him was making his head hurt a bit now. He felt drunk, or how he would imagine drunk would be. He also knew that both he and Kitty were in deep shit. Sly's expression didn't change.

"Whoever you posted them to is also going to get a little bit hurt, so I suggest you tell me now before you read about them in the paper"

Jed realised that Kim must have called Sly. He was proud of his new mobile phone. She must have called before he arrived back home. Sly walked over to Kitty who was drooling down her dressing gown. He grabbed her and she moaned softly

"Leave her alone" Jed wasn't sure if he made himself clear. He sounded like Kitty did the other day. He paused. "OK". Sly stopped and looked at him. Jed fished out his locker key. "Here".

Sly took the key and looked at it

"The college? You left then in the fucking college?" his voice rising in anger and bewilderment. "Here Kevin, go fetch" Kevin caught the key Sly had tossed him. "be discrete, don't want any trouble" Kevin nodded and walked out the door, closing it behind him.

548

Sly pulled up one of the dining chairs and looked at Jed. His expression was almost beautific

"Now things are going to change Jed for you and for Kitty. She will still be our star songbird in the casino, but she will also be a companion for some of our more discerning clients as well. No sex, we don't want to spoil her too much, just smile and flirt"

Jed moaned out loud, Kitty was in more danger now than he could ever have imagined

"And you will both now be on a different pay scale. It's obvious you worked out the courier scam, so now you will only be on deliveries of a certain type, and you will also be getting a little bonus both of you. That drug I gave you. You will be craving more in a few hours, so some of your pay will be in a different form, just enough to make you both docile and less likely to ruin me" Sly's smile widened.

"Oh and your tenancy here will be ending this week. I don't think you appreciated the gifts you have been given. I've found a different place for you both, somewhere a little more to your previous taste. Gloucester Road, its not mine, but Kevin managed to persuade the previous squatters to leave. He'll move your stuff when he gets back from picking up your grassing notes".

* * *

The noise of Kevin coming back into the room woke Jed up. He hadn't realised he had slept. Sly was right, whatever they had been given was toxic but also a warm hug inside. He should be more worried than he was about the coming changes, but his head felt like it was packed with cotton wool. he looked over at Kitty who was still sleeping

unconscious?

Jed staggered off the sofa and tried to shake Kitty awake. She moaned softly but didn't wake up. Jed crouched down and whispered

"I'm sorry"

"She's alright" said Sly who was flicking through one of the notebooks. "You fucking had it all didn't you, you little shit" Sly waved the notebook at Kevin "You've got all of them?"

Kevin patted his pocket "Little bonfire later boss" he said with a grunt.

Sly looked at Jed and said "You're on holiday today. Kevin will take back your bike and bag, but I expect you bright and breezy ready for a long day of deliveries tomorrow. He will move your stuff into your new place tomorrow" Sly stood up "Come on Kevin, we have a little fire to start"

* * *

35

Hell on earth

Jed's head felt like cotton wool for only a few hours. Then the craving set in. Kitty hadn't woken for hours but eventually she had stirred and on seeing him had burst into floods of tears.

"I...I'm sorry" she yelped "Kevin burst in when I finally went to answer the door"

She held out her wrist which Jed could see was bruised

"He grabbed my arm and twisted it" She licked her lips and added

"Why do I feel so rough?"

Jed pulled up his sleeve, then hers

"They drugged you, and me. It's over, they know, they have all of the notebooks"

Jed wanted to weep when he saw Kitty's face crumble.

"And they are making us pay for our grassing, even though no one else saw apart from Thomas. You, are going to be a 'companion' for the casino Sly said. And I am going to be only delivering drugs."

"Can't we run? back to London?" Kitty implored "Get away?"

Jed looked sadly at her

"You could, you don't have any family they could hurt Kitty, but I do. Sly knows about Mike and Cathy, about our friends in the squat, probably anyone I know, even my friends in the children's home. I can't run. I just have to hope they don't do more than they have".

Jed took her hand

"They are moving us out of here too. To some crappy squat they have in Gloucester Road".

Kitty wailed to hear this news. She loved the apartment, had thrived in her own place. Jed felt sick but he continued. She had to know the worst

"And what they gave us by force yesterday, soon enough we will be craving it."

Kitty turned and fled to the bathroom where he could hear her being sick. He felt like vomiting too. He closed his eyes.

* * *

Kitty slept in the chair overnight. Jed heard her walking around, her restless wanderings a sign she was starting to come down from the drugs she had been forcibly given. He heard her weeping too, but his body ached so much he couldn't even lift his head to see where she was. He awoke exhausted at dawn and crawled out of the sweaty bed. His head, his whole body ached.

As he walked out into the living room he spotted an envelope on the dresser. The writing was Sly's 'a little pick me up' it said. Inside was a small clear packet with a white powder and a note inside. 'sniff me'. Jed stared at the note which was like some parody of Alice in Wonderland, though this was not a fairytale.

He took the packet into the bathroom. Kitty had a cosmetics mirror in her bag which Jed took out. He'd seen drug addicts in the squats he had lived with his mum 'do drugs' so he worked out what needed to happen.

He poured a small amount of the powder out onto the mirror, and ripped up a toilet roll cardboard inner he'd fished out of the bin, then made a tight tube of it before cautiously sniffing the powder. He sneezed and it blew some of it down into the sink. He groaned then tried again. This time it worked. His brain fizzed like he had just inhaled sherbet lemon powder. He grasped the sink with both hands and tried not to vomit. After a few minutes he felt much better.

Jed went back out into the living room and shook Kitty

"mmm tired" she moaned. He shook her more fiercely

"Sly left us something"

She moaned and tried to curl back up

"It's going to make you feel better, I promise"

Kitty stirred and looked at him from under her tangle of dreadlocks

555

"Promise?"

"I promise"

Jed dragged her to her feet and propelled her into the bathroom. She stood swaying as Jed picked up the cardboard tube and demonstrated to Kitty what she needed to do. Kitty took the tube and stared at it like it was something from Mars. She bend down over the sink, and copied his actions. She too grasped the sink for a few minutes but unlike Jed she didn't sneeze.

She looked at him and said bleakly

"We are in real fucking trouble now"

Jed couldn't disagree with her.

* * *

Jed went to the courier office. Kim was still absent. Jed figured that she wouldn't be in for at least a couple of weeks. Her skill with makeup was beyond what was possible for her facial and other injuries. Jed hoped Sly was paying her for her 'holiday'.

Jed's bike was indeed back on the rack and Sly greeted him with a cheery "Good morning" as he spotted him in the foyer.

Sly put his meaty arm around Jed and propelled him into the office, shutting the door. He looked at Jed carefully

"You saw my gift then?"

Jed nodded. He couldn't speak. Being in this man's presence, knowing what he had already done to Kenny made him feel very sick indeed.

"You will get enough for you and Kitty to function, keep me and Emir happy and we will all get along just fine. Fuck with us again, you and your girlfriend will end up in the river, just like Kenny did."

Jed had never been more scared in his life.

* * *

The next few weeks passed quickly. Jed was moved solely to the 'special' deliveries which meant that his college work suffered. Thomas had tried to speak to him one evening after his last class but Jed managed to avoid him on the basis of needing to collect Kitty. The next intervention came one afternoon as Jed was eating his lunch in the park close to the casino.

"Been looking for you lad" a familiar voice said "Been avoiding us?"

Jed looked up. Mike was standing in front of him and his face showed his worry and concern.

"Cathy wanted me to invite you round for wrappies. You and Kitty if she's free?"

Jed sighed.

"I've got a lot of work on Mike, exams are coming up and I'm working even longer hours at the couriers too. They've got evening rounds on now."

Mike nodded "You've moved again?" he said "Thought you were set at your place, nice and cosy?"

Jed looked at his friend and knew he couldn't tell him the truth. If he did, Mike could be in danger, him and Cathy. His heart sank but he knew he had to keep them safe.

"You checking up on me?!" Jed stood up his anger not for his friend but for the brothers. His face got red as he continued "In case you forgot, I have been looking after myself for years Mike, me and Kitty both. I don't need you checking up on us, we can manage just fine"

Mike looked horrified as he watched Jed get more and more furious. He stepped back his hands in the air like he was surrendering.

"Just worried about you" he said "Thomas said you haven't been at college a few times this month, and he's not managed to speak to you. What's going on Jed?".

Jed picked up his half eaten sandwich and turned to leave

"Just fuck off Mike, leave me alone"

He stalked off not looking back, knowing if he did he would run to and weep in Mike's arms, and that would be the end of them all.

* * *

Mike was so worried about Jed, he walked over to the hospital and managed to catch Cathy on her break. He told her the story and waited for her to think it over.

"Something's definitely wrong" she agreed "They were so happy at their new place. Do you know where they are living now? Have they split up maybe?"

"Nah, he talked about Kitty in the present tense, if they had broken up, he would have said. No this is something more, something else. The new people at the flat didn't know where they went, no forwarding address, and he's not back at the squat Keith said he would put the word out. Jed looked tired, really ill"

"Could be the effort of working and studying, puts a strain on anyone, look what happened to me in my final year of nursing training. I was a mess"

"You were and still are beautiful" Mike replied

"Right answer" Cathy said with a laugh. She looked at the clock "Sorry I have to go now, shift ends at 8pm, perhaps we can go for a drink and talk more?"

Mike kissed her and left. Cathy was worried though. She had seen people go downhill and often there was a reason for it. She decided to pop into the courier office the following day and see for herself how Jed was doing.

* * *

Kitty's life also changed. She became depressed and sullen with Jed. He knew she blamed him for the mess they were in, despite her also being a part of the plan. She hated their new digs, and started to hate the casino too. Sly had stopped her singing sad songs now,

"Too depressing for the punters"

Her voice and mood didn't make her happy songs any more fun to perform and her 'extra' duties made her want to be sick.

561

Sly had taken to giving her vodka in her drinks before a big party of special VIP guests arrived. She found the booze helped her perform better so her regular drinks were topped up as well.

Her first time in the VIP room made her shudder to remember. Sly had grabbed her wrist and almost dragged her off stage between songs. She nearly dropped her guitar but managed to lay it down before he strode over to the male group waiting outside the VIP door, Kitty following in his wake.

"Smile for fucks sake" he hissed. "Gentleman, I wanted to introduce our songbird Kitty" he pulled Kitty forward and put his meaty hands on her shoulders.

"Hello darling" said the tallest guest "You are a pretty thing aren't you? I'm Harold Minster, Head of the Planning department at Exeter Council" he held out one of his hands.

Kitty looked at his sweaty hand and offered hers. Harold took it in both of his and stroked her wrist suggestively. Kitty wanted to vomit, but she managed to smile though the effort was showing in her posture. She was introduced to the rest of the party. All of the men were keen to show their importance. Two of them were senior policemen.

More on the take, More for the books now burned and gone

Kitty thought sadly.

She was ushered into the VIP room and plonked on a sofa furthest from the door. Sly nodded to the barman who took orders from the group.

"Kitty's usual" Sly said to the barman.

A drink was put in front of Kitty on the table. She tried to resist but as Harold slid onto the sofa next to her, she grabbed the drink and took a long hit. The vodka went straight to her brain, numbing it to the point she could bear to look at Harold. She plastered a kind smile on her face.

"Planning department - that sounds fascinating. You must be a very important person?"

Harold visibly preened himself and placed his sweaty hand on Kitty's knee.

"Oh yes my dear, I really am".

* * *

Sly kept the VIP guests from getting too touchy feely with Kitty. He didn't want to spoil the goods, despite sly offers from some of his guests about whether Kitty "did more than chat". He reluctantly declined knowing she was on the edge mentally. He needed to bring her back from her sullen demeanour. He knew just the thing.

At the end of her shift Sly came over to her and sat down. All of the VIP guests were now gambling at the other end of the room. Harold had tried to get Kitty to join him "for luck" but one look from Sly and he had slunk back to the poker table.

"I have a gift for you Kitty, a shopping trip" Sly announced "Trip to London, the west end, buy you some suitable clothes for your new role as hostess, night in a hotel, my treat and you can keep them here at the club so they don't start a row with Jed and they won't get that horrible damp on them from your accommodations"

Kitty wasn't thrilled to hear this, but a chance to get away from the Gloucester Road squat and Jed who had started to frustrate her would be good.

"Separate rooms?" she asked "I'm not sleeping with you Sly"

"Of course my dear, wouldn't dream of it, never mix business and pleasure"

Kitty knew this was not correct. Sly had made his way through most of the female staff including Kim and most of the staff despised him more. Only Kevin the bouncer seemed loyal to him, but then Sly didn't fancy men. Kitty mentally shook herself

"OK then, when?"

"Tomorrow, pick you up at 10am from the casino".

Kitty made a mental note not to tell Jed. This might be her way out of this mess.

* * *

Cathy arrived at the casino at 9am the following day. A large man dressed in a too tight black suit was standing just inside the entrance. Kitty could see several couriers in the lobby collecting their parcels but didn't spot Jed. She opened the door but the man put his hand out to stop her.

"Casino isn't open till 11 am, love" he said gruffly.

"Looking for Jed Long" Cathy said brightly

"And you are?" the man replied still looking intimidating

"His mum" replied Cathy.

The man looked bemused

"His step mum" Cathy clarified. "His dad is my boyfriend, is he around?"

"He's out on deliveries, won't be back for hours" said the man

"and you are?"

"Kevin"

"Can I leave a message for him?" Kevin looked a bit annoyed Cathy thought, but she didn't like him "Can you ask him to call Cathy when he gets back. He's left a jumper at our place and I wanted to give it back to him".

Kevin grunted and held out one meaty hand "Give it here, I'll pass it on"

Cathy blushed "Oh it's not with me, its drying back at our place. Fell down the back of the washing machine"

Cathy didn't do lying very well. She ended up blushing which often gave the game away.

Kevin grunted again "Jumper, step mum's place, collect, right, that's all?" Cathy nodded and let the door go.

As she turned to walk away someone behind her said

"You looking for Jed?" she turned. "I'm Greta his friend, or at least I thought I was" She was pushing one of the branded Cetin Courier bikes and had a similar bag to Jed's slung over her shoulder.

"Think you could do with a coffee?" Cathy asked. Greta looked in her bag

"I've got three deliveries but can I meet you later?" They arranged to meet at the cafe adjacent to Cathedral Square in an hour

"That long enough for you?" Cathy asked

"I fly like the wind on this bike" replied Greta with a smile.

* * *

Greta arrived on time at the cafe.

"Coffee? Tea? Cold drink?" asked Cathy as the waitress came over.

"Coffee please"

"You're worried about Jed?" Cathy asked as she took a sip of her drink. Greta sipped her coffee before replying.

"You're his step mum? You told Kevin that, but Jed told me he didn't have any family living?" Cathy explained the relationship between Mike and Jed.

"Oh I see".

"What's going on with Jed? He blew up at Mike in the park and it's devastated him. Mike loves Jed as if he is his son."

"Jed is now working a different round system to the rest of us couriers, very secretive, doesn't spend much time in the courier room, and I haven't seen him get his course books out for weeks" Greta paused looking upset. Cathy realised that this girl was worried about Jed too.

"Kim the manager doesn't pass his rounds to him in the same way as us. We get ours in the lobby full view, his are given to him behind closed doors - the office. She looks like she got hit by a truck as well. She was off on holiday, or that's the story the boss Sly gave us, when she came back, thick makeup, the sort you see people on stage wearing, and she moves like it hurts."

Cathy was horrified to hear her suspicions confirmed.

"What do you think he is delivering?"

Greta thought for a moment

"My guess is something illegal, probably drugs"

* * *

36

Not a way out

Kitty was standing at the corner as Cathy came out of the casino after speaking to Kevin. She saw Greta approach Cathy and then go off. Kitty knew Greta briefly, they had spoken one day as Jed and Kitty had arrived for Kitty's shift. She wondered what Cathy and Greta had to talk about. She made a note to mention it to Jed when she got back. Jed had been morose when Kitty had told him about the trip.

"Might be a way out? Get back into Sly's good books?" she had implored.

She had initially wanted to keep the trip from him, but she realised that being away from home for the night, was going to put Jed's paranoia on full alert.

In the end he had grunted and been morose all evening.

Kitty was waiting for Sly's car to arrive. She had waited inside the lobby after Greta and Cathy had left but didn't speak to anyone including Kevin. Sly's sleek Jag pulled up to the kerb. Kitty knew Sly was wary of traffic wardens pouncing on his car, so she quickly left the casino and slid into the passenger seat. She had brought a small overnight bag with her.

"Lovely to see you again Kitty, this will be a nice break for you"

Sly said smoothly. Kitty smiled but didn't reply. It would be nice to be in a warm room this evening, and hopefully bring back some nice new clothes as well. The journey to London took about three and a half hours. Sly was a good driver, he kept to the speed limit, which initially puzzled Kitty.

"You don't drive this like you stole it?"

Sly smiled "I have too many reasons not to be pulled over by some traffic scum"

Kitty realised this made a lot of sense. The car pulled up to a sleek hotel. The sign read 'Radisson Blu Portman Square'. There was a glass and metal canopy over the entrance.

"I chose this hotel because it's close to my favourite store Selfridge's" Sly said as he handed the key's over to a porter and opened Kitty's door.

Kitty picked up her bag but was surprised to see one of the uniformed porters take it from her. "They deliver to your room" Sly said with a smile holding the door for her.

She followed him inside. At the reception desk was an attractive woman wearing a smart blue suit jacket with 'Mandy' on a lapel badge. She looked up from her desk as Sly and Kitty came closer.

"Ah Mr Cetin, nice to see you again" she said with a bright smile. "We've got your favourite suite for you and your guest" She looked at Kitty with a smile that didn't reach her eyes. Kitty knew she wasn't the sort of guest they normally had here. Her dreadlocks and clothes were not their usual attire. Sly accepted the key card from Mandy and turned to the lifts. Kitty thought

Well he obviously knows where he's going then

She followed him to a bank of lifts and waited as one came smoothly to them. Sly guided her into the lift then pressed for the top floor. As the lift opened the view out over the city was breathtaking. Sly grinned

"You wait till you see the view from the suite"

He walked to a set of double doors and clicked the key card which released the lock. He pushed the door open and beckoned her inside. Sly was right, the view was even better. Kitty looked out over the city, most of which she didn't know well. Her time spent in Acton was more suburban than she had realised. The view over the park

Hyde Park

made her realise how different her life was to how she imagined it would be back when she was younger. Sly stood next to her and didn't talk. She knew he wanted to possess her, but she was loyal to Jed despite the mess they were in now.

After a few minutes of watching the view Sly coughed and said

"Your room is at the end of the corridor down there" he pointed to a corridor she had not noticed. "I have arranged dinner downstairs for eight pm. There are a few outfits in the wardrobe you might want to have a look at. Something more suitable for the occasion"

Kitty walked down to the room, her overnight bag on her shoulder. Inside the room was a floor to ceiling wardrobe, and indeed inside were a selection of outfits. Some were more like the things Kim would wear, but near the back she found a black halter-neck top and a pair of silky trousers. Kitty decided to wear her DM's instead of any of the high heeled shoes in the rack beneath the clothes.

She flopped onto the bed and was asleep in moments. She woke after a couple of hours, her head was hurting. She recognised the cravings and went out into the main room to find Sly watching the TV. He smiled as she appeared.

"Good nap?" he asked smoothly "There's a little pick me up over there" he pointed to the dining table in the corner.

On the top was a small case. It was open and inside were a selection of pills and powders all in sealed plastic bags. One of the bags was open and two lines were laid out on the mirror in front. A metal straw was nearby. Kitty walked over to the table and picked up the straw. She was used to the motion now and as she inhaled the powder, her brain sparkled. She clutched at the table for a moment. Turning she saw Sly smile but it wasn't a kind smile.

Trapped, all trapped now

Despite her fears Sly was the perfect gentleman. He escorted her to dinner, shared stories about his family and his brother, though Kitty knew she could never repeat these. He walked her back to the room, and chastely kissed her cheek before wishing her a good evening.

The following day Kitty emerged wearing another outfit from the wardrobe, grey trousers, a white shirt and a cashmere blue jumper. Breakfast was laid out on the table, the case now hidden away. Sly spotted Kitty looking for it.

"What you need is in the bathroom, we had breakfast delivered. Not good to have that sort of thing out on display" he said.

Kitty went into the bathroom where again the case and items were laid out. She snorted another line and felt better. She came back out and sat at the table. Sly poured coffee for her. She took a sip and picked up a pastry from the plate. During breakfast Sly was charming telling her about his plans for the day.

"Selfridge's, for clothes, then I think a trip to Harrods. I need a few more shirts". Kitty chewed her pastry but didn't comment. After breakfast Kitty went to clean her teeth. The case was now closed. She was tempted to take another hit, but she was already realising that this was a bad habit.

* * *

Kitty had never seen so much money being spent. She was given over to the Selfridges personal shoppers Laura and Jonathan on arrival. Sly was busy buying some new suits and shoes. He waved her off.

"They'll look after you" he said. Kitty followed the personal shopper into a large and spacious room. There were racks and racks of clothes lining one wall.

"Mr Cetin was very specific on what you like" said Laura.

She walked over to a rack of outfits. The shirts were just her style, retro collars, fitted with quirky buttons and clasps. She picked out three shirts and passed them to Kitty.

"Dressing room is over there".

Kitty took the shirts and tried each of them on. All were a perfect size for her. Next came both skirts and trousers, all glamorous but also quirky and just her thing. She glanced at one of the labels on the first pair. Over £200. She had never worn anything worth more than £30.

Finally came the shoes. Dr. Martens but shoes not boots. She liked all of them, but a silver and red pair were her favourites. By the end of the session a large pile of clothes and accessories were being folded by Laura and Jonathan for those items Kitty had indicated she liked. Kitty was escorted back out into the store. Sly was waiting for her by the cash desk.

"We'll have these sent to the casino. They will be couriered today" Laura confirmed.

"You had fun my dear?" Sly smiled as he looked at Kitty.

Kitty was reluctant to admit it, but she had enjoyed the experience of trying on lots of beautiful clothes.

"Yes, they have some lovely clothes here"

"Good good. Well, I've booked us a light meal in
Aubane down the road before we need to head back to
Exeter, Harrods will have to wait unfortunately,
business at home takes priority" . Kitty wondered
briefly what business forced Sly to cut short his trip,
but realised she didn't want to know.

Sly escorted Kitty out of the store and hailed a taxi.
The restaurant was as plush as the store had been. Sly
ordered the meal and Kitty enjoyed it. She was
beginning to enjoy this life, these experiences and she
worried about returning to her life in Exeter.

In the car on the way back Sly was aware of Kitty's
fears. He knew showing her a life she could have
providing she would comply with his wishes, he
wanted to possess this woman, this girl but he knew to
do so, to force her would drive her away back to her
junkie boyfriend. He would play the long game.

* * *

As they pulled up in the car to the casino Kitty turned
to Sly

"Thank you for a lovely trip"

"My pleasure" Sly handed Kitty one of the small plastic bags. "A little bonus, don't share" he said smiling smoothly.

Kitty took the bag. It was double what she and Jed were being given as their wages. She tucked it away inside her jacket pocket.

* * *

37

Rock bottom

The downfall came swiftly for both Jed and Kitty. Jed had developed sores on the inside of his nose from the constant snorting. Kitty too was feeling the physical effects of the drugs she was taking and started to need more and more.

Kitty noticed that Sly was less and less enamoured of her and that made her more and more clingy towards him. She seemed to irritate him, but couldn't stop her humiliation. After a few days she began to miss her singing sessions at the casino and those she did do ended with her slumped down in her chair until an embarrassed Kevin was ordered to take her away.

Jed had spoken to one of the other couriers about injecting drugs and had been given a master class one evening down the back of the casino. The difference was intense, and much better.

Sly had eventually sacked Kitty from her singing job. She was becoming an embarrassment and the punters didn't want a slumbering singer, but someone who gave them energy to carry on losing their money.

Kitty returned to her first job busking in the cathedral square and Jed was her minder though Kitty was aware that he wasn't much protection these days. After a few days of not earning much she started to harass passing tourists for cash, and would rage at any that didn't give freely into her guitar case.

The final straw came when a group of male university students had jeered at Kitty and her songs. She had launched herself into the group, dropping her guitar without a thought for its safety. As she battered one of the group, several of the others grabbed the money she had earned in the guitar case. Jed hadn't noticed. He had been asleep. Kitty had stalked off in a rage and Jed had just slumped back down on the bench he had been sitting on.

Their combined need and love for each other faded but both could see no other way out. Mike had repeatedly tried to get Jed into a rehab facility when he realised that drugs were the reason Jed had turned away from him. Cathy too had failed to help Jed, but she explained to Mike he could only help Jed when he was at the very lowest point, and that was not likely to be yet.

Emil had taken both Kitty and Jed under his wing after Sly had sacked both of them. Sly had got tired of Jed missing his courier shifts and Kitty was no longer the beautiful and entertaining singer but Emil had persuaded his brother that Jed and Kitty could be more use within the drugs business and their addiction could be the persuasion needed.

Emil had visited Jed and Kitty in their shabby room and explained that they would be involved directly in the drugs business. Emil had set up a packaging unit in a run down house he had recently bought. The basement was dedicated to growing of cannabis thanks to a clever switching of electricity supply from the house next door. Emil explained that Kitty would be looking after the cannabis plants

"as my brother tells me you had a Swiss cheese plant"

Emil smiled as he said this but Kitty knew that he had been told, or had found out about their disloyalty.

"And you Jed, you will be in charge of taking in the parcels. Our Kenny used to do this job, but sadly he drowned because he tried to stiff me, and was taking a cut off the top. I know you won't make that silly mistake"

His eyes roamed over Jed's body. Jed had lost a lot of weight as the drugs had made him lose his appetite.

"And get some meat on your bones Jed, otherwise you'll blow away in the wind".

* * *

Mike spotted Jed in the city centre. Kitty was nowhere to be seen but her guitar and case were lying on the ground near Jed. Jed was curled up on one of the benches near the Cathedral. His appearance had got considerably worse since Mike last saw him.

Mike walked over to the bench and crouched down and shook Jed's shoulder gently. It had no effect other than to prompt a groan from him. Mike shook his shoulder harder which resulted in Jed leaping up and looking around him, his fists clenched.

"It's me Jed"

Mike said softly. Jed's eyes came back into focus and he mumbled something Mike didn't catch before sinking down onto the bench again.

"What's wrong?"

Mike was aware now that Jed was totally addicted. His appearance showed that. His jacket was torn and had food stains down the front of it. His jeans were hanging off his waist.

"s' OK" Jed mumbled louder.

He looked up at Mike his eyes bloodshot.

"I'm OK" he said more clearly.

He licked his lips which looked sore and dry

"Do you have cash for a drink?"

Mike shook his head. He knew the last thing Jed needed was money.

"I'll go buy you one, Coke OK?"

Jed nodded and sank back onto the bench. Mike noticed that the passing tourists and locals were giving Jed and his bench a very wide berth. Mike didn't blame them, the smell coming off Jed made him wince, but he was also angry, and tempted to shout at them

"He's a good lad, just gone off the rails a bit. He'll be back".

Mike picked up a pack of sandwiches along with the drink and took them back to the bench. Jed's eyes were shut but when he heard Mike come closer he opened them and looked at his friend. Mike handed him the sandwich and coke and sat down next to him.

"You're in trouble aren't you Jed?"

Jed didn't reply immediately but carried on chewing his sandwich. When he had finished he looked at Mike.

"It's OK, we are OK, Kitty and me, we have just fallen down a bit, but Mr C is looking after us now"

"How is he looking after you Jed? You look awful, you smell pretty bad, and you look like you haven't been eating judging from how you are woofing down that sandwich."

Jed knew he couldn't tell Mike what had been going on, his only option to protect his friend was to make him leave them alone. Jed stood up in a rage, not at Mike but how shit his life was now. He knew his mum would be furious with the Cetin brothers

but she's not here now

"He has given us jobs, good ones too. Kitty isn't singing for her supper now, and I am looking after things for Emil. Now leave me alone!"

Mike sat back shocked. The expression on Jed's face scared him but he didn't leave.

"It doesn't look like that from where I am sitting Jed, you smell like you haven't washed in days. When you are ready to accept help, you know where Cathy and I are? We love you, we are worried about you."

Mike stood up then, he couldn't look at Jed, he thought he might cry himself. He'd seen the tears running down Jed's face and wanted to sweep him up and take him home for a bath, but he knew that wasn't the right thing to do. He didn't look back.

Jed stood watching his friend leave. He was at rock bottom.

* * *

About the Author

Janet lives in Oxfordshire UK, when she isn't writing, she enjoys knitting socks, watching cooking and sewing programmes and making her own clothes.

You can connect with me on:
🐦 https://twitter.com/dustbooksauthor
🅕 https://www.facebook.com/DustBooksAuthor

Also by Janet Humphrey

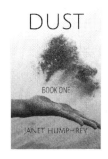

DUST Book One

Sixty tons of cosmic dust fall on the earth every day

What would happen if some of it was more intelligent than us?.

What if it wanted to live, even if you were dying?

Follow the continued story of Jed, and seven other British people Ezake, Cheri, Samir, Marilyn, Barry, Joshua & Brian

Eight people connected by a unique event

#notdead #deadnotdead #sixaliveagain

DUST Book Two
Coming soon

The DUST has been deliberately spread by the original #sixnotdead. More people around the United Kingdom are infected, the world is not prepared for the outcome. Can the DUST be stopped before catastrophic events unfold.?

Would you like to read Book Two before publication? Apply to be a beta reader by contacting me via the Facebook link on the author page